# PARISIAN PROMISE

## (Book 2)

## Ella McLaughlin

**Publisher:**
ASPG (Australian Self Publishing Group)
P.O. Box 159, Calwell, ACT Australia 2905
Email: publishaspg@gmail.com
http://www.inspiringpublishers.com

National Library of Australia Cataloguing-in-Publication entry

Author: McLaughlin, Ella

Title: **Parisian Promise**/*Ella McLaughlin*

ISBN 978-0-6453974-6-8 (Print)

ISBN: 978-0-6453974-7-5 (eBook)

# INTRODUCTION
## THE STORY SO FAR

### BOOK I – FINDING ME AND YOU

After being let down at the last minute, Chloe Clarke finds herself alone on a fourteen-night Mediterranean cruise, frightened and lonely. Jack Mclean, from a small fishing village in Scotland, has been jilted by his long-timegirl-friend, so she could move on to start a relationship with Jack's brother. His worried mother persuades him to take the cruise, and travel as his father had always wanted for him. Jack, feeling just as lost and lonely, meets Chloe.

A beautiful friendship begins, as they set out on a culinary journey of a lifetime. Meeting four other couples, and together, they explore exotic locations, experiencing scrumptious cuisine and great wines, music and dancing. Jack and Chloe's friendship quickly blossoms, turning into a burning desire for each other. They both try to protect the friendship, trying not to let it go any further, until one night as they danced under the huge Sorrento moon, they are mystically drawn to each other. Unable to control their passion and desire any longer, they fall into each other's arms, where they want to stay forever, starting a passionate love affair neither of them could deny any longer.

Upon returning home, a huge storm erupts, fuelled by jealousy and hate. Chloe receives heartbreaking photos of Jack apparently with another woman. Deeply hurt, she instantly cuts off all ties with him. Jack, unable to fit back in at home and losing Chloe, tumbles down a spiralling depression.

He finally picks himself up when his brother agrees to buy him out of the family trawling business. Jimmy has found out that his wife-to-be has sent the photos to Chloe with devastating results and now he has to explain everything to Jack.

Jack packs his bags and heads to Australia to find Chloe and explain everything that has happened. Making his way to Umina, he is anxious, not knowing what the outcome would be. All he knew was that she had seen the photos and cut off all contact with him. He was hoping to find her at the surf club alone and still single. When he eventually does find her, he declares his love for her and reminds her of the promise that he had made to her under the Eiffel Tower. He had come back to get the love of his life and hold her in his arms forever. Unable to be mad any longer and willing to give him a second chance, she falls into his arms, where she belongs.

# CHAPTER 1

# A VISITOR ARRIVES

As Chloe sat and stared into the sea, she was tranquillized by the waves as they roared and crashed, then gently cascaded onto the sand. A soft reminder of her own emotional rollercoaster, her life! Her ups and downs, her freak-outs, then calmness. The good days, the bad days, and the exhausting, emotional strain that lingered. Since she lost Jack, she had hit rock bottom. Just getting out of bed some days was a grand achievement that deserved an Academy Award for Best Effort, and then, there were days she didn't even try. Finally, arriving at the conclusion he was never coming back, she pulled herself back together, piece by every agonising piece. Pushing herself along, mostly on autopilot, the days rolled along, until today. The day he appeared out of the blue, looking better than he had ever looked before.

One minute she was going about her normal routine at the surf club and the next he was calling her name from behind. The shock at the sound of his voice hit her like a bullet, followed by an eclectic whirlwind of emotions. It stunned her, shocked her, panicked her, and filled her with love, excitement and pure delight all at once.

She was instantly captured by his smile, the one which made her legs tremble and made the butterflies in her stomach dance.

Could she resist him? Not a chance. She loved him, that would never change; she was willing to give him another chance in a heartbeat. She knew she was taking a huge risk forgiving him, but the option of living without him was too painful to even consider. He had asked for a second chance and that was precisely what she was going to do.

What they had in Europe was the most incredible love affair. He had stirred feelings in her she never knew existed, and she fell head over heels in love with him in a heartbeat. The time they shared together was filled with laughter and love. When they parted in Paris, he had promised to follow her to Australia as soon as he sorted things out back at home. She waited every day for months for him to tell her he was on his way, but that day never came. Instead, she received photos of him and an old girlfriend getting it on together at his sister's birthday party.

That was the day her world fell apart. She blocked him every way she knew how. For her, it was over! *Forever*. But for him, it was only just the beginning. The day he found out she saw the photos was the day he threw everything into finding her and winning her back. He would stop at nothing until he had her back in his arms, forever.

That morning he surprised her on the beach, he had cried with joy as she turned and ran into his arms. But after she had time to think, she had been more reserved. He managed to explain to her the truth about the photos, and she had agreed to have a walk and talk things over.

He was ecstatic she forgave him, and wanted to try to work things out. But as they sat on the beach, both were nervous and uncomfortable.

They sat cuddling together as they gazed out over the ocean. He had her in his arms again, his wee little kitten, the one he had missed so much while he slowly went crazy without her.

He was out of his mind with panic she might reject him, but she had kissed him with passion and threw her arms around him. They were wonderful signs, but she had gone quiet again. What was she thinking? He had every finger and toe crossed she had not changed her mind.

She startled him as she looked up. "I notice you are still using the same body wash I love." She was smiling.

He could not believe it, he had a grin from ear to ear. "Oh aye, when you told me you liked it, I went to every shop in Aberdeen and bought every bottle."

She nodded. "It smells divine," she said.

"It is made in the highlands at a fine, family-run soap company. I am impressed you have a keen highlander's nose." He smirked at her, and she smiled. "Plus, I had to pay excess weight on my luggage because of your favourite wine I packed to hopefully make you love me again."

Her head spun quickly surprised by what she heard. "You bought a bottle of our Tuscan wine with you?" She said with a huge grin. "Chianti Classico?"

"Aye, of course, maybe two or three. It worked once. I was hoping it might work again."

She threw her arms around his neck. "I love you, Jack. Please don't ever hurt me again. You broke my heart."

He cherished every moment as she wrapped herself around him. His heart was beating a million miles an hour. "Well, to be totally honest, I wasn't the one who broke your heart. It was the lies you believed."

She pulled herself away and stared deep into his eyes. *Oh!* He was right. He hadn't actually done anything wrong. Her heart sunk. She was too quick to blame him for everything and did not give him a chance to explain what happened. The photos she thought his brother sent were not from him, they were sent by his ex,and were of him throwing Shauna out of the party while she was so drunk falling all over him. There was so much more to the story, that she needed to know.

"So, whatever happened to Jimmy and Mary's wedding plans?" She looked up at him with one eyebrow raised.

"Jimmy cancelled the wedding plans and Mary was so wild with rage she went into his Facebook and sent the photos to you."

She nodded, looking back out to sea silently. It was one hell of an incredible story, but she believed him. She had no reason not to.

They watched the dogs and kids play, lost in their own thoughts. He peered at her from the corner of his eye;he could see she was trying to register the whole sorry story and hoped she was willing to put it behind them, and try to start again.

They ducked as a dog's toy went flying over them and a tiny pooch went scurrying past, covering them both with sand. They laughed as they stood up to dust themselves off.

"Sorry," yelled the owner, and they waved with a smile. He had her hand in his from helping her up and did not want to let go. He rubbed her ring with his thumb and looked up at her.

"You are still wearing my ring."

"I promised you I would never take it off."

They smiled before a wave of discomfort hit them once again. " I am staying over there," pointed Jack.

"You are staying at the caravan park?" she said, surprised, happy he had defused the situation.

"Aye, I wanted to be close to you, and as I sat here on my first night, I thought about your stories you used to tell me, and I felt close to you. I knew by your stories you were around those rocks." He pointed towards the headland, and she nodded.

"I was going to walk around and try to find you, but I was a bit scared you might hate me."He smiled down at her.

She elbowed him, laughing. "Well, you are probably right about that one."

"I am staying in a cabin with beautiful water views, would you like to see it?" He asked with a hopeful glint in his eyes.

"I would love to. You were lucky to get a booking, it is such a busy time of year."

He took her by the hand as they started walking up the sand towards the path to the caravan park. "Over here,"he said, leading the way. "There is a tap to wash our feet."He turned it on and held her by the elbow to steady her, as she rinsed the sand off her feet and legs before he did the same.

"Come this way we are nearly there."

She followed closely behind. He was right, it was a lovely spot, sitting at the end and right on the water. "Wow, this is fantastic! This is the best cabin in the whole park, with views of the ocean all the way around to kiddies corner!"

"Sensational views! Come inside. I will grab us some water."

He began to open the door,fidgeting with the lock and dropping the keys. It was obvious he was nervous. She followed him inside. The scent of his body wash filled the air; she took in a deep breath and released it. She had longed for that smell for so long. Her heart started to pound with excitement. He was really here. This was happening.

Sweating profusely after the beach walk, he knew he needed to freshen up. "I need to adjust to your Australian climate. The air conditioner has been on non-stop since I arrived."

She took the water bottle he had offered her and stopped to peer out the front window. "This is such a lovely spot."

He guided her outside, and they took a seat on the veranda looking out over the water. She had never seen her town through a tourist's eyes before; she gazed out as she slurped on her water bottle.

"Aye, I like it a lot, but I am a bit scared of the monkeys in the trees. They wake me in the morning, and then as the sun sets they are so loud. But so far I have not been able to catch a glimpse of them," he said, looking up in the trees.

"Monkeys," she laughed. "What monkeys?"She pulled her head back with a disbelieving squint.

"Aye, monkeys."

"We don't have monkeys."

"Maybe they only live here in the caravan park. I heard them. I know a monkey when I hear one," he said, still gazing high into the trees.

Chloe was laughing. Whatever he heard it was not monkeys, but it made her laugh. Probably one of those wild Scot stories he liked to tell. Whatever it was, it did not matter. He was here.

"Do you mind if we go inside for a bit? I love air conditioning. I am not handling the heat."

"Of course." She stood and followed him inside as he sighed at the relief of the cool air. They were all of a sudden alone and both extremely uncomfortable with each other. They had been through so much since Paris. Were they still the same two people? She needed to find out. Without thinking, she heard herself saying, "Why don't you grab some things and come and stay at my place tonight. I don't have any plans, and I would love to catch up with you properly, I can make you some dinner."

"Sounds great! I haven't been eating much since I left Scotland, and I would love to see your cabin."He smiled, grateful for the invite.

"Wait here, I will freshen up and throw a few things together."He was striding into his room in a panic, looking excited. Chloe laughed.

"I will wait outside for you."

"Aye, I won't be long,"he yelled back from the bedroom as she walked outside to take in the view again.

*He is coming to my place. I ran out the door in a panic this morning, so it is probably a mess,* she thought as she placed her hand on the railing and sipped her water bottle.

She didn't care. All she could think about was him and his touch. *His touch.* Her mind went straight back to their last night in Paris, the night she replayed in her mind over and over again, the dinner at the fancy restaurant and then their last night as he held her in his arms and told her he would love her forever. The way he looked at her burnt into her memory and then the way he touched her. Those soft wet lips that she could kiss forever.

"I am ready," he said, breaking her thoughts as she spun around frantically, finding him staring at her, looking amazing. He had changed into a soft blue cheesecloth shirt she remembered him buying in Santorini. It brought out the colour of his eyes that bored into hers as she stared. His sandy blonde hair was shorter than she remembered, falling just above his shoulders and blowing gently in the soft breeze. His lips grew into a grin. "What?"

She had been standing in a daze staring at him. "Sorry, I was thinking about something. Shall we go?" She pushed past him, and he followed, throwing his bag over his shoulder and grabbing her hand with the other.

They strolled along the track back towards the surf club. She made small talk to break the silence. "So this is the kiddies' skate park and the children's playground on the left, the football and cricket oval and the BBQ huts I told you all about," said Chloe.

"It was a strange feeling. I felt as though I knew everything so well but had never been here. I spotted Seasalt also."

"Ah, yes, well you can't miss that one, sitting proudly on the beach. I will take you for dinner one night."

They approached the surf club, and she ran ahead. "I need to grab my things. I won't be long."

He gave her a wink, and she was off. She found him reading the cafe menu on the wall when she returned.

"I can see you had a hand in putting this menu together. French crepes, very nice."

"Yes, and they are a huge money-spinner. Seasalt serves Bloody Mary's for breakfast and sunset spritz."

"Then we need to go."

"We will. My family runs it, remember?" She unlocked the doors with the remote, opening the boot he threw his bag in.

"I like your car. Small but sporty, just like you."

She smiled as they both jumped in and put on their belts. "Great on fuel, also. Always handy when you live on a budget," she added as she looked over her shoulder, reversing out of the parking spot.

She gave him a commentary story all the way home. His eyes darting from one thing to another, asking questions all the way.

"One thing I love about here is the sunshine. The sun doesn't shine too much at home, it's grey and misty. But here, it's bright and sunny all the time. Don't get me wrong. Scotland is beautiful but in a different way."

His hand had been waving around as he spoke and placed it on her thigh as he finished, and she jumped.

"Oh! Sorry, I didn't mean to scare you," he said, clearing his throat and removing his hand as he looked out the side window.

*Why did I do that? Oh, no, now he thinks I am not interested. Shit.* She was nervous beyond words, her hands were so sweaty she had to wipe them on her shirt one at a time.

He peered out over the headland as they passed above kid-dies' corner and was in awe. "Wow, you get views all along the coastline from here."

Chloe nodded, watching him, butterflies dancing in her belly. "You cut your hair," she said as she took the turn and drove down the winding bushy road to Pearl Beach.

"Well, I had to. I let myself go. I was a mess, so I cut it before I came here."

"It is shorter than before." She gave him a quick sideways glance.

"Do you like it?" he asked with a squint.

"Yea, I do. It suits you." She gave him a quick smirk, and he looked back out the window unable to control his huge smile.

"You have not changed a bit, I still can't take my eyes off you," he said with his sexy grin, and she blushed. "I can still do that, now that makes me happy." He looked proud of himself.

She stopped the car and turned it off."We are here." He looked around as they took off their belts, and got out of the car. It was exactly as she had described it. Simple but beautiful homes lined the streets that were tarred and framed by grass with sandy soil and no foot paths or gutters."Follow me down this side path,"she said as she opened the boot, and he fetched his bag.

As he followed her down the path, past the main house and out the back, his mind was spiralling out of control with thoughts of what lay ahead. He had wanted this for so long and now he was scared to death. They arrived at the French doors, and she unlocked them before opening them up.

"This is my home." She outstretched her arms showcasing it all. He dropped his bag and looked around.

"I love it. It is so you."

"Come inside. I will show you around."

She showed him around the kitchen and lounge room before taking him down the hall and pointing to the rooms to the side.

"Done, petite but comfortable." She turned to walk back out and bumped into him standing right behind her.

He grabbed her and kissed her for what seemed an eternity. She realised she was still in her bikini and rashie from the surf club and knew almost certainly she was still covered in sand.

"I need a shower," she said, and he mumbled, "Me, too. I sweat too much," still kissing her, wild with desire. She started to undress him and then ripped off her rashie, standing in her bikini as he felt her all over. He undid her top and took it off as she turned to set the shower while he managed to undress.

Slipping off her bikini bottoms, she took him by the hand into the shower. If they still felt awkward it didn't show. They steamed up the room with passion and then moved to the bedroom and continued. Hours passed before they lay sighing in each other's arms. "My God, we still have it," she laughed.

"I thought about that so many times. So many nights I couldn't sleep thinking about you."

"Me, too, Jack. It was such a long, horrible four months," she said with a distant stare.

"I didn't think I would survive at times. It was hard for me also."

He was delicately caressing her body with his fingers as he sat upon one arm looking over her.

"You have no idea how good it feels to wrap myself around you again." He leaned in to kiss her as she lay motionless.

"You had me in a trance. I remember how you do that to me now."

He smiled, "It brought back wonderful memories for me also. I thought I would never feel like this ever again when I lost you.

For me, I knew no one could ever make me feel the way you make me feel"

"That feeling, the way you make me feel, is so strong, there was never a chance I wouldn't find you. I would have scoured every inch of land and sea till I did, and when I did I would not rest until I convinced you that we were forever and take you back in my arms where you belong"

She lay staring into his eyes, how did she ever let someone come between them like that. She had never had anyone love her the way he did. How did she almost throw it all away.

"I am so glad you came here, Jack."

"I was always coming, there was never a chance I wasn't"

"Thankyou for not giving up on me"

"Well, believe it or not, it was Paddy once again who thinks he had a hand in me coming."

"He did?" That was a surprise.

"He told me to jump on a plane, find you and win you back."

"So you kept in contact with him?"

"Yea, he sent me an email one day out of the blue, so I rang him. I was lost, broken and I guess he picked it up in my voice, so he asked me to stay with him."

"You went to Paddy and Maggie's house?"

"I did and met the whole family. I guess he was like a father figure for me. He helped me a lot."

"We made some wonderful friends on that cruise, didn't we?"

"Aye, we were blessed, that is for sure."

"I need another shower," she laughed.

"I better let you enjoy it on your own."

She didn't last too long on her own before calling out for him. "I am too lonely in here. We never shower alone, remember?"

He was off like a rat up a drainpipe, throwing open the shower curtain and jumping inside. After a vigorous shower,

Jack was the first to get out, leaving Chloe to finish. He dried off and put some boxers on.

"I will wait for you outside," he said as he peeked inside.

"Beers are in the fridge. Grab yourself one. I won't be long."

She pulled out a box from deep in the rear of the wardrobe. Placing it on her lap, she read the note on top written with a black marker pen: "DO NOT OPEN EVER AGAIN, PAINFUL MEMORIES INSIDE." She smiled and thought about it for a moment before ripping off the tape. She sat staring at the contents. One by one she pulled out her French negligees. And then at the bottom was Jack's t-shirt that he had given her on their last day in Paris in exchange for one of her nighties he wanted to keep. She looked them over as she smiled, recalling all the memories each of them held. She had not been able to throw them away, but seeing them hurt too much so boxing them away was the best solution.

But today, Jack was back and it was time to come alive again. She selected a mid-thigh length lace negligee and covered it with a pale blue satin dressing gown. Pulling her hair up into a loose bun, she checked her look in the mirror and smiled before pushing the box back into the wardrobe and heading out to find Jack.

He stopped dead in his tracks as he saw her coming towards him. "You still take my breath away even after all that. I am the luckiest man alive."

"I just like to tease you." She smiled cheekily.

"Aye, well you do a very good job. Do you know how many sleepless nights I had thinking about you in those nighties, especially the ones that were very revealing," he said with a cheeky grin.

"Well, we are not in France now. That was just a funny thing to do on holidays," she said as she walked to the kitchen."You must be starving."

She opened the fridge to take a peek inside while Jack pulled out a stool at the breakfast bar.

"I have some grass-fed t-bones here. The butcher told me you can cut them with a butter knife, raised in the high country. I couldn't say no. I was going to freeze them for Dad and Johnny but now that you are here we can enjoy them." She placed them on the counter and Jack inspected them.

"My lucky day. My mouth is watering."He sat and chatted while she knocked up a quick salad and put some fries in the oven.

"All set. Is it too hot for you to go outside?" She asked as she grabbed beers out of the fridge.

"No, it has cooled down a bit. Let's go out there." He grabbed the beers off her, and they headed out the back to the BBQ. She followed and sat with him on the lounge, curling her feet up, getting comfortable. He was looking all around sipping on his beer. It was so private, framed by the bush that had the most incredible scent of eucalyptus.

"This is beautiful, Chloe, a lovely wee spot, you are spoilt." She smiled as she looked around; she loved it as well.

It was dusk, and the kookaburras had started their evening chant as they settled in for the day. They were so loud it drowned out their conversation. Jack looked startled. "It's them."

"Them? Who?" asked Chloe, confused.

"The monkeys," he said, looking freaked out.

"How come you never heard them before? They must have followed me here." He jumped up, looking around in all the trees.

"Monkeys? That's not monkeys. They are kookaburras." Chloe couldn't stop laughing at him.

"Kookaburras? You mean, birds?" he said with his eyebrows knitted, looking confused.

"See, over there in the big gum tree next door."

He walked to the fence and looked up the tree.

"Oh, kookaburras. They are so loud."

Chloe was laughing, and he looked very embarrassed."Wait till the cockatoos start. They are even louder."

She could understand how he thought that. They did resemble the sounds of monkeys now that she thought about it. Chloe went inside and returned with the meat, placing it next to the barbeque before covering it.

"One rule you can never forget is to guard your meat with your life. They are excellent at swooping and stealing it."

He looked up at them with a baffled look on his face."Really?"

"Yes, really, they steal from your plate while you're eating if you are not careful. You are a bit protected in the courtyard, but out in the open, lookout."

"I am starting to feel like I need to be on my guard every minute of the day," he said, sitting back down.

"You will learn to love it," she said.

"I already never want to leave," he said, looking around."Here, let me help you with that." He took the lighter off her as she was struggling to light the barbeque.

"I happen to have very good barbeque skills, but I am normally cooking in the snow," he joked.

His mind went back to the night of Jeannie's birthday, when Liam came over to help him. He wondered how close they were, and if they had the strong love between them that he had found with Chloe.

"You are far away somewhere. Can I join you in your thoughts?" she asked, walking back out with two more beers.

"Aye, I was thinking about my sister back at home, at her birthday party. She told me she and Liam were going out together. He is a decent lad. I had an idea they were close but I wonder how long ago they got together."

"Tell me all about it, Jack. I miss your stories."He told her the story about Jeannie and Liam as she sat on the day bed and listened while he cooked. Oh, life was perfect again. She loved listening to his stories, and she knew he would have plenty to tell.

"I still can't believe you are here. Tell me everything that happened in Scotland. I believe nothing happened between you and Shauna, but what 'exactly' went on over there?"

"Okay, where do I start?  Well, it wasn't easy right from the beginning. Jeannie told me Jimmy and Mary were planning the wedding, which I didn't care about, but then she told me Mary had been hanging around with Shauna, and she was as mad as hell about everyone saying how happy I was and people were also giving her a bit of a hard time for moving onto Jimmy also."

Chloe nodded, sipping on her beer. "So it appears Shauna told them she was going to Barcelona for a long weekend with a friend and Mary stepped in, and the next thing she ended up in Dijon. I started to realise what was going on, so cutting a long story short, they put me through hell. I had enough, so like I said before, I went and stayed with Paddy and Maggie for a few days to get away from it all and clear my head. Paddy advised me to go back to work to save sitting around doing nothing, so I took his advice and I went back to work on the trawlers and just ignored them."

"Paddy to the rescue once again." She pumped her fist with a grin.

"Aye, and if it wasn't already bad enough, my wee dog Jock died."

Chloe looked horrified. "I am so sorry."

"I had hit rock bottom, hitting the pub every day, had brawls with my brother every other night, and continually forgot to ring you."

He stared over at her and knew she was feeling guilty. He took a huge swig of his beer before continuing. "Then it was Jeannie's birthday. Mum sat my brother and me both down and told us we were to behave for one night, for our sister. So the night of the party I was staying in the background handling it, until Shauna walked in. I could feel my blood starting to boil. I spoke to Mum, and we agreed she needed to go. I asked Shauna if I could have a word with her, as I was going to ask her to leave and took her to a quiet spot in case she caused a scene, but she had too much to drink and was all over me, trying to kiss me and all. Mary took the photos while I struggled with her to stop."

"What a horrible story. You have been going through hell," said Chloe sympathetically.

"Aye, but the best part was Jimmy witnessed it all, he had been standing in the wing under a tree, and was disgusted and asked them both to leave. After that, he agreed to buy my share of the business. The wedding is cancelled, so I guess that is why she snuck into Jimmy's Facebook and sent the photos to you."

Chloe couldn't believe what she was hearing. Here she was thinking he was having a red-hot love affair, and he was going through absolute hell. She felt so bad. "I am so sorry, Jack, I had no idea," she said, sadly rubbing his arm.

"I understand. I would have thought the same thing if I were in your shoes and saw those photos, especially after meeting her in Dijon. I couldn't tell you any of what was going on, I didn't want to hurt you. I knew I had to come over and see you in person." He smiled, patting her hand on his arm.

"So that is how she ended up in Dijon. I knew there was something funny about all that, it was too much of a coincidence."

"I thought the same, and Mary was there the night of Mum's birthday. Remember the night I rang Mum, it was the night before our wine tour."

"Yes, I do remember, they were all there for dinner."

"Well, after I got off the phone, Jeannie told them everything about the wine tour we had booked for the next day. She said she remembers now, how Mary went off to make a phone call. She must have rung Shauna telling her all about it, and she had a gamble on which wine tour we were on, and booked a ticket. Unfortunately for us, she got the right one."

"Why did they gang up on us like that?"

"Who would know? Bored, I guess. She knew Shauna from school and it appears they met back up recently at a party. I guess Shauna had a gripe with me also. She was hopping mad when I dumped her, so they combined forces."

"That's just nuts. Anyway, that is all behind us now." She got up and turned the meat before sitting back down.

"Oh, sorry I forgot about the meat. I got lost in my storytelling," he chuckled.

"So how was your trip here, and how did you manage to find me?"

"Aye, well, firstly, I can tell you it's a very long way. The plane ride took forever, but when I got off, I was so excited to see you, I was on autopilot. I knew I had to get a train and then I grabbed a taxi to the caravan park."

"You did well, finding your way."

"The next day, I went to the surf club and I met Bob. We had a long chat."

"So you met Bob," she said with a warm smile.

"Aye, he took me out to the Deck of Excuses,Chloe. I got to see the Deck of Excuses,"he said with a sparkle in his eye.

Chloe laughed as she listened.

"Bob was a bit unsure at first I was asking about you, then he recognised me from your photos. We went out onto the deck, and I told him everything. I just poured my heart out to him after all I had been through. I guess I was a bit emotional. He must have felt sorry for me cause he told me that you were going to be at the surf club today, so I came back today and hung around for a while. Then after I saw Bob have a chat with you, and you walked down onto the beach, I knew it was my call. I threw Bob a wink and followed you down there. That is it! You are all up to date."

He took a large gulp of his beer and placed his empty bottle on the table.

"You know what is funny is that he was always on your side. He kept telling me something is wrong, that there is something that I don't know. Wow, and he had never even met you."

"Well, he was right, and here I am." He had a huge smug look on his face, which made her laugh. The story was incredible.

She took a sip of her beer and sat back, taking it all in. "So you sold the business to Jimmy. What are your plans now?"

"I have no clue. I just needed to get here and sort things out with you. I didn't think past that."

"Well, the first thing we have to do is check you out of the caravan park and bring your things here. This is your home now, Jack, here with me," she said, taking his hand. She stared deep into his eyes.

"That is what I was hoping you would say. I never want to leave you ever again, I am so sorry it took me so long to get here." It was the words that she had wanted to hear also. It was happening, he was here and he was staying. Jack,the beautiful strong highlander, was here with her and wanting to stay forever. Her eyes were glistening with tears as she struggled to hold them back.

"You are here now, that is all that matters, we are back together, forever." She managed to say with a strained voice. Jack had tears running down his face. She leaned across and hugged him.

"I am so sorry. Look at me, a grown man crying like a wee baby, but it is just so comforting to hear you say that."

They had so much to talk about over their meal together that night. He opened the bottle of red, and they chatted for hours until Jack started to yarn. "I think that steak has done me in," he said sleepily.

"I don't think it is the steak, you are still suffering jet lag. It's late, we lost track of time, let's head in."

They tidied up before heading into her room to get organised for bed. He walked over to her side table and picked up the painting of them that she had framed. It was the portrait of the two of them painted by the man in Santorini.

"I had this on my bedside table as well." He smiled."I used to stare at it every morning and night."

"I just love it. Funny, even though I was so mad with you. I still couldn't take it down," she sighed. "It was the most beautiful memories for me."

"I just love the way he has captured the warmth in your eyes. He was a very talented painter," he said.

"I thought the same thing about you, Jack. He has captured your gorgeous smile that I love so much."

They crawled into bed, and he cuddled her, both of them exactly where they had wanted to be for months, they had irrevocably found it. Immensely happy and content they both fell sound asleep.

# CHAPTER 2
## WELCOME TO THE JUNGLE

Jack woke up, terrified by the sound of monkeys. He sprung out of bed. Chloe jumped startled, then realising what had happened and fell back onto her pillow. "Kookaburras, Jack, remember? Lovely little kookaburras. It is okay."

"Oh, aye, they startled me, that's all. I am not used to living in the jungle yet," he said with weary eyes peering out the window.

"Come back to bed," she said, still half asleep. He closed the blinds and crawled back in beside her.

"Sorry, I feel a bit silly." He was snuggling into her.

"Relax, you are here with me now, I will protect you," she said teasing.

"Hey, that's my job, remember? I will be the king of the jungle, I just need to get to know the beasties that I have to deal with, and this is the first one that I need to tame, my wee Jaguar here."

She was giggling as he started to hold her down looking over her, as if he was remembering what he had been missing. The gentleness on his face, as he looked over her body, was of pure adoration, and then he smiled at her as she melted. She lay mesmerised by his body as she watched his muscles flex with every movement. He tranquillised her as he bewitched her with his alluring charms. She lay motionless, as her body quivered with delight as he rediscovered every inch of her body.

"Mo leannan," he whispered, and that wave of uncontrollable desire took over, and they became one, both breathing heavily as his body shimmered with a thin layer of sweat, until they were lying back on the bed panting uncontrollably.

"I'm tamed," she smiled still out of breath.

He looked over at her, and she had drifted back off to sleep. He loved waking up with her. He had missed this so much when they were apart. He had laid awake many a night, unable to sleep, thinking of her, and he was lapping up every minute of waking up with her once again.

Reminiscing of their days on the ship as he lay and a smile crept to his face. He was the happiest man in the world, taking a gamble, rushing off and heading on such a long journey to Australia to find her. But it had paid off, and he had never been happier.

Awakening once again she stirred; he slipped out of bed and headed to the kitchen to make coffee. Without any idea where everything was kept, he looked around; he was sure that he would work it out. She smiled as she listened to him searching through cupboards and drawers. He stopped at his duffel bag and grabbed his flask of whisky. It was tradition when they didn't have to be anywhere to have a nip of whisky in the morning.

As he walked back in, she smelt the strong aroma of the whisky in the coffee. "Oh, I love relaxed mornings with you, Jack." She smiled as he put it on her bedside table and sat up as he opened the curtains and crawled back into bed.

"'You must be starving," said Chloe. "I am not too sure what I have in the fridge. I wasn't expecting visitors," she teased.

"I will eat anything as long as I am here with you, as long as it's not snakes and spiders. I think I would probably prefer to go hungry in that case."

"Well, I will find something and cook you up a meal fit for a Jaguar tamer." She laughed as she sipped on her coffee.

After breakfast, Chloe took him up to the main house and introduced him to Mrs. Whitaker. She was sitting in the sun room as usual, doing a puzzle. Looking up at them, she removed her reading glasses as they approached. "Mrs. Whitaker, this is my friend from Scotland, Jack. He is going to be staying with me, if that is okay with you, of course."

"Oh, yes, I remember you showing me photos. Hello, Jack, it is lovely to meet you. You are more than welcome to stay as long as you like. It will be handy to have a man about the house."

"Thank you, I will try not to be any trouble."

"Well, this calls for a cup of tea and I have made some lovely lamingtons. I will go and organise it." Getting up agilely, she made her way into the kitchen.

"What is lamingtons? Is it a cake?" whispered Jack with a thrilled smirk.

"Sort of. You will love them. I will go and give her a hand," she laughed.

As Chloe left, Jack's eyes looked out over the yard. It was neat and tidy with a rose garden down the side and an old hills hoist at the end of a small path from the laundry room. He wiped his brow. It was so hot and it was still only mid-morning. How would he cope when summer came? Flies started to annoy him as he swatted them away.

"It's like living in a jungle," he said to himself. A bird landed on the hills hoist clothes line. He listened as it sang a beautiful song. Chloe came out with a tray full of cups, milk, sugar, and a plate of lamingtons. Mrs. Whitaker followed behind with a teapot, neatly covered with a knitted tea-cosy. Jack was eyeing off the lamingtons with intense food envy.

"You should try one. She is an excellent baker."

"Oh, thankyou, dear. If you like treats you are welcome to come and have a cup of tea with me anytime. I love doing all sorts of baking."

Chloe smiled as a smile crept to his face.

"Well, I think we are going to be extremely good friends indeed," he said as he started on one without needing to be told twice. "These are the best thing I have tasted. Soft sponge, rolled in chocolate covered in coconut. I could eat that whole plate."

The bird started singing again, and he watched as Chloe handed him his cup of tea. "It's a currawong. They look like a magpie but they have the sweetest sound."

Another two landed beside it as the rickety old clothes line began to sway, and they all started to sing together. They watched as they waited until they stopped before being able to hear each other speak.

"They are so loud," said Jack, watching them with an inquisitive glare.

"Not as loud as the cockies," added Chloe. "Jack is not familiar with our wildlife. We will need to teach him," she said, turning to Mrs Whitaker.

"Well, you shouldn't have any spiders bothering you. I had the place sprayed only last week," she said, stirring her tea. "The snakes come out to sun bake. Just stay away and they won't hurt you. They are as frightened of you, as you are of them."

Jack stopped half-eating a lamington and stared unable to believe what she had said.

"Snakes? We have snakes here?" A large crumb fell from his lip and they both laughed.

"Mostly just red belly blacks and death adders. They come out of the bush and love the warmth of the sunshine. This time of year they are just waking up, they sleep during the cold months."

Chloe could see Jack was starting to look panicked and stepped into the conversation. "However, we have wallabies and possums and all cuddly wildlife also," she said as she handed him the plate of lamingtons, hoping to take his mind off the snakes. He smiled and took one before looking around under the table with haste.

'What are you doing?"

"I thought I felt something," he said, still looking around.

"They won't come around us that close," comforted Mrs. Whitaker.

"You just have the jitters now," added Chloe with a chuckle.

Finishing their tea, Chloe decided it was a good idea to make tracks, after Jack more than once sent everything flying off the table as he jumped continuously and swore something was lurking around. They thanked her and went back to the cabin. Grabbing her keys and bag she turned to Jack. "Come on. Let me show you around a bit."

"Sounds like fun. Where are we going?"

"I thought we might go around to Patonga, there is a fish-and-chips shop there I know you will love." She laughed as his eyes lit up with the mention of food. "It is only about a ten-minute drive from here. I am sure your belly can wait."

He peered intently out the window as they made their way down the winding track. The bush flowers were all in bloom and appeared to be greeting them as they swayed in the breeze as they passed. Pulling up they nosed into the parking bay, and they both jumped out looking around.

"Let's take a walk down the wharf." She grabbed his hand and led him along the path.

Looking around, he was impressed. There was hardly a soul around. The beach was framed on both sides by beautiful bush-land and the smell of the bush and the sea made a delightful mix. If it wasn't for the sounds of the birds singing loudly, it would be completely silent. They walked all the way to the end of the wharf, looking curiously into the water along the way.

"This is a very unspoilt part of the world," he said, turning back towards the shoreline.

"So that is the town, the pub and the fish shop," he asked as he gestured towards them.

"Yea that is it, it's a fancy pub. Boats come over from the Pittwater and Sydney to go here, don't be fooled. It is very busy on weekends." He looked back out to sea and spotted a trawler coming back in.

"This is where the trawlers come back in after fishing?"

"Yea, this one coming in now will pull up here and offload."

"Do you think they would show me their catch?" he asked, shading his eyes.

"Sure, they won't mind showing you." He scrutinised the boat as it drew near. He was mesmerised by it. His stare was so intense it made her laugh. He smiled back at her.

"What, was I staring at it? Sorry, I love boats, don't laugh at me."

She wiped the smile of her face. "Sorry, it made me laugh, promise I won't do it again." She smirked.

He continued watching until they tied it off, and then walked over to them. She sat on the old timber bench seat at the end of the wharf as he chatted to the fisherman. She knew by his interest and the huge smile on his face he was enjoying himself. After a while, he came back with a huge grin.

"I just got a job. Turns out, they are short and offered me a start." Things were starting to look up for him. He had only had his feet on Aussie sand for a few short days, and he had not only won back the love of his life, but landed a job also.

"Wow, fantastic news! Well done, see Australia is not that bad after all, is it?"

Settling down on the end of the wharf, with their wrapped bag of fish and chips, she told him stories of the town. Pelicans started hanging around, eyeing off their lunch He stared as they waddled closer, with a look of fear on his face. Standing around half a meter high in height, the pelicans seemed for him such a monstrous bird. He grabbed Chloe's arm as they approached.

"What are those huge things? They look like they want to eat me?"

"Pelicans, lovely, aren't they?" she said as they watched and one opened its wings and began flapping. "Look at the size of its bill, and that wingspan!"

"They have the longest bill of all birds and their wingspan is close to two and a half meters," she explained proudly. "They are fishermen just like you, Jack," she teased. "Whatever you do don't feed them, they won't leave you alone if you do."

"There is not a chance of that happening," he said, horrified. "I don't like sharing food all that much, remember? And plus, they look very frightening."

"How did I ever forget?" she laughed.

Back at the cabin, Chloe was busy showing him where everything was kept. "I have a shift at the restaurant, so I want to make sure you are comfortable," she said.

"Relax, I can find my way around a kitchen, and believe me, I never starve. Get going, I will be perfectly fine."

"Okay, okay, then I am going. Enjoy your night. I will be home straight after my shift." She kissed him and made her way out the door.

As she got in the car, she wanted to turn back around and go back to him. How could she go to work when she had him inside her cabin? She sat for a moment before she started the car, knowing she had to go. They were busy, and she would never hear the end of it.

Chloe almost floated inside as she arrived and gave everyone a big hello before heading out the back to put her apron on. When she returned, Johnny Finn and Kait were waiting as they stared at her. She had been moping around for weeks and everyone was starting to get over her moods.

"What are you so happy about?"Kait said,with an astonished look on her face.

"Oh, nothing. Just maybe the fact that Jack is here," she said, almost jumping out of her skin.

"Here? Where? What do you mean?" said Kait as she flicked her head towards the doorway.

"Not here. He is in my cabin," she squealed.

"He is here? When did this happen? I thought that it was over," asked Kait, shocked.

"Me, too, but as it turns out, it was all a big mistake. I wouldn't answer his calls, so he came over to work things out. It's an epic story, I will fill you in later. He is back, I can't believe it, and I am over the moon."

"Well, I am tickled pink for you, Chlo," she said as she went back to setting the tables.

It was busy so the shift went quickly, and when they closed the doors for the night Kait was waiting to hear all the details. She raced over to her the first chance she had.

"Alright you have had me busting all night. Tell me every juicy little detail," she said, taking off her apron and Chloe laughed because she knew how crazy it had been driving her.

"He found me at the surf club yesterday. He explained everything to me, and I am happy with it. I fell head over heels again, I am crazy about him," she explained, grabbing her bag. "I can't wait to get home to him."

"Oh, that is such great news, Chloe. I am so happy for you. Plus, we were all over your shitty moods," she laughed,

"I am so sorry I have been a bitch at times, but I was hurting bad."

"Yea, we were all aware of the reason, but you were still a nightmare at times."

"Eeks! I am so sorry," she said, pulling a face.

"You are lucky you are so cute, and we love you," she said with a squint, hanging up her apron.

"I am going home if we are all done."

"Well, seeing you have one foot out the door already, I kind of guessed that."

She waved and started down the stairs.

"Wait! When are we going to meet him?" she yelled out to her as she was running to her car.

"Soon! He is all mine at the moment," she yelled back as she got into her car with a grin.

She beeped as she drove past Kait,who waved before turning and heading back into the restaurant with a smile.

Jack was inside watching TV with all the doors closed when she walked in and threw her keys on the breakfast bar.

"Hi, I am back."She went over and gave him a kiss. "What are you doing in here? I thought that you would be outside. It's a lovely evening."

"I was, but then two creatures came from around the stone wall, and sat over there staring at me, I thought they were going to eat me."

Chloe laughed. "That would be the possums. They won't hurt you, they were just looking for a treat. I forgot to mention that to you."

She opened up the doors. "It is lovely out here. Come and join me for a wine." She grabbed two glasses from the cupboard and Jack grabbed a bottle of red from the wine rack. It wasn't long and the possums were back. Chloe gave them a strawberry each, and as they ate she showed him how to pat them. Jack cautiously came closer and patted one. After they finished eating they happily went on their way.

"I told Kait that you are here, and she is so excited, she can't wait to meet you. But I told her to give you some time to settle in," she said as Jack poured her a wine.

"Well, I have been thinking, I still have a few nights at the caravan park, why don't we hang out there for a while, and maybe we might be able to all meet in the park and have a barbeque."

She looked up at him with a squint. "Are you sure? I don't want to push my family onto you yet. You only just got here."

"I would love to meet them, and invite anyone else you like. I may as well meet them all," he said, settling back on the lounge.

"That sounds like a lovely idea. We could do it on Sunday," she said happily.

"Sunday it is."

"Thanks, Jack. Kait is just busting to meet you, and believe me she is hard to shake."

They hung around the caravan park for the next few days, swimming, sun baking and just relaxing. When Chloe had to work, she walked there and Jack would walk up to meet her after her shift. The first night he picked her up, Kait came running out and invited him inside.

"So you are Jack," said Kait, tossing her hair back.

"Aye, that is me," he said nervously, clearing his throat.

"I am Kait and this is Johnny. We finally meet. You have come a long way."

"Oh, it is a very long way. Now I understand why everyone in Europe kept saying that to Chloe," he said, rolling his eyes.

"Well, welcome to Australia, Jack! We are all happy that you are here. Chloe has finally stopped breathing fire at everyone," she teased and Chloe turned red with embarrassment.

"Great to meet you, mate. Let me show you around our little shack." Johhny walked Jack towards the kitchen.

"He's just gorgeous, Chloe" whispered Kait.

"I know. I still can't believe that he is here," she said with an excited grin.

"Mum is going to love him. Is Sunday still on?"

"Yes, I am sure she is going to love him. What is there not to love?" She said with a dreamy look as she gazed his way. Kait had never seen her sister like this. She smiled at her as she thought back, her cards were right. This was the one she would marry.

## CHAPTER 3
## THE PICNIC

The days were going quickly and Sunday morning arrived before they had time to think about it. They were buzzing around getting everything organised for the picnic, packing the esky with the meat and drinks.

"I thought this was a good idea at the start. I should never have suggested this," said Jack uncomfortably.

"Listen to you. I can't believe you are getting so nervous." She laughed as she passed the meat from the fridge.

"Aye, I am. I am meeting your parents. What if they don't like me? They could ship me back off to Scotland," he said with a furrowed brow.

"They wouldn't do that. You have nothing to worry about, they are going to love you," she grinned.

"Well, it is easy for you to say. I will breathe a lot easier when the whole day is over."

"You have met Kait and you like her, and she loves you. They will be just as impressed as she was."

She placed their two little whisky glasses on the table, beginning to pour a nip into each as he intently stared, thanking his lucky stars she was full of great ideas.

"Here, drink this, it will settle your nerves." She handed him the glass, and he smiled at her as he took it gratefully.

"Thanks, I need this today," he said as he shot it back.

"It is normally you calming me down. This is one for the books." She laughed.

"Now, I understand how you feel." He looked over at her with a face full of worry.

"Can I have one more wee whisky?"

"I am never going to let you live this down. You know that, don't you?" she teased as she poured him another nip.

They were the first to arrive at the park and chose the barbeque hut beside the children's play area and oval. The boys loved playing a game of cricket and the park would be handy for Sophia. Chloe put the table cloth on the table, while Jack started to clean the barbeque. He was so quiet Chloe had never seen him so nervous before, and she smiled as she studied him. She liked how it meant so much to him meeting her parents and how making an impression was so important to him.

As she looked around, she spotted Kait and Johnny walking towards them. Kait was pushing the pram and Johnny was wheeling the esky. They were both dressed for a fun day of cricket. Kait was in denim shorts, a white T-shirt, and sandshoes, and Johnny also in T-shirt, shorts, and thongs.

"Hi. we are a bit early," she yelled out as they approached and Jack's head spun, thinking it was her parents. "Sophia was ready for a nap, so we put her in the pram and walked here before she crashed. We both want a couple of drinks today as we welcome Jack," said Kait as she threw Jack a welcoming grin. Chloe took a peek under the cotton throw rug loosely covering the pram.

"Oh, she is so sweet, fast asleep."

"This was the best thing Kait ever bought me, this esky on wheels. You can wheel the whole thing behind you, plus I can fit a whole slab in here," laughed Johnny as Jack walked over and shook Johnny's hand before giving Kait a kiss on the cheek.

"G'day, Jack."

"He is extremely nervous today. He is panicking meeting Mum and Dad."

"Whaaaat? Really? You have nothing to worry about," said Kait with a dismissive wave.

"I keep telling him not to worry."

"No, serious, mate. They are super cool people. I remember when I met them for the first time. I was freaking out also, but when I met them, I was super happy," added Johnny as he placed his esky next to the barbeque.

"Well, you are about to find out for yourself because here they come," said Chloe, and they all turned to catch sight of them, unloading the boot of the car in the car park.

Jack stared intently as they walked towards them across the field. They looked friendly enough. Her mum was dressed in a long beige flowing dress with a camel wide-brimmed hat with her blonde hair pulled to one side. She gave off the aura of a lady as she walked tall with elegance. If Chloe was going to look like that in thirty years, he would be extremely happy. His eyes turned to her father, who had the style of an old surfy. Sandy blonde ringlets and a tanned face, dressed in tailored shorts, a hot-buttered surf brand t-shirt with a mambo shirt unbuttoned over the top, sandals, and a large straw sun hat, waving frantically as they got closer. They were chalk and cheese. It was like Lady Diana had arrived with Paul Hogan. He instantly knew where Kait got her personality.

"Hello, everyone," said Olivia cheerfully as she placed her bag of goodies near the table.

"Mum, Dad, this is Jack," said Chloe proudly.

*Shit, she put me straight in the limelight.* He leaned forward and shook her father's hand. "A pleasure to meet you, Mr. and Mrs. Clarke."

"Hooly dooley, you don't need any formalities here, mate. We are a fairly down-to-earth mob. Call me Rob," he said, patting him on the back.

"Yes, please call me Olivia," said her mum as he leaned in and gave her a kiss.

Olivia walked over to Kait and took a peek at Sophia sleeping. "Oh, bless her cotton socks, fast asleep," she said as she covered her over again. Rob put his esky down next to Johnny's, and returned with a beer. Chloe followed her mum to join the girls in placing their treats on the food table.

"So you are the bloke whose hand I need to shake for looking after my little girl overseas. I owe you a beer, mate," he said, handing him a beer. He took it gratefully, needing a drink to calm his nerves.

"Oh, aye, sir, I mean, Rob. But it wasn't a chore. We had the best time."

"Well, Kait tells me if it wasn't for you, Chloe never would have made it. She was on her way home before you came along."

"We were both a wee bit scared. It was pure luck we met each other."

Olivia returned with a wine Kait had poured for her. "No luck involved. Nana sent him to me,Mum," yelled out Chloe as she wandered back. "I prayed for her to guide me and I met Jack." she put her arms around him and snuggled in closer.

"That's a sweet thought, Chloe. She loved you very much, so I would like to think you are right," smiled Olivia as she started to hand around a platter of nibbles she retrieved from the esky.

"It was my tarot cards we need to thank, without them she would never have got on that frigging plane in the first place," yelled out Kait from the food table as she poured wine.

"Hey, here you all are!"

It was Angie who had walked up behind them and walked straight over to Jack.

"So you must be Jack. Chloe never stops bragging about you. I am Angie."

"A pleasure to meet you also." She dropped her cold food bag on the table and started to unpack it, placing bags of chips onto the table and ripping them open before grabbing out a beer.

"I like the idea of the park barbeque. We can all enjoy a drink and walk home," she said, walking back.

"We drove, but I am only having a couple today. Robby can enjoy a few beers with the boys," said Olivia, putting the platter on the table with the other items everyone had bought along.

Rob walked back from the car with two camping chairs and opened one for Olivia, helping her settle into it.

"Thank you, Robby."

They spotted Bob walking towards them with his esky in one hand.

"Here comes trouble," yelled out Rob.

"G'day, Rob. I will have to empty this esky a bit. I am stuffed and I only had to walk from the surf club," said Bob as he placed a box of nuts on the table and returned with a beer.

"G'day, Jack! Good to see ya, son," he said sincerely.

"Hi, Bob. Thanks for all your help the other day."

"That's my pleasure, mate. Glad I could help." He winked and opened his beer, pulling his UBSLSC beer cooler out of his pocket.

Chrissie and Finn were the last to arrive and came straight over to Jack.

"Hi, I am Chloe's sister, Chrissie, and this is my boyfriend, Finn."

"Happy to meet you both."

Chloe was watching him closely, the nervous frown on his face told the picture, and she gently smiled. Chrissie flicked her long blonde curls out of her face as she dug deep in the bag for a beer cooler.

"There is wine over here," yelled out Kait.

"No worries, Kait. I am sticking with beer today. We need to go to a party later."

"I have a nice coldie here for you, Chrissie," said Finn.

It was obvious to Jack she looked like her mother, but with her father's curls and her personality,she was also a bit of both mixed together.

"That wasn't too bad, was it?" Kait had arrived back after helping her mum with the salads.

"No, everyone is friendly. I think I have survived."

"I tried to tell you, there was no need to get worked up," said Chloe as she handed him a chip.

"Yea, no need for that around here, mate. You have met a girl with the nicest family. They are all super cool people," added Finn, rocking on his heels.

"I am lucky, all right. It was my lucky day when I met Chloe in that bar in Barcelona, that is for sure," said Jack, finally relaxing enough to lean in and grab some cheese and biscuits he had been eyeing off for ages.

"What are you doing here, Finn?" said Olivia as she walked over to join them. "I thought you were working. Who is at the restaurant today?"

"Johnny has organised a Sunday Italian day, so we all get Sundays and Mondays off now. It helps with family get-togethers like this."

Johnny walked over with a bowl of chips he started to hand around.

"Yea, it has worked out alright. It's just pasta and salad bars, so we prep beforehand. And we leave it to a few casuals who run it for us. Easy work for them, not hard prepping for us, and we all get to have some family time."

"I love having him home on Sundays. We get a chill-out family day together," added Kait, smiling.

"I am about to put the meat on the barbeque if everyone is hungry," said Rob.

"Let me know when the snags are done so I can make Sophia a sanga."

"Yea, right O, Kait, shall do," he said, swatting a fly away with the tongs he was carrying.

"I will give you a hand," said Jack.

"No, you're the guest here today, mate. Take it easy. Johnny can give me a hand." He leaned in and whispered, "Plus, he takes over and I end up doing nothing except drinking beer. Works out bloody fantastic." He winked before turning and heading for the barbeque.

They all laughed; they knew it was true. Johnny was off like a frog in a sock. "Wait, I have appetisers to go on first."

"You can hang out with me for a bit. Lap it up, mate. I never get asked to cook, either. I think they have a bit of a competition going between the two of them," explained Finn.

"Sounds like it. We will be drinking buddies, then."

"You catch on quick. You'll fit in well around here," said Finn.

"Where's ya hat, Jack?" yelled out Bob as he returned with a can of aeroguard and everyone started taking a step back. They all knew what Bob was like with a can of aeroguard.

"I have one here somewhere" he said, looking around.

"Well, ya better put it on. The sun can be a bastard. It stole my beautiful wife and gave me a run for me money, also," he said as he bent over, removing his terry towling hat and showing him the top of his head where a skin cancer had been cut out.

"Sorry to hear that, Bob. I have a lot to learn. Chloe is always reminding me to put on sunscreen. She lathered me up this morning."

"Chloe should know better. You don't put sunscreen on ya melon, do ya? And yours would be snowy white, son."

"I didn't think about that. I will have to be a bit more careful. I am still not coping with the heat very well, either," he said, swatting a fly.

"Well, I see you have the Aussie salute mastered," he laughed. Jack stared, confused. "You know, swatting a fly."

Jack nodded as Bob sprayed himself all over with the can and handed it to him, before turning to Chloe.

"I saw that lout you used to go out with yesterday, Chloe. Did you hear he went on a surfing safari up the coast with his mates after he dumped you?"

"Craig. Yes, I heard a whisper," she said a bit uncomfortable with his name being brought up.

"Yea, he doesn't hang around too much anymore after I did my block at him for leaving you hanging, to go on that trip on your own."

"Well, it turned out to be the best thing that could have happened," said Chloe.

"You're right. I told him so yesterday, said you were too good for him, and a few other things. He didn't stick around for too long after that."

Chloe laughed. She could just see it now. Bob would have made sure he told it to him straight, and Craig would have been looking for the nearest escape route out of there.

"Well, it all worked out in the end," said Bob, taking the can back from Jack, giving his hat one last spray as everyone stepped back coughing.

"I am super glad he didn't go," said Jack and everyone laughed.

"We all are," yelled Kait.

Jack started to relax as they all settled in for a laid-back afternoon. The conversation was easy as they shared the meal together. After lunch, Angie retrieved a box of Cadbury chocolates from her bag and handed them around as everyone grabbed one eagerly.

"Hey, how do you stop your chocolates melting on the way home from the shop on a hot day?" asked Rob. Everyone shrugged with a smile knowing he was about to tell one of his bad dad jokes.

"No idea,Dad," said Chrissie.

"Eat them in the carpark," he said with a smirk, throwing a chocolate into his mouth and everyone laughed.

A game of cricket kicked into action, which lasted the whole afternoon. Angie was first to leave and said her goodbyes. The girls all sat it out for a bit leaving the men to finish it off,sitting on the picnic blanket as Kait placed a platter of cheese and biscuits in the centre.

"Mum, would you prefer your chair?" she asked, ready to retrieve it for her.

"No, sweetie. I can still sit on the ground. It's getting up that's getting a bit harder, but my yoga is helping," she said as she slowly sat, fluffing her dress neatly around her.

"Has everyone got a drink before I sit down?" said Kait, looking around at everyone.

"Yes, thanks, Kait. Come and sit," said Chrissie. "Stop fussing." Kait removed her sandshoes and sat on the blanket.

"Is that a new toe-ring?" asked Chloe, stretching her neck to get a better view. Kait laidback on her elbow and proudly displayed her toes to her inquisitive audience.

"Yes, stunning, isn't it? It has an amethyst stone to help promote relaxation. I bought it at the markets last weekend. Johnny took Sophia down to the sand to play and I had an hour to wander the foreshore markets on my own. I lapped up every minute. It is so great having Johnny home on Sundays."

"Yea, it makes a huge difference. Finn and I can stay at parties a bit later now. Awesome not being clock watchers, anymore," added Chrissie, hovering over the cheese platter with a toothpick, unsure what cheese to select.

"Try that one, Chrissie. I bought that one. It's a French cheese and soooo yummy."

"Oh, thanks. I love having a well-travelled sister around, introducing us to all-new foods"she said as she popped the cheese in her mouth and rubbed her belly, humming. Chloe instantly thought of Jack and her head spun towards the cricket field.

"You have found a lovely man there, Chloe. He appears to like you an awful lot," said Olivia, watching her closely.

"Thanks, Mum. He has made me very happy. I can't believe he is here."Her eyes were all over him as he laughed with Bob having a wonderful time. Olivia scanned Chloe's face as she smiled, watching him, and recognised that dreamy sparkle in her eyes. This was the one. Her daughter would marry this man, and she was more than happy with her choice. He seemed sincere and kind, and was fitting in well with the family. Kait poured herself another wine, offering it around, but they all declined.

"I still cannot believe 'you' of all people did Europe before me 'and'found some hot guy to hang out with, I must add," said Kait and everyone laughed.

"You were so brave doing the cruise all on your own," added Olivia.

"Well, I was kinda pushed into it, remember?" she said, glaring at Kait with a smirk.

"Yea, you could have sat here in your tiny little world, hanging out with Craig and the surf club, instead of having sex in every exotic European city with a red-hot lover," teased Kait.

Chloe was having a sip on her beer and almost choked.

"Kait, my god, Mum is here, remember?" said Chloe loudly, shooting her sister daggers.

"Mum already knows all about it," answered Kait, waving her off with her hand and sipping on her wine with the other one. Chloe was as red as a beetroot."Well, I am glad everyone's favourite subject seems to be all about my sex life."

"No one told me," said Chrissie, smiling with delight wondering what saucy things she might find out.

"All you need to know is that the cruise opened up my eyes. I am not the same person, that is for sure. I really found myself on that holiday."

"I always miss out on the juicy stuff," said Chrissie, deflated. And everyone laughed.

"You are right, Chlo. It was the best thing that could have happened to you. We were so proud of you. I called Kait daily to see if she had any news from you," said Olivia, twirling her wine glass in her hand as she thought about how overwhelming it had been as a mother.

"And I told her everything," winked Kait with a smirk and Chloe's cheeks turned pink once again.

"She is teasing, Chloe," she comforted her as she slapped Kait gently on the arm.

"It was hard as parents to push you out of your comfort zone, and then second-guess our decision every single day.

Your father kept telling me to let you go, so I did, but when Kait told me you had met a boy, well that is when your father started freaking out, and you can imagine what that was like." They all laughed.

"And going by what I heard, so he should have been,"added Kait, popping a cheeseball into her mouth with a teasing smirk.

"Ssh,here they come," said Chloe with a frown, the last thing she wanted was Jack to hear her sisters and mother gossiping about him.

They all turned to see them arriving back, wiping the sweat from their brow and laughing.

"Looks like they all had a great time," said Chloe, staring with a nervous grin.

"He is fitting in well, Chloe, don't worry. He will be fine," said Olivia, patting her hand.

"He was so nervous today,Mum, meeting you all."

"That is a wonderful thing. It says you mean a lot to him."

"Nothing wrong with him now," said Kait. They turned to catch him having a hearty belly laugh with Johnny as they walked back."Well, he is definitely some nice eye-candy you have welcomed to the fam bam, Chlo,"she teased.

"Far out, Kait, give it a rest. He could hear you from there."

Kait winked with a smirk as she sipped on her wine.

"Who's up for a coldie?" asked Johnny, heading for the esky.

"Not for me. Chrissie and I have another party to go to, a birthday dinner for one of her friends," said Flynn, resting the bat next to the table.

"Yea, damn, is that the time? We have to jet Finn." She jumped up and ran around to pick up her things."Lovely catch-up, everyone! Welcome,Jack!" She yelled as she kissed everyone, and they left in a flurry.

"I guess I will ring an uber after this beer," said Bob. "It was a big morning at Nippers, I think I am getting a bit too old running around after all those kids," he said yawning.

"We are just finishing our drinks and leaving. We can drop you home, Bob," said Olivia.

"Oh, thanks, Livy, that would help me out a lot. She's a good old stick, your mum, Chloe, and still a bloody good sort, too," he winked.

"Hey, what's this old thing?" said Olivia as she started to pack up the table.

"I knew you would bite at that one," laughed Bob. "And ya didn't disappoint me."

"You can't leave the surf club, Bob. The place would never be the same without you. Bloody hell I can't remember a time you were not at the surf club, showing everyone the ropes at Nippers," said Rob, opening a beer.

Bob chuckled. "Now you're making me feel old."

"You put all our girls through Nippers, and Sophia will be there in no time. We need you around, Bob." He smiled and Bob gave a half-hearted shrug. It made him feel proud inside. It was true he had given more than half his life to the club and the thought of Sophia and who knows how many more from this family were still to come, well it gave him the courage to soldier on. He had a few years left in him, yet. He looked around. This was his family now. They were everything to him. His kids were too busy with their families, and didn't care too much for the surf club, either. He had been gutted when he lost his beloved Patty, but this family had rallied around him and helped him get through his deepest darkest days. He would never, ever forget the love and time they shared with him. Not even his own son had the decency to check on him as much as they did, but he guessed he was dealing with it in his own way.

That night they ordered in a pizza and opened a bottle of chianti classico as they relaxed at the table and chairs on the veranda of the cabin. It had been a big day for them, and they were both happy it was over. Jack was part of her family now. He knew everyone he needed to know, and they all got on well.

"I worked out your family today," he said with a smug look.

"Oh! Did you, now? OK, I am all ears," she said, flicking him a quick glance as she picked an anchovy off her pizza slice, hurling it out over the veranda railing.

"Well, you are a hundred percent your mum, looks, personality the lot, except for your anxiety, of course. Kait is a hundred-percent your dad in personality with your mum's looks, and Chrissie is half-and-half, both in personality and looks; she has your mum's face and your dad's curls."

"Mmm," she nodded with an inquisitive stare chewing on her pizza.

"But your parents are like chalk and cheese. How did they ever meet?" he asked. It had been erking him all day, they got on like a house on fire, but were the most unusual couple.

She settled back, putting her half-eaten slice down, washing it down with a sip of wine, ready to deliver her story.

"Well, you nailed it. Dad has always been a coastie, grew up here all his life. Mum grew up in North Sydney, went to one of those posh la de da schools and then deportment school after that. She was an up-and-coming model, working for some Sydney-based company. Her family had a holiday home here, so they spent every chance they had, relaxing here on the coast. That is where she met Dad. They spent endless days hanging out at the beach together." She stopped to take a sip of her wine before she continued. "Mum always told us girls the story, how she fell in love with a hippie surfer, from the North Coast, how it started as a holiday romance but grew into so much more. Pop thought he was just a larrikin and wasn't too fussed, but Nanna didn't like him too much. She always called him the Galah from the coast. She was worried Mum was throwing away a promising modelling career on a no-hoper surfy bum." She took a bite on her pizza as Jack stared, intrigued with the story, waiting to hear the rest.

"But she did throw it all away," he said.

"Yep, she sure did. She says he made her laugh, and she wanted to laugh a lifetime with him."

"That's a nice thought." He nodded, rearranging the cheese hanging from the side of his pizza. "So what happened to your nanna? Did she hate him forever?"

"No, both her and pop grew to love him. He got a good job on the council, bought a beach shack, and asked for her hand in marriage."

"And that's it, happily ever after."

"Yep, pretty much. She gave up modelling when she fell pregnant with Kait and Nan and Pop ended up loving Dad and his crazy ways. They had a very close relationship in the end."

"So your mum was a model. I can see that in the way she walks and holds herself."

"Mmm," she nodded with her mouth full. "There are some lovely photos, I will show you one day."

Jack nodded, chewing on his pizza, thinking about the story of her family. "So where did your anxiety come from?"

"Nanna, she was always freaking out, apparently, but no one put two and two together until I came along with the same issues, and they worked it out. She ended up a recluse in the end. Too anxious to go out, I suppose. She was the sweetest lady. I wish you met her. She would have loved you." She threw him a smirk, sipped her wine, lost in thought for a moment before continuing. "Pop was a conductor on the interstate trains, gone days at a time. He had a beautiful kind nature, everyone loved him, and he was popular on the trains. A real character."

"I feel I know and understand your family so much more now."

"We're a pretty simple mob, as Dad always puts it," she laughed.

They sat staring at the sky lost in their thoughts. Jack was comprehending the story had just heard. They were lovely people and he was so happy to have met them.

"Look at the stars tonight," said Jack as he peered into the sky.

"I am pretty proud to have you sitting under the Southern Cross with me tonight," she smiled. "See that cross up there in the sky, in the bright section of the milky way? The cross is pointing direct south. If you ever get lost, it will help you find me. I will be here, waiting for you, looking up into the southern sky."

He watched intently.

"Well, that is comforting to know. But I am never leaving the southern sky again," he smiled. He had never given it much thought before. He was sitting under a completely different sky. It was Chloe's sky, and he was thrilled to bits to be there. But not even the Southern Cross could hold his attention when one last slice of pizza was sitting lonely in the pizza box. "Would you like the last slice?" he offered with a face that said, *please don't say yes*.

"You crack me up. Lucky for you, I still have one. It's all yours. Enjoy!"

More than happy with that answer, he eagerly grabbed it before she changed her mind.

"I need to meet your family now, Jack."

"Aye, I would love you to meet my mum," he said, staring at his pizza, chewing, lost in thought, thinking of his mum.

"She sounds like a lovely lady. We will have to take a trip to Scotland one day," she suggested as she pulled a string of cheese from her slice and popped it in her mouth.

"She will love you. I will be so proud to introduce you," said Jack as he topped up her wine glass.

"Just like I was today." She smiled at him. "You were a total hit. I told you they would love you, but I would be a bit careful around Kait if I was you, she thinks you're a bit hot."She smiled as he stuffed almost a whole slice of pizza in his mouth. She laughed.

"You haven't changed."

He gave her a closed-mouth smile and a wink as he chewed.

# CHAPTER 4
## THE LETTER

They checked Jack out of the caravan park the following day, and when they arrived back at her cabin there was a parcel waiting for her on the doorstep. She turned it over and read the sender: *Ava Buckman 1289 Scenic Dve Florida.* "Look, Jack, it is from Ava."

She took it inside and eagerly opened it. There were a few creams and lotions she looked over and then spotted a letter. She unfolded it and read it as she sat at the kitchen table.

*Dear Chloe,*

*I hope this finds you well. We all seemed to lose contact with you and are all a bit concerned. I forgot I had your address tucked away from the day on the cruise when I promised you that I would send you some of my favourite creams. I hope these find you. Catalina has been trying to contact you; they set a date for the wedding. Danni and I keep in regular contact and she said to pass on her love. Please write and let me know that you are okay. We are all back at work now and have a bit of the blues. But we are all now excited to catch up again at the wedding. We hope that you can make it.*

*Missing you,*
*Ava*

*P. S. And we are all keen to know:Did you keep in contact with Jack?*

She hadn't realised that when she shut down her Facebook, she blocked all contact with everyone. She ran straight to the computer and logged back in and watched, as all her messages popped up. She opened the message from Cat and yelled out to Jack, who was unpacking his bag near the washing machine. "Cat and Cruz are getting married in June."

He wandered out, eagerly stopping behind her as he leaned over her shoulder.

"Jack, can you believe this? Cruz and Cat are getting married in June, and we are invited. Do you think we could go?" She looked up at him excited.

"Oh, that is lovely, yes, of course. I am casual, so can tell Pete I am unavailable, and June would be quiet, anyway."

"Same for me. Looks like they made it a year since their engagement. It will be such a treat to see everyone again."

Jack wandered back off to his washing duties and she excitedly sat and wrote a blanket message to them.

*I am so sorry that I lost contact with you all. I went off the air for a little while, but I am back. Jack is here with me in Australia and we are extremely happy. We were so happy to receive the news about the wedding. Can't wait to see you all again.*

*All my love,*
*Chloe*

She added a photo of her with Jack and sent it before sending one to Cat.

*Hi Cat and Cruz,*

*That is wonderful news you are getting married. We would not miss it for the world and will definitely be there. We hope you are getting lots of work and some on the cruise ships as well.*

*Looking forward to seeing you,*
*Chloe*

She then sent Ava a separate one as well.

*Hi Ava,*

*Thank you so much for the parcel. I can't wait to try your creams. I will post you some of my favourite creams in return. The wedding sounds like a wonderful catch-up. We are so excited to pick up where we left off and have some fun again.*

*We miss you guys.*

*All my love,*
*Chloe*

After a few minutes, she got a reply from Cat about the wedding.

*So wonderful to get news from you. Yes, wedding is 1st June in Barcelona. More details later. We are happy you and Jack are together and will be coming, cannot wait to catch up, we are both well over here, getting lots of work and some on the ships as well. We just finished a show and heading for a drink.*

*Love,*
*Cat*

She sat back and thought about her friends and the time they had spent together and smiled. June would be here in no time, and she was very excited to be heading to Europe again.

It was Jack's first day on the trawler, and he was a tad nervous. He left Chloe sleeping as he tip-toed, quiet as a mouse, and made a quick bite to eat before he left. Chloe had made him a packed lunch which he took out of the fridge and placed it in his cooler bag with some water bottles and grabbed the car keys. He took one last look over her, before he headed out the door. She didn't need her car, and he would be home by lunch.

It was still dark as he drove around the headland and down into the little fishing village. It was a pleasant morning, a bit fresh but the best weather for a first day on the waters. The man that he had to meet was Pete. He stared down at the trawler and noticed a man already, getting things organised. He jumped on board and Pete turned to greet him. He was a middle-aged man who had a friendly face that was aged, tanned, and wrinkled by many days spent in the hot sun.

"You must be Pete. I am Jack." He shook his hand.

"Welcome aboard, Jack. So they tell me you're a fisherman overseas."

"Aye, my family owns trawlers in Scotland."

"Well, you arrived at the right time. I have been short of staff for a few weeks and glad to have you around," said Pete as he threw him a pair of gloves.

Jack knew everything there was to know about trawlers; he just had to learn the tides and species of the fish. They immediately hit it off and by the time they were offloading their catch, they were bantering with each other like old mates. Pete told him he had work all week if he wanted it, and Jack graciously accepted.

Chloe was waiting for him when he arrived home, anxious to hear how his day went and hoped it worked out well for him.

"Oh, I have landed on my feet. I had the best day ever. Pete is such a nice man, and we got on very well. I need to get used to your Aussie slang a bit more, so I can understand him better but other than that, the day went great, he gave me work all week. I will be happy to work with him. He is a very hard worker and knows his way around the boat, that's for sure. He taught me a lot today about the waters."

She listened to his stories as she set out a plate of assorted sandwiches and a pot of tea. "You must be starving. Here, come and sit down."

She listened as he didn't stop for air, telling her all about his day, stopping just long enough to stuff a sandwich in his mouth and washing it down with a mouthful of tea.

That evening, Jack felt every muscle as they began to stiffen and ache. "After not worked on a trawler for a wee bit, I am feeling every bit of it tonight," he said as he lay on the lounge. "I will run you a bath. It will help loosen them up."

She ran him a bath and added some salts to help. He soaked in for around an hour while she sat on the toilet seat and chatted to him while they had a beer. It was a fairly small bath, and he only just fit in. Chloe went into the bedroom and lit some candles and placed some massage oils on the side table. She heard him getting out of the bath and called out to him.

"Come in here. I will give you a massage. I have some lovely oils that will help you."

"Oh, you are too good to me. I will accept that offer with open arms."

He lay on the bed on his belly, and she started to rub his back down.

"Oh, that feels amazing! Don't stop."

She continued as she rubbed down his back from the shoulders all the way down his back and down his legs. His body was gleaming in the candlelight, and she was drinking it all in. It was like a piece of artwork, meticulously sculptured to perfection. She continued on for a while and then realised he had drifted off to sleep. "Well, that's the first time that has ever happened," she smiled as she said to herself. "He must be exhausted."

Things were working out for them as they both settled into work. Pete started picking Jack up on his way in the mornings as Chloe was getting lots of morning shifts at the café which suited them to enjoy more time with each other in the evenings. She still did a few shifts at the restaurant, requesting mostly lunch.

# CHAPTER 5
## CHRISTMAS

Christmas was around the corner, and they were in full swing getting things organised. The seafood trade over Christmas was demanding and Jack was gone early every morning, returning home late. Chloe's schedule with the restaurant and cafe was just as hectic, being tourist season. By the time Christmas day came, they were both exhausted.

It was Jack who stirred first, used to getting up early. He couldn't sleep in. He sat looking over her as she slept. It was their first Christmas together, and he had wanted to make it one to remember. She must have felt him looking over her, and she woke smiling up at him.

"Good morning, Princess! Merry Christmas," he said as he leaned to kiss her.

"Merry Christmas! How long have you been awake?"

"Oh, a little while. I will make us coffee. You just lie there and wake up in your own time."

She heard him out in the kitchen and she smiled. She could never have thought in a million years she would be waking up with Jack on Christmas morning.

He arrived back with the coffee naked, and she couldn't take her eyes off him. His body still gave her goose bumps.

She looked him over as he got back into bed. "Come and lie with me. You are driving me crazy, walking around naked like that."

"Ah, my wee little jaguar is back. I have missed you."

They played around with each other and then when it was finally over they lay exhausted. Chloe had gone back to sleep. "Come on, let's have our coffee and get this day going."

Reluctantly, she made her way to sit up, and they sipped on their cold coffee.

"The coffee is stone-cold," said Jack.

"OK, it's my fault. I will make us another one."

"Well, I agree that one was your fault, hands down, and don't forget a splash of whisky."Arriving back with the coffee and ran off, returning with her presents.

"Merry Christmas, Jack!" She handed him two presents wrapped exquisitely in gold Christmas paper with a big red bow on each.

"Thanks! They are too pretty to undo," he said as he started on the bow. He unwrapped the first one with care as he stared up at Chloe at times as she smiled, looking on. Then without haste, he opened the box inside the wrapping, and pulled out a beautiful pair of RM William boots.

"You have no idea how much I love this present!" His eyes were wide as he looked over each boot in detail.

"I can change them if you would prefer a different style."

"No, I love them. Thanks so much! The craftsmanship in this is incredible. It is all one piece of leather."

"Yes they have a reputation for quality work. They will last you forever. You re-sole them when the soles wear out."

"Thank you so much! This is a wonderful present." He gave her a kiss, and he put the boot back in the box as she handed him the next present.

She stared as he unwrapped the next one and gasped. "You bought me an Akubra hat?"

"I wanted you to have a very Australian Christmas, your first one here."

"Chloe, this is incredible! How does it look?" He placed it on his head.

"Well, let's just say RM Williams could have their next model. It looks amazing on you. How's the fit?  You can change the size."

He jumped out of bed and ran to the mirror. "No way! I love it. How did you know the size right?"

"I measured that peak hat you wear to death."

He came back and leaned over and kissed her. "I love them both. Such thoughtful presents."

"Your boots will be lifetime friends,and your hat will get better with age. We can go down to the shop and change them if you would rather have a different style."

"No, I love them. I am wearing them today. Wait till I show Bob I can *slip slop slap* now."

"Yes, he will be impressed," she laughed.

"What does he say? The sun is a bastard."

"Yea. That and a few other things." She rolled her eyes with a grin, thinking of him."He will be there today," she yelled back.

"What about his family?"

"Oh, they call around in the morning, and then he comes over when they leave. It's been a tradition since his wife died."

He nodded, thinking how lonely he must be."He's one of a kind, that is for sure. Come on, let's go for a beach walk before I give you mine. Such a stunning morning out there, I don't want to miss it."

"Sure, I am always up for a beach walk."

They dressed and strolled down the road to the beach. Lots of families were setting up picnics and everyone was in a festive mood. Kids were running wild, burning energy, showing off new toys. They walked the length of the beach up on the rocks, and around the corner where it was quieter and had a complete view of the coastline. They sat and looked out to sea away from the crowds as they started to gather.

"I can't believe how busy it is down here," said Jack.

"Yea, it is a popular thing in Australia, spending Christmas day at the beach. You won't be able to see any sand by lunchtime."

"Well, I can understand why. Check this place out, it's stunning," he said, looking around.

She chuckled to herself; he was starting to sound more and more Aussie every day, with little comments. Pete was a huge influence on him.

"Oh, what a beautiful morning. This is my first Christmas day I am not cold."

"Yes, without doubt a very beautiful day," she said as she watched him. To her it was an everyday thing but to see how meaningful it was to him, made her re-think everything she took for granted. Sitting quietly, they were hypnotised as the waves crashed over the rocks, one after the other. Seagulls dived into the water to catch their breakfast as the sun sparkled on the water.

"Did you ever hear the story about the lonely Scotsman and the beautiful princess?"

Chloe began to smile; here comes one of his stories she loved. "No I don't think I have heard that one. Please tell me."

She snuggled in closer to him as she listened.

"Well, there was this lonely sad Scot who didn't realise how lonely he was until he met a beautiful princess, whom he fell in love with at first sight."

"Oh, he sounds lovely. What happened to him?"

"Well,she was so beautiful and had cute little faces that she would pull, and he loved every minute he was with her, but she was scared and lost and kept wanting to run away from him."

"Oh, silly princess,"she said with a sad face.

He smiled and carried on. "So he had to keep making her happy and feel protected, and very much loved. Then one day she ran away from him again, but this time he feared it was forever, he was heartbroken and very sad. He couldn't live without her, so he packed up and set off to find her."

"Oh, what a horrible princess!"

"Aye, she made him very sad."

"And did he find her?"

"Yes, he did, and he managed to convince her to take him back and love him."

"And then what happened? Did he love her forever?"

"Aye, he did. But what he wanted to know more than anything else was would she love him forever?"

Jack reached into his pocket and pulled out a small red box with a gold ribbon around it. "I wanted somewhere nice to give you this, and I don't think we could find a nicer place than here,"he said as he gazed around.

She knew straight away the box contained jewellery. She slowly pulled the ribbon off and opened the box as her eyes darted between the box and him. An exquisite single diamond ring, which was set into a Celtic band, stood sparkling in the sun.

"So what I want to ask is, will you love me forever and be my wife?"

Tears sprung to her eyes as she wiped them away. She cried,"Yes, of course, Jack, my goodness! Of course, I want you forever!"

He slipped the ring on her finger and kissed her.

"You are amazing! I loved your story."

"Well, I am not as good as Cruz he is the true romantic."

"You chased me half-way around the world. That is the most romantic thing I have ever seen. You win, hands down, as the true romantic." She laughed.

"Aye, well, thank you. So does this mean the chase is finally over? You are done with running away from me now?"

She giggled, looking up at him.

"I am trapped in your invisible chains of love forever," she laughed. "I want you to be the first thing that I see every single day of the rest of my life."

They both laughed, and he pulled her in close and cuddled her."Poor you, you are going to get sick of me, I can tell you." She laughed.

"Never. I will always lie by your side, and protect you and take care of you forever, my beautiful treasure that I adore," he said, looking at her with a serious gaze. They cuddled as she wiped away her tears. Chloe put out her hand, staring at the ring he had slipped onto her finger.

"Jack, it's stunning. Where did you find such a beautiful ring?"

"So you like it?"

"I love it! It is so unusual, I can't stop looking at it."

"I bought it in Scotland before I came over. I was hoping that you would like it. I have been waiting for the right time to give it to you. And I thought our first Christmas together is it."

"It fits perfectly."

"I remembered your ring size from when I bought you the ring in Corfu."

"So special." She sat staring at it before looking up at him. "So we are officially engaged," she said excitedly.

"Aye, we are, and I got your father's approval."

"You did?" she said, shocked.

"I went over the other day after I dropped you at work and told him what I had in mind, and he gave me his best wishes."

"So everyone knows you are giving this to me today?"

"No, I swore him to secrecy, and he gave me his word."

"I can't wait to tell them all today at lunch," she said excited and jumped up."Come on, this is the best Christmas ever."

Strolling home, they were in no hurry as she continually checked her diamond as it sparkled in the sunshine. They had a shower and dressed for the day. Christmas lunch was at her parents' place, and she was busting to tell them their news.

The temperature was rising fast. It was going to be a scorcher of a day, but she knew that would not stop her mother putting on the traditional roast. As they walked down the path and around through the gate, they could smell the roast cooking and hear the laughter and chatter. Everyone was seated out the back. Chloe yelled out, "Merry Christmas, everyone!"

"Ho ho ho! Merry Christmas," yelled back Kait. She spotted the ring straight away and gave Chloe a wicked smile.

Chloe knew she saw it, but ignored her, as she turned to grab drinks, before sitting down next to Jack. Kait was opposite her and looking at her with inquisitive eyes and Chloe was trying not to laugh. She couldn't wait any longer. She scanned around the table first and everyone was seated. Chrissie and Finn were next to them chatting across the table to her parents. Kait and Johnny were opposite them with little Sophia happily playing with her new doll. Everyone had drinks and looked settled. The time was right.

"I have an announcement to make," said Chloe. Everyone stopped and looked.

"I bet you do," said Kait with a wink. Chloe smiled back at her.

"Shh, let her talk," said Olivia with a scornful gaze at Kait.

"Jack and I got engaged this morning."

"Oh, my, that is such wonderful news," said Olivia, gasping.

"Yea, I will second that. Well done to you both," added Rob.

Kait and Chrissie came running around to look at the ring. "It's so unique and beautiful," said Chrissie. "It's Scottish. Jack bought it in Scotland."

"Well done, Jack," yelled out Kait. Rob came around and shook Jack's hand.

"Congratulations to you both! Welcome to the family, mate."

"Thank you! I know it's quick, but we know what we have is special, and it will last forever," said Jack.

"Does your family know?" asked Olivia, looking at the ring on Chloe's out-stretched hand across the table.

"Not yet. We will Skype them tonight."

"I think I speak for both Livy and myself when I say we couldn't be happier."

"So what's all the fuss?"

They all turned. It was Bob who had walked in. Chloe walked towards him and showed him the ring."Well, I'll be buggered" was all he said and cuddled her. He walked over to Jack and shook his hand. "Congratulations, mate! I always knew your word was worth something. You have a good one here. Look after her."

"Thanks, Bob. I told you how I felt about her that day on the deck of excuses, and I meant every word."

"I always knew it," he said, winking at him. "Well, this calls for a drink."

Rob was there like his right-hand man and passed out beers. Kait was doing the wine top-ups around the table. "Well, here's cheers, big ears," she said, holding her wine glass towards them and everyone raised their glass.

"Cheers!"

"Where will the wedding be, here or Scotland?" asked Olivia, still beaming. They looked at each other and laughed.

"We have no idea. This is all new to us both."

"You would love the beer in Scotland, Bob," said Jack.

"I like my feet flat on Aussie soil, son," he said as he waved it off.

All the women were all in the kitchen preparing lunch, laughing and enjoying their new conversation, "the wedding."

"A wedding in the Scottish highlands sounds so romantic," said Kait as she got the roast vegetables out of the oven, placing them on the sink.

"Yea, it does, but we will need to think this one out" said Chloe, as she passed her a platter for the vegetables.

"Maybe I should bring the cards out and see if anything pops up. They were spot-on last time."

"Yes, they were. I have to admit I thought that you were a bit of a nut case with those cards, but it appears that they were one hundred percent correct." She hated admitting that she was right.

"I am hoping that the wedding is in Scotland. Finn and I are already saving for an overseas trip," added Chrissie, busy stirring the gravy.

"Well, that is a wise comment, Chrissie. I think we will all have to start putting our pennies away, your father and I have been talking about doing Europe so this might be the start of our trip."

"Wherever it is I can tell you one thing. It is going to be low key. I don't want anything fancy. I would be happy barefoot with no fuss," said Chloe.

"Well, that sounds perfect to me. We can have it right here in the backyard, a few kegs and a barbeque, and we can all be in shorts and thongs," added Rob as he arrived to carve the meat.

"How did I know you would say that, Dad?" Chloe laughed.

"I like your dad's idea. We can order stubby holders with you and Jack on it and the date," added Johnny, coming in to collect his platters of seafood from the fridge.

"That's a bloody good idea, Johnny," said Rob, waving his carving fork at him.

Olivia swatted him on the rear with the tea towel. "Don't listen to them, Chloe. You will have a beautiful wedding wherever it is."

The platters of food were all placed on the outdoor table, and they all served themselves and took a seat at the table. Olivia had set the table with all the best Christmas plates, wine glasses and vases of Christmas bush, placed in the centre of the table. Bon bons were all waiting patiently with each place setting to be cracked as they all sat down to their feast. Her father wore his traditional Christmas shirt of Santa in the old Holden pick-up truck and her mother was in a long sage green dress with matching gold Christmas earrings, bracelet and necklace. Everyone else wore their favourite Christmas outfit, and Sophia was in a red tulle dress and looked adorable.

The Christmas carols were playing loudly and everyone was in a festive mood. They were all discussing with Sophia how Santa came, and she was showing them her gifts.

"Sophia, what is invisible and smells like milk and cookies," said Rob.

"Here we go. One of Dad's bad jokes," said Kait. Everyone laughed as Sophia stared at him with a distant look.

"Santa's burps," he said loudly and Sophia laughed.

"Not at our house," said Olivia, looking at Rob who was opening another beer.

"Nor ours," said Kait.

Just then, Bob sprang into action. "Alright, why did Frosty stick his carrots up his nose?"

"To stop his boogies freezing," yelled Chrissie and Sophia laughed.

"No. His fridge was full and had no room for them."Everyone laughed.

They were sitting, having a quiet drink in the courtyard later that night when Jack Skyped Jeannie. They were nervous who would be there and were grateful that Mary was nowhere to be seen. They all wished each other merry Christmas and chatted about their day. It was still morning over there and bitterly cold. Jeannie was complaining that it was just rain, and they were hoping for snow later that day. Jack could see that everyone was sitting around together. Liam was there with Jeannie and wondered if he arrived early or had stayed the night. His brother seemed cheerful and his mum was running around giving everyone a wee whisky for their traditional family Christmas toast. Chloe jumped up and poured them a whisky each to join them.

"To Christmas!" said Jimmy. They all toasted and had a sip of whisky. "Wait. While we are toasting, Chloe and I have some news that deserves a toast," said Jack as he smiled at Chloe. "This morning I asked Chloe to be my wife, and she said yes!" He grabbed Chloe's hand and showed it to the camera.

"Oh, that's such wonderful news. I told you the wee lassie would be waiting for you."

"You did. Thanks,Mum. I am glad you are happy for us."

"I love the ring, Jack. You have excellent taste," said Jeannie, leaning into the camera to obtain a better view.

"Thanks, Jeannie. I bought it at the local jewellery store before I left."

"I am happy for you both. Congratulations! I guess you will be planning a wedding, then. Are you coming home or will it be in Australia," asked Jimmy.

"Thanks, Jimmy. Well we haven't thought that far ahead yet. I just wanted to get this ring on her finger before she runs away from me again," he laughed.

"I am so happy for you both. I can't wait to tell Pat. He will be excited for ya."

"Have a beer for us, will ya. I wish I could join you."

"Of course. If Pat has anything to do with it, it will be more likely a dozen."Jack laughed at the thought of it and knew he would be right, and for one slight moment wished he could be there to join them for those beers.

After they got off the phone, they sat back and felt relieved it was done. They had told their families and everyone was happy. There seemed to be one problem that they had not thought of before, and it was where the wedding would take place. It was something they would need to discuss and think about in detail. It was the first question everyone asked. It meant some- one would have to travel and a long way at that.

Over the next few weeks, they tossed up various solutions. Jack wanted to marry on the Deck of Excuses and Chloe loved the idea of getting married in Scotland. They looked at both and then decided it was unfair for one family to have to do all the travelling. They couldn't come to a conclusion so decided to worry about it later.

# CHAPTER 6

## SPAIN

The months passed quickly as they worked hard putting every penny away, and their savings were looking very healthy, indeed. It was getting close to the date they had to leave for Spain. They were receiving messages daily from all the gang off the ship, as they were all packing and getting ready to meet in Barcelona. It was all getting very exciting.

The morning of their anniversary arrived, the day they had met in the bar, and Jack had gone off early to work. Chloe wanted the day to be special; the first time she had ever had an anniversary she had got excited about. They were saving money so didn't want to go out, so decided to cook at home together and share a bottle of wine. She had decided to make paella out in the back courtyard. The meal they had shared the night they met at a little Spanish restaurant in Barcelona. She had lined up with Johnny to borrow a paella pan, and she had planned to pick up all the ingredients along with a bottle of Spanish wine later in the morning.

She was excited as she jumped into the shower and was heading out the door in no time. First stop was Dan Murphy's. She remembered the wine she drunk that night was a rioja and headed to the red wine section of international wines. There was quite a few to select from. She grabbed a couple of bottles of the middle-of-the-road price range and headed to the check-out with a spring in her step.

Next stop was the fruit market. They sold the rice she needed along with some capsicum and tomatoes. She had asked Jack to bring home the seafood, so she called into the restaurant to pick up the pan.

"Hello, Johnny, Finn, anyone here?" she yelled out as she entered the restaurant.

"Out the back in the kitchen," she heard Johnny yell back.

"Oh, there you are, I am here to pick up the paella pan."

"Oh, that's right, I forgot all about that. I will grab it for you."

"So it's been twelve months since Kait forced you onto that plane. Hey, wow, time goes by so quick."

"Yea it has flown and so much has happened. I feel like my feet have not touched the ground, thanks for the pan I will bring it back tomorrow. Wish me luck. I have never made one of these before."

"It's pretty easy, kinda like making a risotto. If you get stuck, yell out."

"Thanks, Johnny." She turned and headed out the door like a whirlwind. Johnny had a chuckle as he headed back into the kitchen.

She arrived back home with enough time to set a table with red and white table cloth outside and put a vase with some red roses she had picked from Mrs. Whitaker's garden, which she had been given permission to do, with a promise for a plate of paella in return. Jack would be home by mid-afternoon so she planned to have an early dinner as he gets so tired at night. It was their last working day before flying out in two days' time. Being a cool late May day and knew the temperature would only drop further, so she lit the chimenea. Done, she looked around and everything appeared perfect. She checked the time; Jack would be home any minute.

He walked inside with a beautiful bunch of flowers and a bag of seafood. He met Chloe in the kitchen.

"Happy anniversary,Princess!" He kissed her as she took the flowers.

"Oh, they are beautiful. I will put them straight into some water, thank you."

He grabbed a beer and headed for a shower while she found a vase to put them in. He was back in no time. Smelling and looking a whole lot cleaner.

"Oh, look at you. Now I can come near you without having to hold my nose," she teased.

"Yea, I know. I am a bit smelly. But the cats love me," he teased. They headed out the back and Jack put another log on the fire.

"What do we have here?" asked Jack."It looks like a paella pan." He was looking at it, turning it over and over again.

"Sure is, I borrowed it from Johnny, I thought we could make a paella tonight."

"Sounds like fun, have you ever made one before?"

"No, but I have watched them being made, and I have the authentic paella spices I purchased at the markets in Barcelona."

"Oh, well, it sounds like you have this all under control."

They sat and went over the flight details, and sent an email confirming their accommodation. They had booked a hotel near the marina and were just about packed and ready to go. It was fun cooking their meal together and opened a bottle of wine to enjoy with the meal.

"So hard to believe we were in that restaurant together a year ago."

"Oh, aye, Chloe, so much has happened along the way. It's been one hell of a rollercoaster, that is for sure," he laughed.

"I remember you coming in and sitting near me in that bar and you kept looking over at me and got all embarrassed when I busted you," she laughed.

"I was instantly drawn to you I could not stop staring," he had a small chuckle.

"So glad you had the courage to ask me out that night. We had a great night,hadn't we?" she said, staring into the fire as she reflected on the memories.

"Oh, we seem to have fun wherever we go. We were meant to be, that is for sure."

# CHAPTER 7

## BARCELONA

They arrived in Barcelona on an unusually clear, crisp morning for May. Turning up their collars as they exited the airport looking around for their transfer, they spotted him holding a sign with Jack's name displayed proudly. "Over here," he said as he grabbed Chloe's hand. He helped them with the luggage and they were at the hotel in no time. Their room was ready, so they checked in and went upstairs.

The room was small but all that they needed. It had a full window that captured marvellous views out over the marina. The décor was modern, decorated in black and white. The bed was king-size and loaded with pillows of all sizes. They had the day and the next to enjoy the city together and get over jet lag before the wedding day. They laid on the bed for a while before showering and getting set to head outside.

"Okay, are you ready to hit the town?" asked Jack.

"Yep, let's go and have some fun," she said as she grabbed a cardigan.

Jack grabbed the hotel key and phone and held the door open for Chloe as she started to put on her cardigan.

"Sorry, I wanted to put this on, it was a bit cool this morning."

"Take it, but I think you will be fine in your long-sleeved shirt, plus you have jeans and boots on." She checked her look in the mirror once more and turned."Okay, I am ready."

They strolled around and ended up near the bar where they met.

"Over to the right, Chloe, the courtyard where our bar is. Would you like to go there for lunch?"

"It is, too, yea let's go. It will be funny to visit it again."

As they walked in, all the memories came flooding back. Nothing had changed at all, and it was even the same bartender. They took a seat at the table, and he came straight over to take their order.

"Two beers, please," said Jack.

"Grande," he asked scribbling their order on his pad.

"Aye, grande."

They scanned the menu as the waiter went to pour their beer.

"What takes your fancy today?"

"Well, I was looking at Gambas Ajillo," she said confidently as she continued looking over the menu.

He looked up at her with a confused stare."Do you even understand what you are ordering?"

"Yea, as a matter of fact, it is garlic prawns," she said, leaning her head to the side with a smirk.

"How do you know that?" he said with an intrigued smile.

"Turn the menu over, Jack."

As he did, he laughed.

"Oh, the other side is in English, you should have led me on,I had no idea."

She laughed and returned her attention back to the menu. "They have Jamon croquettes and manchego cheese plus meat platters. I think we had that last time."

"Yea, we did. I love that cheese. There is a plate of varied croquettes Jamon, porcini mushroom and chicken maybe that, and the cheese platter to start," she said as she flicked her hair and sat back in her seat.

"And some Butifarra pork sausage skewers," he added as he also sat back.

"Hope you're hungry, have you forgotten how massive the servings are here?"

The waiter arrived back with their beers.

"I forgot the size of their beers also." She laughed as the waiter put two giant beers in front of them and a bowl of olives. Jack quickly started to order before Chloe could change his mind.

"Oh, it is so wonderful to be back here, isn't it?" said Chloe as she sat back and gazed around.

"Aye, I remember it well. I had to sit here and chase all the men away from you." He smiled as he took a sip of his beer.

"Oh, one man came over, that is all" she laughed.

Chloe sat and peered around. She spotted a woman sitting alone in the corner eyeing Jack off.

"Well, it might be my turn today. There is a woman over there who keeps on staring at you."

"Where, what woman?" His head starting to dart around, he spotted her staring as she slowly blew out her cigarette smoke his way.

"If you are trying to make me uncomfortable, you are doing an amazing job."

Chloe laughed and the waiter arrived with the platters of food.

"Would you like another beer?" asked the waiter. Jack glanced at Chloe, he was more than sure that she would.

"Sure, why not? We don't have anywhere to go," answered Chloe with a smile.

The waiter started telling them all about the products on the platters and Chloe was intently listening as the waiter spoke. Out of the corner of her eye, she spotted the woman approaching Jack.

"Excuse me, do you have a light?" she held her cigarette out towards him that was in an elegant holder. She moved so close to him that her breast brushed his shoulder as she leaned in close.

"No, I don't smoke," said Jack in a nervous voice.

"Oh, sorry to bother you. Are you with this lady that you are sitting with?"

Jack was unsure what to do next, and Chloe stepped in.

"Yes, he is with me. He happens to be my fiancé," she said firmly.

"Oh, well you have done very well. He is extremely sexy, I hope that you are aware."

"Yes, I am, we are more than happy."

The woman gave Jack a seducing stare as she returned back to her table.

"Can you believe what just happened? That woman tried to seduce me right in front of you," Jack looked startled as he took a long gulp of beer.

"Yes, women do that quite often, and men also. Sometimes it works for them, sometimes not," explained the waiter before he moved off to another table that was beckoning him.

"I think it's hilarious. Now you understand how women feel when it happens," she giggled.

"Don't leave me. If you need to go to the bathroom, I am coming with you."

She was giggling out of control with the sight of his face.

"You are no help. You think it's funny, don't you?"

She nodded, unable to answer.

"Well, it's not." He tried to keep a straight face but could not hold back his laughter any longer, and started to laugh along with her. Ruby red lips, as Jack called her, finally left the bar, and they relaxed. Not being in any hurry, they grazed there for a few hours.

"Wow, check out the time. We should make a move," said Chloe as she drank the last of her beer.

"Don't you have to buy a hat or something for the wedding?" asked Jack.

"Oh, yea, I do, thanks for reminding me. I almost forgot. Catalina said every woman wears a fascinator and stilettos to weddings, so I definitely need to buy one, I just don't know where."

"Here, I can find a place." Jack waved his hand in the air and the waiter came running over.

"We need to shop for a sunhat or fascinator. Do you know where we should start?"

"Oh, I am sorry. We don't mean to waste your time. Jack, how would he know where to buy one?"

"No, no, please, I am happy to help. I know a lady who sells them. A few blocks from here if you head up the Las Ramblas you will come across her stand. She sells lots of tocados and fascinators. I am sure she will be able to help you find one to match your exquisite eyes," he said, staring at Chloe as she became embarrassed, sitting with her cheeks glowing.

"Oh, thank you," said Chloe shyly.

He smiled at her and was off waving his red rag at the table where people were starting to sit before he had a chance to clean it from the other patrons.

"I knew he would help," smiled Jack as they both stood up to leave. "Don't forget your cardigan, hanging on the back of your chair," he said and she turned to grab it as she whispered, "Thankyou."

They found the stall set up inside a small marquee, right where the waiter had said, and he was right: it had lots of beautiful hats. Chloe got straight to work trying them on, checking herself in the mirror and then spinning towards Jack for his yes or no nod. The lady came over to help and could speak broken English quite well.

"I can help you find the most beautiful hat. Do you have a colour in mind?" she said as she started to look Chloe over.

"Yes, I am wearing a blue dress. It is for a wedding."

"A daytime or night-time wedding?"

"Afternoon. Does it matter?" questioned Chloe innocently.

"Oh, my. Yes, of course, a daytime one you can wear all the beautiful tocados and pamelas," she said, waving her hand towards all the beautiful stands of hats. Rushing towards one that just took her attention she handed it along with many others to Chloe as she tried them all on one after the other, turning to Jack for his nod of approval. He always said no.

"What is wrong with my beautiful pamelas, you not like?" she said to Jack with one hand on her hip. Her brunette hair was pulled up on top of her head and secured with a hairpin. Her pencil skirt and tight-fitting top also told him that she was not one to tangle with, and he instantly backed off.

"Well, she is asking me, so I am telling her what I think. You are covering her face with all those huge hats and I happen to love looking at her face."

"Pamelas."

"What?" he said, confused with one eye squinting.

"They are called pamelas," she answered with a frown.

"Oh, sorry. Well, the pamelas are too overpowering."

She turned to Chloe with a surprised gaze."Your man does not like you to dress up too much, he thinks you are sweet enough on your own. Not many like that around here, hang onto him tight."

Chloe just smiled as she looked over at Jack who was edging closer to the door.

"Here, this is a spectacular 'small' tocados," she said, giving Jack a stern glare.

"Oh, that is exactly the same colour as my dress," she turned side to side, looking in the mirror then back at Jack who gave her the nod of approval."I will take it, thank you, you have been so helpful." She slung Jack a poised lip smirk before heading to put it in a box, and they were on their way.

"You don't like shopping much, do you?" She asked as she quickened her pace to keep up with him.

"No, not unless it's for your sexy negligees. Now then, I would love shopping, should we go?"

"No, I don't need any more," she said, digging him in the ribs with a smile. "Come over here. Let's have a drink before we head back."

They made their way slowly to their hotel having fun, stopping and looking at everything along the way. Jet lag was setting in, and they were starting to crash, so they ordered dinner in, and watched television in bed.

"I can't find a television station that speaks in English," grumbled Jack as he pointed the remote at the television pushing the channel button.

"That's because we are in Spain, dopey," she giggled as she applied night cream to her face.

"I like that scent, is it a new one?"

"It is tea tree oil. I brought along some travel-size creams I have been collecting."

"I have never heard of it."

"It's an Australian native tree. Captain Cook found it when he came on the first fleet. He used to make a pot of tea out of the leaves."

"And you put it on your face," he said with his face screwed up.

"Yes, they have since found out it has wonderful healing powers. Wait, stop, go back."Jack moved the channel back and stopped.

"I thought it was. It's Crocodile Dundee in Spanish."

"Oh, I have seen this movie once," he recalled.

"Once! I could recite almost every line to you. I have seen it so many times, that is so funny watching Paul Hogan speak Spanish."

"He reminds me of your dad," he said, putting the remote back on the side table. "Yea, I can see how. He is a bit of a character," she said as she watched intently. She was giggling so hard, it made Jack laugh along with her.

"Have you been on that prosecco again?" he said with an inquisitive stare.

"No, it's just funny. Don't you think that it's funny?"

"Not as much as you do, obviously," he said with one eye squinted. He continued to watch her before throwing his hands in the air. "Well, you're the next best thing to English television we have at the moment, may as well enjoy it."

Jack got out of bed and went to the minbar and handed her a piccolo of champagne. Then poured himself a dram of whisky. "Seeing you're in a giggly mood you may as well have some bubbles."

"Ooh,great idea," she said, sitting up straight.

She giggled all the way through the movie, keeping Jack entertained with her commentary; he started doing the lead role, making up funny lines that made them both laugh. A couple more piccolos and whiskies later, and they were roaring with laughter, and when it was over Chloe snuggled in beside him with sleepy eyes, and he knew she wouldn't be awake for too much longer.

"Thanks for a fantastic day today." She sighed as she snuggled down lower.

"I had the best day also, you're the one that makes it fun."

"Don't have any bad dreams about ruby red lips," she teased, patting her pillow into shape before laying her head down and closing her eyes.

"Oh, thanks, I forgot about her, now I definitely will for sure."

She giggled and he rubbed her back. "You have been coping with all of this extremely well."

She smiled up at him with sleepy eyes. "That is because I have you, I am safe when I have you by my side."

"I am glad to hear that, Princess. Goodnight!"

"Love you," yarned Chloe.

He looked over her as she drifted off to sleep.

The next morning, they woke early taking in an early breakfast. Then they went for a walk around town before heading up to the rooftop pool and bar. It had amazing views of the city and marina. They enjoyed a cool swim and relaxed on the sunlounges while they listened to the music that was playing over the speakers. After swimming for a few hours Jack's worms started to grumble, and they decided to dress and search for a restaurant for lunch. They wandered the streets and then Jack had an idea.

"Let's check if our restaurant is open for lunch, the one we went to on our first date."

"It is close to where we are. That is a great idea."

They wandered the streets for a while heading in the direction that they remembered roughly where it was.

"Over here, look there it is, and it is open."

He held her hand tightly as they crossed the road and opened the door for her to walk inside.

"A table for two," asked the waitress.

"Aye, could we please have the one in the back corner. It is where we had our first date," explained Jack to the waitress who smiled and led them straight to it.

"I will give you a minute to study the menu. What would you like to drink?"

"A beer for me. Chloe, what would you like?"

"Oh, a beer for me also. Are you still keen on seafood paella?" she asked Jack.

"Aye, that would be lovely."

"I will give the chef your order. Paellas take around twenty minutes. They are made from scratch," advised the waitress.

"Of course. Thank you," said Chloe.

"We loved the last one. I think that is why she is still with me," joked Jack.

"I will tell the chef,"laughed the waitress and headed back to the kitchen.

"Oh, the smells of all the spices coming out of that kitchen is making my mouth water," said Jack.

"It is going to be incredible," she added, rubbing her hands together with excitement.

The waitress was back with the beers and placed them down on the table.

"Lunch will not be long."

"Thankyou."

They were both looking around at the décor.

"Nothing has changed."

"No, I hope it never does. It's perfect, it will always be our favourite little restaurant," said Jack.

"So you are calling that our first date now."

"Aye, well, it sort of was, wasn't it?"

"Yea, well, seeing we are still together, I guess it was."

The paella arrived, steaming as the waitress placed it between them.

"Would you like another drink?"

"Yes, could we have a red wine?"

"Of course."

They both leaned in and smelt it as they did on the first night and laughed. The paella was just as amazing as they remembered. Both of them agreed it made their paella at home appear bad, but they had loved it and had fun making it.

"This wine is delicious," said Chloe as Jack served her a spatula of paella."I knew you would want a wine. You never stopped talking about the wine here last time."

She took a mouthful of food and made a humming noise. "Oh,Jack,it's delicious."

He put a spoonful in his mouth and nodded. "The best."

As they finished, the waitress bought them out two Spanish flans.

"It is from the chef. He was happy to hear the story that you were here on your first date and have returned,"she beamed as she proudly placed them on the table.

"Oh, that is so lovely. Please thank him for us,"said Chloe as she threw Jack a nervous smile and watched the waitress disappear back into the kitchen. Jack knew exactly what Chloe was thinking and before she could open her mouth said, "You have to eat it, Chloe, every mouthful, or he will be offended," he whispered.

"But I am too full!" She leaned in, holding her belly.

"You have to try," he said sternly.

"Okay, okay, I will try." It was a delicious treat, and they managed to eat every last crumb, thanks to Jack, of course, and wandered back to the hotel for a rest and a swim to work it off.

They booked a flamenco show for that night and as they walked out, after the show, Chloe turned the phone back on and she spotted a message.

"It's a message from Danni, it came in an hour ago, they are in a bar drinking champagne and want to know what we are doing," said Chloe, looking up at Jack.

"Well, knowing them they are still in the bar. Are you up for a drink?"

"Yea, I don't feel too bad at all tonight. I had a decent night's sleep. How about you?"

"Yea, a whisky sounds good. Find out where they are."

The message came back almost instantly.

"Well, they are not too far away. The bar is near the Las Ramblas somewhere."

"Here, show me, I will google it." Jack took the phone and within a minute had the directions.

"It's this way, not too far." Jack grabbed her hand and led her in the direction of the bar.

"I am so excited, we are about to catch up with Danni and Rocco,"she said with a spring in her step.

Before long they arrived and Jack opened the door and as they stepped in they both gasped."Wow, check this place out!"

"It is totally amazing. We have stumbled into a Mediterranean garden," said Chloe with delight.

They stood looking up and around, looking at it all. There were plants everywhere, vines and Spanish lanterns hanging from a high-pitched roof. Different coloured lights all made the scene enchanting. Soft green lights lit up the vines and a lilac lit roof giving a magical illusion like a spectacular sunset. It was crowded as they walked along, scanning all the tables that lined the walls until they spotted them.

"Over there," yelled Jack above the music that was playing.

"Oh, yea, I see them." She followed him as they made their way to their table. Danni jumped up as she saw then approaching.

"Aah, our friends from down under," she screamed, and they all embraced and greeted each other.

"This is some funky bar you have found here, guys," said Chloe.

"Awesome, isn't it," replied Danni, waving her arm around at the scenery.

"How are you, guys? I cannot believe we are here with you both again."

"Me,neither, and you are getting married also," said Danni excitedly.

"Yes, we are, following in Cruz and Catalina's footsteps."

"I am going to the bar. What do you want to drink, Chloe?"

"Oh, they do wicked cocktails here," said Danni.

"Maybe they will do a spritz."

"OK, I will try. Are you both okay for drinks?"

"Yea, we are fine. Thanks, Jack. Danni has a bottle, and I am sharing it with her."

"Okay, I will be back."

"Here, sit down. Tell me everything that I have missed," said Danni, excitedly pulling her to sit next to her.

"Give the poor girl a chance to take a breath, Danni" said Rocco.

"Yea yea,I am just excited." She waved him off and he shook his head.

"Hi, Rocco, she is ok. You two have not changed a bit."

"Neither have you. So Jack followed you to Australia. How romantic," she said with a shoulder shimmy.

"Yes, he did," Chloe laughed. Danni was still full of life, like she was on a diet of yippy beans. She had missed her a lot and glad she had not changed a bit.

"Oh, I remember on the ship you saying it would not last, that it was probably one of those holiday romances," she said, sipping on her champagne.

"I know, I was totally freaking out."

"What, you, Chloe, freaking out?  No, never," said Jack as he returned with two spritz, handing her one.

"Oh, ha ha, very funny. You just told me last night that I was super cool now," she pouted.

"Well, yes, you are. I must admit you have been very laid back and calm. Well here is cheers!"

Everyone raised their glasses.

"To old friends," added Rocco.

# CHAPTER 8
## A SPANISH WEDDING

The morning of the wedding had arrived. Chloe wore a beautiful navy-blue skater dress, which was soft and flowing and had matching stiletto heels and her hat she bought the day before. Jack was in a navy suit with a soft silver grey shirt. There was no doubt they would turn heads together. They had the address and grabbed a taxi to the villa on the invitation.

The driver entered a long driveway, sweeping upwards and stopping at the top, under an oversized canopy. It was best described as rustic luxury. They were shown through a grand reception room and out the other end through huge glass doors. It was breathtaking.

The lookout, which was straight in front of them had glorious views, over Barcelona. A waiter went past with champagne on his tray and stopped to offer them one. *Oh, God! Champagne and stilettos, it's not a good combination,* Chloe reminded herself. The last time she combined the two was at the horse races, and it ended quite messy. She got her stiletto heel stuck in the ground and fell flat on her face with her dress around her head, so after that she was barefoot swinging her heels. She peered around and decided it was definitely not the place to let that happen.

"Do you have a beer?" asked Chloe politely.

"Yes, Madame. I will be right back."

"Make that two," added Jack.

They spotted where the wedding was to take place. The sweeping look-out was set up for the vows and chairs were lined up on either side of a long red carpet. People were mingling to the side in a courtyard area. You could hear the distinct sound of people talking in different languages.

"Oh, how I love Europe," whispered Chloe as the waiter came back with their drinks.

"Thank you," she said as she took them. "Jack, all those women over there are wearing those huge hats like the ones I tried on yesterday."

"Aye, and they need them."

"What?" laughed Chloe.

"Aye, I bet their husbands bought thosefor them."

"Ssh,what are you saying?"

"It is true. They have to wear the oversized hats to hide their faces."

"Jack, you can't say that!" She gasped.

"You mark my words. Keep an eye out, you will see."

All of a sudden, they heard a roar of laughter coming from the other end of the courtyard. "Paddy" they both said at the same time and laughed. They made their way to where the laughter came from, and they were right. There they all were. Paddy and John were talking and Ava and Maggie were listening and Rocco and Danni were busy arguing about something. Paddy spotted them as they walked towards them and yelled out, "I see what the wee cat has dragged in here." Paddy went running to Jack and threw his arms around him, slapping him on the back.

"It's a treat to see you, and with Chloe also. I am so happy to see you both together."

He was extremely emotional as his eyes started to sparkle with a tear. Everyone was hugging and kissing each other as they genuinely were ecstatic to see each other. Danni was in a sage green one shoulder-side-tied dress that she wore well, looking elegant with a small sage hat, gold heels and dripping with gold jewellery. Ava had worn a pink knee-length asymmetrical dress with mint flowers and mint heels along with a matching fascinator, looking beautiful and sweet as usual. The men were all in suits. Voices and laughter grew louder as they were happily catching up, while a waiter approached and started to collect glasses, asking them to take a seat as the ceremony was about to begin. They joined in as everyone walked to the chairs and settled in. They all sat together and waited.

Cruz walked down the red carpet, greeting everyone along the way. He was in a black suit, no surprises there, as he always wore black. But he appeared happy and relaxed. Music started and all heads turned to the back as Catalina appeared with her father at the start of the red carpet. She was absolutely stunning in a tight-fitting pencil gown, which flared at the bottom with layers that resembled a flamenco dress, the lace veil trailed behind her in true Spanish tradition.

They made their way to the front and her father handed Catalina's hand to Cruz. He bowed to him as he took it. The look he gave Cat was so moving, asking if she was OK. She nodded, smiling at him, and they turned to the front to take their vows. It was all in Spanish but you could keep up with what was happening. They placed the rings on each other's finger, and he kissed his bride, before turning to the congregation and everyone clapped as they made their way along the red carpet.

They were escorted to a courtyard where a cocktail hour was to begin while they went off for photos. They all stood around as waiters circulated the room with champagne and taking drink orders.

Danni and Cruz came over towards them."How is your head today?" asked Danni.

"I was a bit dusty this morning but coming good now," said Chloe.

"I had a wee headache also, but more tired than anything," added Jack as he grabbed a waiter's attention. He came over and Danni and Cruz took champagne each from the tray.

"Could we please have two beers?"

"Por supuesto," nodded the waiter.

"Oh, sorry about that. I had to find the powder room," said Maggie as she and Paddy joined them. "You're always running off to the toot, one of your favourite places it is, as soon as we get anywhere, she starts whining about needing to go to the loo," grumbled Paddy.

"It's a sin to get old. You can't complain, you wee old bastard, always whining about something," she gave back to him.

"Alright, you two, here, grab a drink," said Jack as the waiter re-appeared with their beers.

"Could we please get two of those also?" asked Paddy. The waiter nodded and turned on his heels.

"So I am on the beer today, am I? Why? You don't trust me with champagne," she sniggered.

"No, I don't. I don't want ya stepping out of your petticoat on the dance floor here," added Paddy as everyone laughed.

"The last wedding we went to, I looked over and here she is with her petticoat around her ankles, and then she just stepped out of it kicking it to the side."

Everyone was laughing.

"Is that true, Maggie?" asked a hysterical Danni.

"Aye, it is true. I was having a bonne time. We all had a wee bit too much whisky and I ended up doing a highland fling with some others on the dance floor, me petty coat elastic gave way, and down she came around me ankles. No one seemed to care, only him."

"That's why you are not allowed champagne tonight," he said sternly.

"It was the whisky, not the champagne," she corrected him with a huff.

"I will get you one later," winked Danni.

"Well, you will be carrying her home on your shoulders, not mine."

Everyone was laughing, having a great time listening to Paddy and Maggie banter with their wild stories just like old times.

A man came over and asked them to start moving towards the courtyard. He ushered everyone through an archway, which led to a beautiful courtyard. The tables were all set under a breathtaking canopy of grape vines. There were beautiful Spanish lanterns of various sizes, hanging from the roof and placed on all the tables, which lit up the masses of flowers. The tables were a mixture of long and smaller ones at the side with seating for around a hundred and fifty people. Shown to their table, they were happy to be all seated together, at a round one set for eight. A heavily decorated table stood at the front, which was obviously for Cruz and Catalina.

They all took their seats and looked around.

"Well, this is very nice," said Chloe and everyone agreed.

"I just love this décor with all these beautiful lanterns and flowers," said Ava, waving her arms around at it all.

"Does anyone know why there were no bridesmaids or groomsmen?" asked Maggie.

"I overheard a conversation and in the ladies' toilet that it was a Spanish tradition," added Ava.

"Why didn't you know that? That is where you always are? You could have answered your own bloody question."

"Now don't you start on me," Ava stepped in to stop the bantering. "Look, Cruz and Catalina just walked in, isn't she the most beautiful bride?"

"I just adore her dress," said Danni. "I must shop for some Spanish dresses while I am here," she said and Rocco rolled his eyes as he poured her some water and she gave him a disgruntled smirk.

"It is similar to the gowns she wore on the ship. It is so her style," added Chloe.

Cruz and Catalina arrived back from the photo session and sat at the wedding table. Wine was brought to all the tables and the meal was beginning to be served.

"Would you like a wine, Chloe?" asked Jack as he picked up the bottle of red.

"Yes, please," she said as she handed him her glass.

"See,Jack is a wonderful lad getting Chloe a wine," said Maggie to Paddy.

"Oh, see what you have done now, Jack. Alright,I will give you one glass of wine," he said as he poured her a glass. "But that is all. We have to behave. These things are supposed to go all night."

"Aye, I know, so keep yourself in check. Don't worry yourself with me."

Over the next few hours, tapas dishes were brought out one after another and the wine was never empty. A roasted fish was served and shred between guests at the table, followed by a beef fillet with vegetables. The dessert was served, a Spanish flan with fruits, nuts and custard. Cruz and Catalina had theirs first, and everyone watched as they fed each other as tradition goes.

"That was a hearty meal, wasn't it, John?" said Jack as he sat back in his chair tapping his stomach.

"You can still eat, I will give you that," added Danni, pouring herself a champagne.

"Aye, and you still don't, I noticed," he teased, and they all laughed. They picked up their friendship like they had never been apart.

"So how was that? I can't believe Cruz and Cat just got married," said Maggie.

"Oh, remember the day he proposed to her in front of us all? At the waterfront restaurant. That was so beautiful," added Chloe.

"Well, it is your turn next, you two. We all knew you would end up getting married," said Ava.

"Aye, I saw the spark right from the first day," said Paddy cheerfully.

"Oh, Paddy, you were matchmaking us. You were so funny."

"So where is the wedding going to be?" asked Maggie.

"Please don't say Australia," said Rocco and everyone laughed. Poor Rocco hated travelling distances and was always being dragged somewhere by Danni.

"Oh, we have no idea yet, but I loved this villa idea. It's so wonderful to have all the families together," said Chloe.

"Maybe you could have it in Naples where you first got together," hinted John.

"Or here in Barcelona where you met," added Ava with a suggestive smile.

"You are all just putting ideas in our head, so we won't have it in Australia," said Jack. They all laughed and agreed. Maggie remembered how hurt Chloe was once before, when they were all putting Australia down, and turned to her spotting a similar look on her face.

"Nothing against Australia, Chloe, it is just a long way away," comforted Maggie.

"Maggie and I are getting too old for those distances now," added Paddy, understanding what had happened.

Chloe gave them a warm smile and Maggie winked before turning back to Paddy. "Speak for yourself, you old fool. He is always whining about something these days, I am still as fit as a fiddle, I will show you on the dance floor later."

"See, what did I tell ya, Danni. I will blame you if she gets up on that dance floor," huffed Paddy, pouring Maggie a champagne.

"As long as it's only her petticoat falling to the floor and not her knickers, who cares," answered Danni.

"Well, you are welcome to do the highland fling at our wedding, Maggie," said Chloe.

"Aye and even drop ya knickers to the floor," laughed Jack.

"Ours will be very casual, and we will give you plenty of warning where the wedding will be," she comforted everyone.

"Where is that husband of yours, Ava? Wherever he goes, there is always trouble," said Paddy, looking around.

"Well, to tell you the truth, I was thinking the same thing, Paddy. I saw him talking to a woman before, and now I can't see him anywhere," said Ava as she scanned the room.

"Did she have on a big hat?" asked Jack, sipping on his beer.

"Yes, she did. Did you see them?"she said with a concerned frown.

"No, I didn't, but ya needn't worry."

"Why, how do you know that?"

"If she is wearing a big hat, she isn't very attractive."

"What do you mean?" asked Ava concerned.

"Jack thinks they wear oversized hats to hide their face," added Chloe with a small grin.

"Aye, I do, it is true."

"Oh, that is not true, there are lots of beautiful women here wearing those hats they are just protecting their skin," said Ava having a relieved giggle at his comment.

"Wait, here he comes now," said Paddy loudly to get everyone's attention.

They all turned and watched him approaching, smiling like a Cheshire cat.

"What has he been up to now?" said Paddy.

"No good, it seems,"added a worried Maggie.

"He does seem pretty pleased with himself," added Rocco.

"Oh,God,I will kill him if he has done something to embarrass us at this wedding," said Ava, covering her mouth with her hands nervously.

He scanned them all as he got closer.

"What? What have I done, why are you all staring at me?"

"That's what the million-dollar question is, John. What have you done?" said Paddy with one eye half closed.

"Yes, you have a bit of a reputation for running amuck," added Chloe.

"Oh, well. Yea, I guess I have, but this time I was behaving, I was just talking to this woman,"he said pointing over his shoulder.

"Was she good-looking?" interrupted Jack.

"I really didn't notice. She had a big hat on. Why?"

"See?  I rest my case. If she were good-looking, she would not have worna big hat to hide it," said Jack, sitting back in his chair with a proud grin.

"Yea, whatever," said John,squinting atJack,before returning to his story. "Anyway,we were talking, and she took me to meet

Cruz's famous cousin, Enrique. He was super nice. He is going to sing at the wedding."

"Yea, and. . . ?" asked Ava with a nervous twitch.

"And what? That is it," he said, turning his palms up in the air.

"That's it? You didn't nearly kill someone or injure them?"

"No, I was busy chatting with Enrique, nothing else," he nodded, sitting back down.

"Oh, phew, I can breathe again. I thought we might be making an early exit," said Ava, taking a sip on the wine.

"The night is still young," reminded Paddy. "He still has time."Everyone laughed and agreed.

"Oh, look here comes Catalina and Cruz," said Chloe excitedly, pointing at them at the next table, walking towards theirs.

"Well, here is the gang, so glad you could all make it," beamed Cruz. Everyone congratulated them.

"You have all come a long way. We appreciate you coming," said Catalina.

"We would not miss this for the world, lassie," said Paddy and everyone agreed.

"It is such a beautiful wedding," added Chloe.

"Oh, so glad you like it," said Catalina. "We have just got the first dance to do now, and then its fiesta time," added Cruz. "My cousin is going a play a few songs."

"I met him," said John excitedly.

"Oh, you did. He is down to earth, a nice guy," said Cruz surprised, as a beautiful woman approached and spoke to him."They are ready for you now."

"Okay, we will be there in a minute," answered Cruz. "That was my sister we have to go, but we will be back afterwards to catch up."They smiled and held hands as they walked off together.

"See? She was a very attractive woman and wore no hat," said Jack.

"That was her. She has taken her hat off," said John, looking back after her.

"Well, there goes that theory. Hey, Jack," said Ava, flinging him a smirk.

Everyone laughed. Chloe looked around the room and noticed a lot of women had removed their hats.

"It must be okay to remove hats now. Look," she informed the others.

"Wait, I will google it," said Danni, grabbing her phone.

"Okay. It says here for an outdoor event, which includes a courtyard like we have here, you can remove your hat when the formalities are over just before the dancing begins."

"Just as the ugly lights are dimmed," added Chloe.

"What are ugly lights?" asked Maggie.

"Well, in Australia, we have a joke that at a night club, all the lights are dimmed and everyone is cute especially with your beer goggles on, and then, when it's over, the ugly lights come on and you get to see what everyone really looks like."

"That is funny. Jack, you might be right. Beware of a woman hiding behind a huge hat before the lights are dimmed," laughed Paddy.

"Well, I think you are all wrong. That woman was beautiful," said Ava.

"There is always an exception to the rule," added Rocco.

Their laughter was interrupted by the dimming of the lights. A man walked out with a Spanish guitar.

"That's him, that's Enrique," whispered John loudly.

"Oh, well, I see good looks run in the family," said Danni, straining her neck to get a better look.

"Hola, my name is Enrique. For those of you who do not know me, I am Cruz's cousin, and I am going to play a couple of Spanish love songs that Cruz and Catalina have chosen for their dance tonight. First, I will play Cruz's love song he wrote for Catalina, 'Lay With Me Forever'. Please help me welcome them to the floor, Mr. and Mrs. Diaz."

Everyone clapped as the music started, and they walked to the dance floor and began to slow dance.

"Oh, I love this song," whispered Chloe to Jack."I know it has special memories for us now." She squeezed his hand that was placed on her leg.

As it finished, another Spanish love song began but the beat was faster, and then they started to invite family then guests onto the dance floor.

"Would you like to dance?" whispered Jack softly to Chloe.

"I would love to dance with you," she said as he took her by the hand.

"Oh this is so incredibly romantic."

"Aye, it is. We have not danced like this since the ship."

Everyone seemed to be enjoying their slow dance to the Spanish love songs and then after a few more, Enrique stopped playing and turned to the crowd.

"I am sure you all need a drink after such wonderful dancing. Please take a seat as we have a wonderful surprise for you all here tonight."

Everyone took their seats again as he waited. "Thank you. Tonight, Cruz and Catalina will be performing a dance for you. It is a very beautiful dance that they call the Bolero." The guests all clapped and cheered as they both took to the dance floor. Catalina had changed into a revealing red flowing dress and Cruz wore a red shirt and black pants. You could feel it in the air that they were about to put on a spectacular show.

The music started and everyone went quiet as they began to dance. It was an incredibly sexy romantic dance, as she weaved in and around him, and then he twirled her, spun her around and tossed her like he was playing with a rag doll and as he put her down she started dancing around him again with her skirt waving around like a tissue in a breeze. Everyone was staring, unable to turn away, not wanting to miss a single beat. As it ended everyone, roared with applause and the music started up again but this time, it was ready for a full fiesta.

Everyone jumped onto the dance floor and partied the night away.

"I need to sit down, Jack," whispered Chloe.

"Aye, I am glad that you said that. I need a drink."

They walked to the table and poured a drink. Chloe started to take off her stilettos and rubbed her feet.

"I can't wear these, anymore. They are killing me."

"Did you bring your ballet flats?" he asked with a furrowed brow.

"Yes, I did. I will slip them on," she said, retrieving them from her bag.

"Oh, we have had enough also," said Maggie as she dropped into the chair.

"You have been out there for hours. You did well," said Chloe as she sighed, slipping into her flats.

They sat and chatted as everyone came and went to and from the dance floor before Maggie and Paddy started to say their goodbyes. Chloe was keen to leave with them; she was tired and had spotted Jack yawning a few times.

"Have you had enough, Jack? I am feeling exhausted. I think it is jet-lag still."

"Yes, of course. I was ready hours ago. We can share a cab with Paddy and Maggie, back into town."

They said their goodbyes also. The doorman organised a tax-i,which arrived quickly.

"Well, I wasn't staying till the end. Those things end up going till after breakfast," yawned Paddy.

"Rocco was already dragging Danni off the dance floor. They wouldn't have stayed much longer, either," added Maggie.

"We are still jet-lagged. I feel bad leaving John and Ava behind," sighed Chloe.

"They will be fine. John was dragging Ava off to join Enrique's table as I left," said Jack, leaning around to talk to them from the passenger seat.

"He had a man-crush on him,hadn't he?" laughed Chloe and everyone agreed.

The taxi pulled up outside Chloe and Jack's hotel."Oh, we are here already," said Chloe as Jack gave the driver money and came around to open Chloe's door.

"What are you doing for lunch tomorrow? Will you still be in town?" asked Paddy.

"Yes, we are staying one more night and are free all day."

"Here is our number. Call us in the morning, and we will arrange something."

"Okay, thanks. Sounds good. Goodnight!"

The next morning, they woke late to a text message on their phone.

"What was that?" said Chloe, looking up with one eye open.

"The phone."

"Who could that be so early in the morning?" She flopped her head back onto the pillow as Jack sat up looking at the clock.

"Chloe, it is eleven o' clock," he said with shock. She sat up, looking at the clock, and then laid back down.

"Why is it every time we hang out with them, we wake up with a huge hang over?" she squinted at him.

"It does appear that way, but we went home at a reasonable hour. I wonder what time it ended."

"That is one of them for sure, wanting more drinks today,"she said, waving her hand towards the phone.

Jack laughed. "And you will be back into it as you always do," he said as he went to make coffee. He came back handing her a water bottle.

"Here, start with this."

"Thanks. How come you are okay?"

"Because I am Scottish. I keep telling you this, but ya don't believe me. I bet Paddy is up already sipping a whisky." He laughed as he brought back the coffee and then jumped back into bed with the phone.

Chloe could smell the whisky in the coffee as a smile crept to her face. "Yep, you are right. It is Danni, wants us to meet them for lunch at a bar down on the beachfront."

"I bet Rocco does not have anything to do with this." She laughed as she sat up to drink her coffee.

"No, my guess is he will be the last to know."

"We need to text Paddy and Maggie. They gave us their number last night," she said as she swept her bedhead hairstyle out of her eyes.

"Danni said she has sent a message to everyone but I will send one anyway," added Jack as he replied to Danni.

"Jet-lag, champagne and wine don't mix very well," she complained as she held her head with her hand leaning back.

"Well, you had better get that coffee into you, because I just sent a message saying we will be there."

"I will be fine after a shower. What time did she say?"

"Not till two, so you have plenty of time to recover," he smiled.

"Oh, yea typical Spanish lunchtime, I can manage that."

After a shower and another coffee, they hit the streets for a slow walk to the beachfront. It was a beautiful warm day, the sun made them feel warm and happy as they strolled along, slowly smelling all the different aromas coming out from all the eateries along with laughter and the chatter of the Spanish tongue.

As they arrived, they spotted Paddy and Maggie seated at the table with Danni and Rocco. Walking over, they waved.

"How is the head today?" asked Paddy.

"Oh, I am okay, poor Chloe is a bit dusty. It took a bit to get her moving." He pulled out the chair for Chloe as she gave everyone a kiss and sat. The waitress arrived and Jack ordered some beers."Did you manage to get onto John and Ava this morning?"

"No, we left a message but so far we have not heard from them. Who knows what time they got home," added Danni.

"What time did you leave?" asked Jack.

"Well, I finally managed to drag Danni off the dance floor, not long after you left," said Rocco, sitting back, crossing his legs.

"Yes, thank you, Rocco. I always sulk at the time, but I am grateful in the morning," she said, flicking him a smile.

"It wasn't early. It was after two," added Rocco.

Danni jumped, fidgeting in her handbag.

"I just got a message. I bet that is John." Danni pulled her phone out and smiled. "They are on their way, be here in ten."

"I bet they stayed late," said Chloe.

"Well, they had moved to the family table when we left," said Danni, putting her phone back into her clutch.

"Yea, he was sitting next to Enrique, with stars in his eyes," added Rocco, sipping his champagne.

"He was so funny," laughed Chloe. "He makes me laugh."

"Poor Ava. I bet he was telling him he loved him," added Jack and everyone roared with laughter.

They arrived soon after, looking a little worse for wear and everyone laughed as they greeted them.

"Well, it looks like you two had a big night," said Maggie looking them over.

"And half the morning," said Ava, nodding her head towards John, rolling her eyes as she pulled up a seat and sat.

"Laugh all you want, but I am the one who sat with Enrique last night, and he is sending me a copy of his new album when it is released later this month, signed of course."

"You have a wee crush on him," said Jack.

"No, I don't," said John with an embarrassed look on his face.

"Yes, you so do. You were all over him last night, telling him how much you love him," added Ava.

Everyone roared with laughter.

"We knew it, we knew it," said Rocco. "You are so predictable."

"I am getting a drink. Who wants one?" said John with a smile. "Ava, what will you have, baby?"

"Don't try to change the subject," laughed Danni. "Ava, I have a bottle of champagne if you would like one."

"Oh, no, I think I will stick to beer today, thanks," she said, shaking her head and pulling out a lipstick from her bag. "Sorry he rushed me out the door so quick I didn't even have time to put on my lippy."

Everyone watched as she manoeuvred the lipstick around her lips with artful style, rubbing her lips together to seal the pout.

"We only stopped drinking a few hours ago. How long do those Spanish weddings go for? They gave us a bowl of soup for breakfast along with crusty bread," said John, looking impressed before turning towards the bar.

They all settled into a long afternoon eating tapas and drinking beer and champagne. They were all sad to say goodbye at the end and liked the idea of all getting together again for Jack and Chloe's wedding. Rocco kept insisting all afternoon as long as it was not in Australia, which everybody agreed with, but deep down they all knew if it was Australia, they would all be there in a heartbeat.

# CHAPTER 9
## SCOTLAND

Chloe's head was spinning with a wild hang-over as they pushed through the gate of the two-story grey stone cottage. Her eyes darted from one side of the garden to the other. The lawn was well-kept with minimal plants and a few garden statues scattered around. As they walked up the steps to the front door, the deafening silence rocked Jack. His little dog Jock would be barking by now; he missed his poor wee dog. As he opened the door, no one was to be seen. "Mum, Jeannie, anyone home?" He peeked inside then he heard a familiar voice and a smile crept to his face.

"Oh, Jack, you're home," cried his mother as she came rushing out from the kitchen. Jack turned and smiled at Chloe as he pushed her through the door first before he ran ahead to greet his mother.

"Oh, I have missed you so," she said, cuddling him. She turned as she remembered his guest and took her hand. "I am so sorry, you must be Chloe. I am so happy to meet you," she said, almost crying. "Please come and have a seat I will pour the whisky. I think we need a wee nip."

Jack was smiling at Chloe and showed her to the table. "Please excuse my mother, she is obviously overwhelmed," he whispered.

"And so she should be. She is lovely," said Chloe as she watched her fetching the whisky bottle and Chloe was more than happy that they were having whisky instead of tea. It would help break the hang-over.

She was back with the whisky decanter and poured them all a nip. "So happy to meet the wee lassie who has made my son so happy and soon to be my daughter-in-law."

"Thank you! I am happy to meet you also."

"Where is everyone?" asked Jack. "Well, Jeannie is out with Liam, they will be here shortly. And Jimmy is at the boat shed. He spends most of his time there these days," she said. "I have a roast in the oven. He should be home for dinner."

They sat and had a catch up and Jeannie and Liam walked in the door shortly afterwards. Jack jumped up to greet them and Jeannie threw her arms around him.

"Oh, I am so happy to have you home."

"Aye, and now I also have my wife-to-be to show off." He turned and took Chloe by the hand. "Jeannie, this is Chloe," he said with a proud smile.

"So happy to finally meet you, Chloe," she said as she gave her a hug. "I now understand why my brother went running off to chase you. Welcome to the family!"

"I have made a pot of tea. Come and sit down."

"Thank you,Mum."

They all took a seat back around the table and chatted. It was a dark timber table with six timber chairs, draped with a tartan tablecloth. Between the table and the television stood the large stone fireplace and on the other side was two L-shaped dark brown well-worn leather lounges facing the television and fireplace.

Jimmy walked in the door and everyone's heads spun, looking at the clock on the wall;time had got away and they realised

Jimmy was home for dinner. The last time Jack was with Jimmy, there was tension in the air and nothing had changed. Jeannie had said Mary didn't hang around anymore, but he had no idea where the relationship was. He was hoping she would not be walking through the door any time soon.

"Welcome home, Jack," said Jimmy as Jack stood awkwardly.

"Thank you,I would like to introduce you to Chloe."

Chloe stood, feeling the tension between them as the butterflies began to dance in her belly. He was tall like Jack and full of muscle with similar features, but his eyes were a darker grey and his hair was a darker shade of blonde and shorter. She sensed he was not as relaxed as Jack. Jeannie resembled Jack. She had the same soft blue eyes and shoulder-length wavy hair, which was left to fall anywhere it wanted, casual and relaxed like her.

"Lovely to meet you." Her hands were shaking as he greeted her with respect but with a cold gaze. Everyone in the room stiffened, sensing the tension.

Jack felt Chloe shaking as he took her by the hand.

"I think we might go up to the room and freshen up before dinner."

"It was lovely to meet you all," said Chloe with a shy smile, and they all said the same to her in return.

He guided her up the stairs towards his room and shut the door behind him.

"I am so sorry. I understand how uncomfortable you must be. You are aware of the tension between Jimmy and I," he said as he put his hands on her shoulders, looking into her eyes.

"Yes, he is cold. But don't worry, your mum and sister are lovely."

"No, it is not okay. He has a problem with me, he should not shut you out also."

"Give him time and he will come around," she said as she smiled, but deep down inside she was rattled. She was uncomfortable around him and didn't like his cold demeanour.

They were all exactly as Jack had described them. His mum was warm and caring, Jeannie was bubbly and carefree, and Jimmy was cold and snarly. All the stories started flooding back as she remembered Jack saying he and his brother fought every night, and she hoped she would not have to witness such behaviour.

Pushing the thought from her mind, she started to peer around the room. The first thing she spotted was their painting on his bedside table. She walked over and picked it up.

"Every morning and every night I would stare at this painting thinking of you," he said quietly as he peered over her shoulder.

"Me, too. I loved this painting so much. It certainly has a hypnotic attraction."

"Aye."

She placed it down slowly and started looking round.

"So this is your room? Where I used to talk to you on the phone?"

"This is my lair." He opened his arms as she turned slowly, gazing around. She had dreamed of him sitting here in his room so many times and now she was here with him. His eyes followed her as she walked to his sideboard and picked up a CD next to his stereo.

"Well, bugger me, you like Rod Stewart?" she said shocked, looking back at him.

"No. That CD is my mother's," he said defensively, looking embarrassed as he tried to take it off her, but she pulled it in closer to her and laughed.

"What would your mother's CD be doing here?" she teased and pressed the button marked "open" as the CD drawer sprung to life and was loaded with the Rod Stewart disc. "So your mother sneaks into your room and plays her music?" she said with a teasing smile.

"All right, all right, I confess it is hers but I was playing it. I can explain," he said as he sat on the bed looking embarrassed, and she sat beside him.

"After I got home, there was a song that used to haunt me. Everywhere I went it was playing. The shops, the car, everywhere. Then, when I was coming home from Maggie and Paddy's on the train, it came on again, *of course*, so I listened to the words as I gazed out of the train window, and I realised this was my song, calling out to you, me in my deepest darkest time of my life, missing you, and at that moment, I realised it was telling me to go and find you. So when I got home, I went down to Mum's music stand, as I knew she had the CD, and I played it every night before I went to sleep."

"My God, Jack, how mystifying, what song?"

"'Sailing'," he said, hoping she would not laugh.

"Such a beautiful song. My mum plays his music all the time. I have never stopped and listened to the words."

She walked over to the CD player and pressed play.

"Here, you need to come and lie on the bed with me as I used to do," he said as he jumped on the bed and patted for her to join him. She lay beside him and listened to the words. Neither of them said a word and Jack took her hand and squeezed her tight as it ended.

"How moving," she said, staring at the ceiling, and he lifted himself up on one elbow to stare down into her eyes.

"Aye, now you understand why I was so spooked."

"Yes, I am totally moved beyond words. I have goosebumps," she said, rubbing her arm.

"Those lyrics are so alluring."

"Aye, it was my motivation to keep my plan going when things were not going so well. It gave me hope."

"You did it. You came and crossed the seas to be with me. Wow, it will forever make me think of you," she said softly.

"Of us," he corrected.

"Yes, of us."

"I give this song to you now, so it can haunt you like it haunted me."

A knock on the door summoned them to dinner.

"Are you ready for this?" he asked.

"Yes, of course. Let us go and spend time with your family," she said smiling.

"Don't let him worry you," she said as she stood up.

"I am worried about you, not him."

"I am fine. Come on, the aroma of your mum's cooking is making my stomach rumble, so you must be starving," she smiled.

"I am always starving," he grinned as he jumped up, giving her a quick kiss before opening the door.

They made their way down and took their seats. His mother was still beaming as she brought out the roast to be carved and a platter of vegetables. Jimmy did the honours and carved the roast and then placed it on the table, serving everyone. Jack got up and poured the whisky. Jeannie was the life of the meal and chatted throughout, trying to clear the air.

"Chloe, would you like to come shopping with me tomorrow? I would love to show you around," said Jeannie.

"I would love to go. Thank you, Jeannie," said Chloe. Jack squeezed her leg under the table.

After dinner, they headed upstairs to have some time to themselves. She sat on his bed and quietly listened as he showed her all his things and his most treasured items like his father's kilts and old family photos. "This is the kilt I will wear to our wedding. I will need to bring it home with me. It's a MacLean tartan and was given to me by my father when I turned 21 so it is very precious." He showed her the sporran and all the accompanying accessories.

"So you are wearing a kilt to our wedding? How lovely."

"Oh, aye, I have to. It's tradition and Jimmy will wear one as well," he said proudly.

"So you have your outfit all done, and we still don't have a country, let alone a location to be married."

"Dunna worry, we will sort it all out soon. But I did like the idea of the villa in Barcelona, where all the family stayed together for a week's celebration."

"I loved the idea also. Do you think your mum would travel?" asked Chloe, sounding concerned.

"I will put it to her before we leave," he smiled. "It's our wedding, remember?  If they don't want to come, so be it."

As night fell, she slipped on his t-shirt and crawled into bed.

"Hey what is going on here?" he said as he was pulling trying to pull it over her head.

"We are in your mother's house. I have to respect that," she giggled pulling it back down.

"Alright, I will give you tonight. But tomorrow, I want my wee jaguar back."

They laid together, talking and giggling as he told her stories about his childhood.

"Do you know you are the first girl I have ever had in my bed, and you won't let me do anything," he teased.

"Seriously? What about Mary?" She said, looking surprised.

"No, she never stayed over. I told you we had a boring relationship, and now I have found a wee wild cat, and she won't let me play."

She giggled, and they chatted for hours before falling asleep.

Waking to the noises of the house, and the aroma of bacon cooking, they showered and sat on the bed, chatting.

"Today, I want to show you around my town."

"I am excited to explore your hometown, but I have to be back after lunch to go shopping with Jeannie."

"I have you all to myself this morning, then. Come on, let's go and eat. The bacon is calling me."

As they walked down the stairs, silence made them aware the others were all gone. His mum called out from the kitchen as she heard them approaching.

"Oh, you are awake. Sit down, I will cook you up some eggs," she said as she came out.

"Morning,Mum! Eggs sound delicious."

"Did you sleep well, Chloe?"

"I had a wonderful sleep, thank you."

"I am taking Chloe out this morning. I want to show her around town."

"Your car is still in the garage. Jimmy started it every week for you."

"He did," said Jack with a startled gaze.

"Aye, he did," she said as she turned back to head back to the kitchen.

After breakfast, they spent the morning sightseeing.

"So you surprised me again. A golf. I thought you would have an SUV, for sure."

"Well, there you go. Jump in. You will be surprised how roomy it is," he said as he opened the door for her.

He got into the driver's seat and put on his seat belt.

"Where are we going?" she asked as she put on her seat belt.

"This morning, I am going to show you a lighthouse, but not any old lighthouse, this one is built into a sixteenth century castle."

"Of course, it is. What else? We are in Scotland," she said with a huge smile, and he laughed.

The lighthouse was stunning, and they spent over an hour looking around and visiting the museum.

"Come in here, you will like this," he guided her into the teahouse, and they found a seat by the window which had stunning views looking out to sea.

"Jack, this is beautiful," she said as she stared out the window

"Aye, I knew you would like it. What you are looking at is The Great Sea."

"It's so stunning," she said, unable to stop looking as a waitress approached and Jack ordered them a pot of tea and some cookies.

"Look over there. I thought I saw dolphins jumping out of the water."

"Aye, porpoises, dolphins, all sorts of wonderful fish. Beautiful to sit and let your mind get lost as they parade and folkloric showing off for you," he smiled.

The waitress arrived and placed the pot of tea and cookies down. Jack began to pour the tea.

"These cookies are homemade," said Chloe, shocked, picking one up in her hand.

"And they are delicious also, you should try one."

"I truly love your home town," she said as she chewed on the cookie.

"Well, so much more to discover. After this, we will go and take a walk on the beach, and after we will have to head back home to meet Jeannie." He studied her face trying to read what she was thinking. "Are you okay with the shopping with Jeannie? You didn't have a chance to say no, did you?"

"I will be fine. She is sweet and I can't think of a better way for girls to blend together," she said, sipping on her tea.

"Aye, she is, and I will make sure she takes care of you," said Jack with a stern eye.

"I am sure you will," she said with a crooked smile and he laughed.

They strolled along the beach and Jack told her all the wonderful stories about his home town as she listened. He ran his hand down at her arm and spotted goose bumps. "Are you cold?"

"Just a little. The breeze is quite fresh."

"I don't feel it. Here, snuggle in closer, I will keep you warm." He pulled her in tight and the warmth of his body instantly warmed her. A smile crept to her face when he snuggled her; she felt so safe and warm with his arms wrapped around her tight.

"I love this place. It is so beautiful," she said as she pulled her hair out of her face.

"Well, you got it on one of its better days." He smiled, looking around. He felt warm inside, knowing that she loved it.

"It might be a tad too cold for me in winter, though."

"I would say that was for sure," he smiled down at her thinking about some of the wild weather that battered the coast. "Before we go home I want to take you to the highlands. If you think this is beautiful, you will love the beauty of the highlands."

"I would love that. My nanna told me numerous stories about the highlands."

"Where was she from?"

"Aberdeen shire somewhere. To be honest, I never really asked. All I knew she was from Scotland, but she spoke of Aberdeen and the highlands a lot."

"Well, you will love the highlands. It will be a real highlight for you."

She smiled, looking around. A trip to the highlands sounded wonderful.

"Come on, let's make tracks, you can't be late for your afternoon shopping."

Trays of sandwiches and a pot of tea were waiting for them when they arrived home. The table was set for four. Liam was at work and Jimmy was at the boathouse. Jack felt certain Jimmy usually came home for lunch, and recognised he was staying away as much as possible.

The girls left for their shopping after lunch, and Jack headed down to the boathouse to find Jimmy. He didn't like the distance between them. He needed to find out what was going on. As he approached, he spotted him on one of the boats, he walked over and jumped onboard.

"What's happening? Do you need a hand?"

"No, I am doing a few wee chores," he said not looking up.

"You were not home for lunch," said Jack as he looked around the boat.

"I got carried away, forgot the time," he said bluntly.

"As long as that's all it is, you have been a bit quiet. Is everything OK?"

He stopped working and stood, looking at Jack for a moment as if he was thinking what to say. He put down his tools and rubbed his hands on his jeans.

"Yea, I am a wee bit embarrassed around Chloe," Jack nodded. Grateful he was honest with him.

"Mary is not around. Are you still seeing her?" He held his breath, waiting for the answer.

"No, that never recovered. She started hanging around Shauna more and more and she changed an awful lot. I was happy just working on the boats."

The relief washed over Jack;he was glad she was gone. He had seen a side of her he had never seen also, and didn't want that for his brother. He knew he would be happy working with the boats; that was what he had always loved to do.

"Well, if you haven't had any lunch, let's go to the pub for a beer," said Jack eagerly. Jimmy stared at him, trying to think of an excuse, but he couldn't think of one, and why shouldn't he go to the pub with his brother? It was something they had not done in a long time and would make a well-needed catch-up. He smiled at Jack and said, "OK, why not?"

Jimmy cleaned himself up, and they walked down the road to the pub. He ordered a meal and Jack had some hot chips, then settled into a booth.

"You have new boots."

"Do you like them? They were a Christmas gift from Chloe," he said proudly as he stuck his foot out.

"I noticed them at the bar. They are expensive looking boots. She spoils you, you are very lucky."

"I am, and I am very grateful."

"She seems like a bonne lass," said Jimmy warmly.

"Oh, aye, she is. You should take the time to discover how wonderful and terrific she is."

Jimmy watched the spark in Jack's eye when he spoke of her. He had never seen him like this with anyone and it was clear to him he was head over heels in love with this girl. He was all of a sudden embarrassed he had given her the cold shoulder.

"You are right I have not even given her a chance. I was just so embarrassed."

"Well, there is no need to be. She doesn't blame you. She knows the whole story," said Jack confidently.

"I will apologise to her when I see her."

"She is easy to talk to. You don't have to worry."

They both sat quietly for a moment, lost in their thoughts about all that had happened. "You seem very happy. You get on like a house on fire. I think now I understand why you ran away to Australia."

"Thanks. I am very happy. I have met the love of my life," he said, staring into his beer.

"I overheard you last night giggling and talking. I lay thinking to myself that's what love is supposed to be like. You found real love Jack, and I am happy for you."

"Thanks, Jimmy. That means a lot," he said as he sat thinking. "So, when you say you overheard us last night, what exactly did you hear?" asked Jack, looking concerned. Jimmy broke out into fits of laughter.

"It's OK, I didn't get an earful of anything except muffled voices and a whole lot of giggling," said Jimmy, laughing as he took a swig of his beer.

Jack was relieved as a smile came back to his face. "Another pint," he asked and Jimmy laughed and said, "I thought you would never ask."

Jack arrived back from the bar with Pat, his best friend. They had gone through school together. He also worked on a trawler and was finished for the day.

"Jimmy, this is a surprise. I can count on one hand the times you two are at the pub together," he said.

"Aye, definitely not enough. Sit and join us," said Jimmy happily. They had a few pints while sharing stories and lots of laughter.

"So where is your Aussie lassie I have heard so much about?"

"She is out shopping with Jeannie." Jack glanced at the time. *Shit, was it that late already?* "Ring the house, Jimmy, tell the girls to come down to the pub. We can have dinner here, give Mum a night off," said Jack.

"Aye, that's a brilliant idea," said Jimmy as he fetched his phone out of his pocket.

Chloe, Jeannie and his mum arrived soon afterwards and Jack was so excited. He ran to the door to greet them as he spotted them walk inside.

"How are you? How was shopping?" he said as he took her hand.

"Shopping was fun! We had a lovely time." She smiled up at him.

He had his best mate, his brother, and Chloe all by his side. He couldn't wait to introduce her to Pat. He was the one who Jack would drown his sorrows with most nights when things were rough.

Putting his arm around her, he proudly introduced her. "Chloe, this is my best friend, Pat."

"So, I am finally lucky enough to meet the girl that made Jack cry, and now I can understand why." He leaned in and gave her a kiss. "Such a pleasure to meet ya," he smiled.

"Hey, I didn't cry."

"Ya did. Ya balled like a wee baby quite a few times," said Pat winking at Chloe.

Everyone was laughing. Chloe instantly liked him. He had a calmness about him with soft brown eyes and wavy light brown hair that fell to his shoulders. He had broad shoulders and was built like Jack and Jimmy from working on the boats. They settled in for the evening and had a great time. After dinner, a band started, and they all got into the swing of things after a few pints.

Jack was at the bar and Chloe sensed Jimmy staring at her from across the table. Nervously she glanced his way and smiled. He smiled back and started to make his way around the table to sit in Jack's seat. "Hi, are you having a bonne night?" he said.

"Yes, it's lovely."

"Chloe, I just wanted to say how sorry I am about everything," he said sincerely.

"Oh, please, don't blame yourself. That is in the past," she said, waving it off.

"I am so embarrassed. I truly am very sorry," he stared deep into her eyes and spotted a sadness in his eyes, and for a moment saw a tenderness she knew all along that was hidden in there somewhere.

"It is over now. Let's just have some fun," she said looking towards the band, to ease the moment.

"Would you like to dance?" he asked hopeful.

"Sure, why not?" He grabbed her by the hand gently and took her to the dance floor. He smiled at her and the tension began to lift. He was quite good looking when he let himself relax, his smile softened his face.

Jack came back from the bar and started looking around for Chloe; he spotted them on the dance floor and smiled. Everything was going to be okay. He sat at the table watching, and let his thoughts drift for a while. Liam was dancing with Jeannie and his mum had wandered off to chat with a friend a few tables over. He studied Jimmy, he seemed so happy, he was a decent guy and hoped he would meet someone special and find what he had with Chloe.

They all wandered home together late that night, laughing and being silly as they walked the cobblestone path. Liam was still walking with them,and seeing no one else seemed concerned, Jack thought that just must be the usual and never said a word. They all had a whisky nightcap and then his mum and Jimmy went off to bed. Jeannie and Liam stayed up to have one more. "So where are you going to be married?"asked Jeannie,as she sat down next to Liam, who immediately put his arm around her.

"Well, we have not had time to determine that yet. We need to discuss ideas with you all, and check how far you are willing to travel, and Chloe's family," he said as he leaned forward to take a chip and offering Chloe one.

"Liam and I will travel anywhere. It is just Mum you need to worry about."

Chloe jumped up and grabbed her phone. "Oh, I just remembered. I haven't had a chance talk to you yet Jack but I got an email from Danni today, and she suggested a chateau in France, called Chateau Bijou. Let me find it."

"That sounds so romantic," said Jeannie with wide eyes looking around at everyone.

"Very romantic and dreamy and stunning, here," she passed her phone around and they were all in awe of the place.

"Danni and Rocco were meeting friends in France after the wedding, and they obviously came across the chateau," Jack explained to Jeannie and Liam before taking the phone from Chloe as she peered over his shoulder.

"Aye, it's perfect. Enough rooms for everyone and huge grounds for the ceremony." They all watched as he scanned through the photos.

"Liam and I want to be married and were trying to find a time when you would be home, but if we helped with the costs we could marry on the day after, everyone would be there, plus it would save a lot of money."

They all stopped and stared at her. "You are getting married," said Jack, stunned at the news.

"Don't look at me like that." She laughed, throwing a peanut at him.

"I am more than happy, just a bit shocked," he said, looking like he had seen a ghost.

"Oh, that is such exciting news. Congratulations! Well,I guess it sounds like a wonderful idea," said Chloe, running around the coffee table to give her a hug. Jack followed behind her.

"What do you think, Liam?" asked Jeannie.

"It sounds like a plan, and a holiday. Perfect!" He smiled.

"I will pour us another whisky. Let's celebrate," said Jack, refilling everyone's glass.

The chateau and weddings were the subject of the night. Everyone was excited and no one wanted to go to bed. They started planning and a few whiskies later, they had planned the whole soiree.

# CHAPTER 10

# THE WEDDING PLANNER

"**G**ood morning, Princess," said a very weary-eyed Jack. They were both hung over, but Jack a tad worse after being at the pub all afternoon.

"Good morning. You look terrible," she laughed.

"Aye, I am glad you find me amusing," he said, looking through squinted eyes.

"I will pop downstairs and make us a coffee and grab some water." She tip-toed downstairs and made coffee. The house was silent. They were already out and about or still in bed. She made coffee and slipped back upstairs without anyone noticing. Jack was still passed out on the bed.

"Here, sleepy head, sit up and have some water and coffee. What happened to my amazing Scot that bounces back?"

"Oh, aye, I will be okay. Here, watch, I am getting up." He sat up and thanked her for the coffee, holding his head.

"Did we happen to arrange our wedding last night?" he said, a bit confused.

"Yes, we planned getting married at a chateau in France along with Jeannie and Liam," laughed Chloe.

"Oh, I thought so," he said, squinting. He sat thinking about the turn of events while they drank their coffee.

"And Jeannie and Liam are getting married," he said surprised.

"Yes, apparently. I hope they were fair dinkum because if not, they will be waking up very troubled today." They both laughed as their thoughts trailed back to the night before.

"You know, Jack, I don't think it is such a silly idea."

He just looked at her blankly before speaking. "Are you okay sharing your wedding with Jeannie?" he asked, surprised.

"Well, yes. Not being the same day, I am more than happy. We will have the chateau for a week. What do you think?" she asked, curiously studying his face. She could almost hear his brain registering what she just asked him. He was so cute when he was hung over.

"I would marry you anywhere," he smiled. "And it would make a lot of sense to save a lot of money."

"Saving money. Well,they are a Scot's favourite words. Sounds like a done deal," she said, smiling. "I am not saying it won't take a lot of planning, and I am not really sure if it is actually allowed, but we have a start."

"Aye,I will take everyone out to lunch today and check what their thoughts are," said Jack,still trying to wake up."I need to take a shower. I would love to invite you but I know you would not come," he said.

"Well, you are right. I will go after you," she smiled.

The plan itself seemed brilliant, but Chloe had to check if her family were prepared to fly so far. She recollected her parents were always talking about doing Europe, and Chrissie would be keen, but Kait, Johnny and Sophia were the ones she most worried about. She needed to ask her what her thoughts were before she went any further. There was no time like the present so she sent her a message right away. It was getting late in their time, but she hoped she would be awake, probably just getting home from the restaurant.

*"What are your thoughts on a wedding in France? Would you be able to come? We would lease a Chateau for a week and all stay, everyone would have accommodation."*

She pressed send and sat back. The more she thought about the idea, the better it sounded. Her phone pinged almost instantly.

*"Wild horses could not stop us. Book it."*

She smiled as she thought of Kait. She was her rock. If she said yes, then she would make sure everyone else did, too. Chloe was so excited. "I am getting married in France," she squealed.

They went to lunch at a nice pub with lovely sea views. He had always planned on taking his mum out for lunch before he went home and now he had an excuse. Everyone arrived except Jimmy; he was still finishing off the boats and would come later.

Liam went to the bar with Jack."I need to know. Was it just the drink talking, what you said last night about getting married in France?" asked Jack, concerned.

"We have never been more serious about anything. And you?"asked Liam with his eyebrows knit tight.

"Of course, that's why we are all here. I will hit Mum and Jimmy up and see their reaction."

"What,now? Here today? I haven't even told her mum we are getting married,"he said with a frantic look.

"Well, today is the day. Buckle up, today is the day you spill your beans," said Jack, laughing. "You will be right. She loves you, and would not have it any other way as long as you two are certain. I don't want to rush you into anything."

"Oh, no, you have nothing to worry about. We were definitely getting married. We just didn't have the details of where and when until last night."

Jack stared at him for a moment. He did not want to push him, but he seemed quite certain he wanted to go ahead.

"Alright, if you are sure, follow my lead, and we will break it to her slowly," said Jack as he was checking over his shoulder to see if anyone was listening. He noticed Jimmy walking in as they got the drinks and headed back to the table. "I got you a pint, Jimmy," said Jack as he saw Jimmy heading to the bar. They all took their seats at the table.

"What's this all about, Jack? I am still suffering from last night, and we are summoned back to the pub for more. When did you say you were going home?" said Jimmy and everyone around the table laughed and agreed.

"Well, I promise I won't hold you here all day today. I just wanted your thoughts on a few things that came to light last night." Everyone looked worried. Liam was nervous, drinking his beer way too fast.

"What's on your mind?" asked Jimmy.

"Well, as you all know, Chloe and me want to get married but can't decide where. If we are married in either Scotland or Australia, one family has to travel. So to be fair, we thought of meeting in France. We rent a chateau with room for everyone to stay, and marry in the grounds."

Silence surrounded the table for a moment and then his mum was the first to speak. "Oh, my Lord, Jack. France?"

"Well, it's a whole lot closer than Australia," argued Jimmy.

"Aye, I guess you are right. But it sounds awfully expensive," she said looking concerned.

Jack looked at Jeannie and Liam and gave them a nod to step in. Liam drained the last of his beer nervously as everyone stared intently.

"What's up, Liam? Does a trip to France scare you?" said Jimmy, laughing.

"No not at all. It's just, well, Jeannie and I were hoping to get married also, if that is OK with everyone here." He gulped as he looked around.

"Jeannie," was all that her mother managed to say.

"Yes, Mum. Liam and I have been wanting to marry for a while, but were having trouble when to plan it for so Jack and Chloe would be able to attend. But last night we came up with this great idea of leasing a chateau in France for a week, and we can each have our own wedding day. Everyone will be there, and we share the cost."

"Well, it sounds like a great idea to me," said Jimmy, jumping up to congratulate his sister. He went around and gave her a big kiss and shook Liam's hand.

"Well, I had better buy my new future brother-in-law a beer. This family is getting bigger every day," he beamed, looking around. He went to the bar and got a round of drinks. Liam jumped up to help.

"So, Mum, is this okay with you? What are you thinking? You look like you are about to cry," said Jeannie, concerned.

"Aye, I am. I have been waiting for this day to come and Liam is a perfect choice. I am very happy for ya both. But it's days like this I miss your father terribly. He would have loved to be here."

"Oh, Mum." She gave her a kiss and a cuddle. They all realised it was hard on her, and Jeannie was glad that was the only reason. She was a bit worried thinking it was because she was wanting to get married.

The boys came back to the table with the drinks and the celebrations began. Chloe showed them the chateau Danni had sent her, and they discussed the details. It was the topic of the afternoon and everyone was putting in their opinions and suggestions.

"What about your family, Chloe? Are they prepared to travel?" asked Mrs. MacLean.

"Well, I have told my sister, and she is happy to travel and my parents have always wanted to tour Europe, so I guess it will be okay. But I will have to check with them, of course, before anything is finalised."

They all agreed she would need to check, due to the vast distance to travel. Jack's mum was getting more and more excited as the afternoon went along. Both her children getting married at the same time and in another country, it was all very exciting.

"One thing that would be important to my family would be timing. We live and work in a seasonal town and June and July are our quiet time when we can slip away easier, if that suits everyone here."

They all nodded in acceptance. It was all starting to come together, as a location and a time was finally agreed on.

They gave up their trip to the highlands to spend the next few days looking over chateaus on the internet, and Chloe and Jeannie had decided that the one Danni had sent them, Chateau Bijou, had the best location and the best price. Being in the south of France, it was just a bit out of town from Montpelier which had lots of accommodation for anyone who would not be staying at the chateau and it also had the warmer climate which they wanted.

The chateau itself had twelve rooms and eight gites around the back and acres of land for wedding locations and a large pool to relax on rest days. Available for the first and last week in June if they were more than interested.

"We need to inspect this place before we book," said Chloe.

"Yes, but you fly out in a few days. We won't have time and I have work, so does Liam."

"Maybe we could go there and wander around, visit them and fly home from France. If it is nice, we could put the deposit down and sign the paperwork," suggested Jack.

"That would work if you trust us to make that decision on your behalf, Jeannie," asked Chloe, concerned.

"Of course,I would trust you both."

"Alright, I will Skype my parents and if they are OK with travelling, we will change our flights."

Chloe checked the time and doing the calculation she was aware her parents would be awake in a few hours, so while they waited they looked over the chateaus one more time. They selected two others that were in the same region, so they would compare. One of them was available for nightly rental, so they could make that their base whilst they wandered around the area. The time arrived for her to call her parents, and they took a deep breath to seal the deal. They answered after a few rings and after the usual greetings, Chloe blurted the whole story out without taking a breath.

"We are so glad you mentioned this, Kait let the cat out of the bag accidentally, and we have been looking at trips to Europe. We love the idea. We were half looking at doing this next year, anyway, so well done guys. We can't wait!"

They had got the answer they needed and relief swept over their faces. Interested in knowing the details, they chatted about what they had decided so far. They hung up with a huge smile on their faces. They would be off to France!

The details were discussed again with Jack's family that night at dinner, and booked their flights for early morning the day after. Packing was the priority the next day. They all went to the pub for dinner the last night and bumped into Pat. Jack asked him to be his best man, and he was so excited and promised that he would be there for him. Jimmy was to be groomsman. The boys all had a beer together and lots of laughs, joking about what to wear and speeches. The women spent the night talking of wedding plans.

Everyone had agreed there would be extremely limited guests, and they wanted the chateau to be big enough for the families to stay together. Being an early morning flight for them the next day, they were keeping an eye on the time. It was easy to get carried away with that crowd. They gave Pat a hug, and he kissed Chloe and thanked her for looking after Jack, saying he was jealous, laughing, and they all left.

# CHAPTER 11
## MONTPELIER

The weather was glorious when they touched down at Méditerranée Airport. They were anxious to check in and spend the time in the pool at the chateau. Finding the car rental office was a breeze, and after a swift transaction they were issued the keys to a small Mercedes-Benz. It was of a perfect size for manoeuvring around the countryside of the Languedoc area. It was a short twelve-kilometre drive to the chateau, and they were beaming with excitement. Jack looked around at the driving controls while Chloe put the address into the Navman, and they were off.

They were quickly out of the city and onto the back roads. The scenery was breathtaking as they opened the windows to breathe in the fresh summer air. After a quick drive down a tarred track, which was lined with fields of grazing horses, they arrived at the gates and headed through them onto the pebbled parking area. It was a grand cream three-story chateau with manicured gardens and life-size statues and pots scattered around. They checked in and headed straight to their room. As they climbed the grand staircase with their luggage, they started to lose the excitement they had of being given a beautiful room on the top floor. They hoped they would be given the deluxe room as they were to scrutinise the chateau for their wedding location, and they were not disappointed.

As Jack pushed open the door of the room, the aroma of fresh cut flowers wafted through the air. A huge vase stood elegantly on a table inside the door. The room itself was of decent size, with a king-size bed with extensive views over the grounds of the chateau. There was a small table with a coffee machine and their own en-suite bathroom. The room itself was painted in a crimson shade of red with purple accessories and all too modern, which disappointed them as it took away the old charm.

After a quick change they were out enjoying the sunshine and heading to the pool area for a swim before dinner. The meal that night was served at a communal table on the terrace. Prepared was a beautiful three-course meal with a French onion soup to start a cassoulet as a main and a flan for dessert. Plus bottles of local wines lined the centre of the table. They mingled with other guests and tried to communicate; some spoke English but most spoke French.

After dinner, Jack took Chloe by the hand and took her for a walk through the gardens. It was a lovely evening and the perfume from the roses and lavender fields was drifting through the air. They came across a bench seat in a secluded garden and stopped for a rest. Jack was instantly kissing her with a passion that was wild.

"Jack, what are you doing?" laughed Chloe.

"Oh, I am sorry I have not held you, and had you like this in days and it's been driving me wild."

She was instantly the same; he unbuttoned her top with urgency and slid his hand in caressing her breast. She undid his pants, and he instantly laid her gently on the ground and pulled off her panties and began to make love to her while they were both breathing heavily with desire for each other. It was over as quickly as it started. They both lay panting.

"I am sorry," Jack finally spoke. "I have been burning for you."

"Maybe we should stay at your mother's more often. I like what it does to you," she laughed.

They woke the next morning to the aromas of cakes baking, mixed with roses and lavender. They had two chateaus on their list to explore. The one Danni had sent them was still their favourite and were excited to visit. They showered and went down for breakfast. The kitchen dining room smelt amazing with freshly baked madeleine cakes, croissants, and coffee. They sat out on the terrace while they went over the day's events. Number one was the grand chateau where they booked as many rooms as they liked and were required to book the grounds separately as they would not have exclusive ownership. The afternoon would finally be filled exploring Danni's pick.

They finished breakfast and headed out to the car, waiting for them in the car park. It was a lovely drive amongst wineries, countryside and animals roaming in paddocks. They were at the grand chateau too quickly; they were enjoying the drive around the countryside. It was grand indeed with dual stairways meeting in the middle on the first floor, with huge wrought-iron doors that led to reception. A French-looking woman who introduced herself as Caroline greeted them and got ready to show them around. The interior was just as impressive as the outside, with moulded furnishings and chandeliers in every room. After they poked around inside, Caroline excused herself, and they were left to stroll around the outdoor grounds themselves. The pool was grand with more gites surrounding the rear. Acres of land spanned the grounds, and they could have picked a niche anywhere and it would have been beautiful, but something was missing. Aware it was not what they were looking for, they thanked Caroline before leaving.

They headed to Chateau Bijou. As they entered the enormous wrought-iron gates,a gut feeling told them it was the one. Being smaller, it had a nicer aura and ambience. They strolled up the pebble path, which led them around the feature fountain reaching the opened double entryway where they were greeted by a lady who appeared friendlier and more interested in them and their booking than the previous lady. She introduced herself as Bridgette and began showing them around.

Some rooms were booked but the vacant ones they inspected were exactly what they were hoping for. A pleasant common room adorned the main living area dressed in baroque style of vibrant colours of rich red gold and blue. Standing lamps and lounges with turned legs were made inviting by scatter cushions and throw rugs. The decent-size breakfast room was decorated in true provincial style with a long timber table in the centre of the room,while a door on the other side of the room led out to an outdoor terrace.

The floors were all stone and the staircase up to the bedrooms was beautiful wrought iron. Outside, the gites surrounded the enormous pool, barbeque and pool house. The grounds were immaculate, and they spotted an area they loved for the ceremony, to the side surrounded by trees Chloe imagined all lit up brightly with fairy lights.

Bridgette let them explore as long as they wanted, waving at them as she rushed off for a pressing issue which needed her immediate attention. Alone at last, they were jumping out of their skin with excitement. "Let's Skype Jeannie," said Jack with a broad grin. Chloe pushed her hands into her pocket and pulled out her phone. She answered almost immediately.

"We are here at the chateau. We wanted to show you around. It's absolutely perfect. I think this is the one, Jeannie, but tell me what you think."

They showed her around as much as possible, both talking over each other in speed. They explained to her the one that they were staying at was too modern and the one they visited n the morning was too grand and impersonal. Jeannie was thrilled to bits with the Chateau and asked them to book.

Nothing compared and having the right amount of rooms for the family, along with a number of gites for guests, it was perfect. They got off the phone and stared at each other, then nodded with a smile.

"This is it,Princess. Let's go book our wedding venue."

Comfortable they were doing the right thing, they went in to Bridgette's office. She sat them down at the desk and went over everything with them in detail, offering them the available dates, and they chose the last weekend in June. It was booked solid in July due to Bastille Day celebrations. They booked out every room and gite to make sure they had the whole place to themselves and because they did, they had the run of the chateau for the ceremony. Seeing they were small weddings, Bridgette offered to do the catering and said she would email some menus to her later, along with details for florists, hairdressers, and make-up artists in the area.

They were excited and felt like they were ontop of the world as they walked out. It was exactly what they had wanted, the wedding was falling into place. They stopped at a restaurant just out of town and celebrated. It was a small restaurant with courtyard dining Bridgette had recommended. It was perfect for what they wanted. A charcoal barbeque was burning away in the corner and the aromas were mouth-watering, so a decision to order off the barbeque menu was easy. The seafood platter was too impressive to ignore, and they spied a bottle of local wine they had had in the little fish shop on the cruise.

They were right in the region where the grapes were grown and the wine bottled. They laughed at the irony of it all. Who would have thought the next time they would come across that wine would be the day they booked their chateau for their wedding? They acted like two young lovers who had just met, so into each other and so happy. The lunch was delicious, and they lingered for a few hours, in no hurry to move on.

They stopped at a few wineries after lunch,where Chloe sampled some wines for the wedding and bought a few bottles to take home. As Jack was driving, he just had to trust Chloe's judgement. She took cards from the wineries and said she would be in touch. They headed home to the chateau and organised their luggage for the train to Barcelona the next morning. They had one night in Barcelona before heading home the following day. She sent all the details she had to Jeannie and then went and relaxed by the pool before dinner. It had been a perfect few days, and they wished they didn't have to leave.

The train ride to Barcelona took only four hours. They went straight to the dining car where they settled into a table with a window view and had a charcuterie platter and wine for lunch. The cheeses were smooth and creamy and incredibly Moorish. The food, the wine, the scenery of lavender fields and farms made it an incredible experience as the train hurdled along at a cracking speed. Arriving in no time, they hailed a taxi to the same hotel they stayed at before. It was comfortable and familiar to them, along with the surroundings. The rooftop bar was calling them, so they put on their costumes and grabbed a towel and headed up without wasting any time. Chloe found two sun lounges while Jack went to the bar and ordered them a beer. They lay on the sun lounges happily, until too hot and then dived into the pool. The views from the pool area were incredible, and they gazed out over the railing as they dried off. The bartender came over and pointed out the sights for them. Two things took their fancy: A look-out they had no idea existed and the old town. They had never even ventured towards the old town. They decided to make that their dinner destination. The lookout would have to be put aside for next time. After their swim, they rested before getting ready for dinner. They strolled while they chatted all the way to the old town, taking one last trip down the 1. 2-kilometre tree-lined LasRamblas.

# CHAPTER 12

## PEARL BEACH

A beautiful summer morning had sprung, and life was pretty sweet. Jack had gone off to work and Chloe was sitting on the computer trying to organise the wedding. As she read over numerous articles about getting married in France, she realised they had a problem. Repeatedly stating you must be a resident for 30 days. Plus, you must be married in the town hall. Frantically she searched, again and again, but still the same answer. Oh no, what have they done? She pushed her chair back and looked to the sky, rubbing the back of her neck. They can't reside in France thirty days before their wedding—why didn't she investigate this beforehand? Oh no, what about Jeannie? She was starting to freak out. Panic attacks were setting in. Why did the chateau take the booking? Surely, someone among them would have mentioned this. She needed to ask someone in France. Bridgette sprung to her mind; she pulled her chair back in tight to the computer and jumped online, sending her a quick email. She had to know something. She closed the computer and stood up, stretching. She needed to walk away, it was stressing her out way too much, so a beach walk would help.

Walking down to the sand, her mood was instantly lifted. She walked from one end to the other, as the cool breeze blew her hair softly. The smell of the ocean was invigorating and the sun on her skin gave her a happy buzz. She stopped at the rock pool, leaning over as she peered in, hoping to spot something interesting that had washed in, but all she found was some small fish chasing each other around the pool. Little crabs would run and hide as she tiptoed around the rocks.

"Hey gorgeous, how are you?"

She spun her head around. Jack was walking towards her with a smile. She waved and made her way to him as he welcomed her with a kiss.

"What's been happening,Princess?"

Instantly, he knew something was wrong. He had seen that look before. She was stressing about something. "Okay, hit me with it. What's wrong?"

She told him everything she had learned as they walked along the shoreline.

"Oh, well. I am sure there is a way to fix this. Surely we are not the only ones who want to have a wedding in France."

There he goes again, always making things better, always putting an upbeat spin on everything. "Don't worry about anything, until you get an email back from Bridgette, come on, let's have a swim."

The water was refreshing, and they felt better after their swim. They dried off and walked home. Chloe went straight to the computer and checked her emails. There was one from Bridgette. She was obviously up very early. She quickly opened it as she called out to Jack. The email from Bridgette confirmed everything she had read, but advised that what a lot of people do is have a small ceremony legally in their own country, and then have the celebratory ceremony in France. This is what she thought they were doing.

Both Jack and Chloe read it over again and then looked at each other. "We have to get married here," said Chloe stunned.

"It would not be too bad. We could have a ceremony on the quiet no one would have to know we are already married," said Jack reassuringly. "I always wanted to be married on the Deck of Excuses, anyway." He smiled. She looked up at him; he was incredible, nothing worried him at all, but Chloe was devastated. She had wanted to take her vows in France not Australia. It was all pointless. "Chloe, Chloe, calm down, we are still getting married, I would marry you anywhere. It does not matter. We are putting on the ceremony in France, so our friends and families can witness our love and become a part of us. It is for them, Chloe. Our ceremony, our beautiful private ceremony, with just us, is so incredibly special, don't you see that?"

He was speaking so softly, staring into her eyes. He was so adorable; she was the luckiest girl in the world. He smiled the smile that used to melt her heart and realised it still did. He was right; she didn't care where they took their vows, just as long as they did. She smiled up at him. "Yea, you are right. As always, we can make it our intimate day, and then share the celebratory service with the family."

She snuggled into him, and he kissed her on the top of her head. "It will be perfect, Chloe, you wait and see."

The computer started to make noises. Jeannie was skyping them. "Wow, she must have ESP. I was about to suggest we Skype her and find out what her thoughts are," said Jack as Chloe answered. They explained everything to her, and she sat and listened carefully. "That is fine with me. I kind of like that idea, actually," said Jeannie happily. "I have some friends who would not be able to come, so they could witness us marry here in Scotland. It works out perfect, really."

Liam walked in and agreed that he was okay with everything as Jeannie filled him in with the news. "Aye, I also have friends who would not be able to make it. Sounds like a great idea."

Chloe felt so much better after talking to them. It was all going to work out. The wedding plans were back on track. They sent save-the-date emails to everyone and closed the computer, feeling good.

They took a drink outside while they organised dinner. Life was good again. Emails started to come flooding back from everyone, saying they were ecstatic with the news, and would definitely be there. It was Just Paddy and Maggie that they had to hear back from as they were away on a trip through the highlands and over to the Isle of Skye. A few days later Jack got a very heartfelt email from Paddy, saying they would not miss it for the world. He also said that they would stay in Montpelier as his son and wife would join them to travel afterwards, and had offered to be a piper, as he plays the bagpipes or the bartenders or waiters if they could come along. They were more than happy to let them have the family gite, they needed a spare pair of hands and thanked them. Cat and Cruz had offered to get the wine from Spain for them, explaining how all French wine was from Spain, and relabelled then doubled in price. They didn't know how true it was, but laughed as they thought it was probably border countries' rivalry, but they accepted gratefully. Chloe loved Spanish wine, and appreciated every bit of help they got. They had their numbers. It was perfect. Chloe made a spreadsheet of the guests and the accommodation. Ten bedrooms in the chateau.

I. Jack and Chloe
2. Jeannie and Liam
3. Chloe's parents

4. Jack's mum

5. Liam's parents

6. Jimmy

7. Kait, Johnny and Sophia

8. Chrissy and Finn

9. Patrick

10. Angie

## The Gites

1. Paddy and Maggie would be in the family gite

2. Ava and John

3. Danni and Rocco

4. Cruz and Cat

5 and 6 were for friends of Jeannie and Liam

They had told them only his best man and another couple would attend. They had made the right choice with the chateau that they had selected. Fitting them like a glove. Any other stragglers could stay in Montpelier being only a ten-minute car drive.

# CHAPTER 13
## THE STORM

The months ahead went quickly and Christmas was upon them once again. It was spent with the family. The week after New Year Jack, went back to work on the trawler with Pete. It had been another busy season and they were making good money, so keen to get back into it again. Chloe was working hard also as it was tourist season. She had finished her breakfast shift at the café and was sitting on a chair outside near the deck, rubbing the soles of her feet. They were aching; it felt good as she massaged the ball of her foot.

"I don't like the look of that," said a voice from behind her. It was Bob, walking over, looking up at the sky.

"Looks like a storm coming," answered Chloe, looking in the direction that Bob was focused on.

"That's not just a storm. The last time I have seen clouds like that, it was a beauty." He was still staring at it. "See how those clouds are rolling like a cigar? And that tint of a green colour?"

Chloe watched and nodded.

"Well, the last time I saw that, it blew half the flaming town away. We are about to get slammed. Where is Jack? I hope he isn't out there in this." He turned to look at Chloe. *Shit! Jack was out there.*

"There were no warnings. He checks the weather and radars every morning."

"Well, I remember there was none last time, either."

He had her scared now; she had to call him and warn him. She grabbed her phone and dialled his number. No reception. "Shit."She dialled Pete's phone. He had no reception, either. She knew that they were heading out to a new location today.

Bob had arrived back. "I just went and checked the bureau and there are warnings out now. It's a massive storm heading straight for us, and its moving quick, too."

"I need to go to Patonga. I need to see if Jack is back yet." She was fumbling for her keys.

A huge wind had picked up; it was the wind before the storm.

"It's too late, Chloe. I don't want you to drive in this. You will have to wait it out here and then we will go together."

A huge crack of thunder hit and a lightning bolt struck almost instantly behind it.

The storm was moving in fast, alright. It had started to rain, huge heavy drops. The sky was now an eerie colour that she had never seen before. It had that green tinge that Bob spoke of. He had lived there a long time and knew what he was talking about. They moved inside to get out of the rain. They had a perfect view of the storm as it moved in closer. The rain was beating down but now it was joined by huge hail stones, some the size of tennis balls. The noise on the tin roof was deafening. Bob was trying to tell her something but she could not hear a word that he was saying. She had never seen anything like it before. The thunder and lightning were ravaging the coastline and the seas were angry. She prayed that Jack was not out in it; surely, they would have noticed it approaching.

There was water leaking through the roof now. Bob and a few others were running around looking for buckets. Kids were crying and everyone was looking scared and rattled. It went as quickly as it had started. All of a sudden, everything went quiet it had moved back out to sea. They went outside to look at the damage. Water was still dripping from the eaves and tree branches and there were massive puddles everywhere. The kids were now splashing around in the warm puddles of water with huge smiles on their faces giggling and laughing. The adults were more concerned with what damage had been done.

Chloe tried Jack's phone again, still no reception. She was freaking out now. If he was out there, he was in big trouble. He started looking around for Bob, but he had run off to help get out tarps and ring the State Emergency Services for help. There was no power, cars were battered and as they looked around houses and shop windows were broken and damaged. It had done a huge amount of damage, that was for sure. But all Chloe could think about was Jack. She felt sick in the stomach with fear. She spotted Bob and ran to him.

"I have to go find Jack." She turned and started to head towards her car.

"Chloe, wait, I am coming with you." He yelled out a few orders to the men behind him and ran after her.

She was already sitting in the car with the engine running. "My car is trashed," she yelled as he was getting in.

"They all are. As long as you have insurance, you will be fine."

They headed off turning down the main street. It was deserted and damaged. All the shop awnings were torn and hanging off, the roads were partially flooded and any car that had been parked were riddled with hail stone damage. Chloe was lucky that none of her windows were smashed as many other cars were. They looked in disbelief as they saw the houses and the damage that the storm had caused. Trees were down everywhere.

They made it up to Patonga road but then came to traffic. Everyone was out of their cars and walking around. Bob went up ahead to see what was wrong and came back after a quick chat to a man up ahead.

"It's a tree across the road. It's blocked. Someone is bringing a chain saw."

He got on the phone to the surf club and asked someone to bring up a chainsaw. "Two will make it quicker."

Chloe just smiled and nodded. Yet, her insides were churning inside out. She needed to get to Patonga to see if Jack had made it back. She tried his phone again but still no signal. Bob had walked back to the tree where a chainsaw had arrived.

Chloe sat in the car and waited. Before too long, Steve from the surf club was yelling through her window. "Bob called and said he needed a chainsaw."

"He is up ahead, not too far. Thanks, Steve."

"Any news on Jack?"

"No, not yet."

"I just heard on the news, a trawler has arrived back but one is still missing."

"Really? Oh, far out. I hope it is Jack's."

"I better go help ahead."

She nodded. He was a nice guy. She remembered when she was first home from Europe and separated from Jack; he used to come to the café on her every shift and asked her out quite a few times. She almost said yes once. He was still single and she wondered why. He was a real catch for someone. Maybe he was just happy the way he was. He spent a lot of time at the surf club, always hanging off Bob.

It was at least an hour before they managed to open the road and Bob got back in the car.

"Sorry about that, Chloe. I can imagine how anxious you are. But good news. We spoke to some people in the cars coming from Patonga. A trawler has made it back, so let's go take a look."

The traffic started to move and they were soon on their way. They soon arrived and her heart was pounding in her chest. She could not see Jack's boat. She burst into tears as she parked and went to open the door. Bob grabbed her back. "If his boat is not here it does not mean anything bad has happened. They are both very experienced fishermen. Jack is from bloody Scotland with worse conditions than this. They might have landed somewhere else on the coastline. Don't panic yet. The last thing we need is you bloody falling to pieces, okay?"

He was looking at her seriously, staring into her eyes. He was right. She needed to pull herself together. "Okay, thanks,Bob."

They both got out of the car and walked to the wharf where a crowd was starting to form. Bob went and spoke to the men on the trawler that had recently returned.

Chloe's phone was ringing. It was Kate wanting to know if Jack was ok. She had heard a trawler was missing and they had organised a search party. A helicopter flew overhead as she was on the phone. It was a nightmare. As she got off the phone, she knew it was Jack's trawler. Bob had walked back with the news that she did not want to hear.

"It's Pete and Jack out there. They saw that they were in trouble. It looks like the engine ceased and they were bobbing around like a wine cork. They tried to get to them, but it was impossible. There are boats out there now."

Chloe started to cry. She didn't know if she could handle this she felt like she was going to collapse. Instantly, Bob saw she was not good.

"Come sit here in the car. I will go and see if there is anything that I can do. You need to try and pull yourself together, Chloe. Jack needs you. We will have his boat back in no time, you just wait and see."

She nodded and settled back into the car. She had a bird's eye view of what was going on from where she was, and liked being away from it all. The interior of the car comforted him a bit. She could not deal with the commotion. After a while, she saw Bob striding towards her.

"They found it,Chloe. The marine rescue are hooking up to it now to tow it back."

She sprung out of the car in excitement.

"Is Jack okay?"

"We have not heard of any news on them yet, I will be back when I hear more."

He was off like a rocket. She sat on the bonnet of the car waiting. The storm had made it so muggy. It was too hot in the car. She was instantly drawn to the thought of Jack's mum, how did she cope when she got the news her husband's boat was washed onto rocks and overturned. Oh, God, his mum, she was aware that she tuned in to watch the Australian news every day now plus Jeannie read it online. Oh,God,if she saw this it would break her heart.

"Oh, please,God,if you are out there, please bring him home safely to me. I promise I will be forever thankful and even start coming back to church."

She was wringing her hands watching out to sea, waiting for the first glimpse of his boat coming around the headland. He is going to be okay, he is going to be okay, she kept chanting over in her head. Then suddenly she saw it;she ran down to the wharf and found Bob.

"It's coming. I can see it."

"Yea, here it comes. It doesn't look too bad. I think everything will be okay, Chloe."

He hugged her tight and felt how her whole body was shaking. They stood together and watched as it came in.

"Is it just me or does there seem to be more helicopters out?"

Bob had noticed that also and hoped that she didn't. It wasn't a good sign. "Yea just TV cameras. You know what they're like."He hoped that he had convinced her but he knew something was wrong. "Wait here. I will go and find out what is going on."

He walked off and started talking to a marine rescue worker as they tied the boat to the wharf. He could hear Chloe yelling from behind him as she ran towards the wharf.

"Jack! Jack!"

He grabbed her and held her as they watched Pete get carried off the boat. But where was Jack. She watched intently but everyone else had left the boat with him. She broke away from Bob and ran towards Pete.

"Where is Jack?" she screamed.

"He went overboard, Chloe. I am so sorry."

He was crying and she was dragged away by Bob.

There were no more tears. She was stunned,shocked. What had she just heard? She broke away from Bob and walked like a zombie along the shoreline. He was gone, Jack was gone. She felt the same pain that she had felt at the airport the day she lost him before but this time she did collapse.

She woke up in an ambulance with Bob by her side.

"Where am I? Why am I in here?"

"They have just given you a shot, something to calm your nerves."

"Jack. Where is Jack?"

"They are out there now looking for him. He had a vest on, so that is good news. They will find him, don't you worry about that."

Bob knew it was critical that they found him before sunset. He had taken Chloe's phone and rang Kait who was on her way, arriving soon after they let Chloe out of the ambulance into her care.

"I am not going anywhere until they bring him home."

"Okay, I know. I will stay with you." She had brought camping chairs with her and settled her onto one, keeping the hospital blanket secured around her.

Kait had Chloe's phone and felt it starting to ring in her pocket. She slipped it out and noticed it was a call from Jeannie. She knew that was Jack's sister. She looked at Chloe as she stared vacantly out to sea, deciding it was best if she took the call.

"Jeannie, hi! It's Kait, Chloe's sister. How are you?"

"Hi, Kait. I am hoping you can put our minds at rest. Mum has woken up and started watching the Australian news and has heard of a fishing boat incident at Patonga. I know she is being silly but since Dad's accident she gets pretty freaked out about these things, I feel silly asking you."

Kait didn't know what to say. *Shit*. She was put in a very awkward position. What should she say? She stared at Chloe and knew that she was not in any position to handle this. It was up to her. She walked away from Chloe.

"Jeannie, I would love to tell you that your mum is freaking out for nothing but I can't. It's Jack's boat."

"Is he okay?"

There was no way she could butter this up. She had to be straight with her.

"They found the boat and retrieved it, but Jack is missing, he was washed overboard."

Deafening silence came through the line.

"But the good news is, he is wearing a hi-vis life jacket and there are lots of planes and helicopters scanning the waters. They are very confident they will find him."

"I need to sit down." There was silence again on the end of the phone.

"How am I going to give Mum this news? It will kill her."

"Don't tell her yet. Give us a few hours to find him."

"That's a good idea. How is Chloe?"

"A mess. She has been given medication to calm her down."

"I think we could all do with some of that."

"I am so sorry that I have to give you that news, Jeannie."

"I understand. I have to go. I need to tell Jimmy. He will know what to do."

"I will stay in touch with everything."

"Thanks, I will keep my phone on me."

After hours of a painful waiting, they got news of a sighting. Bob was running up to them

"They found him. A fisherman has spotted him washed up on rocks around the headland," he panted out of breath.

"Oh, thank God! Is he okay?"

"No one knows yet, but the care flight helicopter is on route to rescue him."

They all waited for the news to arrive that he was safely in the chopper.

Bob came running up again.

"He is alive and well. They are taking him to the hospital now. They won't know anything else until tests are done."

"I am on my way," said Chloe frantically.

"I will drive you. Bob, you can take Chloe's car and can you let Johnny know what is happening?"

"No worries, love, keep me in the loop."

They ran to the car and were off in no time. When they arrived, they were ushered to a small room where they were told a doctor would come and brief them.

Kait wanted to call Jeannie but didn't want to leave Chloe; she thought she would give it a while to see what the doctor had to say. Hours were passing and no doctor arrived. Just as she was about to leave to call her, the doctor arrived.

"He is a very lucky boy. He seems to be okay but he has a nasty bump to the head, which we are concerned about. We will need to run a few tests to check if everything is okay. He may have been knocked unconscious at some point. You can see him soon. I will get the nurse to come and get you when they are ready. Grab a coffee and just stay here in this room for a while and relax a bit."

"Thank you so much,Doctor. I am so glad to hear that." Chloe was shaking and crying. Kait cuddled her and settled her before making her escape to ring Jeannie, who answered instantly.

"He is okay, Jeannie. They found him. He was washed up on rocks and they rescued him."

She could hear Jeannie crying, unable to speak.

"They still need to run tests, but they seem confident he is okay. A very lucky boy."

"Thank you so much! My God,what a nightmare. Dad's accident is still so raw. I am sorry I fell apart."

"That's understandable. I was trying to send you a message but things got frantic."

"How is Chloe?"

"She is better now, but was an absolute mess."

"Oh, God, Jimmy, he is on his way, he would be on the plane."

"He is?"

"Yea, he booked a ticket as soon as I told him the news."

"Okay, well, we will sort things out here for him when he arrives."

"Too late to stop him now. I will try and get a message to him."

"Great! Give him my details. I will organise for him to be picked up at the airport."

The nurse finally arrived to let them into see Jack. They followed her down the hall and into his room. Chloe stopped dead in her tracks as she saw him. He was terribly battered and bruised with tubes running off him everywhere.

"Jack," she cried as she ran to him. "My beautiful Jack. What has happened to you?"

He smiled gently at her. "I am okay,Princess,you don't need to worry." His voice was weak and husky.

"What happened to you?"

"I swallowed a bit of water. They are worried about it, but I am okay. Come here, I need a cuddle."

She ran to him and he threw his arms around her. She lay in his arms and sobbed as he whispered quietly in her ear, comforting her. Kait sat in the visitor's chair, wiping away her own tears. The love that these two shared was immense and she thought about how it could have been so easily quite different.

They stayed until the nurses came and kicked them out, and Kait took Chloe home to her place to keep an eye on her for the night. Johnny was still up waiting when they arrived. They poured a drink and sat down to fill Johnny in on all the details.

"Chloe, I didn't mention it before, but Jimmy is on his way here."

"What? Here to Australia?"

"Yes, apparently he booked a ticket as soon as Jeannie told him. He was already on the plane by the time I rang to say he is okay. I guess he was panicked after his Dad's accident and expected the worse."

She was staring at Kait. "Well, that will be okay. It might help with his recovery having family around. I know that is what I would want."

Johnny filled their glasses again. "My God,I can't believe what happened today. It's been a nightmare."

"Yes, it could have been so much worse. We are so lucky," said Chloe with a lost look in her eye. He had been given to her back. Her prayers had been answered.

"Did anyone call Bob?" asked Kait with a frantic look.

"Yea, I sent him a message. He sends his love. It's just poor Jimmy who doesn't know," said Johnny. "When is he arriving?"

"Jeannie said he is trying to get onto him not to get on the plane but she is going to call me with any details," said Kait.

"Well, we need to get some sleep. It will be another big day ahead tomorrow," said Johnny. They were all exhausted after the day's events and knew the next few days would be just as busy.

Chloe was up early and headed straight to the hospital. Jack was sitting up, waiting for her. He smiled as she walked in. "Look what they have done to me, Chlo. They have dressed me up like a race horse," he said, pointing to the leads running from him like a bridle.

She laughed. "At least you have your sense of humour. That's a good sign."

"Well, they are running more tests today, but so far it seems I have been extremely lucky."

"Oh, that makes me very happy to hear that."

She leaned over and gave him a big cuddle.

"You scared me half to death."

"Aye, I scared myself also. That was one hell of a storm. We saw it too late, we started to head in but it beat us. How is Pete?"

"I had a call from Bob this morning. He has a broken arm but other than that he seems to be okay."

"It was a wild storm,I will tell you that. We are both lucky to be alive."

"Have you heard any news from your family?"

"No, I don't have a phone anymore, remember?"

"Well, I just thought they may have rung the hospital."

"They know about this?"

"Yes. Jeannie rang when Kait had my phone. They heard it on the news."

"Oh no, that would have nearly killed Mum. Does she know I am okay?"

"Yes, but last we heard Jimmy was on a plane coming over, but no word since."

The nurse arrived and said he was going for more scans. She kissed him and they wheeled him off.

She went home, had a shower, and headed back in later that afternoon.

# CHAPTER 14
## PATONGA

The following day, Chloe was sitting in the chair reading a magazine, while Jack lay back resting when the door slowly opened. Chloe lifted her eyes expecting a nurse to appear and was shocked when Jimmy walked through the door.

"Jimmy, you are here," she said, jumping up,throwing the magazine to the side.

Jack opened his eyes and began to sit up and gave Jimmy a half-smile as he walked around the bed and gave him a huge man hug.

"Of course, I am here. You scared us all to death."

"We have been waiting for you to call. We would have come to the airport and picked you up," said Chloe.

"I found my way. I got in fairly late last night, I didn't like to bother anyone," he said, looking deep into Jack's eyes.

"Where are you staying? You must stay with Chloe."

"No, I am fine where I am. I have a lovely room at Patonga Hotel."

"How did you end up at the pub at Patonga?" said Chloe,astonished.

"I was told it is where your accident was, so I headed there. Why? What is wrong with Patonga?"

"Nothing, it's just tiny. I am surprised you found somewhere to stay," she said with a shocked gaze.

"A lovely waitress looked after me, helped me checkin. Plus I got a massive hot English breakfast this morning. But more importantly, what about you? How are you?" he said with knitted eyebrows.

"I have had all my tests and they are all are coming back with nothing to worry about."

"Well, that is fantastic news," he said as he flicked a smile towards Chloe, and she nodded.

"I am a wee bit guilty, I am afraid to say. You have come a long way for nothing."

"Oh, not for nothing. I visit my brother and his lovely fiancé and where they live. What a gorgeous spot you have here."

"Aye, I have been telling you this. I have to pinch myself I can't believe you are here," he smirked excitedly.

"Lucky I applied for a passport when you left, just in case I wanted to come and visit one day. But wow, what a hell of a long way. The plane ride almost killed me," he said as he rubbed the back of his neck.

They all laughed. All of them had been through the tedious flight and were well aware of exactly how draining it was. They stayed for hours sharing stories and laughing before the nurse asked them to let Jack rest.

"I can drive you home, Jimmy, and you are welcome to come and stay with me."

"Thank you, Chloe, but I am more than comfortable where I am. I love the town. It reminds me of home a long time ago, before it expanded."

"Okay, but if you change your mind, yell out. We have a spare room. It is tiny but free," she offered.

"Thanks, but honestly, I love where I am. I am going to have a walk around the place this afternoon. I loved watching all the trawlers going out today. It's a real fisherman's village," he explained.

"Okay, but at least let me drive you home."

"Thanks, I will be back in the morning to visit you brother," he said with a double handshake. Then turned to Chloe. "I will let you say goodbye."

"Thanks, I will only be a minute." She turned her head towards him as he headed out the door.

"Can you believe Jimmy is here? What a surprise," said Jack.

"Yes, such a surprise. I will drive him home and will be back later. You have the rest you need, so I can take you home soon. I miss you. I am lonely without you." She hugged him tight and stepped back with a soft smile.

"I better rest. I need to be released out of this place. I am going crazy. I am trapped like a caged animal," he said as his eyes darted between her and the door as if planning an escape.

"Rest up, Jack." She smiled, turning and blowing him a kiss as she closed the door behind her.

Jimmy was waiting for her down the hall.

"So what is the real story?  What isn't he telling me?"

"He has been extremely lucky. It could have easily been so much worse."

She filled him in with all that had happened as they walked to the car and drove to the pub. "I appreciate the lift and the update."

"You're welcome. Yell out if you need anything. I am just around the headland."

He stared at her in disbelief. "Yell out? I don't think you would hear me. I can't yell that loud."

She laughed. "No, dopey. I mean give me a ring."

"Well, why didn't you say that?" He turned to leave and then turned back with a grin."Never mind, I get it, it's an Aussie thing, isn't it?"

She nodded. "You'll be right." She laughed as she waved him off.

"Thanks, Chloe."

She waited as he waved and walked into the pub.

Every day was just like the other for the next few days. Chloe would head to the hospital for as long as the nurse let her, and Jimmy would come in and out. He appeared happy to do his own thing so no one pushed the issue. After her morning shift, she headed straight to the hospital. Poking her head slowly around the door, carefully in case he was sleeping. She smiled as she spotted him looking at her with an excited grin.

"You are very happy there, grinning like a Cheshire cat. Did they give you some good drugs today?" She teased as she kissed him.

"Just happy you are here," he said, tapping the bed for her to sit.

"You look like a mangy cat. Look at your hair. It is standing up on its ends," she said as she looked over his chart.

"I can't find my comb," he confessed.

"So how are you?" She said placing the chart back on the end of the bed.

"Ready to go home," he said with a deflated look.

She sat on the chair next to him. "It won't be long now. Has Jimmy been in today? I thought he might have contacted me for a lift."

"He came in early this morning for an hour. He appears to be in fine spirits, sounds like he is enjoying the town."

"Did he grab a taxi here?" she said with a curious gaze.

"I didn't ask."

Chloe sat back in her chair deep in thought. Something wasn't adding up. She wondered if Jimmy still had issues with her, but she was certain it was sorted out back in Scotland. But it was strange he wasn't keeping in touch with her. Even if it was only for a ride to the hospital. She had hoped she and Jimmy would have a closer relationship, but it was obvious now that would never happen.

Jack cleared his throat. "Pete called in today."

"Oh, how is he going?" she said as she tried to push the thoughts of Jimmy from her head.

"Physically, he is okay. Only the broken arm. But mentally he is a bit screwed up. He said his fishing days are over. He asked me if I wanted to buy the trawler, at a mate's price."

Her eyes darted to Jack's and locked.

"I don't like you going back out to sea again, Jack," she rubbed his arm as his eyes dropped with sadness.

"Well, I can't anyway, for a while. But I thought I might do it up while I recover and sell it or see how I feel afterwards."

He looked up hopeful. She sat and stared at his sad face. He dropped his lip and pulled the face that always made her surrender.

"Don't give me that face. I know what you are doing," she smiled.

"What am I doing?" he said with a smirk.

"Alright, I guess it would give you something to do while you recover."

He pulled her in and cuddled her. "Thanks, Chlo. It will be the best looking boat in town by the time I have finished."

He had won her over as he always does so easily. She was happy for him to have the boat, but she was petrified of him taking it out to sea again.

"You have no idea what state it is in, it might be a wreck." She secretly hoped it was.

"Jimmy said it is not too bad. It is tied up on the old abandoned wharf, near the boat ramp. He inspected it for me the other day."

Her thought instantly went back to Jimmy ignoring her, and the uneasy sensation took over once again. "Is he okay? He is spending a lot of time on his own at Patonga,and believe me, there is not a lot to do except the pub and the boats," she said with one eye squinted.

"Don't worry about Jimmy. He would be loving both. That is exactly his scene. He would be hanging out with all the fishermen and having a wonderful time. He is in high spirits when he calls in."

"Oh, well, if he is happy that is all that matters," she said quietly with a shrug, but her suspicions grew. He was okay with Jack so it was her he had aproblem with. She pushed it from her mind as the door opened and the nurse walked in with the doctor.

"And how is the patient today?" asked the doctor as he picked up his chart and looked it over.

"Fighting fit," said Jack with a raised chin. Hoping he would give him the okay to go home.

"Well, everything here appears to be okay," he said, still staring at the chart.

Jack looked at Chloe with a nervous stare.

"I think we can let you go home."

Jack's eyes were as big as saucers as Chloe grabbed his arm in excitement.

"What, now? Really?"

The doctor laughed. "Well, unless you want to hang around for any reason, yea, now." Passing his chart to the nurse, he smiled broadly at Jack.

"No, no, I want to go home. Thank you, Doctor, thank you!"He jumped out of bed and started organising himself.

"Quick! Help me pack my things before he changes his mind," said Jack as he grabbed his bag from underneath his bed holding the back of his open hospital gown.

The doctor laughed and left the room while they scurried to get out of there.

They were in the car and on their way in no time. Jack squinted as they exited the multi-story car park and the sunshine hit him in the face.

"Oh, the sun is so bright, but I am not complaining." He put his arm up to shade his eyes.

"Your sunnies are in the glove box. I have been preparing for this day," she smirked as he opened the glove box and put them on.

"Aye, this I why I love you to bits, always looking after me. I remember a time when I had to look after you," he teased.

"Well, it is my turn to take care of you for a while."

He smiled, patting her on the leg before turning his attention to the scenery flashing past the side window.

"Can we call into Patonga on the way home? I want to let Jimmy know I am out."

"Yea, of course," she said, giving him a quick sideways glance. That would work out well. She wanted to check Jimmy's reactions with her while Jack was around. She was hoping it was only her imagination. They had a long chat and a few laughs when she drove him home the other day. Nothing made sense.

They drove around the town looking at the wharf and beach but couldn't see him anywhere, so she parked.

"He must be in his room. Come on let's go ask at the pub," said Jack, still looking around.

They headed into the pub and walked up to the bar where the waitress was watching as they approached.

"Hi, what would you like?" she said with a welcoming smile.

"I am looking for my brother who is staying here. Do you have an office?"

"Oh, you must mean Jimmy."

"Aye, that's him," he said, surprised.

"You will probably find him at the boat ramp with Chelsea." She shrugged in the direction of the ramp.

"Thank you," he said, turning, heading towards the door with Chloe in tow.

"Who is Chelsea?" whispered Chloe.

"I guess we are about to find out," he said holding the door open for her before waving thanks again to the waitress.

They drove down to the boat ramp and found Jack with a girl, fishing off the old abandoned wharf. She was tall and slender, wearing jeans and a singlet top with long copper hair and both were wearing huge smiles as he helped her cast a line. It was quiet, no one else was around, and they had their own bit of paradise all to themselves.

"So it is not only the fish keeping Jimmy busy," said Jack with a smile and Chloe let out a relieved sigh.

"She is extremely attractive. No wonder he has been quiet," said Chloe as they got out of the car and walked towards them. Neither of them heard them approaching, lost in their own world, laughing and chatting.

"Catching anything?" asked Jack in a loud voice. Jimmy turned startled.

"So they finally let you out?" smile crept to his face as he chuckled and walked over to give him a man-hug.

"Aye, they finally realised there was nothing wrong with me head."

"Maybe because there's nothing in there," joked Jimmy with a smirk.

They all laughed as Chelsea walked over to greet them.

"Oh, sorry, this is Chelsea."

"Oh, it is nice to meet you. I am Jack, Jimmy's brother as you have probably worked out already. And this is my fiancée, Chloe."

"Hi, it's lovely to meet you. I have heard a lot about you," she said, laying the fishing rod on the ground.

"Chelsea works at the hotel. She has been looking after me, showing me around."

"Aye, that's great. He needs all the help he can get anywhere he goes," said Jack and she chuckled, turning her gaze back to Jimmy, flashing him a beaming pearly white smile.

Chloe was relieved it wasn't her after all. He had met someone. She had detected a British accent and had not seen her around before. She had gorgeous hair and striking features that would not have been easy to forget. Huge almond green eyes were framed by long thick lashes and perfectly groomed brows. Her left arm had a trailing vine tattoo with two purple rosebuds that swept across her shoulder and started to creep down towards her chest.

"Do you live local?" asked Chloe. She was intrigued with her beauty, and keen to know more.

"Well, briefly at the moment. I am from England on a working visa. I have been travelling. This is my last stop before I head home in a month."

Chloe noted how her beautiful eyes lit up with charisma as she spoke. She understood how Jimmy could have been easily besotted, and a warm sense of relief washed over her again.

"Oh, how exciting! Did you enjoy your stay?"

"I did! I have been lucky I have met so many lovely people while I have been out here, but who would have thought I would meet such a wonderful Scot, here in sleepy Patonga."

She smiled warmly at Jimmy, and he was beaming as he looked back at her.

"Yea, it's a bit unbelievable, isn't it?" said Chloe, realising they only had eyes for each other.

Jack spotted the trawler tied to the wharf and headed over, casting his eyes over it as he began his inspection. Jimmy tagged along.

"I have been looking over it, and I think it is a decent buy, especially at the price Pete offered you," he said, jumping on board to inspect the interior.

"I thought the same thing," he said. They all stared as he looked it over carefully. He jumped on board with Jimmy and walked around with a distant gaze in his eye. You knew by the sorrowful look he was reliving the moments of the storm. Rubbing his hand gently along the paintwork, he turned to Chloe with a serious stare.

"I think I might buy the boat, Chlo."

She nodded as she looked at the determination on his face. It was apparent there was no way he could be talked out of it.

"It would give you something to do while you get back on your feet," she said uncomfortably.

"It's a solid boat, that is for sure. It stood up to that storm quite well," added Jimmy.

"Aye, it did. Better than me and Pete," he said with a lost stare, deep in thought once again.

"I will give Pete a call later today," he said confidently.

"I will keep a close eye on it for you, while I am here," said Jimmy, but Jack was already lost in thought. Everyone remained silent as they looked over at him, gliding his hand over the boat like he was stocking a prize-winning mare. Chloe finally broke the silence.

"Why don't you come and join us for a meal tonight?" she said, turning to Jimmy.

"Great, I would love to! I can never resist a meal," yelled out Jimmy as he jumped back off the boat walking towards them.

"And you also, Chelsea," she added cheerfully.

"Oh, thanks," she said as she slid her hands into her jean pockets.

"Jimmy, do you still have the address?" asked Chloe as she shaded her eyes with her hand as she squinted, looking into the burning sun.

"I do and Chelsea has a car, so I am sure I can twist her arm to take me." He smiled excitedly at Chelsea. Chloe realised there was more there than just friendship between them and smiled to herself.

"Is seven okay?"

"Yes, that is perfect? What would you like me to bring?" said Chelsea, flicking her long copper hair out of her face.

"Nothing at all. Jack and I would love to put something together for you. Is there anything you don't eat?"

"I eat anything, thanks. We will bring a wine," she added as she spun around to confirm with Jimmy.

"Aye, sounds perfect." Jack walked over and stood beside Jimmy, still looking back over his shoulder at the boat in silence deep in thought.

"You will be able to announce you are the proud owner of a boat."

"Maybe," muttered Jack quietly.

Everyone said their farewells, letting them get back to their fishing, as Chloe grabbed Jack by the hand and they headed towards the car.

"Are you okay? You are a little quiet," she said as she studied his face.

"Oh, I had a wee deja vu being back on that boat, but I am okay now." He smiled warmly as he put his seatbelt on.

"You know if you ever need to talk about what happened, I am here for you. Speak up. Don't just stick your head in the sand," she said, looking deeply into his eyes, checking if he was as okay as he said he was.

"I do know that, and I appreciate it, thanks," he patted her leg gently.

She knew all too well how men were, they bottle things uptight and it isn't at all healthy. Her thoughts went back to how worried her parents were about Bob, when he lost his wife.

"Just keep it in mind, that's all. You are a pretty good story-teller Jack, but this is an extremely important one," she said as she continued to stare. He nodded and turned his gaze to the side window.

They drove in silence as they made their way up the bushy road. The smell of the eucalyptus hung heavy in the air as they drove past with the windows down, enjoying the fresh air blowing in. It felt good after being cooped up in the hospital, and he let out a long sigh of relief as she spied him cautiously from the corner of her eye.

"So now we know what Jimmy has been up to, no wonder he has been quiet," said Jack as he finally spoke.

"Yes, that explains a lot. I was worried he still had issues with me."

"No, he loves you. You have nothing to worry about there," he said, looking back out the window. Chloe nodded happily, hearing his comment.

"She is attractive," she said, glancing at him. "They are quite comfortable together."

"I didn't pay too much attention," he said, flicking his attention back out the window.

"Well, I spotted a few looks they were giving each other. I think they are an item."

"I would be surprised if they are. I couldn't imagine Jimmy moving that quick."

"I am not too sure about that. Guess we will find out all about it tonight," she smiled.

Jimmy and Chelsea arrived right on time. Jimmy was casual in jeans and a Celtic football T-shirt, while Chelsea wore jeans with a sleeveless white shirt unbuttoned hallway to show a white lace top underneath. They looked relaxed around each other and Jack escorted them to the courtyard after showing them around.

"We brought a bottle of wine," said Chelsea, holding up Jimmy's arm which held the wine.

"Oh, I will grab you some glasses," said Jack, turning back to the kitchen.

"I have put a lasagne in the oven, and made a salad. Is everyone okay with that?"

"Sounds and smells delicious," said Jimmy as he sat next to Chelsea on the lounge.

"Well, I am pleased to announce, Chloe and I are the proud owners, or will be, of a blue trawler." Jack turned to Chloe with a huge smile, and she knew she had done the right thing agreeing to buy the trawler. He had been down in the dumps and it helped to cheer him up.

"Oh, you rang Pete," said Jimmy pouring the wine.

"Aye, I did, and I will meet up with him tomorrow with a cheque."

"Congratulations! I think you have done the right thing," said Jimmy, raising his glass.

"Thanks! I am looking forward to restoring it. It's very exciting."

The boys started throwing ideas around about the best way to restore the boat and Chloe excused herself to check on dinner. Chelsea picked up her wine and followed her.

"So how long have you been at Patonga?" said Chloe as she opened the oven door to take a peek. She liked Chelsea. She was friendly and chatty and easy to talk with.

"Oh, about two months now, but I am due to go back home soon."

"What do you do at home?"

"Well, I don't pour beers," she said with a smile. "I am actually a florist."

"Oh, a florist. That sounds like a lovely job, spending the day surrounded by beautiful flowers," she said, getting the salad out of the fridge.

"Yes, it is. My mum was a florist, so I followed in her footsteps. I started working in her shop straight out of school," she said as she settled herself on the bar stool.

"So are you travelling alone?" she asked curiously. She could not imagine anyone travelling alone after her experience.

"Well, I am now, but originally I was travelling with a friend. She had to go home early as her mum fell sick, so I continued on my own," she said, sipping on her wine.

"You are very brave. I didn't like travelling alone, but thankfully I met Jack."

"I have met a lot of people along the way, so by the time she left, I still had people I knew around me, so it helped a lot. I have only been alone here. We came here to meet a relative of hers and ended up with jobs at the hotel."

"I was wondering how you ended up in a sleepy town like Patonga," she smirked. "It's not exactly on a tourist's list."

Chelsea nodded as she put her wine glass on the table and picked at a mosquito bite on her arm, which drew her attention to her tattoo.

"I like your tattoo. I guess you chose flowers, being a florist," said Chloe, intrigued.

"Oh thanks, it is a work in progress. The rosebuds are Mum and me. I will add to it one day, when I have my own family and have more loved ones, I will add a rosebud for each of them."

"That's beautiful, you are very creative." She wondered if Jimmy would be the next rosebud added. How incredible if he was. Finding love because of a tragedy."Thanks. Do you have any tats?"

"No, I am a clean skin. I like them, I just never took the time."The real reason was she would totally freak out if anyone came near her with a needle, but she kept that to herself as she always did. Chelsea nodded happily with her answer, as she peered around while Chloe took the lasagne out of the oven.

"Can I help?" she said, grabbing a tea towel.

"Sure, can you grab the loaves of garlic bread and the salad? We will take it outside to serve."

They placed the food on the table for everyone to serve themselves and the boys were straight into it. They made themselves comfortable around the outdoor table and Jack topped up everyone's wine before sitting next to Chloe to eat.

"I have to go home soon, Jack," said Jimmy.

"Aye, I am surprised you stayed this long," he said as he put a large piece of lasagne into his mouth.

"It is a beautiful spot here. I now understand why you are so happy."

"But you have to get back to work, right?" he said with a disappointed frown. Work was outweighing everything once again.

"Well, yea, I dumped it all on poor Pat, and don't want to leave him hanging too long. Believe me, I would love to stay," he said, turning to Chelsea with a dreamy smile.

Chloe and Jack turned to each other with a grin before returning to their meal. Two possums came creeping around the corner and Jimmy jumped. Jack went inside and grabbed them a treat and showed Jimmy and Chelsea how to feed them. She sat back with a warm fuzzy feeling at how Jack had settled in so nicely, and loved the scene of him laughing and sharing the possums with Jimmy and Chelsea. She slipped away quietly to put a pie in the oven for them to finish off the meal.

# CHAPTER 15

# A SHADE OF GREEN

Jimmy left a few days later and life started to settle back into a normal routine. Chloe dropped Jack off at the boat every day on her way to her shift and collected him in the afternoons. It was a warm afternoon when she arrived to collect him and for the third day running, Chelsea was there with him. Chloe could not help but notice that she was hanging around Jack a lot lately.

"Hi, I see you two have been painting today," she said.

"Yes, doesn't it look good?" Chelsea jumped up with her hands on her hips.

"Oh, I couldn't have done so much without your help, Chelsea."

Chloe watched carefully, hoping not to spot body language between them.

"You seem to be hanging around a lot, don't you have any shifts?" enquired Chloe.

"Yes, I have been doing breakfast shift, so I come down here to help Jack afterwards," she grinned.

"Aye, and I am grateful for the help," he smiled at her as Chloe scrutinised the situation.

"Well, I think we should go, I need to put a chook in the oven," said Chloe.

"Yea I have to go also. I will see you tomorrow, Jack," said Chelsea as she grabbed her bag and said goodbye to Chloe as she passed her.

"No, I have to do a few chores around the house tomorrow. Mrs. Whitaker has asked me to help her with a few things."

"Oh,okay see you later in the week."

Chloe was starting to get awfully suspicious of her. First, she was with Jimmy and now she appeared to be extremely interested in Jack now he has gone. That night over dinner, Chloe decided to investigate the situation.

"So Chelsea is hanging around a lot, don't you think?" she said, pushing her peas around her plate.

"Oh, aye, and it is extremely lucky for me. She helps me a lot," replied Jack, attacking a drumstick.

"Don't you think it is a bit strange?"

"What? Her hanging around? No, not at all. She is lonely, you know," having another gnaw on the bone.

That is what worried her. She didn't know enough about this girl and felt uncomfortable with her spending so much time around Jack.

"Your boat is starting to come together. What are you going to do with it when it is finished?" she said, wanting to change the subject from Chelsea.

"Well, funny you should ask. Chelsea and I were talking about it today, and she came up with an idea of buying the seafood off the trawlers, and selling it off the back of the boat."

Bang there it was;he was changing the subject straight back to her.

"Oh, did she now? And I suppose it will be you and her doing the trading," she said with slanted eyes.

"Do I detect a wee bit of jealousy there?" He teased, opening a beer and handing it to her.

"Maybe, I don't like her hanging around so much," she said, still pushing the same peas around her plate with her fork.

"Well, you have nothing to worry about,I can assure you of that," he said, giving her a reassuring kiss on the cheek. But it didn't satisfy Chloe's itch, and she stewed on it all night.

The next day the shift was quiet, so she left early and headed to Patonga. Parked, she looked at her watch and going by what Jack told her she knew Chelsea would be finishing her shift. It only took a few minutes before she spotted her walking to her car. She jumped out of the car and walked towards her. Chelsea spotted her approaching as she opened her car door and smiled.

"Oh, hi, Chloe, Jack isn't here today," she said, flicking her hair. She was instantly annoyed how she thought she knew more about Jack's whereabouts than her.

"I am not here to see Jack. I am here to see you," she said as she stared at her with ice-cold eyes.

"Oh really, why what's up?" she said, eyeing Chloe with an inquisitive stare.

"I wanted to check why you were hanging around Jack so much. It's starting to make me a bit uncomfortable."

She closed the car door. "Let's take a walk for a minute," said Chelsea. Chloe looked at her with curious eyes, and without saying another word they crossed the road to the water and started walking along the beach. She had not thought this through, what if she was interested in him, what if she told her something she didn't want to hear? What if something really was going on?  Panic set in. What did she need to tell her?  Her hands started to sweat and her heart raced, but she had to know.

"So what is on your mind?" asked Chelsea as she stopped walking, staring into her eyes.

Chloe was hoping she could not see the panic in her face."You, hanging around Jack," she glared.

"Oh, I am so sorry, I didn't realise. Of course, you would be thinking the worst," said Chelsea as she grabbed her arm gently.

"Well, I can't see any other way to look at it. First, you were all over Jimmy, and then as soon as he left you moved on to Jack," she said as she took a step back, releasing Chelsea's hold on her arm. Her fear was raging in the pit of her stomach and hoped it did not show in her eyes as they grew wide with fear.

"Yes, I can see how that appears, but I can tell you it's not like that at all." She dropped her eyes.

"Then how exactly is it?"

She lifted her chin, staring straight at her, looking so strong but falling apart on the inside.

Chelsea looked at her gently before throwing her hands into the air and sighed. "Okay, I have to tell you."

Chloe froze; her eyes were wide, glazing over with tears. Her heart was pounding so hard she thought Chelsea would be able to hear it. Did she want to get wise to what may be going on? She wanted to turn and run, her legs began to turn to jelly. Her inner voice grew louder. *Run, Chloe, run, you don't want to hear this!* She would have listened to it if she could, but she was frozen. Her legs would not have moved even if she begged them.

"Jimmy and I are seeing each other. We just clicked and it was huge, he asked me to keep an eye on Jack after he left, and I guess I felt close to Jimmy being around Jack. I am so sorry I didn't even give it a thought how it looked through your eyes. I am so sorry, Chloe."

Did she just hear it right or was that her inner voice talking again? *Please, let that be true.* She managed to utter a few words.

"You and Jimmy are seeing each other." Tears of relief started to burn her eyes.

"Yea, I miss him so much, that is why I am going home early."

"You are? Why didn't you say anything?"

"Well, I feel a bit silly. We have only just met, and I am running home to chase him like a teenage school girl, but this is huge for both of us."

"Oh, Chelsea, I am so sorry I had no idea." She hugged her as they both cried.

"Well, of course, you wouldn't." She pulled away, wiping her tears. "Please forgive me."

"Of course, I am the one feeling silly now. I guess I am still emotional after almost losing him," she said blowing her nose.

Chelsea lent in and cuddled her. She felt terrible Chloe had been through so much already, and she did not need this. She felt her whole body shake as she sobbed. After a few minutes she regained herself and pulled away. Chelsea handed her another tissue.

"Are you okay?"

Chloe sighed and fixed her hair, regaining her composure." I am so sorry. I guess I really needed that cry. It's been a tough time."

Chelsea nodded with a sympathetic face. "I am so sorry," she whispered.

"Phew, I am ok now, sorry, when are you leaving?"

"Next week. Jimmy has found us an apartment."

"You are moving in together?" she said, shocked with a giggle.

"Yes, I am so excited. I wish I could jump on that plane right now. We were on the phone last night for hours planning it, after Jimmy told me about the apartment."

"I am so happy for you both. I had an idea something was going on, but I thought it finished when he left. Can I tell Jack?"

"Yea, of course. Oh, Chloe, I am so sorry that I made you think I was getting onto Jack. He made me feel like I was close to Jimmy. They are different in personality but similar features and then the accent," she said, throwing her head back. "I just love that accent, I am crazy for Jimmy."

Chloe put her arms around her and gave her a long hug. "No need to say anymore, hang around him as much as you like, if he helps to heal a lonely heart, I know how painful that can be."

"Thanks, Chloe, but I will be busy organizing my trip home now. There are so many things I want to buy. I have fallen in love with your frangipani flowers, and found a shop that sells all things frangipani. I want to buy a table cloth and tea towels for our apartment."

"That's lovely and don't forget some paw-paw cream."

"Already done, and lots of Tim-tams for Jimmy. He loves them."

Chloe laughed. "So does Jack. I taught him to bite the ends off and suck his tea through it, and he loves it."

"I will have to teach Jimmy that trick," she said, flicking her long hair back.

"Well, I better go and let you start packing but promise to visit us before you leave."

"Of course, thanks for the chat."

On the way home, she couldn't stop thinking about when she met Jack. She knew exactly what she was saying. She knew instantly she had fallen hard for Jack, and it wasn't just a casual love affair. As she walked through the door at home,she spotted Jack walking down the hall looking like he got out of the shower in a pair of boardies and wet ruffled uncombed hair. She couldn't stop smiling as she threw her keys and bag on the table.

"Well, you would not believe what I found out today," she smirked.

"Well, by the smirk on your face it is very juicy news." Jack opened the fridge, took out two beers, and handed her one.

"Let's sit and have a beer while you tell me all about it."

She followed him out to the courtyard, and they sat on the lounge opening their beers and placing them on the outdoor coffee table.

"Okay, fire away. Tell me all your juicy gossip," he said with a teasing smirk.

"I stopped by to visit Chelsea this morning on my way home, and she has informed me that she and Jimmy are an item."

"They are. Well, you did have an idea about that."

"So much so, that she is leaving next week, and they are moving in together."

"They are?" His eyes were as big as plates.

"Jimmy asked her to keep an eye on you, and she felt closer to Jimmy being around you."

"So that is why she has been hanging around. Jimmy never said a word."

"They were embarrassed because they have only just met, which is silly, but I understand."

"Well, I never…the sly dog! I am so happy for him. I will send him a message. Moving out…Wow! That is huge for Jimmy. He must really like her."

"It is a huge thing for them both, head over heels, hooked."

Chelsea hung around them for her last week in Australia, and they drove her to the airport when the time came. She was so excited it made them both laugh.

"Well, this is it. I jump on that big British Airways plane, and it takes me home to Jimmy. Thanks for everything, both of you."

"Give everyone our love. You will adore Jimmy's family. They are lovely people," said Chloe with a warm smile.

"I can't wait to meet them. We will stay in touch." She gave them a wave, and she was off.

Jack put his arm around her as they walked back to the car.

"Well, I still can't believe it. If I didn't have that accident they would never have met," he said, staring down at her.

"Oh, I am not so sure. I think if it was meant to be, the stars would have lined something up for them over there." She smiled back, and he laughed.

"You are probably right there, Princess."

They both worked on the boat regularly whenever they could. Then one warm summer morning they finished the painting and stood back to admire their work. It looked beautiful. It was white with pale blue contrasts and looked like a million dollars. Chloe was still panicking about him wanting to go back on the trawler and had been thinking hard about Chelsea's idea she had suggested to Jack before she left.

"I have been thinking about that idea Chelsea had, about selling the seafood. It might just work," she said.

"Anyone can sell seafood, Chlo. You don't need a boat to do that."

"Yes but what about setting up a long table on the deck, and selling the trawlers catch of the day, dining on the boat we could cook it up and serve it fresh."

"What do you mean?" he said, scratching his head.

"Well, we could turn the boat into a pop-up casual restaurant."

He stared at her then back at the boat.

"Do you think it could work?"

"Let's take a look."

They jumped up onto the boat and started to pace it out.

"You could fit a table for ten on here, it would be tight but you could do it."

"Finn could help me do the cooking at the restaurant before it opens. I am sure Johnny would not mind."

"You might be onto something here."

"We could sell beer and wine out of the esky," he said, walking around looking with enthusiasm.

"Yes, we would need to apply for the appropriate licenses and permits, but Johnny will help us with that."

"Let's give this a go,Princess," he said with a huge smile, and she ran over and cuddled him.

He wasn't going back on the seas; she felt her eyes well up with tears of joy and wiped them away before he could see. He would be safe out of harm's way. She just needed to make sure that this project worked. She would stop at nothing to make sure that it did.

Over the next few weeks, they made the enquiries with the trawlers, and they all loved the idea of selling off their unclaimed seafood. Jack went and enquired at the pub if anyone knew who owned the wharf and a few days later, he was given the papers to lease the jetty from the overseas owners. It was all coming together. They made the huge table and set up eskies to hold the beer, wine, and soft drink. They decided to call it "The Crab Pot"and painted a sign which they hung overhead.

Word got around about the opening of "The Crab Pot"and the first day of trade went well. By the end of the first few weekends, they had people lined up waiting for a spot onboard. The idea was a total success. Customers would feast on lobsters, balmain bugs, prawns,oysters and whatever else the fishermen dropped off to them each day. By the end of the season, they bought another trawler to work on over the winter to join "Crab Pot 1"on the wharf.

Winter arrived and every day they could, they worked on "Crab Pot 2."Chloe was sitting in bed with the laptop one morning when Jack walked in after working on the new trawler.

"Oh, there you are. I was looking everywhere for you."

"It's cold, so I jumped back into bed. Come and join me, I want to show you something."

"I can't. I am dirty." He pulled the bedroom corner chair across and sat next to her. "What would you like to show me, Princess, is it saucy?" He said with a cheeky grin.

"It's nothing like that," she laughed. "No, I am looking at honeymoon destinations."

"Oh, well, we had a chat about this the other day. What did you come up with?"

"Well, I have been looking at Venice. It's the perfect spot for a honeymoon, it is so romantic."

"Perfect! Venice it is," he said as he started to get up.

"Wait, sit down. You mentioned Germany the other night."

"Aye I would love to visit Heidelberg."

"I have found a route from Venice to Heidelberg with a stop in Austria."

"A road trip? ."

"Yes, a road trip like last time."

"Keep going, you're doing a fantastic job, Chlo," he said, getting up ruffling her hair.

"Jack we need to organize this, it is very important."

"Let me have a shower and I will come and give you my undivided attention," he said as he waved her off and headed down the hall to the bathroom. Jack was out of the shower and dived into bed with her. "Okay, I am back let's book our honeymoon."

"While you were in the shower I looked at flights, and how to get to Venice, and if we fly into Sorrento we can pick up a car from there."

"Oh, Sorrento, home of the seductive moon that will make a very saucy honeymoon,"he said, snuggling into her neck.

"You do realize I am naked under here, don't you," he whispered.

"I am trying very hard not to think about that, you are not helping here," she said with a frown.

"I am sorry. Okay, serious, well I have always wanted to visit Capri, I want to see the Blue Grotto."

"Oh, yes, the grotto. If I remember, it is just a ferry ride away."

"See, I am being very helpful here," he said,his hand roaming up her leg. "What have you got on? Let's take this t-shirt off, you will be much more comfortable."

"Jack, stop. Let's just get this organized."

"How can I? I just realized you are not wearing any underwear, and all this talk about honeymoons leads my mind to one thing," he said, kissing her neck.

"Jack, stop, please can we organize this first?" she giggled.

"Okay, leave Capri and Venice to me. I will book somewhere special for us as my gift to you and you can book Austria and Heidelberg for me, deal?"

"Deal!"

"Perfect! Now that is organized, come here let me show you what our honeymoon will be like."

He was moving his fingers up to her breast and started stroking the nipple.

"I can't concentrate on this now, anyway."

"That was the idea," he said as he removed the laptop off her lap and placed it on the floor.

"Now, let's practice being on our honeymoon," he said with a dreamy look in his eye. "I am sure you would not be wearing this," he removed it over her head and tossed it to the floor.

"That is much better, I have full access now."

He bent to put his mouth to her breast and gently caressed her.

She started to sigh as he lowered her gently to lie beside him.

"Let me touch you gently all over," he whispered and she nodded.

Jack had his way as she let him manoeuvre his way around her body as she groaned with desire. The cold winter afternoon was spent warmly under the sheets as they played and then napped wrapped in each other's arms.

# CHAPTER 16

## THE SHACK

Chloe was tidying the house one afternoon when Jack came in excited. His voice was echoing through the cabin as he yelled out to her.

"Chloe! Chloe!"

She put the washing she had been folding onto the bed, and went to meet him with haste. "Jack, what's happened?"

"You will never guess what we have been offered."

"Well, I am guessing it's exciting!"

Jack grabbed her by the hand and led her to the outdoor lounge. "You will need to sit down for this."

She sat smiling at him."What is going on?"

"The proprietor at the pub came to the boat today. The people who own the wharf also own the attached house."

"The abandoned one?" she asked as she listened carefully, wondering where this was going.

"Aye, well, they want to sell and have offered the house to us."

Chloe went to stand up as she heard his story. He had no idea of the real estate market and this was totally out of the question. Placing his hands on her shoulders he guided her back onto the coach.

"Well, that is decent of them, but we could never afford that. I know the crab pots are doing well but that place would be worth a fortune. Do you have any idea about the real estate market here?"

"No, they have offered a generous reduction in price, if we don't go through the real estate. Chloe, I have enough money put away, we can do this."

"What money?" she said with a squinted eye.

"When I sold the business to Jimmy I put that money in a bank account and didn't touch it."

"Well, I know that, honey, but it wouldn't be enough to buy that house. Sure, it is rundown but it is right on the water."

"Chloe, when I came to Australia, my money doubled due to the exchange rate. We can buy this house if we want to."

Chloe's jaw hit the ground."We can?"

"We sure can. What do you think?" She jumped up and started to pace the courtyard as she thought about his idea. He stared with wide eyes waiting for an answer. Finally, she flicked her hair and turned to him with raised eyebrows.

"We could do all our own cooking without having to use the restaurant."

He was up and pacing the courtyard now as she stood, quietly thinking. "Aye, it's the missing link. It would complete our business, and we would also have a house of our own."

He spun on his heels to face her, and she registered the situation.

"Sounds too good to be true." She had started to dismiss it once again. He grabbed her gently on the shoulders and stared deep into her eyes."BUT it is true."

She stared into his eyes lost in her thoughts for a moment. "Okay, slow down. Let's check what sort of state it is in. Remember, it has been abandoned for a long time."

That is all he needed to hear."No time like the present. Grab your keys."

They were driving down the bushy road in no time, stopping briefly at the pub on the way to collect the keys.

Sitting at the far end of the four little fisherman's cottages, standing proudly at the end of the old concrete path, which weaved its way from the car park to the rocks. They parked the car and walked the path along the front of the houses until they reached the rusty wire gate.

Standing out the front, they stood and looked at the pale green painted fibro cottage with a dark green colour bond roof and yellow tin sunshades on the two front windows. The gate creaked loudly when they pushed it open. Pieces of rust started falling to the ground. Looking around the overgrown grass, Chloe picked up a long stick. They walked the cracked concrete path, as she used the stick to beat down the spider webs and climbed the stone stairs to the front porch.

"This place is full of spiders," he said with a horrified look.

"We can spray. That's an easy fix," she said, looking around at the view.

"We can easily extend this veranda and take out these windows and put in big bi-folds to take in that view," he explained, and she nodded, rubbing her hand across the flaky window sill.

"Well, it definitely needs something."

He put the key in and swung the door open The strong smell of stale dusty air hit them as they coughed and walked inside.

"Easy to tell how long it has been vacant. It stinks," she said, holding her nose.

"Needs an air out, that's all."

They entered straight into the lounge room. "The bi-folds and extended veranda would work well, taking in that million-dollar view."

"Yes, I can imagine it all," she said, staring out the dirty window using the stick once again to clear the webs.

The front rooms looked straight out towards the wharf with 180-degree water views. She turned and walked down the hallway, stopping to take a peek at the bedrooms along the way. Wallpaper was hanging half off walls covered in cobwebs. At the end was a kitchen and dining room that led out the back to a sun-room, before leading down three stone stairs to the rear yard that backed onto the bush. A laundry room was to the side.

"I could easily move the laundry inside for you and I could use this as a gym," he yelled back, looking in the door of the outhouse, but Chloe was walking the path to the clothesline looking around at the yard.

"How private."

"Aye, it seems to be made for you,Princess. Nice and peaceful, and you would still get visitors from the bush."

She slowly scrutinized everything, her eyes scanning frantically, darting from side to side as he waited. It was rundown and a mess but looking past that,she could visualise it with a clean-up.

"This is perfect, Jack. There is a lot of work but it has strong bones, certainly wouldn't take much to bring it back to life," she said, choked up.

"You're crying." He stooped, staring down at her with a smile.

"How crazy. I got all emotional." She wiped her eyes with the back of her hand as she smiled.

"Well, if it has affected you that much, I think this place is ours."

"Let's find out what we can negotiate," she said, laughing through her tears.

They signed the paperwork a few weeks later after some good negotiations, and bought it for a song. The owners wanted to sell in a hurry and didn't want any messy real estate involved, which suited them also. All the appropriate paperwork was done and then the mammoth task of the clean-up began.

All the family gathered around to help. They scrubbed, demolished, painted and cleaned until it finally resembled a decent cottage. New carpets went into all the bedrooms and the floorboards in the main rooms that had been hidden under the dirty old carpets were in perfect order. Light sand and a coat of gloss were all that was required to restore them to their former glory.

A flat pack kitchen from Bunnings was made to fit. The bathroom was gutted and filled with cheap but comfortable products and brought it to life with some beautiful tiles that they picked up for a song at an auction house. At the same auction house, they bought the bi-fold doors and timber for the deck. Rob and Olivia arrived on the last day, with a trailer full of plants and they all set to work in the gardens.

The day they moved in, Jack carried her over the fresh hold, and they opened a bottle of champagne as everyone arrived and joined in for a toast to the new home, which looked a million dollars.

Before long, both crab pots were up and running and they were always booked out. Finn and Chrissie helped out as much as possible and Chloe loved having Jack on solid ground. The months passed by quickly as they had their hands full decorating the house, working and running the crab pots. Every spare penny they put away for the wedding. Emails were flying thick and fast between Chloe and Bridgette and everything seemed to be on track, which kept Chloe calm. Every morning she would go to the calendar and cross off another day as it crept closer and closer.

# CHAPTER 17

# AN INTIMATE WEDDING

The morning of their wedding day was spectacular; a glorious sun-filled winter day. They went over everything and checked their outfits one last time, each of them hiding them away so the other did not see. He had decided not to wear the kilt as they were trying not to attract any unnecessary attention. He would wear it in France instead. Today, he would wear the shirt that resembled a pirate shirt and navy pants. He knew Chloe had chosen a plain dress as well.

A clan tartan ribbon was a must for a Scottish bride so he bought one online from Scotland to give Chloe. It was the MacLean tartan and as she became a MacLean today, it was important to him that she did not miss out. He took it out from his draw where he had secretly hidden it for weeks, walked out to her and extended his hand towards her.

"What is this?" she asked, lifting it to study it in detail.

"Well, it's the MacLean tartan and as you become my wife today, I was hoping you might carry this. It's kind of tradition, so I bought it for you." He smiled at her looking very sincere.

"Oh Jack, that's so beautiful. Of course, I will carry it today and treasure it always."

She had not thought of that before. Not only was she marrying Jack, she was marrying into a clan. It gave her a strong feeling of a family bond, as she fingered the ribbon looking at every detail.

"It is beautiful, Jack, thank you." She leaned towards him, and he bent down, so she could kiss him. She put it away with her dress and came back out to the kitchen.

They had planned a picnic in the bush, just the two of them; it was their special way that they wanted to spend their day together. Kait was coming over later to do her hair and Johnny would take Jack to the wedding. Cars would be left at home, and they would Uber to the beach. They didn't want anyone noticing their cars. The spot they had chosen for the ceremony was an isolated part of the beach. Praying for an empty beach, they selected that time of day, and in winter, especially on a Monday, it could hopefully be achieved. They had managed to keep the whole thing a secret, which was an incredible task in itself.

Packed for their picnic, they drove ten minutes away to a spot they liked to go to when they had a chance. They laid out the picnic blanket in a sunny spot to catch the winter sun and set out a charcuterie board full of cheeses, cold meats, pickles, and breadsticks. Opening a bottle of wine, they laid around on the ground, eating, drinking, and relaxing. Exactly how they wanted, just the two of them and no fuss. Keeping a close eye on the time, they soon had to pack up and head back to the house to meet Kait and Johnny.

They arrived on time, and Chloe helped Kait bring everything in from the carboot and then the boys drove the car back to Kait and Johnny's place to dress. As soon as they left, Kait opened a bottle of champagne.

"It is not very often I get a kid-free night and attend my sister's wedding,sooo I plan to let my hair down," she said with a playful smile as she poured the champagne. Chloe laughed.

Her sister was always great company and knew the day would be filled with lots of fun. There was no fussing, no huge rush; they had a few hours to enjoy together as Kait did Chloe's hair. All that she had wanted was long soft curls and Kait had practiced for weeks on her own hair using iron curling tongs. No make-up lady or photographer or bridesmaids running around madly. It was a lovely quiet afternoon that they shared.

A private sunset wedding on the beach was achieved. The girls had managed to dress and get an Uber to the location and arrived to find the boys were already waiting with the celebrant. Chloe wore a long beige linen dress with ballet slippers that matched and a few flowers in her hair. She had a small bouquet she had tied with the tartan ribbon Jack had given her. Her hair hung loose with long curls and minimal makeup. Kait had worn a three-quarter A-line dress in sage. Jack was waiting for her under the wisteria and smiled as he saw her approach. She looked beautiful so childlike and natural. He could not take his eyes off her as she walked towards him. The celebrant welcomed the four of them and gave a quick service before turning to them to say their vows.

"Chloe, I made a promise to you at the Eiffel Tower, one I have never forgotten, and never will. I am here to protect you, and love you forever. You have made my life complete." He slipped the ring on her finger.

"Jack, my true love, the one I will cherish forever, the one that I thought I had lost twice before but now, no one can ever tear us apart from this day forward, we are one." She slipped the ring on his finger.

"You may kiss your bride."

They looked at each other, tears streaming down their faces as they leaned together, and he gently kissed her. They smiled at each other, wiping each other's tears away. He put his forehead to hers. No one else was around as far as they were concerned; they were entranced in their own little world. The celebrant walked off to get the register organized and Kait and Johnny stepped back to give them their privacy. Kait was crying as well.

Still embraced with foreheads locked together, staring into each other's eyes. "I meant every word of my vow to you. I promise to love you, protect you forever, you will be looked after like a princess, and I will make sure you are happy every single day forever. All that I want from you in return is your love."

Chloe nodded, tears still running down her face.

"My highlander," she whispered.

"Aye," he smiled and he softly kissed her. "Mo Leannan falaich, Mo Chloe."

They stood together for a moment longer, having their intimate time, before turning and walking over to the others and signed the register. Kait and Johnny were clapping and waiting to congratulate them.

It was the most moving and beautiful wedding Kait had ever seen. They had done it with love and privacy in their own unique way just for them. No one else mattered. Kait had taken a few photos she would send to her later to keep in their own private collection. It was a private secret ceremony; she would never forget and was so happy that she had been a part of it, to see her sister wed the man she truly, deeply loved.

She remembered the day she had done her reading with the Tarot cards and how she made her take the cruise that she was refusing to go on. She smiled to herself; the cards never lie. They signed the register and then chatted with the celebrant for a while before they left and walked along the beach to the restaurant where they had reservations.

Chloe was cautiously scanning the room to see if she recognised anyone as they were seated. It was a small restaurant and Chloe was confident no one resembled anyone she knew.

"Well, how is that?  You two have officially eloped," said Johnny as he poured  them all water from the water bottle that was placed on the table.

"It was so beautiful guys," said Kait with a dreamy smile.

"Yes, we are married. I can't believe it," said Chloe, looking at her ring."I know I have to take it off after tonight. It is such a shame."

"It won't be long until we have the big wedding," comforted Jack as he patted her on the arm.

The waitress came and took drink orders and explained the specials of the day while they browsed the menu.

"There is kangaroo on this menu," said Jack, shocked.

"Yea, you should give it a go, mate. If it is cooked right, it is really good," said Johnny.

"You eat what's on your coat of arms." His eyes were wide, unable to comprehend.

"Yea, they are a bit of a pest, so lucky they are so bloody delicious, and very lean,so really healthy also," answered Johnny convincingly.

"Alright, I will give it a crack," he said, closing the menu.

"You are getting more and more Aussie every day," laughed Kait.

"It was Pete. He had a swear jar that I had to put money in every time I said aye, I seemed to be paying for the cartons of beer every week," he laughed.

"He's a good bloke,Pete. You must miss working with him."

"I do. He was funny. He brought me vegemite sandwich's every day and tried to make me eat them." Everyone laughed at the face Jack had pulled at the mere thought of it.

"You won't eat it?" asked Kait, astounded.

"You Aussies eat some strange things, even your coat of arms, I now see."

"Well, you don't say that when you are scoffing down Mrs. Whitaker's lamingtons," added Chloe with a smirk.

"Oh, no, I love Mrs. Whitaker's lamingtons."

"Okay, I will have the grilled Barramundi," said Kait as she looked back over the menu, spotting the waitress heading back to take their order.

"No fish for me tonight. I am having the chicken parmigiana," said Johnny proudly, placing his menu back on the table.

"Oh, Johnny, you have that everywhere we go. It's Chloe and Jack's wedding meal. Can't you try something special?" said Kait, annoyed.

"It is special. I have never had a parmi topped with avocado and garlic prawns before," he said with raised eyebrows, look-ing around the table for support.

"That sounds better than the kangaroo. Think I might join you in a parmi,"said Jack.

"Well, I will have the roo and you can try some of mine," added Chloe. They closed the menus just as the server reached their table, pen and paper in hand.

Over the next few hours, they shared a beautiful meal with lots of laughter and wine. As they looked out over the ocean, the moon was full and lit it up like daylight. Jack devoured a huge serving of pavlova, as everyone watched, unable to fit another thing in. He sat back happy with himself as he finished.

"I liked the kangaroo, but that pavlova was just the best," he said, licking his lips and then dabbing them with the serviette.

"You need to walk that off," laughed Chloe.

"I can do better than that. Wait here."

There was a man playing music softly in the corner of the room. Jack went over and requested "Sorrento Moon,"and as it started, he walked towards Chloe.

"My god, Jack, he is playing our song!"

"I know. I asked him to play it. Come on, I need to dance with my wife." Holding out his hand, he smiled that smile, and her heart melted.

"Woohoo! Off you go, young lovers," said Kait loudly after a glass too many of champagne.

"Okay, okay," she said as she took his hand, and he led her to the dance floor. She leaned in and put her head on his chest just like she did the very first night, and they slow danced like there was no one else around. They were back on the ship in their minds, taking their first dance together, and now they were taking their first dance together as husband and wife. It was the perfect ending to a very special wedding.

# CHAPTER 18

## PARIS

Every day was a flurry of excitement as everyone was preparing for Europe. It felt good to be packing summer clothes and leaving the winter behind. Rob had been on Bob's case for months about coming with them to the wedding, and he had finally given in. He had applied for a passport and bought his ticket on the same flight. Lucky for him,there was one gite left as Jeannie and Liam's friends preferred to stay in the city where the action was.

They arrived in Paris mid-morning and headed to the hotel by taxi. Their room was ready. It was beautifully decorated with Parisian prints on the wall and matching curtains and bedspread in a cream and gold floral and stripes.

"I am exhausted. That bed is calling me. I could climb in there and stay," she said as she flopped on the bed.

"Let me make you a coffee. It will pick you up. I am sure they have something here," he started to peer around the room.

"I am going to freshen up. It will help."

"Coffee will be waiting when you are finished."

She met him at the table on the balcony with views out over the boulevard, where he was reading the newspaper. She sat and studied the passing parade below as she sipped coffee. It was a perfect day and they had it all to themselves to do whatever they wanted. She had dressed casual in a blue and white striped t-shirt and jeans and dressed it up with a matching blue scarf and a light jacket. She noticed Jack had not changed and was eager to hit the town.

"Are you going like that?" she asked, putting on a lip balm. He took his eyes from the newspaper, looked himself over and then at Chloe with a stunned gaze. "I was, why? What is wrong with this?"

"Nothing. You have been in those clothes for the long flights, I thought you might feel better in something else."

He looked himself over once again. "Ohh well, I will leave the jeans on and change my shirt. We are in Paris, after all." He shrugged and came back looking fresh and clean in a dark grey long-sleeved shirt rolling his sleeves up. "Better?" he asked.

"Much better," she smiled.

Finally venturing out of the hotel around lunchtime, they happily wandered the streets. "Jack, look," said Chloe as she pointed to a place across the road.

"I know about this café. It's very famous. It has been around since the early 1800s. Hemingway and all his literary friends would meet here and sit and drink coffee."

Jack peered over. The sign out the front said "Les Deux Magots." The grand facade certainly had history and also looked extremely classy. It was proudly sitting on the bottom floor of a six-story old Parisian-style building. Sprawling around all three sides of the block, it had Parisian tables and chairs with pretty umbrellas all placed out onto the paved street.

"Well, as I have a fresh shirt on, let's check if there is a free table," he teased and she smiled, grateful he had changed.

They were escorted by the waiter to a nice outdoor table and handed menus. The drinks menu was extensive, offering all the best wines, liqueurs and spirits you would expect such a place would serve.

"All the best champagnes are on this menu. Moet, Dom Perignon, Bollinger Special Curvee, Oh and Moet et Chandon a rose. Danni would love this place."

"Aye, and Rocco had better bring his cheque book if he is going to let Danni sit and drink here all afternoon," said Jack, taking note of the prices.

"Oh, yes, but what a wonderful experience. I will take a photo and send it to her. She has to come here."

She plucked her phone out of her pocket, took a few photos,and sent them.

"They have Aperol Spritz on the menu, Chlo. Would you like one?" said Jack.

"Oh, yes, that would be lovely," she answered, still staring intently at the menu.

"What would you like to eat?" said Jack as he opened the food menu and Chloe did the same.

"Let's just order something we can graze on and soak up the enchanting atmosphere of this place."

"Well, I was thinking about the mixed charcuterie and a cheese platter," said Jack, looking at her over the menu.

"Perfect! That should keep us happy for an hour or so."

Jack got the waiter's attention and Chloe listened as he ordered in French.

"I feel like I am in the movies, sitting here at this wonderful café with you ordering in French. You can sense the history of this place, along with true Parisian atmosphere oozing out of every nook and cranny, can't you?" she said, looking around.

"I am glad you are enjoying it. This is a perfect start, as you are on your way to your chateau wedding."

"I know I am spoilt. I can't believe we are getting married in a few days in a chateau in the south of France."

"You feel spoilt. I am just a fisherman from a wee town in Scotland. Imagine how I feel."

The waiter arrived with their order and placed it neatly on the table.

"Well, that is relief after you gave me such a wrap ordering in French. I was a wee bit worried I may have ordered the wrong thing."

Chloe laughed as she stirred her cocktail.

"I have to go to the lavatory. I want to check out the inside."

"I thought you might." He laughed.

He watched as she disappeared inside. *I am sitting here in a famous Parisienne café with the girl I now call my wife. Am I freaking out? No, I am actually the happiest I have ever been,* he thought, smiling to himself as he waited. It's all because of Chloe. If it was any other girl he would have run a mile as he usually did when a woman showed any interest. He smiled as he spotted her coming out through the doorway, making her way through the barricade of tightly placed chairs and people.

"So incredible in there. I spotted the two famous statues and I spoke to an American woman who said if we like this place we have to visit Angelina's, another famous café, where all the famous elite used to meet, like Coco Chanel along with all the other glamorous fashion designers."

"Then we shall go. Let me Google their website." Jack took his phone out of his pocket as she waited.

"Booked. I am taking you there for breakfast tomorrow before we check out."

"Online bookings, you are the best! Thank you," she said, nibbling on a biscuit with cheese.

"That is Angie's name. I will take photos for her."

"Oh, Angelina. I thought it was just Angie."

"We shorten everything in Australia. Give an Aussie a word, and they will shorten it," she said sipping on her cocktail and he nodded thinking about it.

"Like Mcdonald's is Macca's," he added.

"Yea, so if you are going to Mcdonald's, you say you're going on a Macca's run," she smiled.

"I notice that a lot, like Sunday afternoon is Sundy arvo."

"Yes and if I say do a ueey, head to the bottle'O, and grab me a goony, I am asking you to turn around and go to the bottle shop for a cask of wine."

"So funny. Pete always says, just taking the piss out of ya, means he is having a joke with me."

"Yep, you got it," she said as he leaned back with a smile, happy he was finally working it all out.

Her phone pinged and she picked it up. It was a message from Danni. She smiled as she read it to Jack.

*Looks like my kind of place. Seeing I can't be there, can you try one of each of those champagnes for me? Danni x*

"I told you she would drink Rocco broke in this place," he laughed.

"Yea, but she is certainly a lot of fun."

They stayed almost two hours before heading off down the street towards the hotel where they relaxed. Chloe dozed on the bed while Jack flicked on the television.

"Oh, I think I dozed off. What time is it?" said Chloe as she woke up and looked around in a groggy daze.

"Dinnertime."

She smiled. "There are only three times in the day for you. Breakfast time, lunchtime, and dinner time."

"Yes, especially when we are in Paris. Let's grab a shower and head out. I want to find a traditional French place for dinner."

It was a cooler evening so they dressed in long shirt and pants. Jack wore his leather jacket and Chloe dressed hers up with a nice jacket scarf and mid-heel boots.

They wandered the streets and found a small French-looking restaurant and ventured inside. The décor was traditional dark wood with wooden tables, and they were shown to a table set for two.

"Bonsoir! Welcome to our restaurant, all the ingredients are fresh from the market this morning, and home-cooked by our talented chef."

"Thank you! I am happy to hear that," said Chloe with a warm smile.

"When you choose your meal I will recommend wines if you wish." He was off heading to the door as another couple had entered, looking around.

"I think you are going to be in for a treat. This place is packed with locals," whispered Jack as he opened the menu.

"It is in French. Can you order for me?" she said with a disheartened shrug of her shoulders.

"It seems to happen a lot to you, doesn't it?"

"Oh, well, we are in France, after all."

"It is a small menu. There is a steak tartar, a beef bourguignon, onion soup, a lemon sole in butter and a chicken cacciatore."

"I will have the soup, please." She cut him off to save him reading the whole menu.

"I will have the beef."

The waiter took their order and headed back to the kitchen. They looked around and realized they were lucky to get a table. Most appeared to be locals, as they chatted happily in French.

"This is getting very real. All of my family should be on their second plane now, flying around out there somewhere."

"Yes, and I had a message from Jimmy, and they are very excited."

"He and Chelsea seem to have hit it off."

"He sounds happy. I guess we will see tomorrow."

The meal was exquisite, and they ordered a crème brûlée and a mont blanc a la crème de marron to finish the meal. They wandered home slowly, stopping at a small wine bar for a drink before heading in for the night.

The next morning, they headed to Angelina's and were shown to a table for two. As they walked inside, the first thing which drew Jack's attention was the huge counter filled with pastries.

"This is a very nice place you have found us here," he said, looking around with eyes full of food envy.

"I thought you might say that," she smiled; it was definitely a place he would dream about for weeks. The décor was beautiful with all the paintings and French mouldings on the walls and ceilings. The tables had a crème and mint marble top and the chairs were typical French café style. A chandelier hung impressively from the centre of the ceiling.

They sat and opened the menu looking around in awe. Chloe could see his mouth watering.

"So I am guessing you are ordering the lot, right?" she teased.

"I don't think even I could eat all of that," he said, not able to lift his eyes from the menu.

"But you would give it a run for your money," he gave her a cheeky grin and a wink and she smiled as he gave the menu his full attention.

"Okay, well, I will have the Angelina's breakfast, consisting of hot chocolate, which is a must, orange juice, and eggs Benedict with Scottish smoked salmon," she said proudly. "Due to present company, the Scottish salmon is a must."

"Scottish smoked salmon," he said with a surprised glance. "I am impressed. I will take you to the best place to have a Scottish breakfast when we go to Scotland."

"I will definitely look forward to that."

"Aye, I am sure you will enjoy your haggis, black pudding, and tattie scones," he said with a smirk.

"Oh, what, now you are teasing me."

"No, I can assure you I am not. So that is why today, I am going to have a Parisian breakfast with all the beautiful pastries including a chocolate croissant, an éclair chocolate, and a Paris -Brest."

"Wow, you certainly are having an extremely sweet breakfast."

"Aye, with a signature hot chocolate, of course."

"Of course, I would not expect anything else." They looked at each other and giggled. They both knew Jack's appetite, and he was especially fond of a sweet breakfast.

The order came out and the pastries looked so lovely, almost being a shame to eat them. Eggs Benedict was served on a gold-rimmed plate with "Angelina"written on the brim. The smoked salmon was plentiful with two perfect eggs on top, and the sauce on the side was served in a small matching gold-rimmed bowl. The hot chocolate was served in gold-rimmed tea cups complete with the Angelina logo. Chloe took a photo and sent it to Angie.

After breakfast, they went back to the room to check out and make their way to the station to board the three-and-a-half-hour high-speed train to Montpelier. They took their seats and Chloe held on tight to Jack's hand as the train took off at great speed. She stared out the window and soon became comfortable enough to let go and relax a little as she enjoyed the beautiful scenery of vineyards go flashing past.

"This scenery is so stunning."

"Aye, it is beautiful indeed," he said as he opened his bag and pulled out a box.

"Our little box of treats from the la charcuterie this morning."

"What did you end up getting?"

"I have some beautiful cheese, and cold cuts and sliced pickles and pâté and in this bag, and she even sliced me some baguette."

"That looks so yummy!"

"Our own little picnic. But wait, there is more!" He put his hands into his jacket pocket and pulled out two bottles.

"A whisky for me and a piccolo for you, and it is still cold."

"You stole those out of the mini bar," she said, shocked.

"No, I paid for them."

"Sure you did. What else have you got tucked away?"

"I have some gin, and some more whisky and another wine," he said as he started emptying his pockets.

"What? We are in France, and I wanted us to enjoy our train ride, that is all."

"You are funny, but it appears we had the same idea. But I only took some soft drink and nuts," she admitted as she pulled out the goodies from her bag.

"I am teaching you well. Together we have it all. Let us enjoy our wee feast," he said as he placed everything on the pull-down trays in front of them.

"Let us enjoy the calm before the storm, you mean," she said as she opened her wine and poured the contents into a plastic cup he handed her.

"Aye, it is going to be a wee hectic. How do you think you will cope?"

"I really don't know. It is going to be stressful, I do know that" she said picking up some cheese and popping a gherkin on it.

"Just let it all happen around you. Don't think too much about it, just let it all flow by itself," he said as he sat back with a relaxed stare.

"That is how you do it, isn't it? Nothing worries you at all. I can't believe how relaxed you are now," she said, nodding her head from side to side as she watched him.

"Aye, there is nothing to worry about. We are here together, on a train enjoying a wee picnic on the way to get married and introduce our families to each other. Why should I be worried?"

She stared at him for a moment and then made him a cheese and pickle on bread and passed it to him.

"Well, for me it's not as easy. You see, first, I had a small panic attack just getting on this train, and then I will have another one when we arrive at the chateau, especially when everyone arrives. And then probably a hundred more throughout the few days that I am there. And I won't finally rest until everyone has gone home, and then I will look back and think, it was so much fun, I had nothing to worry about after all, but then I will worry how much I missed."

"Mmm, it appears that you have a very busy schedule with yourself. Before anything else happens, you must be totally exhausted." He smirked.

"Stop teasing. I am being serious here."

"I am sorry, I am aware of all that you have told me. That is why I have a very busy few days also."

"You do like what?" she stared at him wondering what he meant.

"Well, to start with, I had to make sure I had plenty of things to keep you occupied on the train, to keep your mind off how fast it was going. Then I will have to keep an eye on you until we arrive at the chateau, in case you start freaking out and stepping out in front of cars or locking yourself in bathrooms.

And then I will be staying one step ahead of you, making sure everything is going smooth, so you won't worry yourself sick or panic."

She looked horrified.

"Why are you still hanging around me?  That sounds just terrible," she said with a sad look.

"Don't be silly. It is nothing. I actually enjoy doing it, it is my job and why do I do it?  You ask, because I happen to love you."

She put down the biscuit with a horrified look on her face. "I hate hearing that I am such a problem" she looked like she was going to cry.

"Come here, you silly thing. I didn't do a very good job making you happy today, did I? I have made you cry."He squeezed her, pulling her a bit closer.

"Before I met you, I did not have to worry about any of that, and my life was empty. I was lonely and lost with no purpose at all. But then I was blessed the day I met you. All of a sudden, I had a purpose, a role, and I fell head over heels in love with you, and still am, if you don't already know. I love fussing over you, looking after you, protecting you, I cannot see a single thing wrong with that. As I told you on the ship, I am happy because I have you beside me, without you I would be that lonely nobody that I once was." She gazed up at him and he smiled gently. "Can you understand what I am saying?"

She sat and stared at him, thinking about everything that he had just said. "Yes, I think so." She thought about it for a moment. "I guess it is the same as the way I feel, but I don't have any chores."

"Oh, I think you do. You always make sure I don't order everything on the menu, or stuff my face with all the wrong things, or drink too much whisky, and you are always kicking me under the table when my filters are off and I am saying the wrong thing. Should I go on?"

A smile crept to her face. "Yea, I guess you are right." She picked her biscuit back up and had a nibble. "I will have to take a leaf out of your book and try and relax," she said, looking less rattled.

"Watch this, sit back, take a deep breath, and let it out slowly. Have a sip of your drink, and relax, easy. You try."She copied him exactly and smiled."There you go," he smiled, tapping her on the leg. "You have that laid-back sexy Parisian look."

He poured her a gin and himself another whisky as they sat eating their picnic as the train hurtled along with great speed. The farms and vineyards flicked past as they stared lost in their own thoughts.

"I haven't stepped out on the wrong side of the road for a while or done anything quite so bad. I think I am getting a bit better," she said, looking at him with a serious stare.

"Are you still thinking about that, you funny wee lassie? No,you have not. You are much better," he said as he laughed.

The train stopped at Montpelier station and they found a taxi rank easily. They gave the driver the address and he sped off.

"Are you ready for this?"

"Yea, I think I am, thanks for your little encouragement chat. It helped. I feel much more relaxed."

He smiled and leaned in to whisper, "Is that you or the Gin Genie talking?"

They both laughed and turned to look out the window. Both were still smiling when they pulled up at the open gates of Chateau Bijou and the driver slowly came to rest on the pebbled driveway.

# CHAPTER 19
## THE CHATEAU

As they pulled their luggage down the path towards the entrance of the chateau, they stopped at the fountain. "Promise me one thing. Try to relax, have fun, and remember I am here right beside you all the way."

"I will, I promise. Let's go do this, I think that I am more excited than anything else at the moment."

"Well, I am glad to hear that. Let's go and have some fun."

She nodded with a nervous smile, and they continued to the foyer. Bridgette spotted them straight away and came out from her office on the left, wearing an apricot jumpsuit and matching stilettos that clicked loudly on the marble floor, tossing her brunette curls as she called out to them.

"Oh bonjour, bien venue Jack et Chloe," she beamed as her voice echoed down the large reception area.

"Bonjour, Bridgette, we have made it!"

"Oh, I apologise. You speak English, of course. Here, leave your luggage. Pierre will take it to your room. Let me show you around."

Bridgette showed them to their room and then gave them a tour of the rest of the rooms and grounds. The huge wedding tent was being erected, and they went over and inspected it while Bridgette filled them in on all the details.

"So what do you think? This is what you were expecting?"

"Yes, it is perfect!"

"It is in the spot we chose, and the grounds are immaculate."

They all scanned the manicured lawns and gardens.

"Of course, I want it to be perfect for your special day. The celebrant has been in touch, and she is organised."

"Oh, that is wonderful! Thank you."

"And you have a florist coming. I understand we will be going to the flower market together."

"Yes, we have a family member who will be doing the flowers. She will need to be taken to the market."

"That is no problem at all. I have arranged food as we discussed and caterers are booked. There is nothing for you to worry about at all. Just relax and enjoy," she said, waving her arms around.

"Well, that is very comforting to hear. Thank you so much," said Chloe with a sigh of relief.

"Now, go and explore. I will be in my office if you need anything. Your family is arriving today?"

"Yes, they are."

"I will be here to greet them. I have set up a table big enough for everyone in the pool gazebo, and there are drinks in the fridge for your guests."

"Sounds like a lovely spot. Thanks again."

They went up to their room and their luggage was waiting inside the door. It was everything a bedroom in a chateau should be with floral matching curtains and duvet,a chandelier and a marble bathroom complete with a white hand-painted rose sink with antique gold taps. The open window let a soft breeze flow with a scent of lavender filling the room. Chloe walked over to it and took a deep breath.

"Oh, check out our view. It is a huge lavender field!"

"That is perfect for you. See, lots of people need lavender. Why do you think they need so much of it?" said Jack as he opened the small bar fridge and peered inside. "Ah, Bridgette has thought of everything. A bottle of champagne," he said as he took it out of the fridge and popped it. "Champagne, my dear."

"Why not?" she said as she was looking around. He poured the bubbly and handed her a glass.

"Welcome to our wedding week! Let the fun and festivities begin!"

"I will definitely drink to that!"

After a quiet drink, they made their way to the pool house and looked it all over, making sure everything was in place. Bridgette had thought of everything. They were all set for their family and friends. It was stocked with plates, cutlery and glasses of all shapes and sizes. She opened the fridge and it was stocked with wine, beer, and soft drinks. She pulled open a drawer that was stocked with serviettes, cocktail stirrers and tea-towels.

The first to arrive was Jack's family. Everyone was very excited, and they all gathered in the pool house gazebo. Chloe put out the platters of nibbles that Bridgette had prepared and placed in the fridge.

"Oh, Chloe, this is so beautiful," said Jeannie.

"Yes, I was a bit hesitant at first, but this is spectacular," said Marl. "I cannot believe two of my children will be married here in these grounds over the next few days." Tears were welling in her eyes.

"Come on,Mum, have a seat here. I will pour you a drink. Thanks for coming such a long way." Jack gave her a hug and settled her into a seat in the shade.

"Both you wee girls are going to make bonne brides," said Marl, settling into her chair.

"Maybe we should have joined them, Chelsea," said Jimmy, putting an arm around her.

"It's not too late. We can fit another wedding in if you like," said Jack with a serious gaze. He saw something in Jimmy's eyes and knew this was no joke.

"Yea, come on you guys, take the plunge," added Liam, laughing.

"Is that a proposal?" asked Chloe.

"I think it just might be," said Jimmy, looking at Chelsea who was beaming.

"My parents would kill me if I went home and told them that we eloped," she laughed.

"Get them on a flight. We can fit them in," said Chloe excited.

"I accept your proposal, Jimmy, but let's not crash these weddings," she laughed.

"Wait does this mean? You are engaged?" asked Jack.

"Chelsea, does that mean we are engaged?"

"Yes, I guess it does," she said, giving him a kiss. "Glad you made it nice and private," she laughed looking around at everyone.

"I don't even have a ring to give you," he said with a sigh.

"We can select it together later," she smiled up at him.

"We can buy one here in France," he offered.

"This calls for a drink" said Jack and he headed to the fridge with Jimmy and Liam hot on his heels eager to help.

Chloe smiled over at Chelsea and walked over towards her. "Chelsea, I am so happy for you and thank you for doing our flowers."

"Thanks, Chloe, I told you that day at Patonga, we were head over heels for each other, and nothing has changed. If anything, we are even more in love now." She gave her a hug. "We will be sisters in law."

"Can I join in?" said Jeannie as she walked over. "So happy for you both."

"Thanks, Jeannie, don't get me all dizzy. I have flowers to think about," she said as she flicked her copper hair back over her shoulder, trying to refocus herself.

"Yes, Chelsea has some wonderful ideas for the flowers,Chloe. I think it will be beautiful," added Jeannie as they all started to sit at the table.

"Bridgette is taking me to the flower markets on wedding day mornings. Marl and your mum, could join in if they like," said Chelsea as she took off her jacket and hung it on the back of her chair as she sat. Chloe could not help noticing a new purple rose bud on her tattoo. She smiled, knowing that it was for Jimmy.

"I would love to come with you, Chelsea, that sounds like so much fun, a French flower market," said Marl.

"I am sure Mum would love it also. They should be here soon," said Chloe as she settled into her chair and looked at her watch. She knew their flights arrived hours ago as she had tracked it all the way on the app.

"I have given Bridgette my dress to hold, and she said she has yours also," said Jeannie as she took a wine from Jack.

"Yes, she has hung them in the grand spa room where we will get dressed," she smirked.

Bridgette walked around the corner with Chloe's family. "We have more arrivals," she announced.

"Ah, you are here!" Chloe raced over to give them a hug and kiss. Jack was right behind her joining in on the greetings.

"Your family is here, Jack," said Olivia.

"Yes, come and meet my family. My mum, Marlene, my brother Jimmy, his girlfriend, I mean fiancée Chelsea," he said, slapping his head with his hand. "And my sister Jeannie and her husband-to-be Liam," he said as he waved his arms introducing them all.

"This is my family. My mum and dad, Olivia and Robert, my sister Kait and her husband Johnny with little Sophia and my sister Chrissie and her boyfriend Finn,our family friends Angie and Bob," said Chloe with a huge smile. "Bob, I am so happy you came. Thankyou so much for doing that long flight for us."

"It's a pleasure, love, although I must admit,it's such a bloody long plane ride!"

She threw her arms around him and cuddled him. "You have made me so happy. It would not be the same without you."

"Angie, you made it! I was hoping you would come!" She ran over and threw her arms around her.

"Yea, I would not miss it for the world." She pushed her back gently, taking a long look at her long-time friend. "You scrub up, alright, after such a long flight," she laughed.

"I freshened up before we landed, plus I managed to sleep."

"You travel well. Come and sit down, all of you," said Chloe. Everyone was busy shaking hands and greeting each other.

"Oh, it's so lovely to meet you all, finally. Please call me Marl. Oh, Chloe, all you girls mirror your mother."

"Yes, everyone says that. It's lovely to meet you, Marl," said Olivia as she sat down next to her. Jack went back to fussing around, getting everyone drinks.

"It is such a long way for you to come. I think we will all be in bed early tonight," said Marl.

"Yes, it is a very long way. We stopped over in Singapore for a few days to break it up. We were worried about Sophia," said Rob. "Crikey's, it was bloody hot there," he added, rocking on his heels. "We spent the days by the resort pool, didn't see a damn thing."

Stories of their travels were shared and Jack and Chloe slipped away quietly as everyone was getting to know each other.

"I wanted a minute with you alone," smiled Jack. "How are you coping with all this?"

"It is all a bit stressful, isn't it? I am coping, just," she sighed.

"Well, the others aren't arriving till the morning, so we have the night for our families to get to know each other and then deal with the rest tomorrow."

"Yes, I just want to check with Bridgette about dinner and then I am going to have a beer," she swallowed dryly, unable to wet her parched throat.

"Okay, I will go and make sure all is going well over there, and now that Johnny is here he can help me tap a keg."

"Waiting for the Aussie to tap the keg," she laughed.

"Aye, we Scots only know how to empty it," he teased.

"I can't believe this is actually happening, can you?" She squealed.

"I have to keep pinching myself." He gave her a squeeze and headed back to the gazebo.

The afternoon was filled with laughter and everyone was getting on well. Finn and Chrissie took Sophia in the pool for a swim, and everyone else sat around, enjoying a few drinks. Olivia changed into a more casual outfit of shorts and a cool flowing sleeveless shirt and Robbie poured her a wine. She and Marl seemed to hit it off, and shared lots of stories and laughter together. Rob was the life of the party, keeping everyone entertained with funny stories and jokes. Chelsea and Jimmy were catching up with Kait and Johnny and everyone became relaxed after a few drinks.

Jack was retrieving more drinks from the wedding ceremony main bar when he heard a familiar voice.

"So have you got one of those for an old friend?"Jack looked up and smiled. It was Pat,his best friend who had walked in. His toffee brown curls bouncing as he walked towards him and his speckled copper eyes gleaming with excitement.

"Pat, you made it!" He gave him a man-hug and slapped him on the back.

"This is all a bit flash," he said as he turned to survey the area.

"It's great, isn't it?" he said proudly.

"Can't wait for a dip in that pool. The weather is so warm."

"It is perfect weather, isn't it? How are you? Thanks so much for coming."

"I couldn't miss this, my best buddy getting hitched."

"Where is your bag? Do you know where your room is?"

"Aye, that is all done. The lady showed me around."

"Well, it sounds like all that there is to be done is have a beer."

"I thought you would never ask."

He handed him a beer, and he took a long swig.

"Oh, that is a nice drop."

"French beer is not bad."

"Aye, it goes down too easy."

"Come with me. I will introduce you to everyone."

Jack walked Pat around, introducing him to everyone, and then he spotted Angie. She was walking back from the pool and smiled as she saw them. He stopped dead in his tracks.

"Who is that?" he said.

"That is Angie, Chloe's best friend. Come on, let me introduce you."

Pat stared intently at her as she approached.

"Angie, I would like you to meet Patrick, my best man."

She tousled her long brown curls as she turned and greeted him, flashing him a pearly white smile.

"Aye, I see he has left the best last."

"Well, thank you, but I have to tell you, I have been warned about this Scottish charm."

"Don't believe a word of it," he laughed.

Jack was looking around for Chloe. He had to keep an eye on her. This was a lot for her to handle and knew she would be hiding somewhere.

"I will leave you two to get to know each other," he said as he patted his old friend on the back.

He looked around and then spotted her talking to Bridgette, near the side of the chateau at the kitchen entry, and made his way over to check if everything was okay.

"Here you are. I have been looking all over for you. Are you okay?"

"Yes, Bridgette was just going over a few things with me, but she has everything under control,"she said, smiling warmly at Bridgette.

"Yes, you certainly have. Thank you for everything. You have got it all organised perfectly."

"Thank you, I will leave you to enjoy then," she said as she turned and headed back inside.

"How is everyone getting on? Are they talking? I have to keep an eye on Angie, she is on her own."

"Not anymore. Pat has arrived and I introduced them. All is going well. Your dad is telling some of his jokes. Don't worry about anything."

"Oh, shit. Really already? He didn't waste any time. I definitely need a coldie now. It will help to relax me."

She licked her dry lips as Jack threw his arm around her shoulder, and they strolled back to join the others.

"I need to make sure Mum has a drink."

"Relax, I am pretty sure she has one, she was talking to my mum when I left."

As they got closer they heard laughter and it appeared everyone was loosening up and having fun.

"And so I was wondering why the frisby was getting larger, and then it hit me," said Rob as everyone roared with laughter and Chloe rolled her eyes.

"Drink up, Jack. Believe me, you're going to need it."

He rubbed her shoulders as he chuckled.

"Leave him alone, he is having fun and everyone seems to be enjoying it."

Dinner was served on the paved outdoor pergola and the table was long enough for them all. Bridgette had cooked a pot of French onion soup and a roast, which they all tucked into while Jack walked around the table pouring wine.

"Tomorrow night won't be as elaborate as this. Bridgette will be busy cooking for the wedding, so I have arranged a local pizza shop to bring us pizzas," informed Jack.

"Plus, all the other guests will be here," added Chloe. "You will all meet our crazy friends from the cruise."

"I, for one, have been waiting for that. They all sound like great fun," said Kait. Chloe was keen to introduce Kait to Danni;they were similar in personality and knew they would get on well.

"So what are the plans for tomorrow?" asked Olivia.

"We have to set up and decorate the marquee. It won't take too long if we all work together. The caterers are dropping off all the plates and glasses and the beer and wine is arriving also," informed Jack.

"We will have it all done by lunch and then have a swim," said Jeannie optimistically.

"We will all feel a bit more alive after a sleep," said Johnny and everyone agreed. It had been a long day for all of them and no one was keen on sitting up too late. After dinner, they all had a few quiet drinks before everyone slowly disappeared for the night.

# CHAPTER 20

# SUNFLOWERS IN THE SUNSHINE

The next morning, they were the first to arrive downstairs. It was a stunning morning as Chloe strolled around the garden while Jack went to check with Bridgette that everything was on track for the day. She spotted him as he wandered back to her.

"Come on, I have a chore we have to do." He took her by the hand and led her towards two mint-coloured pushbikes complete with tassels and baskets on the front. "We have to go to the bakery and pick up the baguettes," he said holding a bike for her.

"We do? Did they forget?" She asked, looking confused.

"No, I offered. I thought it would be a nice outing for us," he said, flicking her a smile and she nodded.

He mounted his bike and took the lead. It was a beautiful ride down the dusty country lane, which had fields on either side full of lavender and other flowers. The sun filtered through the trees, shining brightly, casting orange and yellow tones as it danced on each tree branch, creating a magical scene. The lavender swayed in the gentle breeze as its aroma lingered in the air. Taking a deep breath, letting it fill her lungs and then gently releasing it back out, she felt calm and relaxed as she rode along, loving the warmth of the sun as it landed on her skin. Jack pulled to the side of the road and stopped, so she pulled up beside him. She spotted two palomino horses that looked inquisitively at them and started to slowly nose their way towards them. "What beautiful horses!" she cried as she lay the bike down and walked to the fence.

"Aye, I was told to keep an eye out for them," he replied as he took two apples from his basket and handed her one.

"Where did you find these?"

"I grabbed them on the way out of the kitchen when they told me about the horses. I knew you would enjoy feeding them."

She smiled, looking deep into his eyes."You're amazing," she said as she climbed the timber runs on the fence to offer the horse the apple. It came over and graciously took the apple, looking at her with his huge dark eyes. "He ate it," she smiled back at him almost childlike, and he smiled back. He loved watching her as she enjoyed rubbing the horse's neck, and he nodded in approval, letting out a long neigh. "He likes it," she smiled back with a giggle. She looked amazing with the sunlight shining on her with her hair windswept from the soft breeze as it blew the hem of her peasant dress gently in the breeze.

He took photos and watched intently as the breeze carried her hem a little higher every time it blew. Jack was praying to the gods of the wind, a huge gust would come and blow that peasant dress high over her head.

"The other horse is here. Can I give him the other apple?"She flicked her hair out of her eyes.

"Sure, you enjoy," he said, clearing his throat but his eyes were immediately drawn back to her slender legs as the wind gave him a few sweet glimpses of the top of her thigh. *This girl is driving me crazy. Has she any idea how beautiful she looks right now*? He wanted to grab her and lay her in those lavender fields and have his way with her more than anything.

He had to control himself. He looked around and spotted an old shed across the road. *I wonder what was in there. Maybe an old car or machinery.* He tried hard to continue his concentration on the shed but was instantly drawn back to Chloe, and as he did the gods of the wind granted him his wish, and blew her dress high up, giving him a wonderful view that made his desire grow to new heights.

He had to move on before he could not control himself any longer."Come on, we had better collect these baguettes," he said as he tried to compose himself and walked over to help her off the fence.

She threw her arms around his neck and his hand gently made its way up her leg, coming to rest on her bottom."What is that lustful look you have in your eye?" she said,squinting in the sun. "I can read your mind right now, Jack MacLean, shame on you," she teased.

"Aye, and I am trying very hard not to think about that, if you don't mind," he said with a dreamy look. She leaned in and kissed him as he threw his arms around her and pulled her into him close. *Oh! God she smells amazing. I have to stop before I rip this dress right off her right here in front of the horses.*

He swung her around and put her feet gently on the ground as he stepped back."That is not fair, kissing me like that. You are driving me crazy, do you know that?"

"As a matter of fact, I do," she teased and then spotted the most incredible view over his shoulder."Jack, look! Sunflowers," she squealed.

He turned to take a quick peek relieved for a break from the thoughts that were making him weak in the knees.

It was the most picturesque sight of lavender fields, then behind it, fields of sunflowers. The yellow framed the purple magically, and she stood to take photos.

"Do you think that they would mind if I picked one for Kait? They are her favourite flower."

"I don't think they would miss one. There are thousands out there, plus I want to see what is in that shed," he said shading his eyes from the sun.

"Race me," she said as she sped off down a small track between the lavender fields, and he took off behind her, watching as her long blonde mane tousled in the breeze as she looked back, giggling as she spotted him hot on her heels.

Just as they reached a clearing before the start of the sunflowers, he grabbed her and kissed her passionately. His hands were all over her as she started to breathe as hard as he was, and he gently lay her on the ground. He put his hands up her thighs and pulled off her panties as she helped.

"Do you think anyone is near us?" she asked.

He lifted his head high and peered over the lavender fields and nodded. "Only the bees," he smirked. With that answer, she ripped his shirt off, and he slid out of his pants. His hands went higher and caressed her breast."Where is your bra?" he said muffled as he started to nussle himself in her breast.

She sat up and pulled the dress over her head, lying back, giving him complete access as he enjoyed every inch of her before frantically making love to her. They lay panting, regaining their breath for a while before they could speak.

"That was totally amazing!" she looked at him with a giggle.

"That was your fault. You were driving me crazy," he sighed still out of breath.

"Well, it's not every day you get to make love in fields of lavender, is it?" She smiled back.

"No, it's not. I couldn't let a chance go by, plus I knew you would want to frolic in here with me."

"Oh, that is what you were thinking, was it? You were looking after me."

"Of course, that is the nice lad that I am, looking after you like that."

"Come on then, lover boy, we better pick a flower and collect these baguettes."

They started to dress as Jack lay back to put on his pants. He yelped out in pain.

"What happened?" she asked with a concerned look.

"Something bit me on the bum," he said as he sprung to his feet, trying to twist around to take a peek.

"It was a bee," said Chloe as she spotted it squirming around on the ground. "Stay still I have to get the sting out," she said as she pressed her nails into his butt cheek. "Got it," she said, checking out the sting with a curious eye before throwing it away.

"I am being very brave here, it's stinging so bad," he said, screwing up his face.

"So was it worth your romp in the lavender fields?" she teased.

"Every bit of it," he smiled.

They strolled to the shed, peering inside an unlocked door and making their way inside."It's a flower picking shed," he said as he looked around.

"Here are some shears. I will pick you some sunflowers," he said as he took them off the hook on the wall.

"Just a few," she reminded him as he made his way outside. She watched as he selected three beautiful flowers and handed them to her. "Thanks, Jack. Let's make tracks."

They shut the door on the flower shed, and made their way through the lavender fields back to the waiting bikes. Peddling along at good speed made a quick trip to the bakery, and had a leisurely ride back along the country road. As they rode back into the driveway from their morning ride, Chloe felt the most relaxed she had in days. They retrieved the baguettes from the basket along with the flowers and headed inside to the kitchen.

"Oh, bonjour, young lovers. What have we here?"

Jack put down the bag of baguettes on the large butler's table."Morning, Bridgette. We stopped to feed the horses and spotted these flowers. The field was so huge I thought they wouldn't miss just a few. They are for Kait, they are her favourite flower."

Bridgette took the flowers and found a vase under the sink.

"I will pop them in some water for her. I am friends with the farmers. They will not mind at all."

"Also, do you have anything for a bee sting? A bee stung Jack while we were in the fields."

"Oh, show me, Jack. Did you manage to remove the sting?" said Bridgette, grabbing his arm and looking all over.

"It is not on my arm," he said shyly.

"Oh, well, show me. I will fix it for you, it stings, wee?"

"Ah, wee, but it is kinda in a private spot."

"A private spot, young Jack?" she said with a smirk looking at his crutch.

"No, not there. On my bottom," he said as he pulled his shorts down, and she started to investigate. He looked up at Chloe who was holding back her laughter.

"Wait, I have just the cream for that." She went to the first aid cupboard and came back, rubbing his bottom with it gently.

"A small price to pay for some fun in the fields, wee?"

"Wee," said Jack with a screwed-up face, wishing the moment would end.

"I will tell the farmers you enjoyed their fields," she whispered, slapped him on the bottom and turned to Chloe with a smirk as she turned as red as a beetroot.

"Come on, let's go freshen before we face anyone else," said Jack as he took her by the hand, and they went the back way to their room.

# CHAPTER 21
## A FAMILY AFFAIR

Everyone was up sitting around the table, chatting, drinking coffee, and eating, when they arrived back at the breakfast room.

"You were both up early," said Jimmy. "Bridgette said you went for a morning ride."

"Yes, we went for a ride to the bakery. It was so beautiful," said Chloe. "Has Chelsea gone to the flower market?" she added, trying to change the subject.

"Yes, along with my mum and yours. They wanted to select the flowers needed for decorating today," he said, stirring his coffee.

"Well, we will have a quick breakfast and jump into it then," said Jack, handing Chloe a coffee.

A job was allocated for everyone and it was all working like clockwork. The fairy lights and decorations were completed first and then the boys set up the trestle tables and the girls followed them with tablecloths, cutlery, and three types of glasses. The women arrived back with the flowers and all the girls sat around the outdoor table as Chelsea taught them how to create the vases of flowers. They went to work as they chatted and laughed. A play tent was erected to the side for children with little beds where a nanny would put them to sleep when they were tired.

Finally, completed after a big morning, everyone stood back to cast an eye over their work. It was beautiful. It had all come together and had created a stunning wedding setting. Ivy and green foliage were cascaded around the inside of the marquee with a solar-powered chandelier hanging from the centre.

Tall vases of lilies, peonies,and roses, in white, soft pink, and lavender made beautiful centre pieces for the tables. Wine barrels of lavender were placed at the entrance scenting the area. Fairy lights hung in all the trees and bushes outside with an archway of flowers for the vows' ceremony. Chloe and Jeannie stood together holding hands in awe of their marquee.

"It is so beautiful! Chelsea has done an amazing job with the flower decorations," whispered Jeannie. "You chose the most beautiful flowers. They all look amazing!"

"Thanks, Jeannie! I am pretty amazed myself how beautiful it has all turned out. But it was all Chelsea. She is very talented. We will be setting up yours in a few days' time, and I am sure it will be just as beautiful."

"Thanks, Chloe, I am so excited. This has worked out so beautiful. Remember the night we were drunk and brought the idea to life?"

"I do. Everyone thought we were nuts." They both laughed as they recalled the night.

As Jack walked over, he smiled as he watched the girls. "Admiring your masterpiece," he said as he turned and looked it over with them.

"It is perfect. Everyone has worked hard to pull it off for us."

Jack turned and called everyone over. "Thank you, everyone. You have all worked hard. Let's have a well-deserved drink."

"Beer o'clock," chanted Rob excitedly. "Gotta love beer o'clock!"

Everyone followed him to the pool gazebo. Johnny, Jack, and Liam poured drinks while Chloe and Jeannie went inside and brought out trays of baguettes along with cheese and fruit platters that Bridgette had put together for them.

All throughout the afternoon, guests arrived. First was Paddy and Maggie with their son and girlfriend, followed closely by John and Ava. They were shown around and given drinks as Danni and Rocco arrived. They all took a second take as they walked in. Danni was revealing a new hair style, cut short into a pixie cut, and she wore it well. It was platinum blonde, and she looked stunning, dripping in gold as usual.

"I thought Rocco had brought a new woman to the wedding," yelled Jack as they strolled towards them and Danni came running ahead, throwing her arms around Chloe.

"Do you like?" she said as she turned with a ballerina spin.

"Like? I love!"

It suited her perfectly, showing off her high cheekbones. She was dressed casual in jeans and chiffon white floral top teamed with mid heels and a fuchsia lipstick that matched to perfection the flowers on her shirt. The sweet aroma of her usual fragrance immediately reminded you of her.

By late afternoon, everyone had arrived and a whole party scene had been created. Everyone was mingling and the pool was put to good use. Jack and Chloe were circling, making sure they spoke to everyone. They spotted Paddy and Maggie near the drinks table and walked over. They both looked very casual in shorts, shirt and sandals, looking around out over the gardens.

"Where else would I bump into you two? Right beside the drinks table," laughed Jack.

"It's so good to see you two," added Chloe.

"This is a beautiful setting you have here. We were just admiring the gardens." Paddy loved gardens and his acres of garden at home were as neat as a pin, now that he had recently retired.

"Yes, it's glorious. We are so happy we found this place. Well,it was all thanks to Danni, she put us onto it."

"We are so proud to be here to watch you both get married tomorrow," said Paddy.

"Well, you have been there from the start," said Jack. Paddy had been his rock from the time they met and was the father figure he needed. It meant a great deal to have him there with them today.

"I remember Paddy trying to match-make you both on the cruise," laughed Maggie.

"I remember how you were all making bets on us," said Chloe as they all laughed.

John and Ava walked up to join them. John was in his usual polo shirt and shorts and Ava in a pink sun dress with huge pink sunglasses and sand shoes. "I remember that, I won," yelled John.

"I came in a close second," added Paddy.

"Oh, John, you are not looking after Ava. She doesn't have a drink," scolded Paddy.

"Oh, no, it's OK. I will have one later. I am having a break."

"That's not like you," yelled out Danni as she approached with Rocco.

"Danni would never go without champagne," said Rocco.

"I am celebrating our good friend's wedding,"she smiled, and they all laughed. Rocco still hadn't learnt to ease up.

Everyone loved her new hairstyle and teased Rocco about her looking even wilder now, and he laughed it off with a half-convincing smile. It was obvious she was still running him all over town, and they all knew she always would, there was no stopping the wild party girl inside her.

"Where is Cruz and Catalina?" asked Maggie.

"Oh, they are arriving later. They are working on a cruise ship which only docked this morning, and then they were flying in from Barcelona late this afternoon,"informed Chloe.

"I can't wait for the whole gang to be back together," said Danni, sipping on her champagne.

"Oh, wait, they just walked in the door," said Chloe and everyone turned to see them walking towards them, and they all cheered.

"Hello, so glad to see you all!"

"We didn't think that you were arriving till later."

"We got an earlier flight and here we are! Love your hair, Danni. Oh, I need champagne."

"I happen to know where to find one. I will be back in a flash!" Danni turned quickly and headed to the drinks table. Jack poured Cruz a beer.

"Ava, would you like a beer while I am here?" asked Jack.

"No, I will sit this one out."

"Oh, no you won't. I have not seen you for so long and the whole gang is back together," said Danni, grabbing an extra glass.

"Wait, no, I can't," said Ava, panicked.

"We didn't want to say anything and upstage the wedding, but there is no way Ava can go without a drink without you lot noticing, so we have to spill our beans. We are having a baby," said Johnny.

"So sorry, Chloe, I did not plan on spilling our news. This is your day."

"What? No way! This is awesome news!" She threw her arms around Ava.

"Danni, you are such a pusher," Ava sighed.

"I had no idea. I just wanted my little drinking buddy back."

"Well, you will have to wait a few months. I am four months, so baby is due in late October."

"You look amazing, Ava. You are absolutely glowing," said Chloe.

"She is always fussing about her skin," said John, taking a beer from Jack as he handed them around.

"I can't believe you are going to be a dad," laughed Paddy.

"Me neither," he said with a scared face that made everyone laugh.

"He will be a fine daddy. Don't listen to him," said Maggie.

"Thanks for your support, Maggie."

"Poor Ava is going to have two wee babies to care for," laughed Paddy.

"Well, it's good to see your nuts weren't permanently damaged after that jump into the ocean in Croatia," said Cruz.

Everyone laughed remembering the day he jumped off the cruiser and landed so awkward he was walking funny for days.

"Do you know what you are having yet?" asked Cat.

"No, not yet, but we are hoping for a boy. John's dad is adamant about keeping the family name going."

"But what do you want, Ava? Don't worry about his family," said Paddy, giving John a stern look.

She looked at John, and he answered for her.

"She wants a girl, but I keep telling her she can have as many girls as she wants after we get the male to carry the name."

"Oh, that is so old-fashioned," teased Maggie. "I missed out on a daughter. I think a woman needs a daughter just as much, plus she gets spoilt by the father, and becomes a daddy's girl. Don't listen to all that nonsense."

"It won't be Bucko's outdoor living with no Buckman's," cried John.

"Well, lucky you don't have any say in it. Just love whatever comes along," said Chloe,rubbing Ava gently on the belly.

The afternoon was kick-back-and-relax style, as music played and everyone swam, and chatted as they got to know each other. Chloe was right; Kait and Danni hit it off, and kept everyone entertained with their outgoing personalities, not to be beaten by Paddy and Maggie as they got into full swing after a few drinks. Chloe walked out with Olivia carrying pickie platters for everyone to enjoy while they had a drink and Chloe stopped and looked around as they placed them on the long table under the gazebo.

"It is a great bunch of family and friends you have here Chlo, you are very lucky," said Olivia.

"I know. I was just thinking that myself."

She scanned the scene. Most were in the pool playing a game of water volleyball. Danni, Maggie and Kait were sitting at the table sharing a bottle of champagne and Ava was sipping on a non-alcohol cocktail. It had all worked out wonderful. She smiled; everything was perfect.

# CHAPTER 22

## THE WEDDING

**M**orning sunlight was shining and the breeze was blowing the scent of lavender and fresh cut lawn through the open window, filling the room with beautiful aromas. It was morning, and not just any morning. It was the morning of their wedding day. It had been a huge event for Chloe with everyone arriving, and she felt that her nerves had been rattled over the last couple of days. She was glad to have some peace and quiet and a moment alone with Jack. She felt him stir and she smiled.

"Good morning," she smiled and he pulled her closer.

"Good morning, come here, my beautiful bride."

"Ah, what are you doing? We can't do that. What if someone hears?"

"I really don't care. It is our wedding day, and we can do as we please."

She jumped out of bed and headed for the coffee machine. "All of our families are here. Let's have a coffee."

"Alright, I give in, I will never win, anyway."

She opened the bedroom door, reached out and grabbed the morning paper which had been delivered to their door. She passed it to Jack and continued to make the coffee.

"So this is what married life is going to be like? I have the paper in the morning instead of you."

She laughed, handing him his coffee and crept back in beside him.

"No, don't be silly. You understand what I mean. This bed slides on the timber floor just sitting on it."

"Well, if you think we are not going to do it the whole time we are here you better think again," he said, looking upset as he opened the paper.

"Well, we will have to be a bit creative, won't we?"

"Oh, now I like the sound of that. Let's go for a shower. You have me feeling all sexy thinking of sneaking around."

"Drink your coffee. We have a hectic day ahead of us today. I can't wait till it is all over."

Jack had been worried about this. He felt her anxiety peaking a few times over the last few days.

"It has been very hectic with so much commotion going on. How are you?  Can I do anything for you?"

"Oh, I am hanging in there. The smell of that lavender is helping. I just need some quiet time, it has been way too full on."

"I would ask you to run away with me and elope, but we already did that."

Chloe laughed. "Yes, this is all for them, our loved ones, but I liked our quiet little ceremony much better."

"But look how happy everyone is, and they have all finally got to meet each other. It is pretty special."

"Yea, everyone had such a great time yesterday,hadn't they? I am not saying I don't enjoy seeing them all, it is all a bit daunting, that's all."

"They were all in fine form yesterday. It's so wonderful to have the gang back together," he chuckled. "And Ava and John are going to have a baby."

"Oh, wonderful news for sure. I am a wee bit jealous of them, I can't wait to start our family."

"Wow, Jack, that is so sweet. We have never spoken about this."

"Well, I guess it's a bit late on our wedding day."

"It is more than too late. We are already married."

"Oh yea, I keep forgetting."He slapped his forehead with his hand.

"When I was in my depressed days, and I went to stay with Paddy and Maggie. I was so envious of what they had. I was envious of their relationship on the ship, but when I stayed with them, and all their family gathered around them, it was there and then I knew that was exactly what I wanted for us."

"I still have the guilt over that, Jack. I am so sorry you went through it all. I should never have listened to those lies."

"Well, it doesn't matter anymore. Nobody can hurt us now. We are married and about to entertain our families and friends with our ceremony."

Breakfast was served in the breakfast room as everyone ate croissants and madeleines and lots of hot coffee. The day ahead would be long. Olivia and Marlene set off early with Bridgette and Chelsea to the flower markets to select the flowers for the bouquets and hair. The men had to organise the bar and Paddy's son and wife had to make sure the kegs were all tapped and the wines were chilled. Paddy's son also played the bagpipes so would have the job of being the piper for the ceremony. Ava and Chrissie would be in charge of the makeup and hairdressing in the grand spa room at the top of the chateau.

After breakfast, Chloe grabbed Jack by the arm and asked him to take a walk with her in the garden.

"What's up? Are you OK?" he asked, concerned. Today of all days would be the day she could easily fall apart.

"Oh, phew, a couple of deep breaths and I will be fine."

He stopped and picked her a sprig of lavender and she smelt it, breathing in deeply.

"It's all a bit full on, isn't it?" he said as he put his arm around her shoulder and guided her along the garden path.

"Yea, just a bit. I needed a quiet walk with you, that's all."

"I will ask Kait to pour you a champagne, and settle your jitters a bit, but only one. I know how you get with those bubbles," he teased, but her mind was already elsewhere.

"And then to top it all off, I went to open my new pack of the pill this morning and I can't find it. If I have lost them I am in big trouble. Maybe the doctor at home can email me a new repeat and fingers crossed I can buy them at a chemist tomorrow."

"What pill are you talking about?"

"You know, the pill, to stop me falling pregnant."

"Oh, well, that is not a problem at all. If that is all that is worrying you, even if you find them, stop taking them."

"What? I can't do that."

"Why not? We are married and I would be over the moon to start a family straight away."

"You are nuts. Did you hit your head somewhere recently. You are not making any sense," she said with a disbelieving smirk. They heard someone coming up the path behind them and turned to see who was approaching.

"Oh, there you two are. I have been looking everywhere for you, Chloe."

It was Kait striding towards them.

"Oh, sorry, we were just having a quiet moment. It has been a hectic time."

"Well, it is about to get even more hectic for you. Chrissie is ready for you, and believe me she has some serious French attitude this morning I wouldn't upset her if I was you."

"What has she got her knickers in a knot about?" said Chloe.

"She is just freaking out a bit."

"Well, off you go. Kait do me a favour and pour her champagne and it sounds like Chrissie needs one, too."

"I already have the bottle opened and if you don't hurry up, Danni will have drunk it all. She is getting her hair done now."

"Sounds like fun. Bye, Jack, I love you!" She pecked him on the cheek. "See you later."

"I can't wait."

She let go of his hand and turned to Kait. "I need that drink. I hope Danni has left us some."

"She has been keeping us entertained all morning. She is a fair dinkum dag, isn't she? So much fun, you must have had a ball with her on that cruise."

"Yea, she is crazy. I wish she lived closer. She reminded me a lot of you."

"We are getting on like a house on fire."

"Is Mum there?" she asked, just realising she had not seen her all morning.

"Yes, she just got back from the market and getting her hair done. She looks beautiful as usual."

"She has a beautiful dress to wear today."

"She showed me but she would look good in anything."

It was all systems go from then on. A few wines later and Chloe had settled down and started to enjoy the time with the girls. They had her looking like the most beautiful bride. Her makeup was natural and her hair was left out with soft flowing curls and flowers weaved through. A small tiara added the finishing touch.

The gown was an ivory straight lace with matching ballet slippers. Her bouquet was small with the French national flower, the lily,surrounded with a mass of peonies and white rose buds.

Everyone left to take their seats and left Kait, Chloe, Chrissie, and little Sophia alone.

"Here, don't forget this," said Kait quietly as she handed her the MacLean tartan ribbon.

"I have been looking everywhere for this. I thought I lost it. Where did you find it?"

"I took home your bouquet after the wedding, remember?" she whispered.

"Oh, Kait, I can't thank you enough. I think I am going to cry," she said, dabbing at her eyes.

"Well, please don't do that. Ava will be after you if you make that make up run. Come on, let me help you with the ribbon." She tied it around the bouquet and gave her a warm smile. "Are you ready for your fake wedding,Mademoiselle?"

"Ssh. Someone will hear you," she said, looking around but Chrissie had walked ahead with Sophia. "Yes, I am ready. Let's get this over and done with, so I can relax."

She gave Chloe a hug, and they walked down the stairs of the chateau where her father was waiting at the bottom.

"My God, you look like your mother today," said Robert.

"Thanks,Dad,you look so good in a suit. I am sooo nervous! You will feel me shaking all the way down the aisle, with all those people staring at me."

"Well, that is what I am here for. I am your pillar of strength today. Just lean on me. You will be fine and you have a wonderful strong Scotsman waiting for you at the other end," he said, looking deep into her eyes.

"My highlander," Chloe smiled.

"See? That made you smile. Let's go find him."

He walked her to the start of the little pathway where Kait, Chrissie, and Sophia were waiting. She remembered Jack telling her that he had picked a song for her to walk down the aisle to and was expecting the Scottish highland wedding song. The music began and Chloe instantly recognised the tune. She smiled at Jack as a tear sprung to her eye. It was "Sailing." She knew how much the song had meant to him, and was humbled that he had shared it with her today, their day, their song now, forever.

Kait helped Sophia throw rose petals as they walked towards Jack.

He was standing tall, watching, looking like the grandest highlander wearing his father's kilt with great pride. Pat and Jimmy stood beside him, also wearing their clan kilts. He spotted Chloe walking towards him and his eyes locked with hers. They both smiled as she walked towards him. Kait and Sophia moved to the side as they reached the front and Rob handed his daughter's hand to Jack.

"The hand of my daughter, I give to you," he said proudly.

"I will cherish it forever."

Tears were welling in both their eyes but they could not stop smiling as their eyes locked together.

"I did not realise you could be any more beautiful," Jack whispered with a smile and they turned to face the celebrant.

"Jack and Chloe have asked me to keep this simple but personal. You have all been invited to join us here today as you are the small group of family and friends that mean the world to these two wonderful people. I have no doubt in my mind that the love between these two people is strong and it will be a bond that will never be broken."

The ceremony started as they stared at the celebrant and Jack held her hand tight all the way through.

"I now ask you both to face one another while you take your vows. Jack, do you take Chloe to be your wife?"

"I do," he said as he looked deep into her eyes.

"Chloe, do you take Jack to be your husband?"

"I do." It was only just audible and Jack wondered if she was holding back tears or nerves.

"They have something that they would like to say to each other today," she said to the congregation and then turned to Jack.

"Jack, would you like to go first?"

He nodded and cleared his throat. "Mo leannan. As I stand here today, I could not be prouder to be taking you as my wife. I want everyone here today to hear how much I adore you, from today forward I will make sure that you are protected, safe, and loved every single day of your life. I will cherish every day we have together to be playmates, lovers, and hopefully one day, parents. You have made me the happiest man in the world and now it is my promise that I will make you the happiest girl in the world,every day, until my eyes close on the last day I am on this earth."

Chloe stood staring at him, with tears rolling down her face.

"Chloe," said the celebrant. She wiped her tears and cleared her throat before she began as he stared deeply into her eyes.

"Jack, my life began when I met you. You made me come alive inside and out. You are my best friend, my security blanket, and my strength. Today, I make my promise to you, to never run away again." She chuckled as he smiled with a tear dropping from his eye. "I am here to cherish you, and be beside you, through every event that our life takes us. I have lost you twice and now I know as we stand here today we will never be apart ever again. Without you I am not complete. You are my everything."

They were like statues staring at each other.

"It is now time to exchange the rings."

Pat came forward and gave Jack the ring. He turned to Chloe and took her hand.

"Chloe, please accept my ring and as I place it on your finger, I hope it reminds you of my unconditional love for you."

Sophia gave Chloe the ring.

"Thank you, Sophia. Jack, please accept this ring to remind you of my love as I wed you today."

"I am here today to announce to you all that Jack and Chloe are officially husband and wife. Jack, you may kiss your bride."

Jack pulled her in close, and they kissed as everyone applauded. They turned to the congregation and with the biggest smile on his face he raised her hand high in the air. "My wife," he shouted as they slowly walked down the aisle as they greeted everyone along the way.

Drinks were waiting at the end for them as a waiter handed them champagne.

"We did it, Chlo, you were amazing," he said, beaming at her.

"Yey, we did. We can now relax and enjoy," she said with a sigh of relief.

While they went for photos, everyone began to mingle and drinks were served.

"Are you okay, Mum? I saw you shed a tear or two," said Jimmy, handing her a wine.

"I am okay. It was a lovely service."

"Yes, it was nice. I know you are missing Dad today, but I am here for you if you need anything."

"Thank you, Jimmy. I would lie if I said I wasn't missing him. I miss him every day, but on days like this, it is a wee bit harder."

He gave her a squeeze as Chloe's family came over.

"Well, I guess we are all family now," said Rob.

"Oh, aye, Rob, and I couldn't ask for a nicer family to join," said Marl, looking at him. Sincerely. They had all got to know

each other so well over the last few days and a bond was form-
ing between them.

"We,also, Marl. We are thrilled to bits. They both held up
well today, didn't they?"

"I am so proud of Chloe. She was a bit of a mess earlier," said
Kait.

"She was shaking like a bloody leaf walking down the aisle,I
can tell ya that," added Rob, taking a beer from the passing
waiter.

"I still can't stop thinking of Jack's face as she walked down
the aisle. He absolutely adores her," said Kait.

"I was able to see Chloe's face as she walked down the aisle
and I can tell you the feeling is mutual. They are so lucky that
they found each other, that is for sure," said Jimmy looking at
Chelsea, and she agreed.

The piper started to play as he stood at the front of the
entrance to the marquee.

"They must be back from their photos," said Chelsea.

"Aye, the piper is welcoming us to the table," said Jimmy as
he noticed them looking around confused.

"Oh, how beautiful," said Kait.

"You don't have to tell me twice. Come on,Livy, I bet Jack has
a feast in here waiting for us," said Rob as he grabbed her hand
and took the lead and everyone followed.

As they returned from photos, they saw everyone moving
into the marquee as the piper played. Chloe stopped dead in
her tracks.

"That is so beautiful, Jack."

"Aye, it is tradition. He is asking everyone to be seated. Are
you ready for this?" He took her arm and started walking her
towards the piper.

"Wait, I wanted to tell you how much I loved that song you chose for me."

"Oh, you liked it. I am glad. You are well aware how deep that song runs with me."

"Yes, it made me cry. It was so moving."

"It was calling me to go find you, and make us complete once again. I had to fly across the seas to find you," he smiled.

"I will love those words forever. They are so beautiful."

"Aye, and look what I have done. We are both crying again." He wiped a tear from her eye.

"You are the sweetest husband. That song will forever be in my heart."

"You are forever in my heart Chloe , I knew it from the first day I saw you, I knew it was forever , I can finally call you my wife," he said, smiling.

They shared a cuddle and heard Kait calling them.

"Come on, you two, the piper is running out of songs. Oh, look at you both, and crying," she said with a sigh.

"We are coming. We were just having a wee minute together."

"Okay, no worries, I will run ahead," she yelled back and turned back towards the marquee.

"Let's do this," said Chloe with a sigh.

"Now is the fun bit. We have a beer waiting for us now," he said with a broad smile as he led her by the hand to the marquee.

# CHAPTER 23
## A FRENCH RECEPTION

"Over here, everyone. This is our table, and we are all seated together again. How lovely," said Ava as she found her name tag and John rushed to help her, pulling out her chair.

"Maggie, you are beside me,"said John, pulling out her chair also.

"How many tables have we sat around together? We are lucky," said Paddy as he settled in beside Maggie.

"And always in different countries, I might add," said Rocco, helping Danni to her chair on the opposite side of the round table.

"Oh, we have. You are right, Rocco, we have dined in so many countries together," said Ava, waving her serviette before placing it on her lap.

"Well, count your lucky stars. We are not in Australia right now, Rocco," added Danni.

"Where are you going after here, Danni?" asked Maggie.

"We are heading to the champagne region. I was pretty happy when we got the news the wedding was in France."

"Oh, you wanted to visit that region when we were on the cruise, I remember," added Catalina who were getting themselves organised beside them.

"Yes, I did. It was too far away, so we went to Monaco instead. Would anyone like to join us? We have an action-packed itinerary." Everyone knew she was not kidding. Poor Rocco's feet would not touch the ground.

"No, we are going straight home. Ava has a scan next week," said John.

"Oh, yes, you both have busy days ahead," said Cat.

"Aye, your days will be busy for the rest of your life. Ours still run us off our feet. They are dragging us all over the countryside after this," said Paddy.

"They have been a huge help doing the bar," said John.

"Aye, you kept them busy, John," said Paddy, and they all laughed.

The entrée arrived at the table.

"Well, you can see Jack had a hand in this. It looks like a main," Danni said, shocked.

"Oh, Danni, you are in trouble. Jack is not here to finish your meal," said Rocco.

"It's only French onion soup, Danni" said John.

"Yes, but look at the size and a bread roll," she said with wide eyes."Bread is very filling."

"Would you like to swap for the quiche?" asked Ava.

"Thanks, Ava, do you mind?"

"No, I love soup."

"Would anyone else like to swap," asked Maggie, holding up her quiche.

Plates started swapping around the table till everyone was happy. The main followed soon after with a coq au vin and beef burgundy and both were delicious.

"Look at Chloe and Jack. They are on cloud nine," said Ava.

"And both their families are so lovely. That Kait is a whole lot of fun," added Danni.

"So lovely to meet them. And we were all there to witness their romance, right from the start," added Cat.

"It makes you feel a bit special, doesn't it" said Ava.

"We will have to make our catch-up in Florida next year now that Ava and John will have a baby," said Rocco.

"You and Danni will have to have one next so you can keep it in America," said John.

"No babies for us, please, I could not think of anything worse," said Danni.

"Paddy and I will be too old to travel too far, so I bid for Scotland."

"Aye, you might have a point there my love."

"Well, wherever it is, I don't care as long as it happens, and we can do this again," said Danni.

"Seriously, Ava and I have spoken about this, and we would love to host it next year."

"But you will be busy with a baby," said Danni, horrified.

"No, we would love to have you. It would make us so happy if you all came. We have plenty of room, plus there is a motel at the end of our street within walking distance if anyone would prefer to stay there."

"Oh, I think Danni and I will book a hotel room. She needs a lot of room for her wardrobe and shoes," teased Rocco.

"Well, excuse me,Mr. Fancy Pants! You run a very close second with all your linen suits," replied Danni, holding her champagne glass up elegantly to the side. "His wardrobe is just as big as mine."

Everyone laughed as they knew it would be true. Both had a love for fashion and always had the best of the best. And never wore the same thing more than once.

"Cat and I will come. We have always wanted to visit America."

"Maggie and I also. I hope Jack and Chloe will be able to make it all the way from Australia."

"They will be there. They are still young enough to do the long miles," added Maggie.

"Then it is all set. Florida it is!" said Danni and everyone raised their glasses in reply.

Chloe watched the gang at their table as she sat at her table with the wedding party. They all looked so lovely. There was Ava looking sweet in a soft pink A line three-fourths-length dress with ruffled skirt and Danni in an emerald green one-shoulder wrap dress in silk with matching silk heels. Catalina in an orange and green short cocktail dress with jewelled neckline and fascinator. Even Maggie wore a beautiful floral maxi dress. They had all dressed up for them.

She smiled as they were all laughing hysterically, probably at something John said or did. She cast an eye around the table; Danni was sipping on her champagne, Rocco sitting, back legs crossed as he always did, John and Paddy keeping the whole table entertained with their stories, and everyone else smiling along happily.

She remembered the night she met them all, and the wonderful times they shared. That cruise had changed her life in so many ways, making lifelong friends, and meeting a wonderful man she had just married. What if she had never taken it or disembarked in Marseille like she had planned. Where would she be now?

"Are you okay? You seem a little lost," said Jack, turning back to her after a conversation with Pat.

"Oh, sorry, I was looking at the gang over there. They are certainly having fun. It is nice to see."

"They would have fun anywhere. You don't need to worry about them. We are about to start the toasts."

"Okay, great, I can't wait to join everyone for some fun. It's a bit stiff, sitting here with everyone staring at us." He tapped her on the leg. "Drink up,Princess, let's enjoy our party."

# CHAPTER 24

## THE TOASTS

Rob was the first one to be dragged up for the toasts. He had a long swig of his beer before taking his place with the microphone.

"Thank you, everyone! I would just like to thank you all for coming. Everyone has travelled a long way to be here for Jack and Chloe's big day and it shows how much these two people mean to you all. Firstly, I would just like to take a moment to tell my daughter how much she means to me. I am sure that she already knows, but today as I pass her hand to another man to hold, I want to be assured that she knows my hand is always here to hold still, if she ever needs it."

"Thank you,Dad. I love you." She smiled sweetly at him. He had made her proud today, holding onto her so tight as they walked the aisle.

"And speaking of the man that I have given my daughter to, I want to tell you all how grateful I am that Jack came along and entered our life. I have had the honour of meeting a very wise lady who my wife and I have become very close with over the last few days, Marlene MacLean. She has informed me that I should have no problem handing my daughter over to Jack because she knows how much he adores her. When I asked her how she knew this, she simply said, because he looks at her with the same eyes his father looked at me. And today, I saw that look myself as he watched her walk down the aisle with me. So with that, I welcome you, Jack, to our family." Everyone applauded loudly before he could continue.

"I have to admit, I was a bit concerned when Chloe announced she had met a good-looking young Scotsman on the cruise to travel with. I think I said to Livy, 'Livy,there is trouble brewing. Why couldn't she find a girl to travel with? 'But it seems they hit it off and I couldn't be happier with her choice, not only did we get a wonderful son-in-law but joined a family that we love. I think you can all see what Livy and I can see, and that is these two who stood before us today are besotted by each other and as a father, the only advice that I can give is that with that kind of love, there is no cure but marriage, and we wish them a long and happy marriage ahead."

Jack stood after the toast as Rob handed him the microphone. Chloe could see he was nervous and gave him a wink of encouragement.

"Well, I just wanted to say thank you for the hand of your daughter. As I have said, I will cherish it forever. I have given you my word on that. I have found not only the most beautiful girl to marry but the most beautiful family as well. I also have to give special thanks to Kait for pushing her onto that plane because if she didn't, none of us would be here today. And I can tell you that if it was Kait's cards that got us together, well, I am a fan forever." He stopped to take a long swig of his beer as he gave Kait a wink.

"I want to thank everyone for travelling here today. I know it is a long way and both Chloe and I appreciate it very much. Bob, I know you were not a fan of travelling and we are so happy you did it for us. And now I move onto the cruise where Chloe and I fell in love with each other, even though our dear friend Paddy over there thinks he matched us together, I think he already knew a flame was burning brightly. I remember when I first saw her sitting there all alone in the bar in Barcelona like a frightened little kitten, I wanted to put her under my arm and never let her go. Lucky for me, she gave me the opportunity to do just that. I am the happiest man in the world right now. thank you for loving me, Chloe, because I absolutely adore you.

He walked over to her and gave her a kiss as everyone applauded. Rob was calling out for Pat, but he was nowhere to be seen. Jimmy stood up and took the floor.

"I don't know where the best man has disappeared to,no one can find him, so I will jump in here first and say a few words." Everyone clapped, and he had one last look around for Pat. "Well, I must admit, when Jack told me he was following a girl to Australia, I told him he was mad. But it wasn't until he brought her home that I realised the special bond that they had together and that he had found the girl he would happily spend the rest of his life with. When they came to visit last year, I was lying in my bed one night and as I lay there listening to the muffled sounds of laughter coming from Jack's room I knew he had found something special. Then when I went to Australia, it just confirmed it. Welcome to the family, Chlo!" Everyone charged their glasses. "And just before I sit down, I would like to raise a toast to a very special person that is missed a great deal tonight. Someone who would have been very proud today. Someone who would have loved welcoming you to our family, Chloe. He would have loved you. And so I raise a toast in his honour, my father, Mr. James MacLean."

Everyone raised their glasses, and he watched as his mother wiped her eyes.

"Oh, wait, here comes Pat now." He handed the microphone to him and went to check on his mum.

"Sorry, sorry, I got a wee bit lost. This place is huge. I am a bit nervous tonight and had to do a nervous one." Everyone laughed as he took a large gulp of his beer. "I am honoured to be here by Jack's side today as his best man. It has been an emotional day. I must say I have spotted so many having a wee cry. As a matter of fact, I just passed the cake on the way back and even it is in tiers." Everyone laughed. "No, I must get serious. Please be gentle with me today, I am extremely hung over and it happens to be the fault of each and every one of you. I hope you are feeling the same."

"Aye, and we will all feel the same tomorrow I expect," yelled out Paddy.

"I have been lucky enough to have had Jack by my side most of his life. I have a book of firsts that I have shared with him, throughout our lives together. I was there when we started kindergarten and I had to pass him my snotty tissue, after I blew my nose, of course, as he cried while our mums left for the first time. I was there as we played our first game of football together, and he got winded and I broke my arm, and the first time we went to see the Celtic football club and got drunk together. And now that I think about it, we shared our first hangover together as well. Then there was the first time we learned to sail together, and he fell out of the boat and nearly drowned, then the first day we walked down the wharf with our lunchboxes in hand to start our work on the trawlers. I guess I can say I was there for most of the firsts of his life and he in mine, and therefore I was there to witness the first time a girl made him cry. The day he cried like a wee baby, at the pub night after night, because he missed Chloe so bad, he thought his heart had broken, and I think it did. Well, now I didn't know our beautiful Chloe back then or what they had shared and so I told him to get over her and bought him a pint. But I am so glad he didn't listen to me. You see, there is a new book of firsts for him to write and it is not with me anymore, although I am still writing mine. As today I wrote a few more chapters to our incredible book of mateship as I write about the first time I took an overseas holiday and the first time I became a best man. Chloe, it is your turn to start your book of firsts and I know you already have. The first kiss, the first anniversary, and I am sure many, many more are to come and I can tell you that you have the most incredible person to share those firsts with. I give you my best friend, Jack, he is the most wonderful, loyal, strong person to have by your side, and you deserve him, together you make the most beautiful couple. I will be forever be in the wing, sharing every minute with you both. I raise a toast to the grandest Scot I know. Jack MacLean!"

Chloe was wiping a tear as he put down the microphone and walked towards her. He bent down and gave her a kiss on the cheek. "I will share him with you," she whispered and he smiled as he walked back to his seat.

With the speeches done and dusted, they cut the cake and the music started. Jack walked over to Chloe and held out his hand. "I need to dance with my wife." She took it smiling and they walked to the dancefloor. Keith Urban's song, "Making memories of us," played loudly as they swayed in tune with the beat. It was the most beautiful song and the words said everything. It was Jack's pick, his song for her. They were joined on the dance floor by the family and they noticed Bob had stepped in to dance with Marl. Cruz and Catalina treated everyone with a dance and chose to do the bolero. They had changed into their dance clothes and the applause was with a standing ovation. They did another dance of flamenco and everyone hit the dancefloor. Jack and Chloe started to mingle and join the crowd in having a good time. The party went on till the early hours of the morning and everyone disappeared to bed anytime they were ready.

# CHAPTER 25

## THE POOL PARTY

The day after the wedding was a quieter day. They managed to tidy up by lunchtime and then sat and ate a platter of banquettes Bridgette had made them. The beer kegs started to get poured and everyone was soon back into party mode. The pool was the attraction of the day and everyone swam and relaxed on the sun lounges. Dinner was a casual barbeque and then a few quiet drinks were enjoyed afterwards.

Everyone had finally wandered off, and Jack and Chloe made their way up the stairs to bed. They got ready and as soon as they got into bed, Jack started kissing her amorously. "What are you doing? We can't make love here, everyone will hear us."

"We are married. I really don't care. Besides, everyone is way past it, they would have crashed."

Chloe lay thinking for a moment. "Alright, but not here. Get dressed."

He jumped out of bed excited and threw on shorts and a t-shirt as she did the same. She took him by the hand, and they tip-toed quietly down the stairs. They made it outside without making too much noise.

"Where are we going?" he whispered.

"Ssh! Follow me." She led him past the pool and into the garden following the garden path. They stopped at a clearing, and he lay her on the soft grass.

"Oh, this is more like it." He smiled, removing his shorts as she did the same. They did not waste any time. He wanted her straight away, and she was more than ready for him. He entered her as he watched her face in the moonlight. It was over quickly, and they lay panting on the grass.

"This was a perfect spot," he said.

"No one can hear us here. We are all alone," she whispered.

He sat up quickly,startled."That's what you think," he said, staring towards the pool. She sat up and looked in the direction he was looking.

Two silhouettes were heading for the pool. They stopped and embraced in a kiss as they watched.

"Who is that?" asked Jack.

"I don't know, I can't get a close look at them." They watched as they stripped each other naked slowly and slipped quietly into the pool.

"That's Pat," whispered Jack.

"With Angie," Chloe laughed.

"I thought they were getting a bit close today."

"Aye, I thought the same but put it down to them being the singles at the wedding, so hanging out together."

"Oh, that is so sweet."

"And we thought we got it together a bit quick."

"Angie doesn't do this sort of thing. She must like him a lot."

"Pat either. He is extremely shy."

"Well, he doesn't appear to be too shy right now," she giggled as they watched.

"Maybe it's not their first time. They stripped off together awfully quick."

"We need to get out of here. We can't stay here and watch this."

"We can't. They will see us."

"Shit! Jack, what now?"

"We can sneak behind the gites and around the other side and go in through the kitchen side."

"Okay, that will work."

They quietly threw their clothes on and started their way towards the gites. They were creeping behind them when they spotted someone walking towards them. They dived into the garden and hid.

"Who's there?"she whispered as he was peeking through the leaves.

"It is John. He saw us."

They stayed low as he peered in to take a closer look. Still, too far away to spot them in the dark,John picked up a handful of rocks and threw them towards them, one by one as they put their heads low, covering them with their hands.

"Go on, you squirrels, get out of here!"

John gave up and started to whistle as he took a pee. He had another peek towards them and a splash in the pool took his attention. He started to walk towards it when Ava called out.

"What are you doing out there, John, are you coming to bed?"

"Just chasing some squirrels away," he said and walked back inside closing the door behind him.

"Far out, Jack, are you okay?"

"I think so, I have a rose bush stuck up my arse. What about you?"

"I am okay except for a lump on my head where I got hit with a rock."

"I think the shower would have been a better idea."

"There is more flaming people roaming around out here than in the chateau."

"Quick, let's get back before anyone else comes out."

They made their way back to their room and had a sigh of relief as they closed the door.

"Let's have a wee dram before we go to bed." He started to pour the glasses and Chloe started to giggle.

"Jack, look at you, you are bleeding."His arms were covered in scratches.

"Those bloody rose bushes. I bet my arse looks the same."

"Show me." She pulled his shorts down and laughed.

"Yep,far out! Look at you!"

"It's itching and stinging."

"Here, give me the whisky. Remember the story Paddy and Maggie told us about the rose bush's. They put whisky on it."

"We have been married a day, and we have turned into Paddy and Maggie already."

"That was your dream, wasn't it, Jack?" she laughed.

"Aye, but not like this," he whined looking back, trying to see his butt.

"And wait until I see John throwing rocks at us."

"You can't say a word. We can never let him know," she said as she patted his butt with a wet whisky rag.

"And what about Angie and Pat?"

"Aye, well, that one surprised me, that is for sure."

"I think it is cute, we witnessed their first kiss."

"I think we witnessed a bit more than that, and I don't think it was the first kiss."

"I think you are right there," she said finishing dabbing his butt.

"There, let's see how that goes. It's super late. We should get some sleep. Tomorrow is another big day."

"Every day is a big day lately."

They both jumped into bed and spooned each other.

"Next time you get some wild ideas about love making, we should think it out a wee bit better."

"Like the lavender fields," she teased.

"Oh, aye, why is it always me getting hurt," he said as she giggled and it brought a warm smile to his face as he listened to her.

"Go to sleep. Everyone will hear you," he whispered and they both fell fast asleep.

# CHAPTER 26

## JEANNIE AND LIAM'S WEDDING DAY

Coffee was the order of the day onthe as everyone gathered blurry eyed at the table. John appeared from the kitchen wearing a thrilly apron and a white chef's hat and pink fluffy slippers, carrying a basket full of croissants and madeleine cakes.

"What are you doing?" asked a weary-eyed Jack, laughing.

"Well, Ava woke up this morning a little unwell, so I came down to the kitchen to get her something to make her feel better and ended up helping to bake these."

"And you stole her slippers. You are just too cute in that apron," laughed Danni.

"Lucky they are slip-on. My toes were a bit cool. It was cool early this morning," he announced, looking down at his feet.

"Bring one of those over here, you crazy wee lad," said Paddy and John walked around placing some on his plate.

Jeannie and Liam arrived; she looked tired, but very excited when they entered the room. Everyone greeted them and then she spotted John.

"What in the world are you doing? You are a wee sight for sore eyes this morning," she laughed.

"I baked the cakes this morning," he said, placing a few on their plates as they sat down.

"Thank you, all you need now is a sexy French maid's outfit and you would look right at home," teased Liam.

"Aye, he would make a great French maid," roared Paddy with laughter as they all joined in.

Jack noticed they both looked worse for wear, and jumped up to pour them a coffee. Putting them down on the table, Jeannie spotted his wounds.

"Jack, what happened to you?" she said as her forehead creased with concern.

"Oh, nothing. I just had a wrestle with a cat," he said with an unconvincing grin.

"Is that what you call Chloe?" John laughed, still handing out cakes.

"That is what happened to you, Paddy," added Rocco.

"Aye, but mine was rose bushes. Show me, Jack, come here."

The colour drained from his face as he reluctantly went over to Paddy who was putting his specs on.

"They certainly look like rose bush scars to me. Here, Maggie, what do you think?"he said as Maggie leaned over to scrutinise Jack's arm.

"Aye, it does. Are you sure it was a cat?  It looks like you have been in the garden."

"Oh, talking about creatures in the garden, there were squirrels running around last night, so beware everyone," said John, arriving back with a basket of muffins.

"Where were they, John?" asked Rocco as he took one from the basket.

"Up behind the gites, in the garden. I threw rocks at them. I was about to suss them out closer but I then heard splashing in the pool so there may have been more over there. I was going to check it out but Ava was calling out for me to come back inside."

Jack and Chloe's head spun around as he sat back down and looked straight at Pat and Angie, who were looking around sheepishly. Pat spotted Jack looking at him and quickly turned away.

"Chloe, what happened to your head?" asked Maggie.

"Oh, I must have bumped it somewhere yesterday setting up," she said as she hung her head rubbing the bump.

"It appears everyone is suffering battle scars today. Some wild parties you throw," laughed Rocco, sitting back crossing his legs.

"Hang on, I know what is going on here," said Danni with a mischievous smile waving her coffee spoon in the air. "These two, here are your squirrels, John," she said, pointing the spoon to Jack and Chloe.

"What do you mean?" asked John with a confused stare.

"Well, look at them. Jack looks like he has been sitting in a rose bush and Chloe like she has been hit by a rock."

Everyone stopped eating and stared at them.

"What would they be doing in the garden late at night?" Jeannie laughed but then realised and shut up quickly.

Pat and Angie both looked uncomfortable again.

"Yea, what exactly would you both be doing in the garden late at night" asked Danni with a smirk.

Everyone was roaring with laughter.

"Okay, okay, it is not as it seems. We were hiding from two people skinny dipping in the pool."

"What skinny dipping? Who?" asked Jeannie with a grin.

"We didn't stop to find out. We were trying to sneak away without anyone seeing us and that's when John came outside and almost peed on us," he said flashing John an excited smile.

"You saw me peeing in the garden," said John with wide eyes.

"Aye, we had to back up quickly or you would have got us, and that's how I ended up in the rose bush."

The laughter around the table was loud. Danni was holding her stomach as she almost fell off her chair and even Rocco had a good chuckle. Finally, everyone started to control themselves and then Maggie yelled out.

"So who are the mystery skinny dippers?"

Everyone went quiet and looked around at each other.

"Well, it wasn't John and Ava or Jack and Chloe and it certainly wasn't us," said Maggie.

"That eliminates a few who is left," asked Danni scanning the room.

Olivia and Robert walked in at the wrong time.

"Good morning. How are you? I hope you had a lovely sleep," said Chloe, grateful that they had not heard the previous conversation.

"We had a great sleep, thank you, Chloe. We love our room. It is so lovely and quiet," said Olivia as Rob handed her a coffee.

"That's because everyone is out running around the garden at night. Were you the two mystery skinny dippers last night?" asked John, handing them a muffin as Chloe almost choked on her coffee.

"My God, John, I highly doubt my parents would be skinny dipping in the pool," said Chloe. But her father liked the idea that John thought it was them and had a chuckle as he sat down next to his wife.

"Well, you never know. We are in France, you know. All bets off in the land of love," he said, waving his hands in the air.

"Skinny dippers! Oh, Robby, our skinny dipping days are over," she laughed, waving him off.

"I can assure you all, we were tucked up in our beds. But ooh, that is interesting. Someone was enjoying themselves," said Olivia with a cheesy smile. "And you look very sweet this morning, John," she added as he handed them each a muffin.

"Well, if it wasn't us, who was it, then?" asked Rob.

"Well, I can tell you it wasn't Jeannie and me. We had an early night. We have a big day today, remember?" said Liam.

"What about Jimmy and Chelsea? They are two new love birds," said Rocco. There was an echoing, "Yeaaa" around the room as everyone yelled it out at the same time.

"Hang on. Chelsea is not here to defend herself," said Jimmy. "Plus she is already up before anyone and gone to the flower market."

Everyone agreed that they could cross them off the list.

"Danni seemed to work out the scenario awfully quick. My money is on Danni and Rocco," said John.

"Yes, I will put money on them also," added Paddy.

"Well, I guess we will have to wait to see if there is a repeat tonight," said Danni, not giving a clear yes or no. Looking at Rocco and he smiled.

"Well, whoever it was, good on them. Wish it was me. Where is your mum, Jack?" added Rob.

"Oh she left early this morning with Chelsea and Bridgette. They were going to the market to pick up the flowers."

"We all have our set jobs again this morning," said Rob, sitting down with a plate of cakes.

"Yes, we will be excellent at this by the end," said Paddy.

"Thank you to everyone for helping out. You have all been marvellous," said Jeannie.

Bob walked in and Chloe jumped up to get him a coffee as he took a seat next to Olivia.

Chloe set the coffee down in front of him and John walked over,putting a chocolate croissant and a muffin on his plate.

"What in the hell are you doing this morning?" he asked with a huge grin.

"Don't worry about me. You better eat up. You will need all your energy for tonight's dancing, Mr. Travolta. You almost out-did me on the dance floor," he chuckled and everyone joined in the laughter.

"Yes, thanks for looking after Mum. She hasn't stopped talking about it, she loves dancing," said Jimmy.

"Well, I can tell you it wasn't a chore. She is a real trooper. We have had a great time."

"I haven't seen her laugh like that in a long time," said Jeannie. "It's really nice to see her happy again."

"Well, I had a bloody good time also. Your mum has made the journey well worth it, I can tell you that for nothing," he smiled as he stirred his coffee.

"Right talking about jobs, I have to go set up the hairdress-ing room," said Chrissie as she threw her napkin on her empty plate and pushed her chair back to stand up.

"Is Ava okay to do the make up?" asked Jeannie, concerned.

"Yea, she will be fine. I took her a cup of tea and a madeleine cake before, and she said she was feeling better. It's just been a hectic few days and needed a rest," said John.

"Well, if she isn't feeling up to it, I can do the makeup also," added Chrissie.

"She will be there. She has been looking forward to it," he reassured her.

Everyone finished their breakfast and went on to carry out their chores. Bridgette and Marl arrived back from the markets with Chelsea with an abundance of flowers and the girls all set up at the long outdoor table, putting together bouquets and vases of flowers. The men all helped with the carrying of alcohol to the bar and a general tidy up. The inside of the marquee was completed and just waiting for the flowers.

Jack spotted Pat on his own securing the kiddies tent that had sagged. Perfect, he thought as he walked over to him.

"Hey, Jack, so I hear you were the squirrel last night."

"Aye, and I happen to know you were the squirrels splashing in the pool."

"You saw us?"His smile drained from his face.

"Aye, we did, but we didn't want to blow your cover."

"Thanks. I am not sure how Angie would cope with that. How funny Danni and Rocco are getting the blame," he laughed.

"I wouldn't worry about that, they can handle it. In fact, I think Danni actually loves it, not too sure about Rocco though."

"Yea, Rocco seems a bit reserved."

"So did we witness the first kiss?"

"No, we have been together since the first night. I just fell for her instantly, and lucky for me, she feels the same way."

"Well, I am very happy for you, Pat," he said as he patted him on the back. "Wow,this is huge," he said as he realised the whole situation. He couldn't remember a time when Pat hooked up with a girl so quickly.

"Yea, it is, she is coming back to Fraserburgh with me after this for a few weeks. I know now how you felt when you met Chloe."

"She is? Wow! Well, I can tell you the logistical headaches are well worth it, my friend."

"I can see that, thanks for keeping it under your hat."

"Am I allowed to tell Chloe? She is going to be so excited."

"Yea, sure, I know Angie will fill her in when she gets a chance."

"She was more than happy when she realised it was you with Angie."

"She was. Oh I am happy to hear that."

"I better go. There is still a lot to do."

"Okay, but hey wait! Exactly what were you and Chloe doing in the garden?" He smiled wickedly.

"Same thing as you, my friend, only on land," he smirked as he walked away. Looking back, they were both chuckling.

Jack could not wait to tell Chloe. He was so happy for his old friend and wished him all the best. He did not latch onto girls all that often even though many hung around.

After lunch, Jeannie and her bridesmaid headed upstairs to get their hair and makeup done while everyone else went back to their rooms for a nap before getting ready. It was a late afternoon wedding so there was no rush. Chloe woke and opened a wary eye, looking over at Jack.

"You are awake."

"Aye, I couldn't sleep; I have a few things on my mind." Chloe sat up on one elbow with a curious gaze.

"Like what? Are you OK?"

He smiled gently at her. "Just how Jeannie is getting married today, my baby sister, and also thinking about how dad would have loved all of this. I can see him now, drinking beers with your dad, and joking around. He would have got on well with your dad. I wish he was here to see it all."

"Yea, I bet your mum is feeling it also," she said as she lay back down and they gazed at the ceiling.

"Aye, she is. But I had a quiet chat with her the other night and she seems a lot brighter now that Jimmy and Chelsea are getting married. She believes Dad sent Chelsea to Jimmy, to show her that after a tragedy, good things happen, and life goes on. I really think this is the turnaround for her. I think she is going to be okay."

"That is such wonderful news, Jack. She has been through a lot. I can now say I know how she would have felt, but I was lucky enough to get you back. She didn't and is now lonely. I don't want to even imagine what that must be like, but I am sure it's hell."

"She will find someone to make her happy again one day, I am sure."

"Well, Bob has been looking after her. They were so funny at the wedding. I didn't know Bob could dance like that." She chuckled.

"They are having a great time, that is for sure." He smiled at her and they lay quiet in their own thoughts for a while.

"I was thinking earlier. I was sure Jimmy and Chelsea would get the blame for skinny dipping in the pool,but it was Danni and Rocco, that is so funny," said Chloe with a chuckle.

"Oh, glad you mentioned that. Before you say anything to Angie, just be careful. I am not sure how she feels, but Pat is really hooked on her."

"He is. You spoke to him?" she said, jumping up on one arm to look at him.

"Aye, this morning he was working on the kiddies tent alone, so I went and had a chat. She is going home to Scotland with him for a few weeks after this."

"She is? Far out. So then it's not just a holiday fling, like we thought."

"Nope, I think they are going down the same path that we did."

"Wow, that's incredible! That is so exciting, Jack! Both our best friends are hooking up."

"Hooked up! It's been on since the first night."

"Wow, that is so not like Angie."

"You wild Aussie women leading us poor Scots astray," he teased.

"Oh, you needn't talk! You swept me off my feet on the first day also."

"Aye, but I didn't take you straight to bed, did I?"

"No, but you could have," she smirked, starting to caress him.

"None of that now. Look at the time. And remember the mess you got us into last time."

"I think it was you who started it last time," she laughed, leaning over him to see the clock.

"Shit, Jack, we need to get ready. We will be late."

"Aye, I have been tellin ya this."

She frantically made her way to the shower, and he followed her in after a few minutes. She stood in front of the mirror putting on her earrings. She loved the dress she had selected. It was comfortable and the aqua looked stunning on her.

"Let me take a look at you." Jack stood back and looked her over. "You are ravishing as always."

"Thank you! So are you. I really love you in a kilt."

"Well, don't get used to it. After this, the next time will be at our baby's wedding or Jimmy's, whatever comes first," he teased, and she laughed.

"Well, going by what I have witnessed over the last few days, it will be Jimmy and Chelsea next," she said.

They were downstairs in plenty of time and everyone started to mingle. Jack spotted Jimmy and Chelsea and made his way towards them.

"How is everyone? Are you ready to do it all again?"

"Yes. Mum is a bit nervous. She is walking Jeannie down the aisle," said Jimmy.

"That is lovely. Very special. Come on, they are calling us," said Jack as he rushed to grab Chloe along the way.

Everyone was exactly where they should be as the music started. The traditional highland wedding song rang out loudly, complemented perfectly by Paddy and Maggie's son the piper. It filled the air and everyone turned. The wedding party started down the aisle. Jack wiped a tear as Jeannie and his mum passed by, Jeannie blowing him a kiss. Chloe noticed Jeannie had two ribbons in her bouquet, one she recognised as the MacLean tartan and the other matched Liam's kilt. She was relieved that Kait had found hers for her. Liam was standing, looking grand in his McNamara clan kilt, unable to take his eyes off Jeannie. As they arrived. Marl handed Jeannie's hand to Liam. "On behalf of my dearly beloved husband James," she softly said and sat down beside Jimmy as he patted her on the hand.

The wedding ceremony was moving and as they turned to the congregation the pipes were played again and there were smiles and clapping all around as they made their way back down the aisle. Everyone followed and the waiters were circling with trays full of champagne and whisky. Jack took Chloe by the hand and went straight over to Jeannie, throwing his arms around her.

"You made a fine bride today, Jeannie," he said, standing tall, turning to Liam. "You have a fine lassie here. Take care of her or I will be knocking on your door."

"You have no problem there. I love this one to death, but I need a drink before they drag me off to photos," he said, looking anxious for a waiter.

"Aye, I have something for you."

He reached into his pocket and pulled out a flask and handed it to him. Liam took it and read the engraving, "To my brother-in-law, may we always share a wee dram together, Jack."

"You are the best brother-in-law and it is full."

"Aye, I learned the other day when they dragged me off, you would need it to be filled."

"Come on, Liam and Jeannie, photo time," said a photographer clapping his hands.

"Best present ever," said Liam, taking a swig as he was dragged off.

"Not a bad drop, either," he yelled back.

"That was very thoughtful," said Chloe.

"Aye, I was tortured I would have killed for a wee drop,so I made sure it was full for him, come on let's go find the gang."

The party went well into the night once again and everyone was weary eyed at the breakfast table the next day. They were all departing that day and going their separate ways. Angie had announced she was going to Scotland with Pat,which meant Bob had lost his travel companion home. Kait and Johnny invited him to join them, visiting his family in Italy and he had accepted until Marl asked him to come and stay in Scotland. He had always wanted to visit the highlands and she promised to take him. They had been the best of friends the last few days and everyone was excited for them. Danni and Rocco were the only ones at the table as Jack and Chloe entered the room.

"Morning! How are you both?" said Chloe as Jack went and poured them coffee.

"We are alive, just," laughed Rocco.

"It was a huge few days, that is for sure," added Jack as he put the coffee cups on the table.

"We are leaving straight after breakfast. We have a long drive to the champagne region,"explained Rocco, stirring his coffee.

"I am ready to do it all again. I am so excited," said Danni.

"Danni and the Champagne region, you are a brave man Rocco."

"Yes and I said to Danni, if you want to do it, do it now, I am not coming all the way back to France again just for a glass of bubbly."

"Yes, you would. You would do it for me," she winked at Chloe and Rocco sighed as they laughed. They all knew he would.

"Morning all. Everyone seems bright and chirpy," said Catalina as she and Cruz entered the room.

"Fresh as a daisy. I am keen to kick on again," added Danni beaming.

"Well, we don't feel that way, I can tell you," said Cruz.

"That was a huge few days," sighed Catalina.

"Yes, we were all just saying that. Do you have a flight today?" asked Chloe as she pulled a chocolate croissant apart.

"Yes, we have an early afternoon flight," she said, watching Chloe's croissant.

"I am going to get one of those. The diet is already ruined," she said as she started to get up.

"Get two," screeched Cruz with a hoarse voice.

"When are your parents leaving, Chloe? They have a long way to go home," asked Danni.

"Mum and Dad are only going to Montpelier today. They have a cruise from Barcelona in a few days ,so they are hanging around to help us tidy up a bit. Kait and Johnny are heading to Johnny's family in Italy."

"I almost had Kait convinced to come with us," laughed Danni. "But Johnny wasn't so keen."

"There is not too much cleaning up left to do. We did a lot last night," said Jimmy as he and Chelsea arrived at the table."You won't see Paddy or John any time soon. They were still drinking when I went to bed after we all finished the clean-up," he laughed.

"That is the only reason they were helping to clean up," laughed Rocco.

"Hey, I heard that," said John as he walked in with Ava.

"See? I can keep going just as good as any Scot. I can't see Paddy at the table yet," he said as he headed for coffee.

"Well, thank you all very much," said Jack. "It's greatly appreciated."

"And thanks for all coming such a long way," added Chloe.

"Who wants one last French croissant before they leave?" asked John as he walked around with the tray.

"No, thank you, not for me," said Danni.

"I will have hers," yelled Jack and everyone laughed.

The goodbyes started as Danni and Rocco packed their car and everyone was sad to see them leave. They were all out the front of the chateau near the fountain waving as the car started to leave.

"Have a wild honeymoon. We will see you in Florida next year," said Danni, waving frantically as they drove out of the driveway.

As the car disappeared out of sight, everyone turned to walk back inside, heading to their rooms to pack.

"I am so sad to see them go," said Chloe as they walked the stairs to their room.

"We will see them again soon. We have Florida next and then Danni will have us all flying somewhere, don't you worry," he said, putting a comforting arm around her shoulder. She smiled knowing he was right.

# CHAPTER 27

# THE HONEYMOON CAPRI

After a morning filled with trains planes and automobiles, they had finally arrived at the stunning island of Capri. Sun, sun, sun, and the glorious views of the Tyrrhenian Sea sprawled out in front of them as they gazed out from the balcony of their top-floor apartment. It had been a week-long party full of emotions and now they were looking forward to a week of relaxation.

"Welcome to our honeymoon! Isn't this a fantastic start?" said Jack.

"These views are incredible, this place is amazing, and we have our own private Jacuzzi here on the deck," said Chloe with excitement, as she wandered around the over-sized balcony, stopping to check the temperature of the water as she splashed her hand into the Jacuzzi.

"Aye, it is the top floor penthouse, a wee pampering for my beautiful wife. I can imagine you relaxing in there with a wine in your hand," he said beaming at her. He had wanted to impress her and was pleased he did. He had spent weeks looking at accommodation online wanting to find the perfect spot for her to relax and unwind after a hectic week. Understanding her anxieties, he was well aware she would appreciate the serenity.

"You are amazing! I need this so much, I want to jump in now."

"Well, don't let me stop you. I will pour us a drink if you like."

"Maybe later. If I jump in now, I will never want to get out. What would you like to do today?"

"Well, it's almost lunchtime. I think we should take a stroll around town and find a nice quiet Taverna to have a wee drink and a bite to eat."

"Sounds wonderful. I will change into something cooler. It is such a warm day."

"We can make use of this when we get back," said Jack as he splashed around in the Jacuzzi with his hand. "The perfect temperature."

"Okay, let's do this. I want to get back here," she said, almost skipping into the bedroom.

Chloe changed into a white flowing button-up shirt teamed with deep blue shorts and mid-heel sandals as she grabbed her wide-brimmed straw sun hat from the table.

"I am ready."

"You seem to have found the perfect 'Capri style'. Very sexy."

"Well, thank you! You are looking sexy yourself. I love the white cheesecloth shirt. It looks amazing on you."

"Well, I don't know about sexy, but it is light and breezy. You see, for me, it's all about staying cool. The heat is killing me."

"I thought you would be a bit adjusted after being in Australia."

"Well, if I am, I would have hated to think how I would be if I wasn't."

"Come on let's go find somewhere to have a cool drink."

Strolling around the town for a while they shopped before stopping at a taverna, which had breathtaking views of the port of Marina Grande. Ushered by a waiter, they were seated at a table where they spied the colourful bobbing boats tied to the marina. Water was placed on the table, which they appreciated after walking in the heat, while they looked over the menu.

"What takes your fancy, Jack?" she said as she lifted her sunglasses to the top of her head to read the menu.

"Oh, it all sounds wonderful. Let's graze while we have a few drinks. Seafood seems to be the speciality here," he said with a knitted brow, giving the menu his total attention.

"Let's start with a spritz, for old times' sake," he suggested.

"Why not? And I am sure you would enjoy a platter of Mediterranean sushi to share, for starters," she said with a smirk.

"Sounds like a great start to me."

The waiter approached and took their order and was back quickly with their cocktails.

"Ciao,bella, my name is Derek and I will be serving you today. When you have finished your sushi please call me over and I will help you with your next course."

"Thank you, Derek. What do you recommend?"

"Well,Madam, if I was ordering I would make sure I try the zucchini flower and the curry flavoured tempura prawns. They are a speciality here and are delicious."

"Thank you, Derek. I think we will try both of those," said Chloe as she looked over at Jack for approval.

"Aye, of course, I will eat anything," he smiled.

They happily grazed for hours as they sipped on their drinks, unable to take their eyes off the views of the Marina.

"Have you had enough to eat?" asked Chloe.

"You are keen to slide into that Jacuzzi, aren't you?"

"Yes, I am busting to spend the afternoon cooling off in that Jacuzzi."

They wandered home and changed into their swimmers and Chloe sipped into the Jacuzzi, while Jack returned with two beers. Making an online request, he had specially asked for the fridge to be stocked with beer, wanting total relaxation, not needing to go out for anything.

"Well, you didn't muck around. You are in, already," he chuckled as he handed her the beer.

"Thank you. Come and join me. This is heaven."He jumped in beside her.

"Now, this is a holiday."

"Cheers to the best husband in the world!"

"And to my incredibly beautiful wife," he added.

"You spoil me. Thank you for everything. This is all so incredible."

"Prego,bella," he said in his best Italian accent.

Placing her beer on the table beside the pool, she closed her eyes and lay back with her head on the back of the tub. He studied her face as he noted the stress leaving her. Staring out over the view, he thought about a tour he wanted to take but was worried as it may be too stressful for her. He had been waiting for the perfect opportunity to bring it up.

"So what have you got planned for tomorrow?" she said with one eye open. This was his chance. He took a deep breath before beginning his sale pitch.

"I am glad you brought that up. There is something I wanted to run past you."

Opening both eyes, she sat up."Okay, I am all ears," she reached for her beer.

"Well, there is something I really want to do, but I am worried it might be too much for you."

"Okay, sounds interesting, go on," she said with a slow curious tone.

"Have you heard of the Blue Grotto?"

"Yes, of course! The sea cave. It is supposed to be incredibly beautiful."

"Yes, I would love to see it. Would you like to go?" He held his breath as he waited for her answer.

"Yea, of course I would love to."

He turned to her with wide eyes, unable to believe what he heard. "Really?" he shrieked loudly;surely, she had misunderstood what he had asked.

"Yes, for sure. Why wouldn't I? You have mentioned this before."

"Are you aware that you have to squeeze through an opening, which is only about a meter high and then you are inside a cave," he said with one eye squinted. Surely, they were not talking about the same thing here. Squeezing inside a small cave was something she would normally run a mile from. Studying her face, he knew she was thinking about it as she sipped on her beer.

"The tour is not just the cave, Chloe. First, you go for a cruise around the island, and I am happy to do the cave on my own if you don't want to," he added with a hopeful look.

"I want to do the cave with you, Jack," she said taking a sip on her beer.

"You do?"

"Yea, of course. You are so good to me. I will be strong and do this for you."

"You are the best! Thank you! But if you change your mind on the day, I am happy to go alone."

"Okay, but I am going to do this for you."

"I have tentatively booked, but I will call and confirm if you are sure."

"Yes, I am sure."

He jumped out of the pool with so much excitement he splashed a wave of water over her.

"Oh, sorry, sorry, I didn't mean to drown you," he said with half a smirk.

"Go make your call before I change my mind," she said drying her eyes with her wet hands as he handed her a towel before drying himself off and grabbing his phone.

She listened as he rang and confirmed the booking. The idea of the cave frightened the heck out of her but if she said she did not want to go, he would miss out. She remembered when they were booking the honeymoon, it was these caves that made him want to come to Capri. Deciding to go on the tour was easy. If she needed to chicken out, she could let him go on his own and stay with the captain on the big boat. She had read all about it,knowing he would want to go.

When he returned, he had a huge smile as he leaned in and kissed her. He was bubbling with excitement.

"All done! You are going to love it! It will be just like when we cruised around the Greek islands on the cruiser with Paddy and the gang."

Jumping back in the pool he told her all about the day as she listened intently. His eyes darting wildly as he told the story full of excitement.

Tired after a big day in the sun and still getting over the week at the chateau, they decided to have a night in. Jack went back to the same restaurant and ordered a takeaway pizza, and they sat under the stars and washed it down with a bottle of prosecco.

Another stunning day dawned, and they were excited to be going on a tour around the island by boat as well as stopping at the Blue Grotto. The boat was similar to the one Paddy had hired for them in Greece and Croatia and the thoughts of those days made Chloe wish they were all with them today. She looked around. It was a small group of ten people, most were keeping to themselves, some sparking up conversations with others. The captain welcomed them onboard and introduced himself as Luca as he gave them a rundown of the day and told them all to make themselves comfortable.

Before long they were off. Jack put his arm around her shoulder, and she instantly felt calm and secure.

The sun beat down as they relaxed on the boat, sipping limoncello and listening to the humorous locality stories of the captain who kept them entertained. Arriving at the Blue Grotto,there was an endless row of bobbing boats lined up at the floating ticket box. It did not take too long before they reached the front and the captain ordered the tickets. Jack was keeping a close eye on Chloe. He was expecting her to change her mind, but she didn't.

"Are you okay with this? I am more than happy to do this alone if you would rather wait here. They are going to put us in little wooden boats."

"Yea, I read all about the tiny entrance. I am scared but I want to do this, just hold onto me tight."

Casting a watchful eye over the captain, they watched as he helped his passengers one by one onto the boats before turning his attention to Chloe. Jack had a quiet word with him earlier, giving him the heads up, about how she was anxious doing it, and he said he would keep an eye on her and take special care.

"Ah, my last two. I have handpicked this top-notch boat for you today. He is the best driver in Capri. Frankie, I want you to look after our Chloe."

"Ah, you give me such a beautiful woman. Of course, I will take care of her," he mocked.

The captain helped them onto a little wooden rowboat, and rowed them towards the cave's entry. Jack held onto Chloe tightly. He observed her shaking as the captain told them to lay down low as he ducked and they entered the one-metre opening.

"Lean back on me, Chloe, and I will wrap my arms around you tight." They laid back just as they entered. He was well aware she was anxious doing it, but she was being brave for him. It was on his bucket list and was ecstatic she joined him for the experience.

Closing her eyes, she held onto Jack tightly. She knew they were inside the cave as darkness came and soft echoing ancient Neapolitan music filled her ears. "Open your eyes, Chloe, you can't miss this. We are in the Blue Grotto," Jack whispered. Realising it must have been extraordinary by the sounds of people *ooh*-ing and *ahh*-ing along with cameras clicking, she slowly opened her eyes. She gasped as her butterflies danced stronger in her stomach. Her heart pounded as she took deep breaths. It was the most beautiful thing she had ever seen.

"I think I have died and gone to heaven," she whispered softly. They were in a dark cave lit by a beautiful azure blue light that made it appear heaven-like. The captain rowed them around for a few minutes, and then they snuck through the opening once again and exited out into the daylight.

Rowing back, they made their way to where their larger boat waited and were greeted back on board with a prosecco.

"I did it," said Chloe excitedly.

"You sure did. I am so proud of you. You are so brave."

"I can't believe I did it. Thank you for helping me to be strong. I am so happy I did it. I can't believe how beautiful it was."

Jack watched as she drained her drink and the captain came over and refilled her glass.

"You deserve this. Well done, you did it!"

"I feel like I am floating. It was the most incredible thing that I have ever seen."

"Grazie! I am happy and humbled that you loved it. We are extremely proud of its beauty, and now you can relax and enjoy the rest of your day."

He turned and continued chatting withthe other guests. Her heart was leaping out of her chest from the adrenalin, but she was overwhelmed by the whole incredible experience.

"Phew!" She let out a deep breath with a huge smile and Jack laughed. "So proud of you," he said as he gave her a cuddle.

After a stop at the cove for a swim and a lunch of sandwiches and rolls, they sailed on to see the other grottos. First, the green, and then moving onto the white one. Both were stunning but the Blue Grotto was a definite show stopper. They sailed around in the warm Mediterranean sun with the warm breeze gently blowing their windswept hair.

"We are heading back now, but as we pass under the Faraglioni Rocks, hold your loved one tight, and share a kiss to be blessed with eternal love."

He told the story of the old Greek myth and everyone was smiling as they approached and all the couples embraced in a kiss.

Their last day in Capri had arrived and after a full day of boating, they wanted a quieter day. They were enjoying a relaxed breakfast on their balcony. Jack had booked them in for lunch at a restaurant that he was sure would impress. He was keeping the location a secret she had been busting to find out.

"This morning, I thought we would go for a walk to a lookout, and then we have our incredible lunch booked."

"Oh, that sounds wonderful. I have been looking forward to that lunch."

"All I can tell you is it is a very popular restaurant."She stared at him chewing on her toast. She wanted to push him a bit more, but she knew there was no use as he had his lips buttoned tight on this one.

They had a leisurely stroll to the lookout; it was a peaceful morning on the quieter side of the island. They arrived after around twenty minutes and looked out of the view.

"What a stunning view of the Faraglioni Rocks and the marina."

They sat on the stone and iron love-seat and leaned back, scanning the view. Jack pulled a flask and two plastic glasses out of his pocket.

"What have you got there?"

"I thought this might be a nice spot for a wee dram of whiskey with my wife."

"Did you, now?" She giggled, taking the whiskey from him. He watched as she took a sip before leaning back and sighing, looking out over the view.

"Oh, this is incredibly beautiful!" She sighed.

"Did anyone ever tell you the tale of the sirens that lived on the Faraglioni Rocks?"

"No, I don't know that one. Please tell me." She smiled as he pulled her in closer, and she snuggled in.

"Well, the sirens lived on the rocks, and when the ships would sail by, they would sing seductive songs. The sailors would be lured and almost always sail to their deaths on the rocks below the cliffs. One day, a Greek warrior was sailing towards the rocks and after hearing many a story about the sirens he asked his sailors to stuff their ears with wax and tied himself to the mast, so he could listen safely to the sirens' alluring songs. The songs made him want to go to them so much, he begged the sailors to untie him, to be free to go to them, but the sailors knew better and would not do it. He lived, thanks to the sailors but so many more did not."

"Oh, that is a tragic tale, such a sad story for such beautiful rocks."

"You liked that story?"

She nodded. "I love those rocks."

"Come on, I have a surprise for you."

They made their way to the jetty where the restaurant shuttle boat was meeting them. After a quick boat ride, they arrived.

"Oh,my goodness! Jack,look at this place. We are right here, right on the water's edge with the Faraglioni rocks."

"Yes, you can't get much closer."

"I am super impressed!"she said as she beamed with excitement.

They were ushered inside and guided to a table for two, right on the water's edge. It was a thatched roof outdoor seating area, where they were seated right at the foot of the rocks.

The table was set with a white linen cloth and blue and white plates, white serviettes, and silverware.

"This is the best view of the rocks. It feels like I could reach out and touch them."

"I thought that you would like that," he said with a smile as he opened the menu.

"Jack, that lady over there is drinking a spritz," she informed him as she peered over his shoulder.

"So she is. I will order us one."

The waiter spotted him looking and came to take their order. "Do you know what you would like?"

"Yes, can we start with two spritzes, please," said Jack, still looking at the menu.

"What was the dish that just went past with all the seafood piled on top," she asked the waiter, and he turned, smiling as he spotted the dish she was referring to.

"Ah, that is our seafood risotto, very popular."

"I will have that," said Chloe with a sparkle in her eye.

"And I will have the aubergine au parmesan and the lamb ragu," said Jack, slamming shut his menu with a smile.

"Another wonderful choice. You will enjoy both your dishes,-Sir," said the waiter with a smirk and was off.

They both scanned the view and listened to the soft music playing. It was a surreal moment as she remembered the captain's story of kissing under the rocks for eternal love and smiled. The mythical stories of sirens and creatures and the incredible hospitality of the people were making her never want to leave.

"Our last day here, it is very sad," he said. "You must have been reading my mind. I was just thinking, let's stay here forever."

"And what about Venice?"

"Well, if we did not have Venice as our next stop, I would be devastated."

"I am also very excited about Venice. I have a few wee surprises for you."

As she twirled her hair, the effervescence of excitement grew inside her as her mind drifted to Venice and all the wonderful surprises that lay ahead. Once again, he would sweep her off her feet as he always did, and she would float along in absolute delight.

# CHAPTER 28
## VENICE

At nine in the morning, the transfer arrived to take them to the airport. They had a twelve-thirty flight and arrived with ample time to checkin and board the plane. After a quick one-and-a-half-hour flight, they were touching down in Marco Polo international airport. The water taxi took them directly to the motel, which was on a back canal.

It was a charming white building featuring reddish-brown shutters and window boxes filled with red and white flowers. A wrought-iron framed balcony stood proudly in the centre of the upper floor with white columns where three Italian flags waved proudly in the soft breeze. Two red and white barber-style poles stood at the water mooring where the water taxi pulled up gently to the deck.

Chloe was mystified as she peered around in awe. A man dressed in a suit came to greet them from the hotel. He extended a hand helping her out of the boat.

"Thank you, this place is so beautiful."

"Grazie! I am happy to hear that you are impressed, Madam," he said as leaned forward to retrieve the bags the water taxi driver was handing him.

Venice was exactly the perfect place for a romantic honeymoon, full of elegance and comfort whilst surrounded by outstanding beauty. The hidden courtyards, which had so many tales to tell with all of its centuries of history, were beckoning her. The tiny bridges magically enticed you to wander along and explore every inch of this enchanting city.

Jack startled her as he walked over and put his arm around her. "Stunning, isn't it?" He said as he stared out over the canal view.

"Oh, it's breathtaking," she said dreamily.

"Come on, let's see what our room is like."

"I can't wait," she smiled as they turned and headed inside. The reception staff had everything ready, and they were in their room in no time.

Her jaw hit the ground as she entered. It was beautifully decorated in Moorish style in colours of gold and cream, with soft lighting, making an exotic scene. The huge bed was elegantly made with gold doona with two large tasselled cream pillows and two smaller gold and cream stripped cushions. The bedhead was cream and gold in a large tulip shape. Strings of rose-shaped large confetti hung from the ceiling above the bed and hundreds of red rose petals were shaped into a large love heart in the middle of the bed.

"Jack, you did this?"

"Yes, it is our honeymoon, so I asked them to make sure everything was perfect for you."

"Simply amazing," she said with a low soft voice. She walked around, looking at everything with a dreamy look in her eyes. An ice bucket stood grandly, displaying a bottle of Moet, two flutes and a box of Italian chocolates. Jack walked over and popped the cork as she wandered slowly around the room in awe. The bathroom was floor-to-ceiling marble with a spa bath in the corner, dressed with gold taps and a large display of bubble baths, shampoos, conditioners, and creams sat on the counter.

As she re-entered the main room, she noticed a window covered by a sheer curtain that appeared to be leading out to a balcony. She slowly walked over. *Oh, please be a balcony with the canal view.* As she pulled open the sheer, she gasped. It was beautiful; she opened the door and stepped outside. It was the canal view she had always dreamed of. A tear sprung to her eye as she turned to Jack, walking towards her with two flutes of Moet.

"I couldn't afford the Grand Canal, but this is my gift to you," he said, waving his arm around the room.

"Oh, Jack! It's stunning. You are too good to me." She took her flute and gave him a kiss on the lips. "Thank you! This room is breathtaking. I am in shock. It is massive."

"It's a junior suite,fit for a princess. And seeing I have one, I booked it for her, plus, the look on your face is worth every penny."

"What did I ever do to deserve you? You are too good to me."

"Well, I think that you had better ask your granny that. She sent me to you,remember?" He smiled. "But now, I would like to propose a toast to my beautiful wife. May we have many years of happiness like this to come."

"To us!" she said as he wiped a tear running down her cheek.

They clinked their glasses together as they looked deeply into each other's eyes.

As night fell, they walked along the Grand Canal before stopping at a bar that was well-known for stunning views at sunset. They found a table and Jack went to the bar for drinks. He soon returned with two aperol spritz. Chloe laughed as he handed her one.

"It's traditional."

"It certainly is. Thank you."

Later, Jack led her along the canal, stopping at a beautiful quiet Venetian restaurant. It was located right on the Grand Canal, but tucked away in a quieter corner.

"I have booked us in here for dinner. I thought that you would enjoy the quieter part of town. I hope you like it."

"You know me so well. Yes, of course, it's beautiful."

They were seated at a table right on the water's edge, just as Jack had requested. The table was beautifully set with a white table cloth, a candle, and a small vase of flowers, along with expertly placed silverware and glasses. The waiter came and placed down two menus and took their drink orders.

"Could we please have a bottle of chianti classico, if you have it?"

"Of course,Sir, excellent choice."

"Our wine. You think of everything."

He smiled as he looked over at her. She was beaming with delight just as he had hoped. The waiter arrived with the wine and poured two glasses after Jack's nod of approval.

"Prego."

"My God,Jack, you are still sweeping me off my feet. I remember the first day on the cruise and you secretly booked us a lunch, you totally blew me away."

"Well, it is my job to make sure that you are looked after, plus I have fun along the way," he teased and opened the menu. Unable to stop staring, she sipped on her wine, taking it all in.

"What do you like on the menu?" she asked, knowing full well he would have it all sorted.

"Aye, well, there is mixed seafood as an entrée, which sounds nice."

Chloe opened the menu and looked it over. "Oh and an octopus and potato salad."

"Sounds wonderful! Okay,that is the entrees sorted, what would you like as a main?"

"Oh, the frutti di mare is definitely my choice."

"Spaghetti seafood. Of course, you love that. Well, for me, it is definitely a Florentine steak."

"Of course."

"Our favourites, so I am guessing if we are going to be creatures of habit, it will be a tiramisu and a panna cotta for dessert."

"You are right. We just ordered the same meals we did last time we were in Italy," she laughed.

The waiter arrived to take their order,then they sat back and relaxed.

He watched her as she looked around in awe. It was incredibly romantic, the way the lights hit the water and lighted up the gondolas. The city of love was alive and showing off in grand style.

Lights glimmered, leading the way along the cobblestone path as they walked along after dinner and ended up at the casino. It was a grey stone three-story building that oozed old time beauty and charm. They stopped to read a plaque at the front before entering.

"This is the oldest casino in the world, dating back to the sixteenth century."

"So are you feeling lucky?"

"Yes, let's have a go."

They paid the entry fee and received a drink voucher and some chips for the slot machines. They spent a few good hours watching the roulette and playing on the machines. As they wandered around the room, the Old World charm embraced, making you feel as though you were in a movie.

"Have you had enough?" he said as they arrived back to the spot where they started.

"Yes, I have had a lovely night."

They strolled home hand in hand, chatting all the way. Arriving home, they opened the door to find their lamps were on,and the bed turned down with chocolates placed on their pillows.

"Wow! Have you ever had that done for you before?" she said,stunned.

"No, never. This place is certainly spoiling us. Let's sit out on the balcony for a wee bit."

He walked over and drew the curtains and led her out.

"I think I will have a wee dram of whiskey. What would you like to drink? There is still some Moet, if you would prefer."

"Oh, yes, that sounds lovely. Thank you."

She sat and stared out over the canal. It was like a fairy-tale. *All those years I lived in my bubble at home, never going any-where. And now, here I am sitting in a junior suite, looking out over a canal in Venice while the man of my dreams is pouring me a Moet,*she thought.

"Look at you sitting there with a wee smile on your face," he said as he handed her the wine.

"Thank you! , I was just thinking how lucky I am, that's all."

"Mmm. I thank God every day that I found you at that bar in Barcelona."

" When I look back, I still cannot believe I got on that plane alone. I remember how scared I was. I guess I got extra strength from somewhere."

"It was meant to be, that's what it was. You are always telling me about mystical spooky tales and cupid bows."

He bent over and gave her a gentle kiss but it wasn't enough and went back for more. It was a long passionate kiss that made them both start to breathe a bit heavier.

"Wait here, I will be back in a minute."

She disappeared as he started to take control of himself.

*My wife, she is my wife, I still can't believe it, that wee sexy beast is my wife,* he thought to himself once again as he had thought a million times over the past few weeks.

He heard her approach him and turned;she took his breath away.

She was in a sexy white negligee that was extremely short with a matching loose dressing gown that was blowing in the breeze as she walked over to him.

"Do you like?"

"I love! You look beautiful."

She put her phone on the buffet and pressed "play." Music started playing and she took him by the hand.

"Come and dance with me."

"Our song."

"Yes,our new song."

He pulled her in closer, and they swayed as the song serenaded them.

He was feeling her all over, and she took off her dressing gown.

She unbuttoned his shirt and gently caressed his chest and hardened nipples as he passionately kissed her. She undid his pants, and they fell to the floor. She watched as he removed them and his underwear. He stood naked as she looked him over.

"I love your body," she said dreamily.

"You do?"

"Oh, I do," she said as she gently caressed him all over. "Then I don't think you need this on anymore." She started to lift the negligee, and he helped her take it off.

It was his turn to stare.

"I love your body."

"You do?"

"Oh,aye,I do."

"Come with me."

She led him to the bedroom and handed him a lotion.

"I bought us some massage oils. I want to rub you down and feel every bit of you."

"Only if I can do the same."

"Of course."

He picked her up and laid her on the bed. "Let me go first."

She laid still as he started to massage her back and then slowly moved down each leg.

Turning her over, she smiled up at him.

"You look beautiful in the moonlight."

He continued to rub the oil all over her, gently caressing her. Her body was shimmering in the moonlight and the sight of her was making him want to take her there and then. He caressed each leg and started to massage them back up until his hand reached the top, and he gently started caressing her with his fingers between the legs.

She started to moan as he watched her.

It was all too much. He was going to explode if he didn't take her then and there.

He laid down on top of her and gently started to enter her as he watched her face in the moonlight. She began to moan and he instantly exploded.

They both lay panting, and he pulled her closer, and she rested her head on his chest.

"I didn't get to massage you," she whispered.

"Tomorrow."

"I will hold you to that."

"I hope so."

They both fell asleep easily happy and content.

Shutters and block-out curtains protected them from the blazing sun as they slept naked, sprawled out on the oversized king bed. They were visiting two of Venice's most beautiful islands later that day and as they were close by and no need to rush, a sleep-in was welcomed. Visiting quieter areas also meant Chloe would appreciate a more relaxed day.

After a lavish breakfast, their first stop was Murano, where they visited a glass factory. Afterward, they wandered around the island before stopping for gelato. Sitting on a bench seat by the waterfront, they ate their two-scoop homemade treat with a cookie on the side.

Finishing their treat, they spied a ferry and boarded it for a leisurely ride in the warm sunshine across to Burano. Photo opportunities were endless, and Jack took lots of photos as Chloe posed as they sailed towards the picture-perfect coloured houses that lined the waterfront.

They strolled along the canals, looking at all the old buildings getting a real feel of the history of the town. Three bridges took their attention as they stopped to photograph the exact spot where the three canals met. It was hard not to have a true feeling of happiness as they took in the ambiance of the lovely little town.

For lunch, they stopped at a family-run trattoria for a typical Venetian lunch. It was waterfront and specialised in seafood, with daily specials for the catch of the day. They shared platters of razor shells and scallops frito misto and finished it off with a freshly made tiramisu.

Music was playing quietly on the deck as they watched the fish swimming in the water below.

"Do you know this song?" she asked.

He listened for a moment. "Maybe. It sounds vaguely familiar. What is it?"

"It is an old 80's song called 'When I am with you', by a band called The Sparks."

"Mmm...it's catchy."

"After I came home from Europe, I was at Mum and Dad's place one day. I was a bit lost and lonely, so I used to help with gardening on the weekends. Dad would be playing his 80's music loudly and this song came on. I listened to the words as I weeded the garden and it made me think of you." She stopped to eat a scallop as she watched his mind race.

"Let me listen." He cocked his head to the side, lifting his ear in the air to capture the sound. "I get it, when I am with you, I am always hot and bothered," he laughed.

"When I am with you I am always hot and bothered, when I am with you I always need a shower," she sung, and they laughed. "But this line is what sold it to me, 'When I am with you I never feel like garbage, when I am with you, I almost feel normal, when I am with you, I meet a lot of people," she sung, and he hummed along.

"So that was my winning charm, I made you feel normal, I like that!" he said as she nodded, sipping on her wine, and he started on another razor shell.

The rest of their stay in Venice was filled with long mornings in bed before leisurely strolls, eating delicious food, and drinking heavenly wine. It was what a holiday was all about—a well-deserved rest.

# CHAPTER 29

## INNSBRUCK

The next morning they checked out early, took the water taxi and picked up the car at the car rental and hit the road. They had a five-hour drive ahead of them, mostly highways, so easy driving for Jack, and they would arrive in Austria by mid-afternoon. Sadness filled them leaving Venice;they had such wonderful few days here.

"Well, here we are driving in Europe again, and it feels fantastic to be back on the road," he said, smiling at her as she was trying to tune in the radio. She turned and looked at him. He was humming the song,"When I am with you."

"You have that song stuck in your head, haven't you?" She laughed.

He looked over at her and hummed louder. "Yes, I do. It has been in my head since yesterday."

"It will start to drive you nuts, you know," she advised. "It happens to me all the time."

"I have had worse songs stuck in my head," he said, flicking her a quick smile.

"You are doing great with the driving, by the way. I am impressed." She pulled back her hair to get a better view at the radio.

"Well, thank you. These main roads are fine. It is the small roads I have a wee bit of trouble," she nodded, distracted by the radio setting.

"So, my honeymoon choices are done, and now I head into the unknown charters of your accommodation choices," he teased with a quick sideways glance.

"Yes, we are, and I have to say after your choices, I hope mine stand up to the high standards," she said as the radio sprung to life with an Italian tune playing loudly.

"Bingo!" She smiled, happy with herself.

"Me, too. I am excited. Austria! Wow! I don't care if we are staying in a phone booth, I would be happy."

"Well, I hope I did a little better than that," she said, settling back, adjusting her sunglasses.

Hotel Monshein stood grandly, looking romantic and pretty with views of the Alps behind, with snow still lingering on the peaks. It was one of the dozen six-story, colourful buildings with pitched roofs, all standing in a row across from the river,each alternating between salmon, grey, lemon and green. Their hotel was the salmon one. They were blown away by the beauty of the town. It was postcard perfect. They were both laughing and smiling, chatting together as they started to pull up out the front to offload their bags before going to the parking area around the back.

Having too much fun together, Jack drove straight up the gutter landing half on the pavement. They both broke into fits of laughter. They did not notice a man from the hotel had arrived, tapping on the window.

"I am sorry,Sir. This space is for guests staying at our hotel," he said with a stern gaze.

"We are staying here," announced Jack proudly.

"You're staying here?" he enquired, looking over the top of his glasses.

"Aye, that's right, we are paying guests."

He looked them up and down before taking a chance they might be telling the truth. "Very well,Sir,I will fetch your luggage out and I think it would be safer if I park your car for you."

"That sounds like a ripper idea, thank you," she shouted, flicking Jack a wink, holding back the laughter.

"Sorry I had to do that."

They were both smirking at each other as they followed him inside. He leaned towards her and whispered, "He was not sure about us, was he?"

"No, but at least you got out of parking the car," she said with a smirk.

The reception staff were lovely, friendly and polite. They checked in and went upstairs to their room.

"What a view!" He threw the keys on the table. It was a stunning river view room with a beautiful bay window, a window seat and a small table and two chairs. The four small windows opened out to welcome the outdoor atmosphere. Featuring beautiful views of the river and the old town was accessible by the bridge conveniently right out the front of the hotel. Chloe joined him at the windowseat and peered out.

"Oh, what a beautiful pub, right on the banks of the river," she said as she spied the other side of the river.

"I can see us having a beer there, maybe even walk over for dinner. What do you think?"

"That would be nice," she said, already more interested in looking around inside.

"This is a grand hotel you chose for us here," said Jack, checking out the comfort level of the bed.

"Glad you like it. It's no junior suite but stunning views."

The next few hours were spent relaxing after the drive. Chloe checked her emails and Facebook while Jack poured them a drink. She read messages from all the gang. They had tagged them in their photos, and she scanned through them all, smiling. There were so many wonderful photos with everyone having a great time. She stopped at the wedding photos of her and Jack and thought how wonderful they looked together along with the setting and location; it had all come together beautifully.

"Oh, I miss everyone already. I can't believe it's all over and half the honeymoon done and dusted."

"Well, let's not worry about all that now. We have a new city waiting for us to explore,"announced Jack as he crawled over the bed to take the phone off her.

"Come and have a shower with me. I have been thinking of you all day, sitting there, looking so beautiful in the car. I wanted to pull over at times and have you right there," he said with a wink and a little grin. She waved him off with a giggle.

"What is wrong with that? It is our honeymoon. I am supposed to be amorous towards you and you should be the same," he said as he pulled her closer."Aren't you feeling the same?" he said with a sad face.

"Extremely amorous," she said in a low sultry voice as she led him to the shower.

They freshened up and strolled across the bridge, stopping for a beer at the hotel by the river. The weather was so inviting they decided to sit outside and found a table with views to enjoy the atmosphere of the Alps behind them.

"What a beautiful view. Imagine how spectacular it would be in winter."

"Yes, spectacular, but you would not be sitting here enjoying the view in winter."

They finished their beer and decided to have a walk through the magical old town, looking incredible,all lit up as the sun set. They strolled hand in hand and came across a restaurant down a back lane, with an extensive outdoor beer garden.

"Let's go in here. It seems to be popular."

They found a table and sat down, picking up the menu, hoping the food would be typically Austrian, and it was. "You are going to have trouble choosing, Jack. It all sounds yummy," she said, pulling her chair in closer for a better view.

"Well, for once I know exactly what I want."

"And what is that? Everything on the menu" she teased.

"Seeing we are in Austria, I am going to order the wiener schnitzel," he said proudly.

"Just the schnitzel," she teased, giving him a quick smirk before returning her attention to the menu.

"Have you seen the dessert menu?  I am saving myself."

"Yes, I have. It has more items than the mains."

"Well, that tells you they are going to be a treat. What is tickling your fancy tonight,Princess?"

"I love the sound of the grilled local trout from the river, but the veal tafelspitz sounds intriguing."

"Here comes the waiter. Which one? Or do I order both?"

"No, I will try the veal."

She sat back and held back her laughter as he struggled to order her the tafelspitz. As the waiter walked away, he leaned in closer to her with pursed lips.

"I have realised why you changed your mind. You set me up."

She giggled at his frantic face. "You kept calling it a spritz. I am not sure if I am getting a cocktail or a meal," she said, unable to control her giggles.

"You need not worry, he politely corrected me, more than once," he said, trying to appear irritated but then unable to hold out broke into a grin."And no bubblyfor you tonight," he said turning away, which set her off again. He turned back and laughed.

A musician began playing and the crowd rolled in, creating a vibe that was happy and relaxed. The waiter returned with the beer he recommended, a German weizen wheat beer, and they both enjoyed. After dinner, they walked back over the river, tired after the drive, happy to have a quiet night.

The next few days were spent looking around Innsbruck. They took the steady twenty-minute walk up to the zoo and spent the day looking at all the animals and the scenery along the way. They passed the cable car entry on the way out, and he stopped looking at it with envy. She knew it was something he really would have loved to do and started to feel sorry he would miss out because of her.

"How far does it go," she bravely asked, looking up the track.

Jack wanted to take the cable cars to the top more than anything but didn't want to push her. "Well, that depends on where you want to go. You see, there are a few stops, you don't need to go all the way to the top."He watched as she looked it over. He could tell she was wrestling with herself and was ready to jump in when she beat him to it.

"I think I would like to go to the next stop. The views would be incredible," she said, hoping he would not pick up on the quiver in her voice.

She looked at the cable car coming up the track. *I need to jump on this thing before I have a chance to talk myself out of it. I need to do this for Jack.*

"You would?" He said, shocked.

"Yes, I will get off at the next stop and wait for you. I want you to go all the way to the top and take photos for me."

He could not believe what he was hearing. He opened his mouth to question her again, but she spoke over him.

"Quick, get the tickets! Here it comes," she said frantically.

He turned and darted off, arriving back with enough time to grab her hand and help her onboard. She was shaking like a leaf, and he knew she was doing it for him, which made it all the more special.

"Are you okay?"

"Yes, you go in first. I don't want the window seat," she said, stepping aside as he scooted into the seat before her.

"You are amazing!" He kissed her on the head as he put his arm around her tight.

The little carriage began to depart as it slowly made its way up the hill. She closed her eyes and licked her dry lips. She would have been unable to speak even if she wanted to. He knew she was in her fight zone using every bit of her energy to not freak out. He held her tight and enjoyed the scenery going past. They were approaching the station where they had to disembark, and he gently shook her and whispered, "It is time to get off,Princess."

She nodded and opened her eyes first with tiny slits and then slowly opened them fully as he pushed her to make a move. The carriage had stopped completely, and she made her way to the door and walked down the stairs until her feet had landed firmly on the ground. It wasn't scary at all. Her butterflies left her. She licked her dry lips to talk, hoping something audible might come out.

"It's not too scary, I did it," she said, looking around with glee. The trees and bushes were blocking the true beauty but it suited her perfect. "I can do this. I can go all the way with you. That train wasn't so scary, after all."

He was delighted he had pushed her out of her comfort zone a tiny bit and it had given her the courage to push ahead further. The only problem was, she had not realised he was going on the hanging cable car the rest of the way. "You are here. Look, isn't this spectacular?" he said with encouragement.

"Yes, I am. I did it. I am on top of the world. Quick, let's jump back on before I change my mind."

"The little train you were on is the funicular. It goes back down. From here you take the cable car," he said as he looked at it approaching over her shoulder. She turned and looked with fear as she spotted it.

"On that," she said with a quivering voice.

"Yes, can you do it? We could go one more stop and there is a fantastic restaurant with views."

He studied her face carefully as she stared at the cable car. She was fighting with herself she wanted to do it, but could she? "We will stand in the middle so you can't see out and I will hold you all the way," he said as he noticed people starting to board.

"I don't have a ticket," she said trying to find an excuse.

"I will fix it at the other end. I don't want to force you but I think you would enjoy this with me. I would enjoy having you with me, and I am a wee bit peckish," he said as he moved her slowly towards the car. Jesus, he wanted her to do it. She didn't have to, but he really wanted her to do it."Do you trust me? You can hang onto me all the way."

She trusted him but at this point in time she wasn't sure if the trust she had for him involved anything like this.

"I have to go now. There is a cafe over there where you can wait. I won't be long," he said as he started to shake her loose and kissed her as he started to climb aboard. He was hoping she would cling to him and follow him on. He turned to say goodbye. "I won't be long, I promise."

Just as the doors started to close, she ran. "Wait, I am coming," she said without giving it a single thought, and he yanked her in just in time as the doors shut behind her.

"You did it!" He said, shocked. "Come here. Let's go to the middle."

She nodded, and they moved to the middle as promised. The car was busy but not overcrowded and everyone went to the outer edge for the views so the middle was not congested. She closed her eyes tight as her legs turned to jelly. She spoke to herself all the way with words of wisdom. *You can do this, Chlo. You flew all the way to Europe on your own in an aeroplane. All you have to do is stand here quietly and then your husband will take you to lunch.* A smile almost came to her face as she saw images of his face appear in her head, of him thinking and looking at food.

It felt like an eternity as she stood there like a Roman statue, but was probably only minutes before she heard the words she had wanted to hear.

"We are here, Princess. Open your eyes."

The doors opened with a loud clang and people started shuffling. She opened her eyes but had them fixed on the floor as she stepped off the cable car.

"You did it! You are here," he said with excitement, but as she opened her eyes completely her face dropped and her eyes went wide with fear. She was frozen, unable to move.

"You need to walk away from the car, Princess." He took her by the arm and led her away.

She was on top off a huge mountain and butterflies were going berserk in her stomach. "Jack, how high are we? I am about to throw up," she said, looking frantic. "Look at the shit you get me into. Why do I listen to you? I am as high as the clouds."

"But how beautiful it is," he said, waving his hand out to the view. He spotted some chairs away to the side and led her towards them. "Here, sit down for a minute. You will be okay. Just take those deep breaths you do so well. I will go and fix up the cable car ticket and book us a table for lunch."

She didn't answer.

"Will you be okay if I leave you here?"

She nodded, and he kissed her.

"I love you! Thank you for doing this," he said as he backed up, watching her carefully before turning and heading into the doorway of the restaurant.

*You frigging idiot. Control yourself, you flip. He is so grateful you did this, you need to snap out of it and try to be normal. See all the normal people, they aren't scared, and the little kid looking over the edge—oh,God, there is that wave of sickness again— God-damn him, why do I trust him? What has he got me into now?* The thoughts went over and over in her head as she sat and did her breathing until she spotted him striding back with huge smile.

"I got us a table on the inside of the room, nowhere near the window," he said, looking at her proudly.

"Thank you," she said with an embarrassed half smile. He gave up so much for her. He would have loved those views from the cable car and the table right at the window looking out at the once-in-a-lifetime view. But no, he gave it all up for her. She took his outward hand, and he put his arm around her as they walked to the restaurant door.

Once inside, the waitress came over instantly and picking up two menus, recognising Jack she said, "Follow me."

"Wait! Is that table over there available?" asked Chloe, wiping her sweaty palms on her pants.

"That one?" she pointed to the table next to the huge window beautifully set for two.

"Yes, that one," Chloe said.

"Umm …Yes,as a matter of fact, it is," she said with a confused stare towards Jack and then realised what was going on.

"Yes, please come. It is all yours," she sat them down, and she saw Jack give her a wink of thanks.

"I think drinks should be the first thing to order," said the waitress, looking at Chloe's panicked eyes.

"Can you bring us two of your best wheat beers?" said Jack.

"Grande," added Chloe.

"My wife is scared of heights," he said.

"Well, I have just the thing,"she said as she turned, throwing Chloe a warm smile.

"You are very brave wanting this table. You have chosen the one with the best views, I appreciate what you just did," he said.

"Well, I am glad you noticed. It makes it all worthwhile." She smiled a crooked smile

"Just do me a favour. Lean to your left a little, so I don't have to look at you on an angle."

"What do you mean?"

"You are sitting on an angle, leaning away from the window. Just straighten up a wee bit."

"I am?" she asked as she straightened herself up.

"Yes, you are. Nowthat's better," he chuckled. "Well, I am very, very proud of you and also extremely over the moon with this view," he said looking out at it, giving her a narrative of everything he could see.

*Oh, God, please shut up, Jack. I don't need to know all about that,I am definitely going to throw up.*

The waitress returned with two shots of schnapps and placed them on the table.

"This will help you relax and enjoy your lunch. It is schnapps from the Alps," she said with a smile and was back with their beers. "Enjoy!"

"Ah, you have still got it. You get all the best treats."

She laughed a nervous laugh as they shot them together.

"Wow! If that doesn't relax you, I don't know what will," he said, shaking his head.

She laughed as she opened the menu. By the time they finished their beer, she was starting to relax and took a quick peek out the window.

"I saw that,"he said with an astonished look.

"How beautiful," she said.

"I am very relieved you finally did that. It's breathtaking, isn't it?"

"Yes, stunning. So are you going all the way to the top?"

"Well, that depends on you. Are you coming?" he asked with pleading eyes.

"No, I can't. I am so sorry. I was a train wreck coming this far, but I want you to go, I will be fine I will wait here."

"Are you sure? I am happy I came this far, I don't need to go any further," he said, sitting back in his chair.

"No, I want you to. I want you to take photos to show me."

"Okay, if you are sure."

"Yes, I am totally fine. I am happy here. See, I even looked out the window," she said, taking another quick peek out the window.

The waitress came back to clear the table. "Are you all done here?"

"Chloe is going to wait here while I go up to the top. Would you like her to move tables?"

"No, you are okay here. Lunch service is over now. It's not busy. Stay as long as you like."

"Thank you. Can you take a photo for us?"

"Sure." She took the phone and took some photos and left.

"Well, I guess I will go. I promise I won't be long."

"I will be fine here. Go and enjoy."

He kissed her and headed out the door just as the cable car arrived. He turned back and waved as the door shut and started his way up the hill.

She sat for a moment deep in thought. What it must be like to live with no fear. She was so envious of him. He was strong and capable of doing anything. She was so lucky to have him, look at where she was. Sitting halfway up a mountain in the Alps, she could never have achieved this before. He made her want to do so much, because she loved him. She didn't want him to miss out because of her. He deserved so much more, and she was extremely grateful

He was back in no time and sat showing her all the photos and she genuinely loved seeing them all. The shots he took were incredible; with the backdrop of Innsbruck and the Alps she was glad he had done it. The smile on his face in his selfies told her how much he had wanted to go.

The time had come to make their way down the mountain, and she coped a lot better going down than coming up. When they arrived, she jumped off and ran to the side, unable to hide her excitement. "I did it, I did it, I went all the way up!"

"You did! You were extremely brave today, but did you have fun?"

"Yes, I had the best fun. Thankyou! I am so happy I conquered it."

"So you don't hate me anymore and I don't get you into shit all the time?"

"I am sorry, I was freaking out. Don't listen to me when I am like that."

"So you want to do it again tomorrow?"

"Noooo! I am so glad I did it, but I never want to do that ever again."

He laughed as he threw his arm around her, and they walked back to the hotel.

Their last day in town they spent wandering the streets of the old town, stopping to admire the Golden Roof. They strolled along lovely old streets, which were full of character, and everywhere you looked was something else interesting to admire. They visited the Swarovski factory, where Jack bought her a stunning necklace. That night they visited a folk show where traditional dancers were dressed in full costume singing, yodelling and dancing. Chloe wore her new necklace and a long green dress that set off not only her necklace but the stones in her ring that Jack had bought her in Corfu. They were swooning with delight as the night was filled with Austrian beer,hearty soup, schnitzel and strudel. Lots of Austrian folk dancing helped to wear off the huge meal afterwards.

# CHAPTER 30

## HEIDELBERG

After a hearty breakfast, they made tracks and were cruising the German autobahn in no time.

"This is totally amazing! Did you notice how fast that car sped past us?" said Jack with pure delight. "I can go as fast as I like! This is so much fun."

"Slow down, Jack. Jesus, we are going to die!"

"Die? No way, this is the best fun I have had in ages. Wow, did you see that? I think it was a Porsche Cayenne but it sped past so fast I could not tell."He had a quick glance at Chloe and saw she had curled herself up into the foetal position, covering her head with her hands.

"What are you doing? Aren't you having fun?"

"No, I am terrified, and I think I am going to throw up."

"Hang in there,Princess, we are almost at our exit," he said, patting her on the head with a smile. She stayed low until he gave her the okay to sit up.

"Jack, that was terrifying, how are you not shaken up?"

"Shaken? It was absolutely awesome. I can't wait to tell Jimmy and Pat we drove on the autobahn. They will be so impressed."

"Well, glad you enjoyed the whole experience but I have never been happier to see the Heidelberg turnoff," she said, looking pale. He suddenly realised she didn't look right.

"Are you okay?"

"I will be, just give me a minute," she said, looking frazzled, and he smiled.

They were soon at Heidelberg and made their way through the town, then headed up a winding road all the way to the top as far as it would go. Making a right-hand turn, they entered the driveway which opened up to a grand old two-story hotel topped with a third-story loft with a slanted roof. It felt like they had dropped in on an old German fairytale house.

"Wow, we have landed in a fairytale." She said, looking through the windscreen as he took off his belt.

"Where did you book this place? On the Walt Disney site?" He said with his mouth open.

"Wooow! How incredibly stunning," she said as they opened their door and got out, stretching as they gazed around.

The remoteness of the location was peaceful and quiet. As they walked on the pebbled ground the crunching of the stones was the only sound to be heard. They walked to the side of the drive and peered down towards the views which overlooked the river all the way to the old town.

"These views are breathtaking."

"Well, the pressure is off,Princess. You have aced it. You have found yourself a fairytale castle complete with out-of-this-world views."

"I can't wait to take a peek inside."

"I am half-expecting Hansel and Gretel to greet us," he said with a grin he could not wipe off his face.

He was more than impressed with her choice, and she was relieved. He had given her the most beautiful places to stay and was happy she could do the same for him. They walked into the foyer and were greeted by Helga, who was a jolly woman, welcoming them with a jovial smile and a tray of cookies.

"Guten tag," she said with a broad smile.

'Thank you, we have a booking for MacLean."

"Oh, welcome, our newlyweds, Mr. and Mrs. MacLean! I have our honeymoon suite ready for you."

"Thank you! We are looking forward to staying."

They climbed the squeaky timber stairs to the loft on the third floor they spotted from the front with uninterrupted sweeping views.

As they stepped inside, Chloe gasped. "Jack, it's stunning!" She walked in and stopped, dropping the luggage. It was like a huge suite, complete with a lounge area that looked out the full-size windows that framed the views of the river below, with no TV to be seen. You could hide up there for a week and not get cabin fever. The bed was enormous and Jack jumped on it and laid down.

"This bed is like in the fairytales. Remember the song about Grandma's big bed?  You better not fall out of this one," he called out.

"Oh, this is so very comfortable, I think I might stay right here. Come and join me," he invited, tapping on the bed, but she had already moved on into the bathroom.

"Look at the size of this spa."

He jumped off the bed and rushed over, poking his head in the doorway. "Now that is going to get some good use." Chloe picked up the spa products and looked them over."Top of the range; nothing shabby about this place," she said as she walked out and spotted the coffee machine "That will be appreciated in the morning."

"Aye and Helga said breakfast was free and served out on the deck, or inside the restaurant, whenever we are ready, come down and enjoy," he said with a smile.

"Well, it was one of the reasons I booked here. I know how you love your food," she flicked him a teasing grin.

"Oh, I am very excited to try a German breakfast. What do you think they will serve?"

"I have no idea, but I am sure it will be plentiful. What would you like to do this afternoon?"

"Let's just hang around here, maybe visit the bar downstairs. I bet they have German beer," he said with an excited smile.

"Good chance, Jack, seeing we are in Germany," she teased.

He slapped his forehead with his hand."I keep forgetting," he said, still looking around at everything. He flicked the switch on the stereo and music started to play. "This place has every-thing. I am so impressed."

She smiled warmly, watching him run around, opening every cupboard like an excited child. "Okay, let me freshen up, and we will head outside and check out the grounds."

They were outside in no time and took a stroll around the grounds.

"Chloe, come over here," said Jack excitedly, and she left the garden she was looking at and wandered over to him. Nothing would have surprised her. As she got closer, she saw he was staring at a billboard half-covered with overgrown trees.

"What is this?"

"It is a funicular. Did they mention anything about this when you booked?"

"I don't think so. Where does it go?" He looked around frantically.

"Wait, come over here." He stopped to read a sign. "There is a station here somewhere," he said, looking around. "It says we can board it here, and it will take us to the castle. The old town or it will take us all the way to the top of the mountain."

Chloe's hands started to sweat at the thought of it. She remembered vaguely reading something about it now but had no idea what it was. She could tell by how excited Jack was she would be sitting on that scary looking thing for sure and heading high up into the hills.

"Stairs! Follow me."

She followed him down the stairs, and they found themselves at an old two-story thatched-roofed sand-coloured railway house. Just as they arrived a train pulled in. It was a small timber carriage that trundled along slowly as it climbed high up the mountain.

"We need to do this. This is so exciting; you have found us somewhere fantastic to stay."

Her heart was pounding and her hands were sweating just looking at it, let alone go on it.

*Oh why did she chose this place to stay?*

She took a step back and let Jack explore as she tried to calm herself down. There was no getting out of it, tomorrow she would have to be brave and do it just for him. He did so many wonderful things for her;surely, she could do this. She did it in Innsbruck, so there was no excuse not to.

"Chloe, I was just reading. The timber cable car is the oldest in Germany and it only takes us up five hundred and fifty metres above sea level. You went higher than that in Innsbruck,the views are supposed to be spectacular, can we do it after breakfast tomorrow?"

He was so excited, how could she say no? "Sure, why not," she said with a quiver in her voice, looking towards the stairs that would lead them back to the hotel, wishing she never ventured down them.

"Come on! Let's go and enjoy the view from the bar." He grabbed her by the hand, kissed her on the head and with a radiant smile then leaped up the stairs, dragging her with him. They found a table on the outside of the grand uncovered veranda with views all the way down to the castle, old town, and river below.

"Can you imagine how beautiful it is going to be from the top?"

"Yes, I can, it will be like the cable cars in Innsbruck," she said, turning quite pale at the thought of it.

"No, no, it is nowhere near that high. I would never put you through that again, it goes up really slow. I think this is your type of funicular. I want to share this with you."

A waiter approached before she had time to answer. "What can I get you to drink?" he said, looking at them from one to another and back again.

"We have not had a chance to check yet," said Chloe, looking rattled.

"A cold beer. What do you recommend?" said Jack, leaning back with one arm resting on the back of the chair looking up at him.

"Oh, well, I can recommend a Paulaner, it is a Munich beer."

"Sounds perfect. Can we please have two Paulaner beers?"

He nodded and he was off.

"Right. Where were we?"

"You were telling me how I will absolutely love the thrill of climbing the mountain," she said biting her nail.

"Well, we will wait and see in the morning, if it is not something you want to do then that is okay, I have done Innsbruck, so I am happy."

"Really, we don't have to do it?" she said with a shriek.

"No, we don't," he leaned into her and put his hand over hers.

"I will never put you through what you don't want to do, ever." He looked deep into her eyes. She took a deep breath and sat back, his eyes were still locked with hers.

"Thankyou," she said, and he sat back as the waiter placed two beers in front of them. He stood proudly waiting as Jack took a long gulp and placed it back on the table. Wiping his mouth, he looked up at the waiter with a spark in his eye.

"That is one hell of a good beer."

The waiter's eyes grew wide with delight. "I have another recommendation," he said proudly.

"And what would that be?" said Jack, looking up at him with a squinted eye.

*Oh, geez, here it comes, I bet it's the bloody funicular,* she thought as she started to wriggle in her seat uncomfortably. She sat up straight and took a sip of beer not wanting to hear what he would say next.

"I would suggest you stay for a few drinks so you can witness the most spectacular sunset."

She slumped back into her seat with relief. "Sunset," she said with surprise.

"Yes, the sunsets here are incredible, and the food is also very good. It is traditional German food."

"Oh, that sounds just wonderful," she said, feeling relaxed and able to breathe again.

The afternoon was spent drinking, relaxing, and enjoying the beautiful day. They needed the rest and it was the perfect location to do so. The waiter came back regularly, chatting and telling hometown stories. Other tables were starting to fill and they were grateful they were staying as so many others had just dropped in for dinner.

As the sun started to set, they were glad they stayed to witness the incredible views. The waiter came back to check if they enjoyed it and offered them the menu. Chloe had the wild salmon as it was locally caught, and Jack the German white sausage, and they shared a large pretzel breadstick. Chocolate mousse to die for ended the meal. They waddled upstairs to the top floor. The views from the room at night were even more spectacular.

As she opened the door, her eyes went straight to the huge window.

"Check out this view," she said peering out the window.

"It is pretty spectacular,"he said, making his way straight to the bathroom to run the bath.

"Oh, now that is a fantastic idea. Make sure you put some of those bubbles in," she said as she flopped on the lounge, looking out the window.

"Done. That will take a while to fill up. Now, what would you like to drink?  A red or some bubbles?"

"Oh, bubbles please."

They sat in the bubbles for hours, happily chatting about the day's events.

"That bloody autobahn has made me so tense. Soaking in here will help relieve the tension in my body,"she said, closing her eyes with her head back on the tub.

"You really did not like it, did you?"

"No, I hated every minute, but you loved it," she said sitting up again.

"I found it exciting," he said, wiping the bubbles off his arm to pick up his drink."Tell me, what made you scared," he said as he sunk back, relaxing. He knew she would have a long story to tell as he lay back, smiling listening to her every detail about the autobahn and then onto the Innsbruck funicular. He was never going to let her know, but he too got a bit nervous at times, but he had to be strong for her. He began realising if he pushed her just a little out of her comfort zone with him beside her,she was accomplishing things she would never have accomplished before.

After the bath, they sat on the lounge at the window, finishing their wine. The scent of the bubbles filled the room, and they sat with no lights to appreciate the ones beaming in from outside. They were delighted as fireworks lit up the sky and the riverbank below;it made the whole scene even more beautiful.

"Can you believe we are in Germany?" Chloe said quietly.

"No, to be honest, I still pinch myself. I am married to a beautiful girl, watching fireworks from the top of a mountain in Germany. How lucky can one person be?" He smiled at her.

"I am so glad you listened to your mother and bought that ticket for the cruise."

"Me, too. Life for me would have been a whole lot different."

"And for me," she sighed.

"And for Jimmy," he added. "Oh, yes, and Chelsea."

"And Pat," he continued. "And Angie. Wow, all because of us."

"Yep, all because of us."

They sat staring down at the fireworks, lost in their own thoughts, realising how lucky they were and everyone else whose lives they had changed, to have found each other.

"I am going to have a wee dram before I go to bed. Would you like one?" he said quietly.

Hearing no response, he looked down at her as she had snuggled in with her head on his shoulder."Chlo," he whispered but she was fast asleep.

He gently woke her and helped her to bed and poured himself a whiskey before crawling in beside her. He sat drinking his whiskey as he looked out over the view from the huge window. She had been incredibly brave yesterday. Going up to the café in the funicular and cable car, he smiled as he remembered her leaning away from the window and the look on her face when she took her first peek at the view. She had surprised him, but going on the cable car was something he never thought he would see. *She did it all for me, that was what was so special,* he whispered quietly as he looked down at her with the moonlight brightening the room just enough. He sat quietly gazing out the window, thinking how incredibly lucky he was. He watched happily humming away, sipping on his whisky and then smiling. *Damn it, that is that song again, she was right, it would drive him crazy,*he smiled down at her as he sipped his whiskey. "When I am with you I almost feel normal, when I am with you I am really well adjusted. Goodnight, Princess," he whispered.

They were up early the next morning and after Jack got back from the fitness room they headed for breakfast. Jack was in his glory. There was everything that you could desire, all laid out on huge long tables that circled along the walls of the dining room. There were different varieties of pancakes, Weisswurst sausages, bacon, a German semolina pudding, raw pork mince served on a German bread roll, and boiled eggs smothered in creamy mustard sauce. They filled their plates and took them outside on the deck to enjoy the views.

"These eggs are delicious," said Chloe. "And these sausages are boiled instead of fried."

"Pancakes are good but I miss all the sweet breakfasts."

"It's my turn to enjoy," she said as he shovelled half a sausage into his mouth, and she smiled as she shook her head. It certainly appeared he was enjoying the feast.

"What would you like to do today,Princess?" he said as he pushed back his empty plate.

"Don't you want to go on the funicular?" she said as she rubbed her shoulder, hoping the answer would be no.

"No, not if you don't want to. Today is your day. You tell me where you would like to go, have a think while I go back for some of those eggs you said were nice."

He flicked her a wicked smile before jumping up and was off. She knew what he was up to. He would be piling his plate again as usual, using the eggs as an excuse. She sat thinking about the day ahead. She wanted to do something they would both enjoy. Then as she stirred her coffee she came up with an idea. He was back and the plate was again full of bacon, pancakes, and sausages. No eggs could be seen.

"What happened to the eggs?" she asked as she stared at his mound of food.

"I couldn't fit them in."

She smirked as he started to devour his feast.

"How about we catch that cable car down to the old town today. You get a ride in the funicular, and I am excited to visit the castle and the old town."

Jack stopped his fork mid-flight and stared at her. Did he just hear it right? She wanted to get on the train?

"If that is what you would like to do, yes, sounds wonderful," he said as he finished eating. He was thrilled to bits by her suggestion and also surprised. He thought she would run a mile before getting on the funicular after Innsbruck, but it was only down to the old town and not up the mountain. But it was a surprising start to the day.

After breakfast, they walked around the grounds in the sunshine before taking the cable car down to the old town below. It was a charming old town, and they strolled around for hours, buying souvenirs and getting a feel of the history. They sat for ice cream in a courtyard and listened to the tales of a local older gentleman that was sitting at the table beside them.

"Where are you young people from?" he said as he leaned closer to pay attention to their reply.

"We are from Australia," said Jack, biting the bottom of his ice cream cone.

"Oh, Austria. You don't look Austrian," he said thinking they were telling tales.

"No, Australia. We are on our honeymoon," added Chloe.

"Oh, such a long way from home. You make a striking couple."

"Thankyou," said Chloe, happy with his nice comment. "We like your town."

He nodded as he thought for a moment and they happily licked their ice-cream, looking around.

"You would be surprised to know how much history is surrounding you, you young folk don't take time to know," he said with a disgruntled gaze.

"Oh, I love hearing stories about old days and towns," said Chloe with an upbeat voice. He sat thinking again and then turned to her. "This square holds so much history. In fifteenth century they used to burn witches here," he said looking around.

"Where? Here?" said Chloe, looking around in disbelief.

"Right over there, next to the fountain," he said and she stared with fright. "They had a cage also. It was called the Twister. Anyone caught for petty crime would be placed inside. It spun around, so onlookers would have fun tormenting them by spinning it," he said, jerking his head in the direction of the fountain.

Chloe froze with a gaze of disbelief on her face, her ice cream dripping down her fingers. Jack stepped into the rescue, handing her a serviette.

"Fascinating history for a grand old town," he said, hoping he had finished his stories.

"Down there on the other side, is a church if you head that way. Take time to look for the carvings of pretzels on the wall," he said as he pointed his walking stick down the cobblestone lane.

"Oh, they must have loved their pretzels," she said with a forced smile.

"They did, that is where the market was held, they sold them along with bread and other groceries, but they didn't trust the bakers and measured the pretzels to the size of the carvings on the wall and if they were not the same, they would throw the baker in the twister," he said, leaning towards her with the corners of his eyes wrinkled.

"Well, I am glad we don't live in those days. I now understand why I don't like history all that much," she said as she rubbed the back of her neck . Jack jumped to his feet, thinking Chloe had heard enough of his stories, and she followed his lead.

"Thank you for your very unusual and informative stories, but we should be off," he said as he grabbed Chloe's hand.

"All the statues have wonderful stories. Make sure you take the time to stop and read the plaques all about them," he said as he waved them off."Typical young folk," he muttered.

"Come on, I think you deserve a drink after that," he said as he quickened the pace, and she nodded.

He spotted a German bar and started dragging her towards the door. As they entered, they immediately realised they had stumbled upon a special place. The interior was all stone and brick with medieval chandeliers, and long heavy timber bench-style tables and chairs. He walked her to one towards the back and she slid into it, looking around.

"Here, you wait here. I will grab us a beer."

Her thoughts instantly returned to the old man's story and she shivered. A beer would be well appreciated to remove the horrors going round her head. He returned with speed and a huge grin on his face, carrying two steins.

"Look how they serve the beer." Chloe's eyes were open wide. "I don't think I will be having a second," she said as she eyed the stein. "I can hardly pick it up," she chuckled.

"I love this place," sighed Jack, smiling, looking around and then his gaze landed back at the size of his beer. He took a long gulp. "The beer is so full of flavour."

"You are going to love the food also," said Chloe as she scanned the menu.

"I have been watching the pork knuckles go past."

"That is the specialty of the house," she added as she spied another going past.

"Well that is me, I don't need to read anymore."

"I like the sound of the pork cheek with sauerkraut, but I am still full from breakfast."

The waitress arrived to take their order and advised that the portions were very big, and sometimes people shared the pork knuckle. Chloe's eyes darted to Jack's with pursed lips, trying not to laugh as Jack struggled with the idea of sharing.

"I am happy to share," he said unconvincingly.

"Are you sure?" asked Chloe slowly with a sly grin, unable to believe what she heard.

"Yes, I am sure. I can order dessert if I need to," he said with a half-smile.

Chloe grabbed the menu again and quickly scanned it. "Could I please add a small salad with chicken strips and yogurt dressing?" she said as she looked at Jack and he smiled. He was grateful that she had read his mind.

Overhearing different languages, they were aware the place was packed with people from all over the world. Some locals joined them at the table and gave them some great tips on their city. Chatting with them after lunch, they got along so well that the Germans invited them to a biergarten, or beer garden that they were going to. Thanking them for the invite, they happily tagged along. They introduced themselves as Franz and Heidi, and they spoke perfect English.

When they arrived at the biergarten, they were introduced to their friends who invited them to join them at the long wooden table under an old tree.

"This place is amazing," said Jack as he glanced around in all directions.

"The beer garden is small compared to the ones in Munich, but still the same atmosphere. We celebrate Oktoberfest here. It all comes to life like a huge festival with lots of stages, and it is a huge party scene,"explained Franz proudly.

They sat and listened to their stories over a few steins that were served in turnstile in and out beer huts. The men pouring the beers were dressed in traditional short lederhosel outfits, while the girls picking up the glasses wore little traditional dirndl blouse and skirt. People were starting to order dinner and Chloe could see Jack's mouth starting to water. He was eyeing off another pork knuckle as she leaned over. "Would you like me to go and find some dinner?" she smirked.

"That would be lovely, but this time I don't think I want to share."

She laughed. "I don't think you shared at lunch very much either. Wait here. I will see what I can do." She wandered off to the food tent, looking around at everything along the way. People were having a great time drinking, laughing and some cheerfully singing old bawdy songs. There were no fights or bad language, but maybe it was just that it was early in the day. Arriving at the food tent, she ordered a pork knuckle, white sausage with sauerkraut and pretzels. The pretzel she thought would be good to soak up the beer. Arriving back, she found Jack telling a grand story. She just smiled as she put the food tray down, noticing others were eating also.

They happily devoured their meal, listening to the music and enjoying the company of new friends. After dinner, Franz called them a cab and gave the cab driver the address where they were staying. They thanked them immensely for a wonderful afternoon and told them if they were ever in Australia to contact them, and they would look after them.

The last day of their honeymoon was taken at a very slow pace. They packed and then packed again, trying to get the suitcases right for the early morning flight. Placing the cases near the door. they lay on the bed going through their photos as they laughed and re-lived each moment with delight.

# CHAPTER 31
## MARRIED LIFE

Settling in at home proved hard after an amazing time in Europe. Jack's crab pots were pulling in the cash and Chloe was asking for fewer shifts, so she could spend more time preparing the seafood.

An early morning shift at Seasalt was proving to be difficult. She didn't feel right waking up with the urge to throw up but pushed it from her mind as she knew they were short-staffed and needed her for the shift. She had to soldier on.

Kait and Chloe both sat at the table with glum looks as Johnny handed them both a plate of scrambled eggs.

"Here, eat this and stop winging. It's time to open the doors soon."

"Don't be so mean to me, Johnny. I care for you when you are sick."

"You're sick?" asked Chloe, surprised.

"Yea, I don't feel right. I think I have picked up a bug."

"Me, too. It must be going around. I am all queasy in the stomach."

"That is what I have, and Johnny is feeding us eggs," she said, throwing Johnny a disgruntled stare.

"He may be right. It might line our stomach."

They both started playing with their meal, pushing their food around as they chatted.

"Are the crab pots booked out again this weekend?"

"Yea, they are booked out every weekend. I can't believe how popular they are. I have been run off my feet since we got back from Europe."

"That is what is wrong with you. Your immune system is down, I am the same, between this place and Sophia my feet never hit the ground."

"Well, this is only the start of the season, god help us. It will get ten times worse in the next few months."

"We need to hire more staff, but it's hard finding the time."

"We were trying to keep it small but not too sure if we can. Angie mentioned she was coming home soon. I think Pat is coming with her, they would be a huge help."

"Such a surprise. They certainly hit it off, didn't they?"

"Yea, they make an awesome couple. So happy for them."Chloe looked at Kait. She was pulling the weirdest face.

"Kait, what's wrong? Are you OK?"

"No, I am going to throw up!" She ran to the bathroom and Chloe chased her.

The sound of Kait throwing up was too much for Chloe, and she was in the next cubicle throwing up beside her. They emerged and washed their faces in the sink. Looking in the mirror they were both pale.

"Bloody Johnny and his eggs."

"Yea, they weren't too good, were they?" They walked back out to the kitchen.

Johnny took one look at them and yelled out to Finn. "Eggs are off the menu today. They have made the girls sick. Here, sit down both of you."

"Without eggs, we have no breakfast menu," yelled back Finn.

"Without the girls, we have no waitresses. Put the closed sign on the door with a note."Finn did as he asked. "Okay both of you home to bed."

They took off their aprons and told Johnny how sorry they were.

The twenty-four-hour bug seemed to last for days. Chloe was busy preparing the seafood trying not to throw up when her phone rang. She picked it up and noticed it was Kait.

"Hi, Kait," she said cheerfully.

"Hi, Chlo. How are you?"

"I can't seem to shake this bug. How are you?"

"Well, if you have the same thing as me, you had better get those extra staff you were talking about because you are going to need them."

"Why? What do you mean? What have you got? Are you okay?" A wave of panic struck her.

"Yes, I am over the moon. I did a pregnancy test and it is a very bright positive."

"Oh, Kait, that is such wonderful news. You have been trying for so long, I am so happy for you."She then stopped dead in her tracks and almost dropped the phone. "Shit! I probably am also."

"Yep. Pretty good chance of it. One thing I do know it wasn't Johnny's eggs."

Chloe dropped to the chair. "I need to do a test."

"I am on my way over. I will stop at the chemist on the way. Sophia is at daycare today."

"Okay. Oh, my God,Kait, what if I am? We have no time for this now. We are flat out."

"Well, I hate to tell you, but I think we are all about to get a whole lot busier."

"Do you think I am?"

"Only one way to find out. I will see you in ten."

Chloe slumped on the kitchen chair. *What if I am pregnant? What if Kait is right?* Unable to move, she was still sitting there when Kait arrived.

"Are you okay?"

"I will be in a minute. Quick, let me do this."

Kait handed her the package and she disappeared into the bathroom a few moments later. She returned as Kait was making the tea in the kitchen. Her face told the story.

"It's positive, isn't it?" She said with glee.

"Yes." Her mind was spiralling out of control as she walked to the dining table and sat.

"What's up? Are you about to cry?"

Looking deep into her eyes she walked towards her and placed the tea on the table. "I am not sure, I don't know if I can do this." She looked up at her with frantic eyes.

"We are pregnant together, Chlo, we can do this together. You won't be alone, I will be beside you all the way, so will Jack." She threw a comforting arm around her.

"Jack, shit," she jumped up, pacing the room.

"Jack doesn't want kids?"

"Yea, he is the one who wants them. I am just freaking out, that's all."

"Johnny is over the moon. We have been trying for years to extend our little family."

"Oh, my God, Kait, I am so sorry. I have not even congratulated you. I am so sorry."She threw her arms around her.

"It's OK, Chloe, you are just in shock. Once it sets in, you will be fine."

"I need to tell Jack."She began to bite her nails.

"I am sure that he will be okay,"she said with a dismissive wave.

"He will be ecstatic. He has wanted us to start a family. That's all he spoke about on our honeymoon."

"Well, sounds like he has got his wish," she said, pouring the tea.

"That must have been a pretty sexy honeymoon." She winked but Chloe was still lost in thought.

"It must have been in France when I lost my pills, and I was on nothing for around a week until I found them again." She took the cup off Kait and stirred it.

"I have an appointment at the doctor tomorrow. I guess I will find out more there, but my money is on France, for sure."

She nodded, sipping her tea, lost in thought.

"How can I be a good mum? I am a walking disaster at the best of times." Tears shone in her eyes.

"You are going to be a great mum, Chlo, I have no doubt about that. You are smart, kind, caring. This little bub is going to have the best mum in the world."She cuddled Chloe and she smiled, wiping her tears away.

"Thanks, Kait, just like you."

"It will be so much fun having our babies together," she smiled.

"You are right. It was a bit of a shock, that is all."

They heard footsteps coming up the front stairs. Startled, they turned around to see who was about to walk in.

"Jack," said Chloe as she jumped up in a panic. He knew something was going on.

"What did I miss?"

"Oh, nothing, we were just having a cup of tea. You're home early."

"Aye, I am. We are finished, and now I want to take my beautiful wife to lunch," he said as he flicked through the mail, sitting on the bench-top.

"Well, that sounds like a perfect idea," said Kate, picking up her handbag, noticing the test kit still sitting on the kitchen table. They gave each other a frantic gaze as she threw a tea towel over it and Chloe let out a deep breath. "I have to jet. Have a nice lunch. Where are you going?"

"I thought about walking up to the pub, but it is up to Chloe. She hasn't been feeling too well," he said, and they flicked each other a quick glance.

"Yea, sounds perfect to me," said Chloe nervously as Kait gave her a quick cuddle.

"Nice. Well, enjoy! I will call you tomorrow Chloe."

"Okay, sounds good." She gave her a kiss, and she turned to walk down the front stairs. They followed to see her out stopping on the front veranda as she waved and walked down the path to her car.

"What was that all about? I can't help but think I walked into something."

"Oh, I will fill you in later. I will go and change."

She disappeared into the bedroom to get ready and when she came back out Jack was looking at the test.

"Is this what I think it is?"

She stopped dead in her tracks, not knowing where to turn. "Umm, yes, it is a pregnancy test."

"It says positive. I knew I walked into something. Kait is pregnant, isn't she?"

She let out a sigh of relief. "Yes, I was going to tell you at lunch. They are ecstatic."

"Oh, such awesome news! They have been trying for so long."

"But you can't say anything yet."

"Okay, I bet it was when we were in France. A holiday can relax you."

"Well, we will find out more tomorrow. She is going to the doctor. Come on, I am starving."

They wandered along the beach slowly towards the pub. It was a pleasant day, and they walked hand in hand as they chatted. "So Kait and Johnny are going to have another baby," he said, bending to pick up a shell.

"Yes. Exciting news," she said.

"I am a wee bit jealous. I was hoping it was us," he said sadly as he threw the shell out to sea.

"So you would be happy if I fell pregnant?"

"It will be a day in my life. I will treasure forever the day you tell me we will have a wee baby."

She studied his face as he looked out to sea.

"I know you aren't very keen, so I will be patient." Turning back to her, he smiled.

The crushed look on his face was tearing her up inside. She couldn't wait any longer to tell him. "Jack, that pregnancy test wasn't Kait's."

"It wasn't?" He turned his head towards her with zest.

"No, it was mine."

He stopped and stared at her with disbelief. "Yours?" A smile crept to his face. "We are going to have a baby?"

"Yes, we are," she said softly with a smile.

He smiled at her and a tear crept to his eye. He started turning around, throwing his hands in the air with delight.

"What are you doing, you crazy galah," she laughed.

"I am sorry. I am just so happy right now." He wiped the tear from his eye and gave her a cuddle.

"I wanted to tell you in a nice way. Do something memorable. But when I saw your sad face I couldn't hold it from you any longer."

"Well, this is a very special lunch now. I think we should go somewhere fancy."

"I have some bits and pieces at home I could put a picnic together, like on the morning of our wedding day, and head off the beaten track."

"That sounds perfect. A celebration lunch for just the two of us." he smacked his forehead with his hand. "I mean, the three of us." They turned and walked back home and had a picnic basket full of goodies packed in no time.

"Oh, wait, before we go I need to make a doctor's appointment," she grabbed her phone.

"Yes, of course, I will take this out to the car."

She was out in no time, beaming as she walked down the path to the car.

"I got in tomorrow. They had a cancellation."

"Oh, that is wonderful."

They drove to the spot that had views out over the ocean and set up their blanket.

"Oh, this is perfect. I love the scent of the bush," said Chloe as she placed the sandwiches and cheese platter on the rug.

"Our favourite wee place, so tell me, how far do you think you are?"

"I am not sure, but a rough guess about three months." She watched him as he was deep in thought."Are you doing some calculations?"

"What! Oh,no, I was thinking, I am really sad for Kait. She will be crushed now that you are having a baby and not her."

"Well, there is one thing I have not had a chance to tell you. Kait is pregnant also."

"She is?" He said wide-eyed.

"Kait has a doctor's appointment tomorrow also."

"Oh, wow! That is unbelievable."

"Yes, it is. We will go through our pregnancies together." He nodded, cutting a wedge of cheese way too big for his cracker. "I am so scared," she said quietly.

He sat and stared at her. He had never given it a thought, how she would be feeling. It was a shock to him but an even bigger shock to her. He put down his cracker and moved in closer to her and put his finger to her chin, pulling her face towards him.

"I will be there with you every step of the way, any time you need me, for appointments, back rubs or just a shoulder to lean on. We will prepare for this baby together every step of the way."

"Thank you. I needed to hear that. You are an amazing husband and you will be an amazing father also."

"As you will be an amazing mother."

He kissed her gently on top of the head, and she snuggled in. "Life is moving pretty quick for us at the moment."

"And it is not going to slow down any time soon," she said panicked.

"Bring it on!" yelled an excited Jack, and she laughed.

"I guess we won't be going to Florida for the catch-up," she said with a sad face.

"No, that much I can definitely guarantee you. But there will be plenty more catch-ups."

The doctor's appointment went well. He confirmed they were having a baby and would be due at the end of March. Sitting quietly, they waited as he made all the appointments for her, and they thanked him and left. It wasn't until they were back in the car that Jack finally spoke.

"We are going to be parents in March," he said, throwing his back in the seat and then turning to her with a face that looked like he had won the lottery.

"But it is so close."

"We will need to start organising everything, decorate a room, buy a cot."

"I am starting to freak out a little."

"No, don't freak out. This is wonderful, we can do this, the first thing we need to do is tell the family."

"Oh, well, my family will be easy. I guess we will do it together with Kait and Johnny."

"My mother is going to be so happy. She may even board a plane and come over."

"I hope she does. We have busy days ahead Jack."

They were looking at the bedroom they had chosen as the nursery later in the afternoon, when Kait rang.

"I just got home from the doctor, and he has confirmed it all. Johnny is over the moon."

"Congrats! I am so happy for you, guys. I also went this morning."

"You did? When are you due?"

"The last week in March. How about you?"

"The same!"

"You're kidding me."

"No, I am not."

"Oh, wow! This is totally amazing! When are you going to tell Mum and Dad?"

"I have not worked it out yet, but I am hoping we could do it together."

"I was thinking the same."

"I can imagine their faces. How about dinner Sunday night?"

"Yes, everyone's day off. Come to our place. Jack and I will put a meal together."

"OK, sounds good! See you Sunday."

She walked back towards Jack."That was Kait. She is due the same week as us, can you believe that?"

"I bet you it was at the chateau. Everyone was relaxed and having fun."

Chloe laughed. "I don't want to think about that, and I was worried about us. Sounds like everyone was bonking."

"Aye, well, we know for a fact Patrick and Angie were."

They both laughed at the thought of the night they busted them in the pool."Speaking of them, I was thinking they could help out here. We are going to need extra help now."

"They are coming home at the end of the month. I got an email from Pat the other day. He is planning on buying a trawler here. He sent me a picture of the one he is interested in. I forgot to tell you."

"Well, there has been a lot going on, but that is perfect. Angie can help me with the seafood for the crab pots."

"I guess we had better start on this nursery. What colour should we paint it?"

"Do you want to find out the sex of the baby?"

"No, I don't think so. I would like a surprise at the end. What about you?"

"It really does not worry me. I am happy to wait."

"Well, a neutral colour, I guess. Maybe white, and we can add some colour with the furnishings."

"Okay, let's go and buy some paint. I am keen to start."

They spent the next few days painting the nursery and the spare room and by the time Sunday came around they were pleased with their efforts. It was painted in crisp white with lime touches. It was all starting to come together. He was more than excited that his mum might come and visit. Maybe even Jimmy and Chelsea would come with her. He wanted more than anything to show off what he had.

# CHAPTER 32
# THE ANNOUNCEMENT

They were ready with a roast in the oven when everyone arrived at almost the same time. They all settled at the large trestle table on the front lawn overlooking the water, as she had dressed it beautifully. Vases of wattle, jasmine and frangipanis not only decorated the table but the scent was fresh and inviting. Jack got beers for the men and opened a bottle of wine, pouring Olivia and Chrissie a glass of wine each.

They were all seated and happily chatting about their events of the week as Chloe placed platters of nibbles on the table. "This is so beautiful here. It is so private and the views are to die for," said Olivia.

"Yes, it will be nice when we get the deck finished."

"Come and sit, Darl," Rob beckoned. "Your mother is right. You have a lovely spot here. Jack, you missed Chloe. She does not have a drink," said Rob.

She sat and Jack walked over with a sparkling water and poured it into her wine glass.

"Water? What's going on here? Are you on a health kick?" Rob chuckled.

Jack walked around to Kait and poured it into her wine glass. Everyone went quiet as they watched.

"Thank you, Jack," said Kait as she winked at Chloe.

"Yes, water,Dad. Kait, and I will be drinking water for a few months."

Olivia's mouth dropped open as she gasped. "Oh, my goodness, you're not."

"Yes, we are!" They both said excitedly at the same time. Kait was clapping her hands with an excited stare. She jumped up and gave them both a cuddle as the others at the table watched.

"What am I missing here? I don't understand" said Rob.

"Dad, we are pregnant," explained Kait with a laugh.

"Well, why didn't you say so. I am not the sharpest tool in the shed, you know." He was beaming from ear to ear. Everyone was up cuddling each other and shaking hands.

"Wait, both of you are pregnant? Did I hear right?" said Chrissie with a squinted smile.

"Yes, both of them. They will go through their pregnancies together," added Jack.

"So when are you due?" asked Olivia.

"Last week in March."

"Both of you?"

"Both of us."

"You will have three grandchildren."

"Now, you are making me feel old," added Rob as he put his arm around Olivia as she wiped her tears away with a tissue.

"Have you told your family yet, Jack?" she asked.

"No, but I am about to. I am about to Skype them. It is morning there now, and they should all be having breakfast. I have asked Jeannie to make sure Jimmy and Chelsea were there, so I can break the news to everyone at the same time."

Chloe was organising the computer for him as he checked the time.

"OK, is everyone ready? Let's visit Fraserburgh."

Jeannie answered quickly with a welcoming smile."Hello, oh, wow! Everyone is there. Hello to you all," said Jeannie waving.

"Jack, what is going on? Getting us out of bed early on a cold Sunday morning," said Jimmy.

"Well, we won't beat around the bush. We have news," said Jack as he turned to Chloe and put his arm around her shoulder, smiling. "We are going to have a baby!"

"I knew it! I had a wee idea this might be why you gathered us," said Jeannie, jumping up and down.

Everyone was clapping and congratulating them.

"Wow! You two certainly didn't muck around. That's great news! Mum,you are going to be a grannie."

Jack could see his mum was crying. "Are you OK,Mum?"

"Aye, I am weeping tears of joy,lad. When is the wee baby coming?"

"Last week of March. You have to come over."

"Aye, I will put some thought into that."

Everyone was chatting amongst themselves about visiting Australia, and they waited till they stopped. "Sorry, we forgot about you for a moment," said Chelsea as they all looked back towards the computer.

"That is not all the news. Kait has news also."

"We are pregnant also and due the same week," yelled Kait with excitement.

Everyone congratulated them and Jimmy poured everyone a whisky as the families chatted for a while and Olivia invited them all over for the birth, saying they had plenty of room for everyone.

When everyone left, they sat back and sighed.

"Do you think your family will come over?"

"Jeannie and Liam might, but not sure about Mum. it is a long way."

"I think she will."

"I hope you are right. She would love to see the baby."

"Well, we have a lot of work to do. We will need to do up the spare bedroom for visitors."

"Aye, we will have it done in time, no need to panic."

Angie and Pat arrived home and came to stay with them while they found a place of their own. They had finished furnishing the room just in time. Pat helped Jack start on the deck out the front and Angie helped Chloe finish re-decorating the inside.

"How did you like Scotland?" asked Chloe as she stood back looking at the curtains they had hung in the nursery.

"Oh, it was beautiful. Pat took me up around the highlands and it was incredible. I loved every bit of it. I would have stayed but Pat was keen to come and see Australia."

"We had to forego our highland trip, to rush off looking at chateaus."

"You will have to do it one day. It was incredible." Chloe nodded. She knew her days of roaming around the highlands were over for a while. But she was happy Angie had got to see it.

"So you two seem to be hitting it off."

"Yes, we are. He is such a great guy, I can't believe I went to a wedding in France and ended up in Scotland."

"Life takes you on some strange journeys sometimes."

"Pat is loving Australia. Who would have thought I would end up with Jack's best friend?"

"Well, I think it is wonderful. Come on, let's go and have a cup of tea after all our hard work."

Angie followed Chloe to the kitchen and helped her make a pot of tea. They filled a plate with some cake and biscuits made the day before and took them outside to join the boys for morning tea.

"Oh, Pat, the girls have arrived with gifts," said Jack as he started to take off his tool belt.

They all sat at the outdoor table on the front lawn and enjoyed the cool breeze as they watched the boats sail past.

"The deck is looking good," said Chloe as she ran her eye over it.

"Yep, just about done. We should have it finished tomorrow, complete with the bi-folds, and then we are going to inspect a trawler Pat is keen to buy," said Jack as he selected a biscuit.

"If it is as good as it says, I will be buying it," added Pat.

"Sounds like everything is working out for the two of you," said Chloe as she poured the tea.

"Yes, it is. We are extremely happy," said Angie as she smiled at Pat.

"Well, you two have certainly landed on your feet," said Pat as he scanned the water views.

"Yes, we have been lucky."

"It is so quiet here. Does anyone live in the other houses?" asked Angie, stirring her tea.

"There is a man who lives in the end house. He is old and alone. Chloe keeps an eye on him. But the others are weekenders, we never see a soul there."

"We are looking at a house on the other side of town over the weekend."

"Oh, it will be nice to have you local," said Jack, looking at Pat.

"Pat wants to be near the boats," beamed Angie, swatting a fly.

"Aye, a true fisherman," nodded Jack.

Chloe's phone pinged and as she picked it up, she noticed it was from John in Florida. She read it and smiled. "Well, John got his son. Ava has just given birth to a boy."

"Well, that is wonderful news," said Jack.

"Any names yet?" asked Angie excited.

"Yes, his name is Riggs William Buckman, weighing a healthy four and a half kilos."

"Oh, I love that name. I knew she would pick something manly," said Angie.

"I can just see John. He will be doing his happy dance," laughed Jack and they all agreed.

They finished the deck the following day as planned before setting off to meet the owner of the trawler Pat ended up buying. Things were busy as Jack helped Pat get the trawler ready to work and helped move Angie and Pat into the house they rented on the other side of town. It was perfect for them and Pat could walk to the boat in the mornings.

Jack took Pat out every morning for a few weeks, showing him the ropes while he learned the waterways. Every day they were gone, Chloe would sit in her rocking chair on the front deck until she saw them return with the seafood. She prayed for the day Pat found someone to help so Jack did not have to go. The following week, Pat had a local boy wanting to try out. He knew the waters well but nothing about trawling, but he picked it up quick, and together they made a good team.

# CHAPTER 33

## COUNTING FINGERS AND TOES

Time passed quickly and the morning of the scan had arrived. They were both excited as they drove to the hospital. "Today, we get to see our wee little baby. Are you excited?"

"Yes, super excited! Are you sure you don't want to find out the sex of the baby? Because this is it!"

"Yes, I am very sure."

"Have you thought about names yet?" asked Jack.

"A few. I like Isabella, my nanna's name."

"Oh, I like that. Well, if it's a boy, I would like to name him James, after my dad."

"Of course, I thought you might. I love it!"

Jack pulled up at the hospital and helped her out of the car. He could feel her hand shaking and knew she was nervous.

"Yes, I am. It's all a bit daunting and exciting at the same time."

"Well, if it makes you feel any better I am also a wee bit scared," he said with a comforting look.

"Really, you don't get scared."

"Well, today, I am seeing my wee baby for the first time. They say the images are pretty clear."

"What chance has this poor little thing got with us as parents?" She giggled as he opened the door for her and they stepped inside.

They were in the room in no time after completing numerous forms, and the nurse started the scan as she showed them everything. She stopped talking, concentrating on something. Jack and Chloe stared at each other with a worried face. "Is something wrong?" asked Chloe.

"No, nothing is wrong," she said as she stood up. "I will be back in a minute."

She left the room and Jack could see Chloe was panic-stricken. "She said nothing is wrong. Don't panic, yet."

He rubbed her shoulder and tried to make out nothing was wrong, but he was just as worried as she was. The nurse entered the room with another woman and they both scanned the monitor carefully.

"Yes, you are right," said the second woman, smiled and left as quickly as she came.

"Sorry I wanted to get a second opinion before I gave you the news."

"What news? Is everything ok with the baby?" asked Chloe, looking like she was about to cry.

"Everything is completely normal. It all looks to be healthy and has all of its fingers and toes."

"Oh, I was so worried." Her shoulders slumped as she let out a sigh of relief.

"Well, the reason I had to get a second opinion was to be sure I was correct. There is a second heartbeat in there."

"A second heartbeat? What are you saying?" she said in a low, panicked voice.

"I think she is telling us we are having twins, Chloe," he said, looking at the nurse for clarification.

"That is exactly what I am saying. Congratulations!"

Chloe sat motionless. The nurse was staring at her and Jack shook her gently.

"I am sorry, I am speechless," said Chloe, smiling.

"Me, too. But in a good way. I am very happy," said Jack, unable to wipe the smile from his face.

"So would you like to know the sex of your babies?"

"Umm...no, we don't. Sorry, I am still getting over the shock. I am going to have two babies?"

"Yes, you certainly are," said the nurse.

"Chloe, we will have an instant family," said Jack with an encouraging smile."I am shocked, but I am happy. Maybe we will get a boy and a girl."

"Well now is the time to see, but if you want to wait that is perfectly okay. Congratulations!"

"We are happy to wait,thank you. We feel blessed," said Jack as he took hold of her hand.

"Well, I will let you get dressed. Congratulations!"

They left the room and walked to the car without saying a word but as soon as they were in the car they sighed and looked at each other.

"Chloe, are you ok?"

She held out her hands and observed them as they shook.

"No, I am not. I am freaking out."

He took her hand in his."It is all going to be ok, honey, we will have an instant family. You will never have to go through this again."

She stared at him, thinking hard. It had been a huge shock."I suppose you are right. I am being silly."

"You are not silly. It is normal to be a bit scared," he said in a comforting voice.

"Thanks, I needed to hear that."

She put on her seat belt and they drove home. Pulling up out the front, he helped her out of the car and noticed she was extremely quiet."Are you sure you are ok?"

"Yea, I will be when it all sinks in."

But she wasn't, she was trembling on the inside. *What if I am a terrible mum? What if I can't handle this,* she thought as they walked through the door.

She made her way straight to the nursery and scanned the room."This room is too small for them both," she cried.

"It's perfect. They don't need too much room, just a wee cot and they share everything else."

"Oh, shit! I can't do this, Jack." She threw her hands to the sides of her head holding it and then covered her mouth with a look of shock.

He grabbed her, pulling her in tight, cuddling her and rubbing her back as she sobbed."Yes, you can. I will be here every step of the way. You are an amazing woman and you are going to be an even more amazing mother."

"I hope so."

"I know so. Now, come on, let's go and shop for some baby furniture. You will see how easy it will all fit in."

"Maybe tomorrow. I have to prepare the seafood for the crab pots," she said, waving him off.

"Angie will be here any minute. I called her and asked her to give you a hand today. I wanted this to be our day,a special day, the day we got to see our baby for the first time."

"Babies," she corrected him with a glum look.

"Oh, babies. Yes, well that is going to take a while to sink in," he said with a smirk that made her laugh. "Ah, that is better, that is the face I love," he said.

"How do you always make me feel so much better?"

"Come on, let me take you shopping." He grabbed the keys and headed for the door as she followed.

They spent the afternoon shopping and had a wonderful time laughing and having fun. Purchasing the rocking bassinets along with linen and a few other cute accessories they couldn't resist. He watched Chloe as she lovingly gazed at all the sweet little dresses;he knew in her heart she was hoping for a girl. He smiled and even though he wanted a boy to carry on his father's name at that moment he knew how much a little girl would bring them so much joy. Maybe they would both get what they were hoping for.

That night, Chloe had arranged for everyone to meet at Seasalt for dinner to announce the wonderful news. They waited until Johnny and Finn finished and came to join them before announcing the news.

"Well, you have been asking all night about the scan and how it all went and we told you everything except one teeny weeny thing."

Everyone was staring at them, waiting to hear what they had to say.

"You found out the sex of the baby," squealed Kait.

"No, Jack, I will let you deliver the news."She turned to him smiling as everyone went quiet.

He took a long gulp on his beer and put his arm around Chloe."We are having twins."

"Twins? We don't have twins in our family," said Olivia, shocked.

"We do now," squealed Chrissie, as she ran around to give her sister a hug.

"Wait, I am going to have four grandchildren in a few months' time," said Rob.

"You girls certainly know how to make us feel old. Congratulations to you both!" said Olivia, looking for a tissue in her handbag.

"I hope they are tears of joy,Mum," said Chloe.

"Of course, they are. It is wonderful news."

"Chloe is worried she won't be able to cope," said Jack.

"You are going to be a wonderful mother, Chlo. You are stronger than you think," said Chrissie.

The months ahead went quickly as they prepared for the babies. The summer months meant a busy season for the crab pots. Pat and Angie had stepped in helping, along with Chrissie and Finn, who juggled themselves between the restaurant and the crab pots.

Jack's family arrived a few weeks before the expected due date. Chelsea and Jimmy stayed at the pub and Jeannie Liam and Marl stayed at the house to give Chloe a helping hand. It was hectic but wonderful for Jack to have his family gathered around. He was so proud of the house and was thrilled to bits to welcome them all. Bob took Marl out almost every second day, showing her around the coast. For a special treat, he booked a Captain Cook long lunch cruise on Sydney Harbour, which they both talked endlessly about for days.

# CHAPTER 34
## COMPLETE

C hloe waddled around with a huge stomach and helped out as much as she could until one day as she bent down to pick up an empty bucket to take to Jack for the seafood,she felt a dribble of water running down her leg.

Chrissie had just left taking everyone for a day out shopping. She looked around and spotted Jack at the boat."Jack!" she yelled out.

He turned and with the look on her face, jumped off the boat onto the wharf and went running towards her, scaling the metre-high rusty wire fence.

"Chloe, what is wrong? What happened?" He put an arm around her, bending to see her face.

"I think my water broke."

He stood up straight,flabbergasted. "What? You mean, now? Are you sure?"

"Bloody hell, Jack, yes, now! I didn't just pee my pants."

"They are not due till next week."

"Well, you can tell them that when you see them."

His eyes dropped as more water ran down her leg. Fear took over him. He was as nervous as a red belly snake in a room full of rocking chairs.

"Shit, okay, I will fetch the car. The bag! I need the bag. Shit, we have practised this and now I have no idea what I am doing," he said in a panic. Running one way, and then turning, and running back again.

"Slow down, it is okay. We have time, I will call Kait, you grab the bag."

"Okay, okay, shit!" He ran inside and was back in less than a minute.

"Let me help you in the car."

He walked her slowly to the car and opened the door.

"Are you okay?" he said as her face grimaced with pain.

"Yes, I had a contraction," she smiled. He ran around to his side off the car and landed in the seat with haste before slamming the door.

"We are about to be parents," he said, holding his head in his hands.

"Yes, we are. Are you okay to drive?"

"Aye, I think so," he said in a panicked voice, sitting there deep in thought.

"Then maybe we should go," she encouraged with a smile.

"Oh, yes, of course!"

He started the car and headed off and by the time they made it to the hospital the contractions were coming along every few minutes. They were escorted to the delivery suite and six hours later the doctor told them it was time to push. After six hours of watching Chloe go through pain, he was a mess. He thought he was going to pass out a few times and then a tiny baby came into the world and was placed on Chloe's stomach.

"It's a girl," said the doctor. "Congratulations, you have a daughter!"

"We have a daughter," cried Jack as he looked her over and kissed a tearful Chloe. "Is she alright?"

"She is perfect," said the midwife. "But we will need to take her for a moment to weigh her, but we will bring her back in a minute." With that, the doctor announced the next one was on its way and before they had time to blink another baby was placed on Chloe's stomach.

"Another girl," said Chloe as she cried.

"Two girls," said Jack, stunned.

The doctor chuckled at his surprise."I hear ya, mate. You will have your hands full now. I have one daughter, and I am going crazy."

The babies were weighed and cleaned, and they were handed one baby each.

"They are a nice weight. Three point four and three point five kilos," confirmed the nurse.

"They are perfect," said Chloe, looking over them. "Which one do I have?"

"That is the firstborn. If you are okay here for a minute, I will go and fetch you both a cup of tea and some sandwich's," said the nurse and left the room. They were alone at last,just the four of them. They sat in silence as they scrutinised them closely.

"They are exactly the same," said Chloe as they looked from one to the other.

"That is going to be a bit confusing."

"They are gorgeous. Look at their little blonde puffs of hair," laughed Chloe as she ran her finger gently over her head.

"Aye, they are. So do we name one each," asked Jack.

"Sounds fair. Do you have a name chosen?"

"No, I only had James for a boy but I don't think she will be too happy with me if I call her that," he chuckled as he scanned the babies' faces.

"I am so sorry, Jack, you didn't get a boy." She glanced over at him hoping he wasn't too crushed.

"I don't care about a son, anymore. I have two beautiful daughters, my goodness! Look at what I have!" He smiled at Chloe. "She has taken my breath away with her beauty."

Chloe's heart melted as she softly smiled, watching him. The baby opened its eyes and looked at him as a tear streamed down his cheek.

"She has eyes as blue as the waters of Capri."He sat and stared at her for a few minutes and then turned to Chloe. "I think I would like to call her Capri. Do you like that name?" he asked.

"I love that name. It's perfect," said Chloe as she wiped the tear which was trickling down his cheek.

"I just gave you the first gift from me to you. Your name," he said, smiling down on the baby.

"And it is a beautiful name. She is a very lucky little girl to have such a wonderful daddy."

"And what about you? Are you still calling her Isabella after your nanna?"

"Well, I have had a name going around in my head for a few weeks and now you have named Capri, it matches. It is Candice. Do you like that, Jack," said Chloe, hopeful.

"I love it! Hello,Candice," he said as he leaned over and kissed the baby on the top of its head."Candice and Capri, welcome to our world!" He smiled.

"We are a family," said Chloe.

"Aye, we are, and a beautiful one at that." He winked and lent in to give her a kiss.

The nurse walked back into the room with a tray, and they placed the babies into their cribs. "So, do they have names yet?" asked the nurse enthusiastically.

"Yes, we just named them," said Chloe. "The one I had, the firstborn, is Candice, and the one Jack had, is Capri."

"Oh, what beautiful names. I will write it on their crib cards now, so we know who is who, and you probably have not had time to notice but Capri has a birth mark on her bottom so it will be easy to identify who is who," said the nurse as she took a pen out of her pocket and walked over to the charts on the cribs.

"We were a wee bit concerned about that," said Jack, with a sigh of relief.

"All done, now we know who is who. I will leave you to enjoy." She turned whistling as she turned back towards the doorway.

He sat on her bed as they shared their cup of tea and sandwiches that were placed on the mobile food table between them as they peered over at the babies sleeping soundly.

"I forgot to call Kait," said Chloe.

"We didn't know what we were doing running around like chooks with no head," he chuckled, stirring his tea.

"That was you. I have never seen you like that before. You had no idea what you were doing."She laughed as she took a bite on her sandwich.

"I have never been that scared," he admitted.

"You were scared? I was the one who should have been scared, not you," she laughed.

"Well, after what I just witnessed, you are never going through that ever again."

"What? Nooo! We need to try for a boy. You really wanted a boy."

"No boy. I have two beautiful daughters. I could never ask for anything more. I will never let you go through that ever again." The stern look he shot her took her back. She knew it was not open for conversation, especially now.

"We will see how we cope with these two first," she said wisely.

The warmth came back to his face. "That is a wise decision, but now I think I need to call the family. They will be wondering what happened to us." He jumped up, digging his phone out of his pocket.

"Let's send out a blanket message to everyone, so we can enjoy our time here together without it getting all too crazy."

"That is a wonderful idea. I can do that." He sat back down on the bed and stared at his phone for a moment then looked over at Chloe.

"What do I say?" Chloe laughed.

"Fair dinkum, Jack, you have totally lost it today. Just tell them they have arrived and more details to follow soon."

"Okay, of course," he said as he started typing.

"Is this okay?" He cleared his throat before he read the message. *I am proud to announce that my beautiful wife has blessed me with two wee baby girls today. All are doing well, and we can't wait to introduce you all to Candice and Capri.*

"Jack, that is more than okay. That is beautiful."

"I have put all of your and my family, so they all receive the news together."

"Don't forget Bob."

"Oh, Bob, of course." He added Bob to the list then looked at her with a satisfied smile.

"Done! It's gone."

They sat there watching as all the messages came flooding in before the babies decided it was time for a feed and the nurse came in to help.

"I forgot I have to share those now," whispered Jack.

"Jack! Shh!" she said as she elbowed him. "It's okay. It is a very common comment out of new fathers' mouths. You are certainly not alone there with that thought."

A stay overnight and they were home. Jack had organised the coming home details with everyone and the welcoming committee were all waiting. As they got closer Chloe spotted pink balloons tied to telegraph poles and as the house came into view, it was decorated head to tail in pink. She covered her mouth with her hand as she gasped. "Oh, my goodness! That is so beautiful."

"I thought you would like it. Our families have been here all morning getting everything ready."

They were all on the veranda, lined up as far as the eye could see, all of them waving frantically as they pulled up. "Every man and their dog are here," she said with a joyful croak in her throat. Kait was sitting in the rocking chair nursing swollen feet, while Jeannie and Chrissie ran to help them take the babies out of the car. Jack looked at them all, pumped his fist into the air and yelled, "The MacLean's are home." Everyone cheered loudly.

Once they made their way through the crowd, they put the babies in the lounge room and everyone looked over them in awe.

Bob bent in to take a peek and turned back to them with a wink. "Well, aren't they just the bee's knees?" He patted Jack on the back. "Well done, son. They are the cutest little bundles I have seen in a long while." He pulled out two red and yellow surf lifesaver hats from his pocket and placed them gently on their cribs. "Just getting in early. You will be with me on the sand, in no time." he bent and gave them each a kiss as everyone watched.

"Two wee bonne blondies playing at the beach," said Marl.

"He will be batting off blokes left right and centre when these two beauties grow up," added Johnny as he handed out the beers. "Time to wet the baby's head."

"Wait, what are they doing to the babies?" said a protective dad.

"It's okay, Jack. They mean let's have a beer and welcome them."

"Oh, well, why didn't they bloody well say that?" he said with a grin.

"You're getting more and more Aussie every day," laughed Kait.

"It was bound to happen, wasn't it? Hanging around you mob," he joked.

Chloe looked around at the family and closest friends, all having a wonderful time. She imagined them all setting up for the homecoming with love and plenty of friendly bantering. She scanned the room, taking in their hard work. It was decorated with pink unicorns, pelicans, balloons, and streamers while the table was filled to the brim with every pink finger food you could imagine. Jack walked over and put his arms around her, eating a pink finger bun.

"Are you okay?" he laughed.

"Look at all this," she waved her arms around as a tear crept to her eye.

"They were all so excited," he smiled.

"They both look exactly the same. How can you tell them apart?" yelled out Kait as she was picking up one of the babies.

"Capri has a birthmark on her bum," said Jack.

"Oh, that is handy. Pity it wasn't somewhere a little easier to spot," said Rob as he ate a pink cupcake.

"Oh, they are so precious and ever so sweet," said Olivia as Kait handed her the baby and Jeannie handed Marl the other one. "Look what they have given us, Marl."

"Aye, bonne lass's indeed. It will be hard to return to Scotland now," she said with a tear in her eye.

"Well, I have a spare room if you want to hang around a while," said Bob and she smiled up at him.

"Be careful, I might take you up on that."

"I hope you do," he said as Chloe elbowed Jack and they smiled. They were the best of friends and they could not be anymore happy for them.

"You will have one of these anyday now, Kait," said Rob.

"Yes and I cannot wait. I am so over being pregnant."

"I bet it's another girl," added Rob.

"Well, you will find out soon enough. We are not saying a word," said Kait, waving her finger at her father with a smile. Only they knew the sex of the baby, and it had been a long-running joke trying to get them to spill their beans. It was no secret he was hoping for a grandson after three granddaughters.

Two days later, as Chloe was doing the seemingly endless task of sorting washing when she got a message from Johnny.

*Kait has just given birth to a baby brother for Sophia. Leonardo Jonathon weighing in at a healthy four kilos. Both doing well.*

She ran out the front and called out to Jack, who was raking the front lawn. "Jack, Kait and Johnny had a boy." She was beaming from ear to ear.

"Oh, that is wonderful news. Your dad will be pleased," he said as he put the rake down and skipped up the veranda stairs.

"They called him Leonardo."

"I like that name."

"Me, too."

The following day, the welcome home party was in full swing at Kait and Johhny's home as Johnny drove into the driveway. The house was decorated in blue, and everyone was excited as they brought little Leo into the house. Sophia spied him carefully, unsure if she liked the idea of him or not and everyone laughed. He had olive skin which showed his Italian heritage.

Chloe looked around at her two bundles of joys both sleeping soundly and thought how much life had changed. Life was crazy all of a sudden, but everyone was more than happy. And as a blue cake with candles was brought out by Chrissie, Rob popped a bottle of champagne, and they all had a toast to baby Leonardo.

Chloe took to motherhood like a duck to water and Jack was right by her side every step of the way. They were both very good babies and good sleepers only waking when hungry. Chloe expressed milk daily so that Jack could also help with feeding, which he loved doing.

As the months passed by, Chloe observed how Jack had special time for Leo. She felt guilty having two daughters, and he did not have a son. She constantly asked his thoughts on having another baby, but he refused.

The years rolled past all too quickly and before they knew it, the twins were two. They were the prettiest little girls with blonde hair and big blue eyes and turned heads everywhere they went. At Leo's second birthday party, she watched as Jack played with all the kids running around being silly as he always did. It tugged at her heart every time he played with Leo, and there and then, she knew what she had to do.

A few months later, she was sitting on the veranda watching the twins play as Jack came home through the front gate.

"Everyone looks happy here today," he said as he climbed the stairs, stopping to give Chloe a kiss who was sitting, watching the twins.

"Yes, they have been happily playing there all morning."

He sat on the chair beside her, taking off his boots.

"I have made us some rolls for lunch. I will go and grab them."

"Oh, thank you. I am starving."

The girls played and Chloe came back with a tray filled with some rolls and a pot of tea.

"Oh, let me help you," said Jack as he took the tray and helped set everything on the table.

"The girls have already had lunch," said Chloe, pouring the tea.

"Life has turned out pretty good for us," said Jack as he looked out over the ocean and the wharf with the crab pots and his two little girls playing happily in the play tent.

"Yes, it has. Actually, you almost have what Paddy and Maggie had, Jack,except there is one thing missing."

"Nothing is missing. I have it all, my wife, my daughters, and my castle."

"Just one more baby would be nice."

"Not that again. I am happy with what I have got, thank you very much."

"Well, I don't think you have a say in this, anymore," she winked.

"What does that mean?" he said, looking confused.

"Well, I have news," she said, beaming.

"You do?  What news?" he said cautiously.

"We are having another baby."

Jack's jaw dropped as he slowly put down his cup of tea." We are?"

"I wanted to give it one last try to give you the son you always wanted, and so I stopped taking the pill."

"You're pregnant?" he said with wide eyes.

"Yes, I am. Are you happy?"

He jumped out of his seat like he had been hit with a lightning bolt and ran around and threw his arms around her.

"Careful, careful, you are squashing me."

"Oh, sorry. I just... I just... I am so excited," he said with his blue eyes flashing with sheer delight.

"Really, you are not mad at me?"

"No, I could never be mad at you, especially for giving me another baby."

"But don't get your hopes up. It may still be another girl," she said, trying to bring him back to reality. He stopped and stared at her.

"I know and if it is, I will welcome her with open arms."

The pregnancy went smoothly and Jeannie and Liam brought out Marl to see the children. Jimmy and Chelsea were awaiting their own bundle of joy in a few months' time. It was a running joke that it was a race to have a boy. His mum stayed with Bob this time, and Jeannie and Liam stayed at the pub. It was wonderful all enjoying the feeling of family again.

James Robert MacLean came into the world, two weeks late to two over-the-moon parents. He looked exactly like his sisters with blonde hair and big blue eyes.

Taking him home, they turned the corner and saw the family all waiting on the veranda with the house all decorated in blue. As they got out of the car and walked up the path with baby James, everyone's eyes were on them.

"Come on, hurry up! The peanut gallery is getting restless," yelled out Kait.

"A man's not a camel," added Bob."We have been waiting to wet this bugger's head for weeks," he said as he put his arm around Marl and she smiled up at him.

Jack pumped his fist high into the air "The MacLeans are home!"

Everyone roared and cheered.

She had done it; she had given him the son he always wanted. After all that he had done for her, she finally got to pay him back.

"We are complete," he said as he kissed her and as she looked around at everyone's smiling faces, she knew she had never felt more complete in her life.

www.ingramcontent.com/pod-product-compliance
Lightning Source LLC
Chambersburg PA
CBHW070045120726
47909CB00002B/305